P9-CRH-203

continued . . .

To
Catch a Wolf

Susan Krinard

B

BERKLEY SENSATION, NEW YORK

This is a work of fiction. Names, characters, places, and incidents either
are the product of the author's imagination or are used fictitiously,
and any resemblance to actual persons, living or dead, business
establishments, events, or locales is entirely coincidental.

TO CATCH A WOLF

A Berkley Sensation Book / published by arrangement with
the author

PRINTING HISTORY
Berkley Sensation edition / September 2003

ISBN: 0-425-19208-3

A BERKLEY SENSATION™ BOOK
Berkley Sensation Books are published by
The Berkley Publishing Group,
a division of Penguin Group (USA) Inc.,
375 Hudson Street, New York, New York 10014.
BERKLEY SENSATION and the "B" design
are trademarks belonging to Penguin Group (USA) Inc.

PRINTED IN THE UNITED STATES OF AMERICA

10 9 8 7 6 5 4 3 2 1

Prologue

Cañon City, Colorado, 1875

Free.

Morgan paused just outside the gates of the Territorial Penitentiary, staring through the bars at the cold, hard faces of the men who had kept him caged for the last five years. He knew that their blank expressions hid relief—relief that the one prisoner they couldn't break was leaving their jurisdiction.

They'd stopped trying to beat him after the first year, because he gave them no reason other than their dislike of his silence. They left him almost entirely alone after the second year, and so did the other convicts. Even though he never attempted escape, they kept him in his cell all but an hour each day, and let him out only under heavy guard with half a dozen rifles trained at his head.

He'd learned how to keep his sanity when the scents of wood and river came to him through the barred window. He'd learned to exist in a place where everything he had been died a slow and lingering death.

It was easier than the one his father had suffered.

With no possessions but memory and the clothes upon his back, he turned away from the high stone walls. The road led east, to the town of Cañon City with its houses and shops and saloons. To the west rose the peaks of the Sangre de Cristos, and to the north Pike's Peak and Colorado Springs. The border with New Mexico Territory lay a hundred miles to the south, as the crow flies.

The road that had led him to Colorado in search of his father had begun in the west, in California. But his mother and sister were no longer waiting in the little mountain cabin. Four years after his trial and incarceration in various jails and then here at the Territorial Penitentiary, he had received the one letter of his nine-year term.

His uncle Jonas had been brief. Edith Holt was dead, and his sister Cassidy had gone with Jonas to his ranch in New Mexico. There she would have a decent upbringing away from the unsavory influence of her kin.

Cassidy had been six when Morgan left. She would be a woman now, familiar with courting and kissing and all the things Morgan had missed. She might even have started a family of her own. She'd have no place in her life for an ex-convict.

Better that Cassidy should forget he ever existed. He had no family. He was alone. And he would remain alone.

There were many ways to be alone in Colorado. Not every valley was a booming mining town, nor was every hill swarming with eager prospectors. There were places where wolves still avoided the hunters' guns and traps.

That was where Morgan would go. North, and west, into the high mountains, the deep valleys. There he would forget he had ever been a man.

His feet, so used to measuring the dimensions of his cell, were slow to remember what it was to stride. Autumn dust rose in little puffs about his dilapidated shoes. He stepped out of the shapeless leather and kicked the shoes away.

He walked a hundred paces down the road and turned north where only animal trails marked the path. No one called after him, neither a curse nor a farewell. He dismissed the humans from his mind.

Time as men measured it had long since lost its meaning. He walked for many days, drinking from trickling streams and springs and rivers, eating what he sensed was fit and safe. Where men made their stink of waste and metal, he passed by unseen. The season they called Indian summer lingered well into the mountains. Golden leaves rustled under his feet. Then snow fell, and he shook off the cold as he had done in the years of captivity.

At last there came a day when he heard the wolves howl.

The scent of men did not reach here. The air stung his nostrils with the promise of winter, and turned to fog with each breath.

He looked up at the unbarred sky and howled. The wolves answered. They came, silent to any who walked on two legs. When they ringed him in, hackles raised and teeth bared, he stripped off the remains of his ragged clothing and walked among them without fear. As they shrank back, he Changed.

The wolves recognized him, though they had surely never seen his like before. They crouched low in obeisance. The mated pair who led the pack whined anxiously, and he told them in a language they understood that he would not usurp their sovereignty as long as he shared the fate of the pack.

So they welcomed him. He made himself known to each wolf in turn, his black-furred shoulders rising above those of the others, twice the height of the smallest beast. Then he sent them away, and became a man for the last time.

He gathered his discarded clothing and laid them in a neat pile upon the virgin ground. With his hands he dug a deep hole, placed the shirt and trousers inside, and smoothed the dirt over the remnants of his humanity.

A snowflake kissed Morgan's shoulder. Another joined it, and its kinfolk danced and spun out of the sky to offer a final benediction. He ran his fingers over his face, feeling the gauntness and the sharp planes, the scar where a fellow inmate had stabbed him through the cheek and left only the slightest mark. There would be no such mark on the wolf. And the weight in his chest, so long ignored, would shrivel and be forgotten.

With a shrug of his shoulders, he Changed. Snowflakes caught in his fur. The richness of the forest poured over him and embraced him.

Howls rose from the nearest slope. He answered and broke into a lope, covering the broken ground effortlessly. The years sloughed away one by one, like human skin and bone, until his heart lay naked to the world. It froze into a lump of ice, untouched and untouchable.

Now he was truly free.

Chapter 1

One by one the members of the Ladies' Aid Society rose from their chairs and sofas in the Munroes' grand parlor and took leave of their hostess. Narrow silk and brocade skirts rustled, confining legs that seldom found practical use save to convey their owners from mansion to carriage and from carriage to shop.

Athena Sophia Munroe did not rise to see her guests to the door. She extended her gloved hand and accepted the offered farewells like a queen upon a throne. A queen as luxuriously confined as the most favored consort in a pasha's harem.

She smiled and found a compliment for each lady in turn, listening to their chatter as Brinkley led them into the hall.

Cecily Hockensmith lingered, waving her fan indolently against the hot, dry air.

"What is to be done about this awful heat?" she exclaimed. "Everyone advised us to go to the mountains for the summer, but Papa did not wish to miss any business opportunities." She made a moue of distaste. "Business, always business. Is it not frightfully dull?"

"The men do not seem to find it so," Athena said. She thought of Niall, hard at work in some stifling office while she sat at her ease at home. "It is true that many families do leave the city in the summer. That is why our attendance today was less than it would be at other times. In the autumn, we will have our full complement again."

Miss Hockensmith closed her eyes and sighed. "We always went to Newport during the summers in New York. Ah, those fresh ocean breezes. How pleasant it was."

Athena nodded with polite sympathy. "It must seem very different in Denver, with the ocean so far away."

"Have you ever visited the sea, my dear?"

"I am afraid not. I was to attend school in the east, but—"

"You must go one day, Miss Munroe. You cannot miss it."

Athena imagined herself by the waves, breathing in the salt air and letting the water bathe her feet. The picture was so enticing that it hurt.

"I would like to take the orphans to the ocean," she said quickly. "They would appreciate it more than anyone."

"Ah, yes, the dear orphans." Miss Hockensmith grew serious, meeting Athena's gaze with an air of troubled concern. "I hope you won't mind a bit of sisterly advice. I have been observing you ever since our arrival, Miss Munroe. I confess that I have never seen anyone work as tirelessly as you on behalf of the masses. Why, even our greatest philanthropists in New York did not become so . . . personally involved in such work."

Athena straightened in her chair. "You compliment me too highly, Miss Hockensmith. I do little enough, and I have the assistance of many others. It seems to me that it is our duty, as the more fortunate, to do what we can to aid the less."

Miss Hockensmith raised a plucked brow. "Naturally. But the orphanage, the fallen women, the unemployed men in Globeville and Swansea—are you quite sure that you have not taken on too much, my dear?" Her dark eyes sparkled with compassion. "I fear that you will exhaust yourself with the Winter Ball, among so many other ventures. You know that I would be more than happy to assist you. I had much experience with organizing affairs of this sort in New York. And I do so wish to help the dear little orphans."

Athena looked up at Cecily, at her height and presence and midnight-black hair above a pale, lovely face. The lady was used to being ruler in her own kingdom, and who could blame her? She had sacrificed a great deal to come to Denver with her father.

"Of course," Athena said. "Your advice and experience will be most welcome. I shall need everyone's help to make the second Winter Ball a success equal to last year's."

"It is a shame that we had not yet come to town then," Cecily said, "but I am sure you made an excellent job of it. Certainly your ballroom is one of the finest I have seen in Denver . . . for a modest gathering. How you must enjoy dancing in it."

Athena made a slight adjustment to her perfectly arranged skirts as if some part of her might have been exposed by an inadvertent motion. She was grateful for Cecily's oblivious comment; far better these occasional pricks than the slash of pity.

Denver society no longer had reason to pity her. Had she not proven herself capable of contributing as much as anyone in her work for those less fortunate? Was her formal parlor not one of the most stylish and tasteful in Denver? Did not the wives and daughters of her brother's colleagues trust her judgment on everything from the latest Paris fashions to the hiring of servants?

I am no different than any of them. No different.

"But oh, how thoughtless of me," Cecily said. "Pray do not think—" With a show of confusion, Cecily created a minor hurricane with her fan. "It was not my intention to remind you—"

"Please, Miss Hockensmith. Do not distress yourself. I assure you that I am not in the least offended by the subject of dancing." She laughed lightly. "It is a ball, after all! And you are a most elegant dancer."

Cecily Hockensmith had perfected the fine art of the blush. "You flatter me, Miss Munroe. It is only natural that a woman should dance well when provided with a superlative partner."

Athena knew to whom Miss Hockensmith referred. Athena made it a point to take note of every ripple in the generally calm waters that made up Denver's elite social circle. The stylish lady from New York—as yet unmarried—had paid particular notice to Niall from the first. It was no wonder. Niall Munroe was a handsome man of dignified bearing and considerable assets.

But Niall had not reciprocated the interest, though he had courteously danced with Cecily at Mrs. William Byers's anniversary ball. Nor was he a particularly fine dancer. Business had prevented him from mastering such niceties.

Inwardly, Athena sighed. What was she to do with Niall? Could Miss Hockensmith be the right woman for him?

The mere thought was uncomfortable. But why? There was much to admire in Miss Hockensmith, and her father might become Niall's new business partner. *You will be seeing much of her now that they have settled in Denver. Perhaps we will become great friends. How wonderful it would be if I could help Niall and Miss Hockensmith find happiness. . . .*

Cheered at the notion, Athena pushed aside her faint unease and pressed Cecily's hand. "I doubt that you shall find a shortage of partners at the Winter Ball."

"Thank you, Miss Munroe. But please consider my offer of help. I should not wish you to tire yourself. Your brother did mention that you work much too hard."

Niall again. "Do you not have a brother, Miss Hockensmith? You know how they are. I think they must secretly believe that no sister ever grows up to be a woman."

"And a woman such as yourself would not wish to remain dependent. I admire your courage." Cecily closed her fan. "Nevertheless, do call upon me at any time, Miss Munroe."

"Athena, please. We are such a small circle in Denver."

"And formality is best reserved for those outside it." Athena had the brief, uncharitable thought that Cecily must have practiced her perfect smile before a mirror. "I am certain we shall become bosom friends, dear Athena."

"Then I look forward to seeing you at our next meeting."

With a graceful turn, Cecily swept to the door. Athena admired the way she moved so that her form-fitting skirts maintained a column almost undisturbed by the motion of her legs.

As if she had no need of legs at all.

Athena wheeled her chair to the window and drew back the curtains. All of the carriages had gone, even Cecily's. Not one of the ladies would consider walking home, though most lived within a few blocks of the fashionable quarter along Fourteenth Street.

Would they choose to walk tonight if they might never walk again?

You are morbid this evening, she chided herself. *Niall will soon be home.*

And Niall deserved peace and tranquility after a long day of business. Athena deftly maneuvered her wheelchair to the kitchen to consult Monsieur Savard about the evening's dinner. She rearranged the roses displayed on a low rosewood table in the marble and oak-paneled entry hall, and spoke with the housekeeper regarding the new chambermaid and the hiring of a laundress to replace the woman who had returned to her native France.

When all was completed to her satisfaction, she took up her usual place at her secretary in the private sitting room and began to sort through the various letters, invitations, and responses to her charitable campaigns. She basked in each small victory and refused to regard the minor failures. Where the orphans were concerned—or the unmarried mothers, or the poor men up by the smelters, looking for work—she could be remarkably persistent. She had something to fight for.

Something that was beyond herself and her petty problems.

In the hall outside the front door opened, and Athena heard the boom of her brother's voice, followed by the cultured tenor of Brinkley's. Niall strode into the room, a typical look of preoccupation on his handsome face. He paused just inside the door and noticed Athena with vague surprise, as if he did not find her waiting in precisely the same place every evening.

"Good evening, Niall," she said. "How was your day?"

"Very good, thank you. And yours?"

It was the comforting ritual they always followed, though seldom had either one something truly noteworthy to report. Niall ran their father's business and handled Athena's inheritance, providing her with a very liberal allowance; she, in turn, kept the house and played hostess when his business associates gathered for dinner or a sociable meeting.

But there were times, like this evening, when Athena felt a treacherous yearning for something more. If only Niall would take some real interest in her activities. . . .

"It went quite well," she said. "The Aid Society met to discuss the Winter Ball—"

"That's months away," he said, pouring his usual whiskey at the sideboard.

"Yes. But the Munroe successes have always come from excellent planning. I only follow your and Papa's examples." She smiled to take the challenge from her words. "I regard my work as worthy of such care."

Niall downed his drink. "I'm not so sure that the beneficiaries of your charity are worthy of your efforts—or the money you spend on them." He poured another drink and frowned at the inoffensive glass. "You are much too generous."

Athena retained her smile. Niall had always been blunt,

and this was hardly a new argument. "We agreed long ago that you would make the money, and I would see that some portion of it went to help the less fortunate, according to my own judgment."

"A judgment based upon emotion and sentimentality."

Athena wheeled closer to him and touched his sleeve. "What is it, Niall? Is something troubling you?"

He set the second drink down untouched and looked directly at her. "One of those 'fallen women' you attempted to reform was caught trying to steal the wallet of a very influential financier from Chicago."

"One of my girls? How do you know?"

"When she was caught, she blurted out your name. She seemed to think that you would intercede for her." He swept up the glass and downed the contents quickly. "It was not a pleasant circumstance to hear my sister's name on the lips of a whore."

Athena stared at her interlaced fingers. "You witnessed this yourself?"

Niall paced to her desk and shuffled the stack of papers and bills. "I was consulting with the gentleman regarding a business venture of some importance when she accosted him on the street. It is fortunate that he caught her. She is now in jail where she belongs."

Niall had always been the hardheaded, ambitious one in the family, Athena the heart and conscience. He was more annoyed with his sister than with the poor young woman who had been driven to such an act.

Annoyed because Athena's work had inadvertently disrupted his business. Because she had failed.

"It is entirely my fault," she said meekly. "I will pay the girl's fine, and—"

"I forbid it. Some people can't be helped, Athena. They only become more entrenched in their laziness and dependence."

She looked up to meet Niall's gaze. The flinty gray of his eyes had softened, and she saw the pity and guilt in his face. Not for those he spoke of, but for her.

"Have you ever tried to help," she asked, "simply for the sake of it? With no hope of profit or gain?"

"Have you?" His mouth was a rigid line, almost cruel. "Hasn't your work paid dividends in the admiration and respect of your ladies? Hasn't it won you a place for yourself where no one can feel sorry for you?"

Athena clutched the iron-rimmed wheels of her chair and jerked it backward as if he had struck at her. "I am sorry that I have disappointed you."

He shook his head and made a slashing gesture with the side of his hand. "No. No. But it is completely unnecessary to exhaust yourself by becoming indispensable to every philanthropic cause in Denver. The Munroes already have the city's—the nation's—respect and admiration. We never had to fight for it. No one stands above us in influence or capital. As long as you are my sister, your position is assured."

Even though I cannot dance, or make a grand tour of Europe, or even enjoy a social luncheon at the Windsor. "Of course you are right, Niall," she said, regaining her composure. "I appreciate all you have done for me."

"Athena . . ." He grimaced. "I'm poor company tonight. Perhaps you should dine alone."

"No, please. I understand the pressures you face. Let us speak no more of this. M. Savard has prepared your favorite meal, and you would not wish to disappoint him."

He sighed. "Very well." It was impossible for her to take his arm, so he positioned himself behind her chair and pushed her to the dining room. He placed her at one end of the table and assumed his seat at the opposite end. Each setting was elegantly arranged, with a cloisonné vase of fresh flowers at the center of the vast oak table, low enough so as not to obstruct the view down its impressive length.

Brinkley appeared to direct the parlormaid and footman in serving the first course. For a time they ate in silence while Athena searched for some innocuous subject to draw Niall close again.

"I saw Miss Hockensmith today," she began. "She is quite taken with you, I believe. She will be expecting your attentions at the Winter Ball."

"Will she?" He never lifted his eyes from his plate.

How little he truly knew of women, for all his vast experience of the world. How lonely he must be with only those dry businessmen as companions, and how oblivious to his own loneliness. His sister was simply not enough.

Until recently, she had not considered the damaging effects of that loneliness. At the ripe age of twenty-six, she had seen more and more of her peers married and managing households of their own. She remembered a time when even she had held such aspirations.

Selfish aspirations, with no thought of others. It was Niall she must worry about now. She knew his real reason for avoiding the bonds of matrimony.

It was she. Athena Munroe, bound to him with the implacable chains of guilt. All he might have dreamed as a boy, all the old wildness, had been abandoned for her care, her happiness.

But how could she be content when she knew that he was not, even if his ultimate happiness meant that she must be alone? Was that not a small sacrifice to make after all those *he* had made?

As long as she had her work . . .

"Miss Hockensmith is rather lovely, you know," she said. "Quite willing to help in the work of the Society, and with the orphans. I seem to remember that you had been considering her father for some sort of partnership."

He peered at her over the top of the flowers. "Do you wish to become my business adviser, Athena, or are you simply matchmaking?"

His attempt at humor warmed her. "It would not hurt you to show occasional courtesies to my friends."

He muttered something too low for her to hear, which was not an easy feat. Her ears still functioned perfectly well, and better than those of anyone she had met in her lifetime.

"I beg your pardon?"

"Nothing." He nodded to Brinkley, who had brought the dessert. He stabbed at the pudding as if it were a tough slice of beef. At last he set his spoon down and looked at Athena. The back of her neck prickled as if at the gathering of a prairie thunderstorm.

"This makes the fifth summer that you have not gone to the ranch," he said. "I don't like it, Athena. The heat and dust is unhealthy for you. You need fresh air and quiet, and by remaining in Denver you are certainly not getting it. I will not have you becoming ill because of your own stubbornness."

Athena sampled her pudding, barely tasting it. "I am in good health, Niall. There is no danger—"

"You think me unobservant, but I have seen the changes in you. You've convinced yourself that you can solve all of Denver's problems single-handedly, without taking any rest for yourself."

"Rest? Look at me." She swept her hand down the length of her body. "I have plenty of rest. It is the people I try to help who have no rest, struggling as they do every day simply to survive."

"Our own father struggled when he first came to Denver, and no one gave him charity. He would have turned it away."

"Not everyone in this world is alike, Niall. You know that as well as anyone."

They stared at each other. There were two subjects they almost never brought up between them: Athena's accident, and the nature she had inherited from her mother. Athena deliberately avoided thinking about either; the first could not be undone, and the second she had left behind forever.

She had not known her mother. Perhaps that was why she felt so deeply for the orphans, who had lost much more.

"I have kept my promise to you," Athena said, the words sliding past the lump in her throat. "You promised not to interfere in my chosen occupation."

He scowled, rising from his chair. "I did not promise to let you do whatever you pleased, no matter what the cost. Your insistence upon visiting the tent city and the warehouse district is foolhardy in the extreme."

Her skin went cold. How had Niall learned of that? She had been so careful to go incognito, cloaked and hooded and accompanied by a brawny former soldier she had employed after her orphanage administrator had urged her to take some protection. Had it not been for her immobility, she needn't have feared any man, even in the worst part of the city.

Do not think of what might have been. Do not.

"You have paid employees to send on such tasks," Niall continued. "No one, least of all the members of your Society, expects you to dirty your hands or endanger your person. You are no common shopgirl, Athena. Your fine Miss Hockensmith could not approve of such impropriety."

In her heart Athena knew he was right, but she had chosen to take the risk, knowing that the other ladies would not expect a cripple to be capable of such adventures.

They were the only adventures permitted her, now. Among the orphans, or the inebriates, or the poor folk in their threadbare tents along the South Platte, she could not possibly be an object of pity. It was she who held the advantages, she who gave. No one reminded her, however inadvertently, of what she had lost.

And they *needed* her.

"They are people, Niall," she said earnestly. "It is not enough to have someone deliver the food and see that they have fresh water and clothing and coal enough to get through the winter. They must be encouraged, led to see that there is a better life to strive for. Without real examples, how can they learn?"

"Let someone else do the teaching. Someone who is . . . unencumbered."

She pushed away from the table and spun her chair about. "Am I not an encumbrance upon you, Niall? Your worry for me is distracting you from your important work, and wouldn't it be so much easier if I would sit quietly and knit stockings until you find some use for me?"

Her outburst hung in the air like a choking haze. Athena touched her throat, amazed and chagrined. Had that self-pitying, selfish tirade come from her, or had some harpy assumed her shape and voice? What had possessed her?

Have you any use at all, Athena Munroe?

Niall walked the length of the table and stopped before her, grave and strangely quiet. "Yes, Athena. It is what I would prefer—to see you safe and content. But I know that is not possible."

"But I am . . . I am content! Don't you see—"

"I am sorry. You leave me no choice. Either you agree to cease these clandestine visits to the slums, and reduce your commitments to a reasonable number, or I must take steps to see that you are removed to a place where you can reconsider your priorities."

Icy terror swept through her. "The Winter Ball—you cannot expect me to give that up, or abandon the orphans. Papa's money made it possible. I am only doing what he wished."

"It is your choice, Athena. I could see to it that you are relieved of all your self-imposed duties—and I shall, if I believe it will save you from yourself."

"If only you thought of something besides making money—"

"The money you are so glad to have?"

Tears burned behind her eyes. "Where did you get your hard heart, Niall? It was not from Papa. Your mother—"

"Leave our mother out of this."

"She was never my mother. She did not wish to be."

Niall's fair skin reddened. "She acknowledged you as hers, when she might have—"

"I know what she might have done," Athena said quietly. "I know." She wheeled about and started toward the door. "If you will forgive me, Niall, I am tired. I will go up to my room now."

"Athena—"

"Good-night."

She heard the bang of Niall's fist on the table as she entered the hall. Brinkley appeared, ever bland and efficient, to help her to her room. He steered her into the Otis hydraulic safety elevator at the end of the hall and closed the gate.

After two years Athena was used to the curious motion of the device, which Niall had insisted was the perfect solution for the problem of stairs. And now, of course, the grand Windsor hotel had an elevator of its own. Niall's foresight matched their father's in every way.

So did his devotion to her. A devotion that imprisoned him as surely as her chair did Athena.

At the second floor, Brinkley met her to roll back the gate and step aside. He had been too long with the family to ask if she wished to be taken to her room. Fran would be waiting in the small chamber adjacent to hers, and all Athena wished to do now was retire.

How had things gone so wrong? How had she managed to quarrel with her brother, when they so seldom lifted their voices to each other? She could never beat Niall in an argument, and she did not make the mistake of doubting his threats.

Fran helped her undress and get into bed, and she lay staring up at the ceiling for a long while. She had wanted Niall's happiness; she needed to continue her work without hindrance. Somehow she must distract Niall from his focus on her, and at the same time prove that she was fully capable of caring for herself.

If you were truly independent . . .

But how? Niall still controlled her inheritance, according to the terms of Papa's will. She could not demand her portion unless Niall agreed. And he saw her as what she was—a cripple.

She tried to move her legs. They remained lumps under the blankets, only the toes capable of wiggling. She had given up on walking long ago.

There must be some other way of convincing Niall that

she was a sensible, mature, strong woman in mind and spirit if not in body. Some way to relieve him of his guilt once and for all.

She drifted into a twilight world between sleep and waking, and it seemed that she was running—running on four legs instead of two. Four whole, healthy, powerful legs. And she was not alone.

In dreams, she could pretend.

Chapter 2

Voices.
They drew him toward flickering light and the smell of human habitation, though he had left that world behind in a time beyond memory. He could not have said, even had he been capable of speech, why he fled the hunters into the arms of other men instead of to the deep wilderness.

Madness. Yet the pain drove him, and the knowledge that he was near death. The voices were very close.

Firelight seared his eyes. He plunged into the circle made by the many human dwellings and staggered to a stop. The baying of hounds resounded from the forest's edge.

Raised voices, cries of alarm, shouting like the howls of wolves. He braced himself for more pain, ready to expend the last of his strength if they came with ropes to bind him.

None did. Tall shapes darted in and out of his blurred sight. Human scent washed over him. His legs buckled, and he fell to his side. Each breath brought searing agony. Little by little, the light and the remnant of his senses faded. Then came the darkness.

Peace.

He returned to himself slowly, and the voices were still there. They flooded his mind like tainted water: human words, human thoughts, human images.

But now he understood what he heard. And he, himself, was human.

"Jesus, Mary, and Joseph! Did you see that?"

"Remarkable," said the second, deeper voice. "Quite astonishing."

A murmur of agreement and disbelief followed. "Since we all witnessed it," said a third voice, marked by a gentle drawl, "we must conclude that it was not a delusion."

"Delusions don't bleed," the first voice said. "Whatever he is, he's been shot."

"He may be dangerous," came a fourth. "Do not touch him, Caitlin."

"Can't you see that he is too badly hurt to be a danger to anyone?"

He opened his eyes and tried to bring the world into focus. His senses were dulled, hearing and smell filtered through awkward human organs. The body he now wore refused to respond to his commands.

Memory came, and understanding. Between his lower ribs lodged the hunter's bullet, the same that had caught him as he fled the human's dogs. It would not have been a fatal injury had he remained a wolf.

But he had not. Somehow, in some way beyond his will, he had Changed. The wolf had run to men, and the man within him had betrayed the wolf. And now he lay in his own blood, firelight dancing over naked skin, suspended halfway between life and death.

He could not make out the faces around him, but he smelled them clearly: woven cloth, leather, sweat, and horseflesh. A dozen men and women whose voices came more swiftly now, like midsummer rain.

"He appears to be regaining consciousness."

"He will bleed to death if we don't help him."

"Help him? We know nothing about him."

"It's possible that whoever shot him had good reason."

"Maybe he can't talk at all!"

He struggled to remember how to move his mouth and tongue to form words, how to speak the name he had worn in that past life.

Morgan. Morgan Holt, who accepted help from no one. No debt, no obligation, and no charity. Yet he had come here. He was completely in their power.

With a fierce act of will, he shut away the distractions of thought and memory. He summoned up his dwindling strength and called upon the wolf within.

Nothing. Nothing but pain, and night. Blood whistled behind his ears. His heart stuttered, stopped, sprang to sluggish life again.

One of his would-be rescuers came near, and he tried to pull away. Calloused skin brushed his. He was too weak to shudder in disgust. He floated, disembodied, in a limbo where only the voices were solid.

"Come, children," the first voice said. "Help me move him to my tent."

"We hardly have enough food left to keep ourselves alive, let alone an outsider."

"An outsider? Just look at him! He's like us!"

"Caitlin and Harry are correct. We cannot leave him to die, and I believe I hear sounds of pursuit."

"You know as well as anyone how the townies are, and how they treat those who are different."

A face, round, male, and bewhiskered, took solid form from the fog. "Can you hear me, young man? We wish to help you. My name is Harry, Harry French. You find yourself among the troupers of French's Fantastic Family Circus. Never fear, you are quite safe here—"

"He *will* die if you keep talking, Harry."

Another face drew near: younger, more delicate, framed by a mass of red hair. "He won't die. He came here for a reason, I know it. To help us, as we help him."

"One of your 'feelings,' Firefly?" said the gentle drawl.

"Something made him come to us. We've needed a miracle. Maybe this is it."

"If he survives and is willing to aid us."

"I agree with Caitlin," the old man said. "He is the good luck we have waited for, and we must save him. Tor!"

Heavy footfalls approached. Broad hands seized Morgan, and he was lifted in arms bulging with muscle and tight as a vise. A great void opened up around him as he lost contact with the earth. From the depths of his throat came a single, pathetic snarl.

"Do not worry, Tor. You won't bite, will you, young man? No, indeed. Caitlin, come with me. The rest of you had better watch for those dogs and whoever is with them."

"They won't make it past us, Harry."

That voice was the last for a very long time. When he woke again, he lay on a cot under several blankets, surrounded by the scents of animals and humans. He tried to sort through the smells, connecting each to its name: canvas, straw, rope, oil, metal, mildew, old cooking. His limbs were weighted; his chest ached with every breath.

But he was alive.

Dim sunlight found its way through the canvas stretched overhead. The small space was crowded with crates, some of which served as platforms for other unidentifiable objects. The cot was the only furniture in the tent, save for a folding chair and small table.

Outside the canvas walls, Morgan could hear the noise of a busy camp. Dogs barked, horses whinnied, and men's voices made a continuous drone.

They had brought him here. They had saved his life. A string of curses came back to him in all their crude inventiveness, but his throat was too dry to speak.

He tensed his muscles. One by one his fingers obeyed his commands. He was not a prisoner. He could tear through those walls of canvas as if they were tissue, once he regained his strength. He felt the healing of his wound, flesh knitting hour by hour.

He concentrated on shifting his legs. A wall of gray pain dropped behind his eyes. He fell back among the blankets, breathing harshly through his teeth.

A wave of human scent blew into the tent, riding on dust-laden air.

"Ah, you're awake! Very good, very good. It did seem touch and go for a—No, no, you mustn't try to move just yet!"

The voice was the first he had heard, the one that belonged to the old man with the whiskers. Harry French. Morgan blinked the haze from his eyes. The bulky silhouette resolved into a stout, gray-haired gentleman in a patched black coat, bright red waistcoat stretched over a prominent belly, and trousers in gray and black checks. A white, upward-curving moustache was the crowning glory of an otherwise homely face, wrinkled with age and burned by the sun.

The ability to laugh had deserted Morgan long before he had chosen the wolf's way. But something in that comical face and broad grin woke a peculiar sensation within him, and his belly moved in a painful heave. He coughed.

"Oh, dear, oh, dear," Harry French's hands sketched a pattern of distress. "You must be dry as a bone. Water— yes, that's what you need, and perhaps a bit of whiskey for good measure. I believe we still have a bottle or two left." He turned as if to leave and then spun about in midstep. "Foolish, foolish. We have not been properly introduced, though perhaps you remember my name?"

His innocent enthusiasm reminded Morgan of a wolf pup still wet behind the ears. "Harry . . . French," he said hoarsely.

Harry clapped his hands. "You did understand! Wonderful. Delightful. Perhaps you also recall where you are?"

Circus. Words were coming thick and fast now, but it took Morgan a moment to assemble the images. He had seen a circus, once, when he was fifteen and without a penny in the world. The wagons and tents had been set up on an empty lot on the outskirts of a prosperous Nevada mining town. He'd sneaked into the main tent and hid behind the risers to watch the show, until a member of the crew had caught him and booted him off the lot.

That boy had not remained a child much longer.

"How . . ." He cleared his throat, remembering how to move his lips and tongue. "How long?"

"How long have you been with us?" Harry French nibbled the edge of his moustache. "Six days, I believe. Yes, six. You've made quite a recovery. A bit more rest, that's all you need." He beamed and rocked back on his heels. "We are your friends. No need to tell us anything you don't wish. You can rest assured that we won't give your secret away—no, no. We understand."

Your secret. Morgan stiffened and slowly relaxed again. His anonymous rescuers could not know anything of his past, but they had seen him Change and hadn't the sense to be afraid.

"We're all a little odd here, you see," French said, as if he had guessed Morgan's thoughts. "Oh, we're nothing at all like the big railroad outfits, with the poor creatures in cages and great star performers. I like to think of us as a family, a family of very special people. Those who have no other place to go—they find their way to me, sooner or later, just as you have."

He drew a pocketwatch from his vest, glanced at the face, and stuffed it back in. "Dear, oh, dear. I had promised to speak to Strauss about the food stores. Strauss is our chief cook. We are running low on victuals, and I fear my accounting skills have never been—" He broke off with an apologetic sigh. "You must think me quite addled. We have not been as prosperous of late as we might wish. A series of misfortunes—bad luck, as it were. That is why we are camped here in the wilderness and cannot offer you a decent hotel bed. I do so worry about my children, and what will become of us—but I am confident our luck has changed. Yes, indeed. You will meet the others soon." He glanced at his watch again. "You will excuse me, dear boy? I'll send someone with food and drink straightaway."

Before Morgan could frame a belated response, French was out of the tent. His words resounded in Morgan's sensitive ears for several minutes after he left.

But what he had said aroused more feelings Morgan had abandoned as a wolf: worry, consternation, and fear. Not the sensible respect for nature's fickleness or the hunter's gun, but a dread far more nebulous.

"He won't die. He came here for a reason, I know it. To help us, as we help him. . . . We've needed a miracle. . . . He is the good luck we have waited for . . ."

Premonitions of a fate worse than mere death seized Morgan with renewed urgency. He braced himself on his arms and pushed up again, relieved to find that his body functioned in spite of the pain. He could escape. It was not too late.

There was only one way to learn if he was healed enough. He closed his eyes and willed the Change.

Deep inside his body, the core of his being began to shift. He felt it, not as pain, but a natural transition. It was as if each atom became fluid and reshaped itself like clay in the hands of a master potter.

But the Change did not complete. It met the barrier of his injury and paused, forcing his body to make a decision based upon a single law: survival.

Survival meant preserving strength instead of draining it for the Change. Morgan opened his eyes and found himself unrecognizable, neither wolf nor human. A monster.

Instinct made the decision for him. He returned to human shape. Dizziness and nausea held him immobile for a few seconds, but he pressed beyond his body's exhaustion and clambered to his feet. Sheer determination propelled him toward the sliver of dimming light that marked the tent's entrance.

Sunset lent the camp a certain softness that almost disguised the atmosphere of shabbiness and adversity. Tents and colorfully painted wagons, marked with hard use and frequent repair, lay scattered at the edge of a wide valley filled with sagebrush and saltbush. A herd of sway-backed horses clumped together in a makeshift corral.

Everywhere there was a certain frantic activity, as if the members of Harry French's Family Circus did not dare to stop moving. People hurried to and fro, wrapped in much-mended coats and blankets. A man juggled several bright red balls without seeming to touch them. An impossibly slender woman balanced on a wire almost too fine to be visible to normal eyes. Dogs ran about yapping and jumping through hoops.

The one quiet place was centered at a fire beside an open tent furnished with rows of rickety wooden tables and benches. There a fat man cooked a dismally small section of meat on a spit, attended by a mob of barefoot children who watched with the grim concentration of hunger.

Morgan knew poverty when he saw it. He had suffered hunger many times in his life, and had traveled with no more possessions than the clothing on his back. His great advantage had been the wolf, which had allowed him to hunt and to survive under conditions that would have killed an ordinary man.

These folk were not so fortunate. It did not take much imagination to see that they had suffered the "bad luck" Harry French had mentioned, though Morgan knew little of circuses and what made them prosper or fail.

He did understand that no man helped another without expecting something in return. Harry French's "children" hoped for something from him, something he could not give them. He might outrun guilt, as he'd outrun so much else. If he left, now, without facing those who had saved him. . . .

"You're not going so soon?"

He looked down at the familiar voice and met a pair of blue eyes in a pixie's face, topped by a blaze of wildly curling red hair. Here was the second of his rescuers—his captors—the one who had claimed some undisclosed purpose for him. She seemed hardly more than a child, flat-chested and narrow-hipped. The tights, knee-length skirt, and snug bodice she wore only emphasized her boyish shape.

She was the first woman he had seen in a decade, and he felt nothing. Neither his heart nor his body stirred. He realized with a shock that this girl reminded him of his sister Cassidy, so dimly remembered. Only Cassidy's hair had been black, like his.

The girl whistled through her teeth. "You heal quickly, don't you?" She clasped her hands behind her back and circled him, clucking under her breath. "Do you always walk around stark naked? I liked you better as a wolf."

"Then get out of my way, and you won't see me again."

She placed her hands on her hips. "Well, at least you can speak."

Morgan bared his teeth. *Too late,* his mind wailed. *Too late.* "Who are you?"

"I'm Caitlin—Caitlin Hughes. Do you have a name?"

"Morgan. Holt."

"Well, Holt, do you know where you are?"

"The old man told me."

"That old man is Harry, who agreed to take you in, and don't you say anything bad about him, or you'll answer to the rest of us." She glared at him. "I doubt that it occurred to him that you would just up and leave without a word, after we saved your life."

The hairs rose on the back of Morgan's neck. "I did not ask you to help me."

"You came to us, didn't you?" She gestured about her eloquently. "We haven't much to spare, nothing at all for outsiders, but we accepted you. Who else would have done that? You owe us more than running away like a whipped cur."

Obligation. Morgan stared across the grounds and at the freedom beyond, so rapidly slipping from his grasp. "You think . . . there is a reason that I came," he said, pitching his voice in mockery.

"I know there is."

"There is no reason for anything that happens."

"You really believe that, don't you?" She shook her head. "Whatever you are, wherever you came from, I think there is some honor in you, or you would already be gone. That's why you are going to help us."

He met her gaze, and she took one step back. "You play a dangerous game."

"You don't frighten me. I've seen too much."

She was a little afraid, but she hid it well. He felt the first stirrings of grudging respect, as he had felt fear of bonds that had nothing to do with prison walls.

"I have nothing to give you," he said harshly.

"But you do. You have something very valuable. We make our living by showing people things they've never seen before. And you are something very few people have seen."

"You want me to . . . go on display?" The idea was so absurd that it erased both doubt and fear. He turned to go.

Her hand caught at him. His first impulse was to remove it by the swiftest means possible, regardless of the damage to her. He held himself rigid instead, and growled.

"I can't let you go. Not until you promise to meet the people who helped you."

Morgan recognized the trap, and that he must pay a price to escape it. He gave the girl a terse nod. The language of her body told him that she had not been sure he would agree and knew full well that she could not stop him. She ducked into the tent and reemerged with his blanket.

"Put this on," she said, "and come with me."

He took the blanket and draped it over his shoulders. Caitlin marched across the camp toward the nearest tent. People called out greetings in the twilight, voices warm with friendship. Morgan hunched into his blanket and deafened himself to Caitlin's cheery responses. They were not his friends, and neither was she.

They reached a tent as shabby and patched as the others, and Caitlin lifted the flap. "Go on inside," she said.

He hesitated. Three distinct and familiar human scents

permeated the air. This was yet another trap, another way to hold him.

"Don't worry," Caitlin said. "You could break Ulysses in two if you wanted, and Florizel is harmless. As for Tamar—" She shrugged.

Morgan tried to lay back ears that remained stubbornly fixed in place and entered the tent.

Two men sat at a pair of folding chairs on either side of a small table, intent on a game of cards. One of them was of average size, but his skin was pale as the moon, and his hair the same ghostly hue.

The other was the height of a child, legs dangling well above the ground. He was dressed impeccably in proportioned trousers, vest, and coat, all made of what Morgan guessed to be expensive cloth. His boots shone with recent polishing. His features were handsome, his thick yellow hair the sort that any dandy might envy. But nature had shaped his body into a parody of a normal man's.

Behind them stood a woman of overwhelming sensuality, lushly curved and with skin that shimmered as if imbedded with a hundred tiny gemstones. Her thick black hair fell almost to her waist. A pair of snakes wound about her shoulders and upper arms, tongues darting.

The serpent woman stared at Morgan with dark, glittering eyes. At the table, the albino threw down his hand of cards with a breath of disgust.

"Don't even attempt to deny it, Wakefield. You let me win again."

The little man lifted his brows. "You need not play if you find it unpleasant," he said in a smooth Southern drawl. "I do apologize if I have offended."

The albino snorted and looked toward Morgan. Wakefield followed his glance.

"Ah," he said. "I see that our patient has recovered." He slid down from his chair. Caitlin went to his side, her slight form towering above him.

"Ulysses, this is Morgan Holt. Morgan Holt, this is Ulysses Marcus Aurelius Wakefield."

The dwarf executed a surprisingly graceful bow. "I am at your service, sir."

Caitlin shook her head. "Your Southern courtesy is wasted on this one, Professor."

"Indeed. And you, of course, have not in any way provoked him, Firefly."

Caitlin snorted. She glanced at the dark woman. "This is Tamar, the snake charmer. And Florizel"—she indicated the pale man with a nod—"is our chief Joey. That's 'clown' in towny talk."

Florizel regarded Morgan with mournful wariness. "This is your Wolf-Man?" he said. "This is our final hope, our savior?"

"Florizel, you talk too much," Caitlin said.

"I do not believe that this is the time for familial squabbles," Ulysses said. He looked up at Morgan with the same fearlessness as Caitlin's, but his came from a deeper, quieter place. He was as removed from passion as Morgan sought to be.

"It is unfortunate that we were unable to consult your wishes, Mr. Holt," he said, "but you were insensible at the time. Caitlin is prone to strong feelings—premonitions, if you will—that move her to rash action. She often fails to apply logic when it would be most useful. She sees your particular talent as a possible solution to our quandary—which you may have observed."

"She wants me to work for you," Morgan said. "To be one of your . . . freaks."

"To be one of us," Ulysses corrected. "You were alone and on the verge of death when you arrived. Have you somewhere else to go?"

"I prefer to be alone." Even as he spoke, Morgan did not understand why he had admitted that much to a stranger. He lifted his lip. "I am alone."

"It is a rare man who truly prefers solitude," Ulysses said. "As for Caitlin's hopes—many of the troupers have no home other than this. It is their family. Harry took in the first outcast ten years ago, and he has never turned away anyone in need. But our troupe has faced one misfortune after another in recent months—theft of our capital, the illness of our horses, and grave mishaps of weather. We have insufficient resources to feed ourselves and nothing saved for winter quarters. We are now in a precarious position that may require us to disband if we wish to survive. You, with your unique gift, appear to have arrived at a most propitious moment."

Morgan thought of his adopted pack, all dead, and what it had been like to be part of a greater whole. Yet he had always been separate, even then. Always.

"I can't save you," he said. "Let me go."

Ulysses studied Morgan for a long stretch of silence. "You are what they call a hard man, Morgan Holt, one who has lived apart from civilization for some time. You are accustomed to caring for yourself. You are exceptionally skilled in survival. You do not care for the entanglements of emotion, and that is why you resent any debt placed upon you. Yet you still suffer the pull of obligation. Why?"

Morgan felt as if he were being taken apart piece by piece like the inner workings of a clock. "You are smart, little man," he said softly. "But you don't know everything."

"I believe you are a man of honor, Mr. Holt, though the world may not recognize that quality." His broad brow creased. "You have faced some great trial that has tested your faith in mankind and driven you into the wilderness. But now you find yourself among those who might begin to understand."

Words. Accurate words, razor sharp, that wove themselves into a wire made for a single purpose. The noose was tightening inch by inch. Morgan backed away, prepared to toss the blanket and run. Caitlin held out her hand as if to stay him again, and for once she appeared as vulnerable as any other girl of her age.

Morgan took another step and struck a warm, firm surface. Hands caught at him to steady him. He spun about to face Harry French, who held a bottle of whiskey in one broad, chapped hand. The old man blinked in surprise.

"You should not be on your feet," he said. He looked beyond Morgan to the others. "Caitlin, why did you let him get up? You are pale, my boy, much too pale."

"Mr. Holt is leaving us, Harry," Caitlin said.

Harry's face fell, and it was as if the sun had gone behind a cloud. "Oh, I see. I see."

The disappointment on this old man's face pierced Morgan's dormant heart more surely than any of Caitlin's reproaches or Ulysses's recital of disaster. For a moment he saw his father's face, and the dying of dreams. The end of all hope.

"Well, well," Harry said, trying to smile, "we must at least share a drink before you depart. I did, as you see, manage to find one bottle."

"The only one left," Caitlin said. "Don't waste it, Harry."

"We place no price on kindness, Caitlin." He set the bottle down on the small table and drew a pair of glasses from his coat. "Let us drink to your recovery, Mr. Holt—and to your continuing good health." He poured and offered Morgan the first glass.

Morgan stared down at it. Had he been able to stomach the stuff, he could not have swallowed it down past the lump in his throat. "I don't drink."

"Ah. Very admirable." Harry lifted his own glass, gazed at it wistfully, and set it back down. "There is no escaping our troubles in the bottle, no, indeed."

Morgan turned his face away. Harry patted his shoulder. "Think nothing of it, my boy. We asked too much of a stranger. But you must not go until morning, after you have had a good meal—"

Morgan shook him off and strode out of the tent. He walked blindly across the lot, shivering though he did not feel the evening chill. He stopped at the edge of the camp, let the blanket fall, and willed the Change. His body protested, but it obeyed. He began to run to the hills.

The low woodland of pinon, juniper, and oak closed in about him, and the voices of the circus folk became the distant cries of birds. Thick fur rippled and flowed about his body. Small game fled before him. His broad paws devoured the miles. The sky lit his path with a thousand stars. The clean air sang to him. Human voices, human thoughts were left in the dust of his passing. Far, far to the north, the wolves called him to the old life of forgetfulness.

He had made it over the first range of pine-clad hills and into the adjoining valley before the tether snapped him to a stop. He raged and fought it, but it pulled him southward, back across the mountains step by reluctant step.

He had never taken charity, nor become dependent upon anyone. He was whole, but only because *they* had made him so. His body was free, but not his heart. Not so long as the debt remained unpaid.

Obligation was not belonging. It did not mean friendship, or love, or any of the worthless words men used so freely. It did not bind him forever.

He would make his pact, serve out his time, and leave without regret.

Sunset was driving shadows down into the valley when he reached the woods above the camp. He sensed the wrongness at once, and the alien scents of strangers. Cries came faintly from the cluster of wagons and tents. Morgan set off at a fast run down the hillside.

The handful of men who were causing the trouble might have been rowdies from the nearest town, grubstakers who had lost their claims, or even desperados from over the New Mexico border. They, like wolves, would attack where they saw weakness, but they took joy in the tormenting.

One brawny fellow staggered under Caitlin's insignificant weight while she pummeled his head and shoulders; Harry was wringing his hands and shouting warnings from the sidelines, and the oversized trouper, Tor, had two of the other townies by their collars. The fourth invader held Ulysses Wakefield suspended in his arms.

"Sir," Ulysses said with impeccable dignity, "You are mistaken if you believe that we have anything worth stealing. I have no wish for violence."

"Violence!" the ruffian spat. "Why, you li'l speck—"

Morgan plunged among them and seized Ulysses's tormenter around the ankle. Teeth pierced wool and flesh. The man yelped and dropped the dwarf. Ulysses curled into a tumble and jumped to his feet, brushing off his clothing. His eyes met Morgan's. He nodded, slowly, unsmiling.

Morgan wheeled about on his hind feet and went for Caitlin's opponent.

"Wolf!" the first man cried. "It's a wolf!" Like the coward he was, he took off as fast as his limp would allow. Caitlin leaped from her adversary's back, and he dashed after his fellow. Tor's two captives picked themselves off the ground and followed suit. Morgan let them go.

"That should teach them," Caitlin said, slapping the dust from her hands. She eyed Morgan. "About time you showed up."

From all parts of the camp, the other troupers gathered close against the night. Children ran from the tents, whooping at the excitement as their parents scolded them. Morgan stood at the center of the loose circle, as alien as he had ever been, and Changed.

There were a few gasps, and murmurs, and one exclamation. No one fled. Harry, Caitlin, and Ulysses drew near, with Tamar close behind. Moonlight silvered the skin of the snake charmer, unearthly in her beauty, whose creatures coiled and rustled about her shoulders.

"So it is true," she said, looking at Caitlin. "He is what you claimed."

"And he can save us, Tamar. He is one of us."

"He is one of us," Ulysses repeated gravely.

"Welcome," Harry said, clapping Morgan on his bare shoulder. "Welcome and thanks, my boy. Your return was most timely indeed." He rubbed his hands and beamed at them all. "My dears, I think it is best if we move on straightaway. If one band of ruffians has discovered us, others may as well. We have much to prepare now that our new friend has joined us, new towns to conquer." His eyes lit up like a child's. "The Wolf-Man," he said. "We have much to do!"

Tamar slipped closer to Morgan. The patches of scaly skin on her bare arms winked and glistened. "Will you share my wagon tonight, Wolf-Man?"

Caitlin snorted. The twined snakes on Tamar's shoulders reared up.

Ulysses stepped between them. "Mr. Holt can, I believe, decide for himself."

"I'll walk," Morgan said. He met Harry's gaze. "I owe you a debt. I will repay it."

"I know you will, dear boy. Your generosity—"

"I am neither generous nor honorable. I don't want your thanks. I don't want anything from any of you."

"Someday," Caitlin said, "you'll need someone, Morgan Holt. I hope I'm there when it happens."

She marched away toward the tents, and the others followed. Morgan remained where they had left him, listening to the snap of canvas, the stamps and snorts of the horses, and the soft calls of the troupers and crew as they broke camp. He made himself blind to the stars that had been his only roof for so many years, deaf to the summons of the wilderness and the deep terror in his heart.

Someday you'll need someone.

Never. Never again.

Chapter 3

"*Is it real?*"

"It can't be. These circus people know every trick there is. Born thieves and swindlers, all of 'em."

The two farmers stood a few feet away from the bars of the cage, just near enough to feel daring. The older one, a frayed bit of straw between his teeth, gave a knowing nod.

"Purest fakery, all of it, take my word." He spat into the trampled straw at his feet.

"Maybe you're right," the younger hayseed said, "but it sure looks real to me." He grinned slyly. "You want to go in there and find out?"

"They won't let no one in there."

"Then just put your hand up to the bar. See what it does."

The milling crowd between the two men shouted mocking encouragement. "Go on!" a store clerk urged. "Stick your hand in and see what happens!"

The farmer glared. "I ain't here for your amusement—" He jumped back with a cry as Morgan lunged at the bars, baring his teeth for effect. The farmer's companion fell onto his knees and crawled away among the feet of the observers. Within seconds, the crowd was abuzz with delight and terror, pressed as far toward the rear of the tent as they could go.

"B'God, it *is* real!"

"Don't you dare swear, Cal!" a woman cried. "It's a minion of the Devil himself!"

"Aw, it's just a man in a fur suit . . ."

Morgan stalked the length of the cage and back again, curling clawed fingers in menacing fashion, and retreated to his corner. Some foolhardy soul poked a stick through the bars; he snapped it in two with a casual swipe of a hand. A lady shrieked and pretended to swoon. He had seen it all a hundred times.

One of the sideshow talkers arrived to herd the townies to the next attraction and on to the big tent for the show. Once again The Terrifying Wolf-Man was a spectacular success.

Morgan released his hold on the Change and let himself become human again. He had grown used to the discomfort that accompanied the unnatural half-shaping, but it was only after the performance that he felt the ache deep in his bones and muscles.

Stiff and sore, he let himself out of the cage and shrugged into his dressing gown. He splashed his face with water as if he could wash away the stares of the humans, the constant smell of their bodies crammed into the small tent day after day. Always the same ritual, the same contempt, the same resolution.

Tomorrow. Tomorrow I'll go. I've done enough.

He laughed and pushed wet hair away from his face. He'd let it grow until it reached his shoulders, heavy and wild like a wolf's pelt. He meant it to remind him of who he was, and who he was not.

He stripped off the dressing gown and pulled on a shirt and trousers. Nearly five months he had been with the circus. Five months, and Harry had said just yesterday that the troupe had enough money saved to set up in winter quarters without the risk of disbanding.

Thanks to the Wolf-Man, whose fearsome reputation had preceded the circus in every town, village, and fly-speck camp they'd visited. It didn't matter that French's Fantastic Family Circus was still a modest wagon show, unable to compete in grandeur with the great Barnum or Forepaugh. Each farmer or rancher, merchant, or whore—young and old, male and female, simple or smart—had to see for himself if the creature was real, or as fake as the farmer had claimed. Some came back two or three times. None of them ever learned the truth.

They didn't want to. And Morgan endured their igno-rant speculation and taunted them with his poses and snarls. He had learned to be amused at the blindness of men.

The troupers were equally blind. They had accepted him completely, welcoming him as if he had always lived among them, but he had done for them all he was capable of doing.

Tomorrow, I go.

He rinsed the sour taste from his mouth and walked out into the night. Beyond the lanterns that marked the perime-ter of the circus grounds lay a swathe of darkness, and be-yond that the lights and bustle of Colorado Springs. The cries and applause of the audience in the big top drowned out the murmur of crickets and the soughing of the wind in the cottonwoods along the creek. Every night he stood and listened, poised to run from everything he despised.

I could leave now, he thought. But he remained where he was, turning his face to the north where men held sway. He had not gone into town since the troupe's arrival three days ago; he never slept in the cheap hotel rooms shared by the troupe's top performers when they could find such accommodations.

But it was not Colorado Springs that drew his attention northward instead of west into the mountains. Instinct, the only part of himself he dared trust, whispered in a lost and unlamented tongue.

You are not alone, it said.

He shivered violently, as if the words were raindrops to be shaken from his coat. He had been alone since he'd left home at fourteen. In all his years of searching for Aaron Holt, there had never been another like him or his mother or sister.

You cannot hide forever.

He snarled and turned south, toward the big top. For once safety lay in the crowd, where the voices of his past did not reach. He strode past loitering townies along the midway and entered the pad room where the troupers dressed and prepared for their entrance. The smell of human bodies assaulted him once more. The crowd roared approval as the clowns completed their performance.

"Is it tonight, then?"

Morgan looked down at Ulysses, who still wore his scholar's robes and mortarboard. The "Little Professor" was, according to the sideshow talker, both the smallest and most brilliant man on earth. He could answer any question, and sometimes made remarkably accurate judgments of character. Morgan knew that only too well.

Morgan showed his teeth in a half-smile. "Reading my mind, Professor?"

"Not at all. Simple logic and observation." He flipped back the sleeves of his robes. "Our finances appear to be in good order. You have achieved what you set out to do. Your debt to us is paid, is it not?"

Us. It was always us, the troupers against the world, and Morgan just outside the circle. He wanted it that way.

"Harry would be most disappointed if you failed to bid him farewell." Ulysses removed the oversized cap with its gold tassel and held it between his manicured hands. "Caitlin, as well."

By unspoken consent, they both moved to the back door, the trouper's entrance, to get a better view of the big top's interior. Caitlin was just beginning her act, balanced gracefully atop the bare back of one of her well-trained gray geldings as it cantered around the ring. With each circling, Caitlin somersaulted over banners held by her assistants, landing perfectly each time. Her bare feet, blessed with remarkably flexible toes, never lost their grip. Red hair bounced above a laughing face.

"Caitlin cannot understand your desire for solitude," Ulysses said. "She, more than any of us, has kept the troupe together. But you have no ties to bind you here. You do not seek a home among others like yourself."

"There are no others like me."

Ulysses raised his brows. "While it is true that I have never observed a second member of your species, I theorize that you do have kin somewhere—family—who share your gifts."

It was not the first time that Ulysses had tried to pry into Morgan's past. If anyone had the right to ask, he did. The two of them shared living quarters, and Ulysses's dispassionate nature suited Morgan's desire for privacy.

Morgan grudgingly admired the little man's detachment from the scourge of emotion. But Ulysses had one besetting flaw, and that was his curiosity. On more than one occasion, that persistent quest for knowledge had pierced Morgan's careful guard.

"I have no family," he said. "Do not feel sorry for me, Professor. I don't need what you and the others want."

"But you have changed," Ulysses said. "Whether or not you wish to admit it, you are different from the man who came to us months ago. Harry and Caitlin saw it in you from the beginning."

"Saw what? That I could be tamed like a dog to a leash? Men will sooner kill each other than give up any part of what they are."

"Men will fight for what they believe in. What do you believe, my friend?"

"That a man who trusts anyone but himself is a fool."

"Perhaps. But to be a fool is better than to be without hope."

"The way you cling to the hope that your family will take you back?"

Such small cruelties were usually enough to stop anyone fool enough to demand amiable fellowship from Morgan Holt. Ulysses was made of stronger stuff.

"Touché," he said. "Pope said that fools rush in where angels fear to tread, and neither of us is an angel." He turned to go, just as the applause of the crowd marked the end of Caitlin's act.

Cursing himself, Morgan stepped in front of the little man. "Damn you," he said softly. "You should leave me alone, Professor."

Ulysses gave him one of his rare and wistful smiles. "Even wise men can be fools in friendship. Alas, notwithstanding my family's disappointment in me, they raised me to be a gentleman."

"And I am not. I belong with the wolves. Not here."

"We all, at one time or another, doubt where we belong. If you will excuse me—"

"I am—" Morgan still had not learned how to apologize without the words sticking in his throat. "I was too harsh."

Ulysses bowed. "It is no matter. And now I have letters to write."

"Your family?"

"A gentleman's duty, I fear."

"Even though they never answer."

"They are family," Ulysses said. "One will do much for family that one will not for a stranger."

The old pain could sometimes catch Morgan unaware, as it did now. "I prefer to remain a stranger."

"Sometimes that choice is made for you, regardless of your inclinations. But if you choose to leave us tonight, do not forget us."

This time Morgan let him go. He had never yet won a debate with Ulysses Marcus Aurelius Wakefield.

"He has feelings also, you know."

Caitlin walked up beside him, dabbing at her face with a cloth. Her bare arms, neck, and face were moist with perspiration, and tendrils of her hair clung to her cheek. The barking of Vico's trick dogs in the ring signaled the beginning of the next act.

Morgan watched the canines' antics with faint contempt, remembering how Vico had tried to convince him to play tame wolf among the curs. "The Professor can take care of himself."

"Is that why you always stick to him like a burr whenever we go among the townies?"

"The Professor is right. Your imagination does run away with you."

"You are a terrible liar. You'd rather die than admit you care for anyone, or anything."

"And why should he admit that to you?" As silent as her serpents, Tamar appeared beside them. "You try to change him into something he is not." The snake charmer's heavy-lidded eyes swept over Morgan. "It is not a mistake I make."

Morgan took a careful step back. Tamar had a unique power of her own—to fascinate nearly every man who came within her grasp. She was tall, lithe, and beautiful, despite the coldness of her eyes. The lilt of her exotic accent worked like venom mixed in honeyed wine. No towny knew that the luxurious wig of raven-black tresses concealed a head as smooth as snakeskin. Most of her suitors would not have cared. They were smitten.

But all of them, towny or trouper, she ignored . . . save Morgan. He avoided her, and so she pursued all the more relentlessly.

She slid close to him, running her supple hand the length of his arm. "You are weary, my friend. Leave these who do not understand. Come to my tent, and I will soothe your brow with scented oils and sing ancient songs of love."

Only a dead man could fail to be aware of the sexuality Tamar exuded with every whispered word, every motion. The circus folk were no Puritans, but he ignored the few invitations he received. To take a trouper as a lover, even casually, meant stronger ties with the circus. He preferred the anonymity of women who sold their services for a price.

Even so, he was tempted. His body was hungry for the release it had been denied so long. Sex was touching without true intimacy, pleasure without commitment—not as it was among the wolves. Tamar might be satisfied to know she had conquered him, if only for a night.

A slow smile curved Tamar's lips. Her hands left his arm and wandered lower. He flinched. She laughed under her breath.

"My poor, poor wolf. You are sick. Tamar can ease your pain." She cupped him boldly. "No one understands you as I do. Come, my fine stallion. We will ride fast and far."

Caitlin made a rude noise, jerking Morgan from his daze. "The man who wrote about the subtlety of serpents cannot have been thinking of you, Tamar."

"And no man would want you," she hissed. "You stink of horses. You are shaped like a stick. Morgan would not have you if you begged him."

"Morgan is my friend." Caitlin cast Morgan an apologetic look. "I don't seduce my friends."

"I do not think you are a woman at all. Why don't you find another girl to play with?"

"That is hardly an insult worthy of you, Tamar. Where's the poison in your tongue?"

Morgan growled. Two pairs of feminine eyes fixed on him, and Tamar shut her mouth. Caitlin folded her arms across her chest and started to speak.

"Be quiet," he said. "If you want to fight, wait until I am gone."

"Gone?" Caitlin repeated.

"I'm leaving tonight."

Tamar clutched his arm. He shook off her grasp and met Caitlin's stricken gaze. "The Professor said I should tell you before I go."

"How very kind of you. How gentlemanly."

"I never claimed to be either. I have repaid the debt—"

"And now you go on your merry way without a thought for what you're leaving behind."

"I made no promises."

"Good riddance, then."

"You are strong, Firefly. The strong survive."

"If you don't say good-bye to Harry, I will hunt you down and kill you myself."

"I would be a fool to risk your anger."

"You would never make a good clown, Morgan Holt," she said, tears thick in her throat. "Go on. *Go.*" She ran back into the big top as the band struck up the finale.

He obeyed before she could change her mind. Tamar had already slipped out of the pad room, for which he was profoundly grateful. But he hadn't come away unscathed. The unfamiliar, bitter taste of regret burned on his tongue.

This was sadness. Guilt. He had let himself grow too close to Caitlin—and to Ulysses, and Harry. There was still one final ordeal ahead.

He waited by himself at the edge of the lot until the stream of townies emerging from the big top heralded the end of the show. Laughter and excited chatter dwindled and faded, only a few children lingering to catch a final glimpse of the freaks by moonlight. The rest drifted past the ticket wagon, down the midway and toward the town lights.

The performers came next—Florizel and the clowns, Vico with his dogs, Caitlin and her assistants leading the horses to their pickets, Regina the bird-boned rope-walker, Tor the strong man, and all the others. They left the tent singly or in small groups, each to his or her own wagon or tent. The roustabouts and crew would work through the night to tear down the big top and prepare the troupe for departure before dawn.

But even the rest would not sleep. It was a time for celebration, because at last the troupe could afford to take up winter quarters and rest until spring without fear of disbanding or starvation. The "freaks" of French's Fantastic Family Circus would keep their beloved home and sanctuary for another year.

And Morgan would abandon it as he had every other home he had ever known.

The last, solitary figure to leave the big top moved with the deliberation of a man who suffered the aches of old age and believed no one was watching. Morgan skirted the edge of the lot and paused just outside of Harry's tent until he heard the sound of pouring liquid and a satisfied sigh.

Bloodshot brown eyes looked up as Morgan entered. Harry set down his glass, and his snowy moustache lifted in a grin.

"My dear boy," he said. "Pull up a stool. I believe that we can call our final performance in Colorado Springs yet another triumph, don't you agree?" He lifted his bottle. "Perhaps tonight? No, no, of course not." He took another swallow and smacked his lips. "All the more for me!"

Morgan ducked his head. In many ways this was the most difficult, this farewell. Caitlin was not naive, in spite of her small size and pixie's face. Ulysses was too pragmatic to believe that Morgan would stay. But Harry . . . Harry French was still a child, unaffected by the punishing hand of experience.

"It's all thanks to you, of course," Harry continued. "We have already found a lovely spot for winter quarters, in Texas. Far better than the old one in Ohio. We will all have plenty of rest and time to improve our acts." He chuckled. "No point in confining ourselves to the smallest towns. All we need do is take care to avoid direct competition with the big outfits. We may not be large, but we have the finest attractions in the west!"

"Harry—"

"Yes? Did you say something, my boy?"

Morgan steeled himself. "I am leaving, Harry."

Harry grew very quiet. He set down his glass. "Well, well. We knew this day would come, didn't we? Though I had hoped—"

"I am . . . grateful for what you did," Morgan said. His voice sounded rough and harsh, and he made an effort to soften it. "You know that gratitude does not . . . come easy to me."

"Ah, yes. Yes, I know." He gave a small laugh that blew

out his whiskers. "That makes it so much more important when you give it."

"Don't, Harry. I am not worth . . . this—"

"Feeling?" Harry didn't raise his eyes. "Feelings are difficult for you. I know that, too. You are a man of few words, and yet . . ." He looked up, tears in his eyes. "I do not believe you are a man of no sentiment. Otherwise you would not have come to make your farewells."

"You see what you wish to see."

"My eyes are old and weak, but some things one sees with the heart. In some ways, for all your abilities, you are blind, my son."

"Do not call me that."

Harry flinched from his snarl but remained where he was. "Forgive an old fool, Morgan. I have made it a policy never to seek into the pasts of my people, and I have broken that rule with you. I only wish . . . that I might convince you that you are a better man than you think."

Morgan's temples had begun to throb. The hair on the back of his neck stood up at the premonition of disaster. "I came to say good-bye, and to . . . thank you." He backed toward the tent's entrance and stood awkwardly for a final second, despising his hesitation, and strode from the tent.

He got no farther than the foot of the hills. He had not Changed. His heart weighed him down, cold and smothering like a heavy snowfall. He would have welcomed a strong snow now. It would disperse the scents of those he left behind, and draw a veil between the world and the wordless silence of the wild.

The solitude. The loneliness. A howl built in the back of his throat, the only sound of grief he could make.

But the snow did not answer his summons. The sense of wrongness he had felt in Harry's tent had grown. An evil scent wafted up from the prairie, the acrid smell of smoke.

He turned to face the east. A roiling cloud rose from the circus lot far below. Something very large was burning.

He ran more swiftly than any human, bare feet finding purchase on loose pebbles and sharp rock. The smoke curled inside his lungs and stung his skin. Soon the light of a towering fire obscured the moon and stars. By the time he reached the lot he had to force his way through the crowd of onlookers drawn by the spectacle of a large and destructive blaze.

Flames devoured what was left of the big top, and several other tents and wagons were burning as well. Troupers stood about in forlorn knots, helpless, as the local volunteer fire department struggled to extinguish the conflagration.

But the damage had been done. The prop wagons had been among those destroyed, along with a number of tents and most of Harry's office wagon—the one that held the troupe's wages and savings.

Sifting subtler scents from the overwhelming stench of smoldering ash, Morgan found his way to Harry.

The old man was not alone. Caitlin and Ulysses stood with him. Firelight picked out the grief on each upturned face. All the progress the troupe had made since Morgan's coming had been undone in an hour.

"Harry," he said.

The old man turned, his eyes wells of misery. "Morgan?"

"You've come back?" Caitlin asked. Her face broke into a broad grin. "You couldn't abandon us, not now. Not ever." She flung herself at him and embraced him tightly. Morgan endured the touch in stoic silence.

Harry's eyes met his over Caitlin's head. "You are a good man, Morgan Holt."

Caitlin stepped back and wiped at her face with her coatsleeve. "What do we do next, Harry?"

He looked at the billows of smoke that rose from the dying fire. "We continue, as we always have. We find a way to go on, even if we must perform through the winter."

"We go on," Caitlin agreed. "And we stay together."

Ulysses moved to Morgan's side. "I hope that Caitlin does not suffer a grave disappointment," he said softly. "It is much worse than Harry admits."

"I know."

"You are remaining with us?"

"I will stay. I have no choice, do I?"

"I sometimes wonder," Ulysses said, "if Caitlin is not right, and there is a reason for such events—one beyond our understanding."

"Then whoever makes such reasons has no love for me—or you."

" 'The heart has its reasons which reason knows not of.' "

"You are a fraud, Professor," Morgan said. "You still listen to your heart."

"And you do not?"

Morgan turned on his heel and walked away.

Chapter 4

The fire had drawn Niall, though he might have missed it had he not left his hotel for a late-night stroll. Colorado Springs was not so great a town to ignore a good-sized conflagration, especially when it was burning up a visiting circus.

So Niall followed the crowds to the outskirts of town, where most of the blaze had already been extinguished. He had not seen the circus perform, preoccupied as he had been with the business he had recently completed in New Mexico, but he recognized disaster when he saw it. He watched with detached curiosity as the circus people ran to and fro, gesticulating and crying out as some new loss was discovered.

He could almost pity them. His father had suffered such setbacks in his early years of business in Denver, but he had persevered and overcome them. He had been daring and ruthless as well as shrewd, as one had to be in these times. Niall had carried on in his footsteps. The Munroe fortune had doubled in the seven years since Niall had taken control.

But he had started with an advantage. These people, vagrants and mountebanks, lived on the edge of ruin. He doubted any of them would accept a decent, steady job in place of the life they lived.

Once he had considered the wandering life himself. Once he'd had no thought of the future beyond the next five minutes. Athena had paid for his folly. Now he spent every day trying to make it right. And failing.

He pushed his hands into the pockets of his greatcoat and remembered his last conversation with Athena. *"Where did you get your hard heart, Niall?"*

She simply could not understand. How could she, sheltered as she was? And he intended to keep her that way. She had no conception of the dangers of the world, the cruelties it held for a young woman foolish enough to believe she could change it.

Niall sighed and looked at the stars, visible now that the smoke had begun to clear. When was the last time he had glanced up to notice the constellations, or walked for the sake of walking? He took for granted what Athena was unable to do, because of him.

Well, now he had an opportunity to prove Athena wrong about the nature of his heart, if he chose to take it.

He dropped his gaze and followed a lone figure as it crossed the lot with a purposeful stride. One of the performers. A woman—by no means curvaceous, almost childlike—but graceful nonetheless. In fact, the way she moved was arresting, and he found himself staring after her when she disappeared into one of the undamaged tents.

It wasn't until he was almost there that he realized he had been walking toward that very tent. He stopped, considering retreat. This was not his world, or his business.

But his sudden impulse to help demanded that he find someone to accept his generosity. He pulled his wallet from his pocket and examined the contents. A hundred dollars would be more than adequate.

A head poked through the tent flap. It was crowned by an untidy cap of curly red hair, and the face beneath was attached to the young woman he had followed.

She stared at him, nonplussed. He tipped his hat.

"Forgive me," he said, "but have I the pleasure of addressing one of the performers of this establishment?"

The girl burst into laughter. "You talk like Ulysses. Who are you?"

It was his turn to be taken aback. That she could laugh at such a time amazed him, but her bluntness was astounding.

"I beg your pardon," he said. "My name is Niall Munroe. I could not help but notice the damage you have suffered as the result of the fire—"

"Did you?" She stepped fully from the tent, and he got his first good look at her. His initial impression had been correct: she was slight, boyishly slim in an oversized coat, and elfin in size and bearing, but her eyes were bright and her smile dazzling. "And why should you care, Niall Munroe?"

Indeed. He thought once more of walking away, but her eyes held him rooted to the spot. "I had thought to offer my assistance," he said stiffly, "but if you have no use for it, Miss—"

"Hughes. Caitlin Hughes. And I still wonder why a towny should care what happens to people like us."

Towny. She spoke the word like an epithet. He drew himself up to his considerably greater height. "In Denver, it is customary for the fortunate to assist those who are less so. When I noted the degree of your misfortune, I hardly thought that you would be likely to reject any offer of help."

"Oh." She widened her eyes. "I understand. You are a very rich man from the big city, and you wish to give us charity."

He slammed his hat back on his head. "I see I have offended you, so I will be on my way—"

"No. Wait." She bit her full lower lip and sighed. "I'm—we are not very used to townies offering help. Most of the time, they—" She broke off. "You'll have to speak to Harry."

"Harry?"

"He is the manager and owner. I'm sure he'd be very happy to see you, Mr. Munroe."

He had the absurd desire to ask her to call him Niall. "I would be obliged, Miss Hughes."

She flushed, raising freckles on her pale skin. He wondered again how he could possibly find such a ragamuffin attractive.

Caitlin looked up the long, slim length of the gentleman and cursed herself for an idiot. She knew as well as anyone that the troupe was in dire straits, even if she pretended otherwise for Harry's sake. If some towny wanted to offer help, who was she to say no? Even if all of the alarm bells in her head were going off at once.

Yet, she had to admit, this fellow was no ordinary towny. He was dressed like someone with a great deal of money. He carried himself like a prince. He was handsome, in a cold sort of way. And he looked at her with a strange intensity she couldn't ignore.

Morgan had that intensity. But when *he* looked at her, she saw only a friend. She felt no prickling in her belly, nor heat in her cheeks.

"I'll tell him that you have come," she said, retreating quickly into the tent.

"Back so soon?" Harry said, looking up from the chaos of ledgers and papers he had salvaged from the office wagon. His face was drawn and haggard. "What is it, Firefly?"

"There is a man outside—a towny—who . . . well, as peculiar as it seems, he wishes to help us."

"Indeed?" Harry pursued his lips. "That is peculiar. Well, send him in, by all means!"

Caitlin nodded and went outside to Niall Munroe. He was fidgeting, something she hadn't expected to see in such a dignified gentleman. It made him seem more human, somehow.

"Harry—Mr. French—will see you now," she said.

"Thank you." He nodded and stepped into the tent.

Caitlin waited outside, pacing back and forth. The scent of burnt canvas and wood was choking, but the tingling in her nerves only heightened her hope. Could Niall Munroe's appearance be yet another miracle? Several months ago, she'd been certain that Morgan had been meant to come when he did. Now her intuition was telling her the same thing of the gentleman stranger.

Your intuition, or something much more physical?

She shook her head in self-disgust, but waited out the long hour while Munroe consulted with Harry. Munroe emerged at last, settled his hat on his head, and buttoned his coat against the night's chill. He did not seem surprised to find her still there.

"Good-night, Miss Hughes," he said. "We shall meet again."

She flushed at his bow and looked elsewhere until he was some distance across the lot and headed toward town. Harry appeared a moment later.

"You will not believe this, my dear, but we are saved yet again!"

"Saved?" she murmured.

"That gentleman, Mr. Munroe, has offered us an engagement in Denver, a private performance for his family's orphanage. The Munroes are very important people in Colorado—I have heard of them myself. They are extremely wealthy and influential. Mr. Munroe's sister is quite a central figure in Denver society and does much good work. He wishes to contribute to her charities in a most novel way. He has agreed to replace our tents, provide us with a lot on land he owns, and pay us very well indeed. So well, in fact, that it will more than make up for this night's losses."

"So much?" Caitlin could no longer see Munroe's form, yet she continued to search against all reason. "It is so late in the season—"

"One last performance, and then we may have enough to winter over as we had planned. How can we turn down such an opportunity?"

We can't. Of course we can't. Yet Caitlin felt a wild see-sawing of dread and anticipation, as if she were attempting a new and very dangerous stunt.

"When are we to leave?" she asked.

"As soon as we can be ready. I shall call the troupers together at dawn and share the good news." He clasped his hands. "Ah, it has turned out to be a much better night than events would suggest! Who knows where such patronage might lead?"

Indeed. Harry always found the good in everything, but she felt the same sense of anticipation.

Of one thing she was certain. Their lives were about to change—hers, Morgan's, everyone's. She couldn't begin to guess where those changes were leading, but Fate had intervened with a vengeance.

After tonight, nothing would be the same again.

The tall, familiar figure strode up the drive, and Athena rolled away from the parlor windows to face the door. Niall had come home.

He had been gone a very long four months. Strange that in spite of their last argument, she had missed him terribly. Not even the constant social and philanthropic commitments had been completely successful in easing her loneliness.

When did it begin? she asked herself, listening for the door and Brinkley's greeting. *When did I become . . . dissatisfied?*

She could not pinpoint the precise day or date, but the feeling of emptiness had been growing, and it troubled her. She had spent wasted hours looking out the window at her friends and neighbors walking and riding in the crisp autumn air, and remembering what it had been like to kick at piles of leaves and dash across the park on a high-spirited horse.

But her friends and fellow Society members had been as attentive as always in their visits, just as generous in their contributions. The orphans and poor folk still responded to her visits with solemn gratitude. There was no good reason for her disaffection.

Surely it was the change of seasons that made her feel so restless. Now that Niall was back, those troublesome emotions would dissipate. His opposition to much of her work might even fire a renewed determination. Yes, that was what she needed—fresh inspiration, something to fight for.

The front door opened. Brinkley's voice welcomed his employer home, and Niall's footsteps echoed in the vestibule.

Athena sat up straight and had her best smile ready for him when he walked into the parlor. She held out her hands.

"Niall, welcome home! It is so wonderful to have you back."

He bent to take her hands and kissed them. "Athena. You are looking well—and lovely, as ever."

Athena searched his face. He, too, was looking well; his ordinarily sober gray eyes were almost sparkling, as if with some hidden mischief. They reminded her of the old days, when Niall had been . . . when it had been so much easier for him to laugh. So much easier for both of them.

"Sit down, and tell me all about your business," she said, signaling for the parlormaid to bring tea, coffee, and biscuits. "Was it very successful?"

Niall smiled and sat in his armchair facing the fireplace. "You have never taken any interest in my business."

"Perhaps it is time I did."

"And perhaps it is past time that I take an interest in yours."

She grew alert. "I am . . . sorry about our argument before you left—"

"No. You were quite right. I have been too harsh, without understanding."

Her heart swelled with hope. "That is kind of you, Niall. Nothing would please me more than if you wished to help."

"Then I trust you will be pleased with what I have brought you today."

Athena did not allow herself to show vulgar excitement. Niall often brought her gifts upon his return from business trips, but never with such pleasure.

"I do not see a package," she said, leaning as if to look behind him. "I cannot imagine what you can have brought from the mines in the south!"

"Oh, it will not fit in any sort of box," he said with mock solemnity. "Indeed, you will have to come outside to see it."

Alarm stopped the air in her lungs. "Here at the house?"

"It would not even fit on the grounds. You must come out with me, in the carriage, if you want your present."

She looked down at her lap and the carefully arranged folds of her gown. "You know . . . that is not easy for me, Niall."

"You go out to the orphanage and among the poor."

"Yes, but that is different—"

"Because they have no right to pity you?"

She flinched at his too-acute observation. For a moment he looked uncomfortable. "I realize that you do not enjoy going into the city, or even on social calls," he said. "But I think you will wish to make an exception in this case."

She met his gaze. There was a hint of a challenge in it, and that was shock enough to win her full attention. He was so apt to want to protect her, and now he urged her to go out. There was something special about this, indeed.

"Very well," she said slowly. "If you will take refreshment while I prepare—"

"Nonsense. You are fine as you are." He rang for Brinkley. "Please call Miss Munroe's maid, and tell Romero that we will be needing the rockaway."

Fran appeared to settle Athena's wrap about her shoulders and pushed her chair down the hall. Only moments ago Athena had been wishing for some new source of inspiration, and her wish seemed to have run away with her.

Fran, Romero, and Niall bundled her into the carriage

and covered her legs with another wrap. She forced herself to look out the window as they set off, catching glimpses of several women she knew walking arm in arm, a new mansion going up on Welton, the streetcar on its way to the business district. Everything about Denver was moving, too busy to slow down for an instant.

She expected Niall to stop the carriage at any time, but they rattled on out of the better part of town, past more modest dwellings with livestock kept in dusty yards, and on to an area near the outskirts of the city. The Munroes owned several empty lots there, and Niall had often said that he expected the investment to pay off when the city expanded and required the land for new construction.

Curious despite herself, Athena looked for anything unusual. The carriage made a turn down a dirt track, and there, spread across a field of autumn grasses, was her surprise.

A circus. She recognized the tents, the colorful wagons, the peculiar folk moving about with their animals and bright costumes. Niall smiled, pleased at her confusion.

"You wonder why I bring you to a circus?" he asked. "Before I left, you chided me about my failure to help those in need. You will be pleased to know that I have listened. I have not only assisted these people in their time of need, but I have engaged them to perform for your orphanage at my expense."

Athena stared at him and realized her mouth was agape. "Niall . . . I am . . . I could never have imagined—"

He signaled Romero to stop at the edge of the lot. "I wanted you to see this for yourself, and meet those I've hired to entertain your children."

"Oh, Niall. The children will be so delighted, I know it."

He reached across the seats to press her hand. "So long as it delights you, Athena. Shall we?"

He and Romero helped her down, and her chair was taken from its special rack in the boot. Athena was too busy absorbing the view to notice the bumpy, uncomfortable ride over the rough ground as Niall pushed her chair toward the tents.

A fat, jolly-looking man with white whiskers came to meet them as they approached the largest tent, the one she supposed must house the main performances. He was eccentrically dressed, but quite normal in contrast to a few of the people she had glimpsed at work or practice on the lot.

"My dear, dear Mr. Munroe!" the stout man said effusively. He pumped Niall's hand and looked down at Athena. "And this must be your lovely sister!"

"Athena," Niall said, "may I present Mr. Harry French, the manager and owner of French's Fantastic Family Circus. Mr. French, Miss Athena Munroe."

"Delighted, delighted beyond words." French beamed at her. "May I say how very charmed I am to make your acquaintance?"

Athena liked Harry French instantly. She returned his smile and pressed his hand.

"I am glad to meet you, Mr. French. My brother tells me that you have come to Denver to entertain the children of our orphanage. I know they will consider it the experience of a lifetime."

Harry blushed, his skin contrasting even more vividly with the white of his moustache. "We shall do our best, indeed we shall. Your brother has done us a great favor. You see, we had suffered a number of misfortunes, and he offered a solution to our difficulties. He is most generous. Oh, yes, most generous."

Niall looked away. "I hope that you will not find it inconvenient to show my sister something of your establishment, Mr. French," he said gruffly.

"My pleasure. Oh, yes. We are still setting up, but I am sure—ah, there are a few of my troupers, if you would care to follow—"

He set off at a waddling trot. Niall sighed and steered Athena after him.

"Do you think this is the right circumstance for introductions?" Athena asked. "Perhaps it would be better to invite them to our home instead."

"You astonish me, Athena," Niall said. "One doesn't invite such people to one's home."

She could not argue. From all she had heard, circus folk were deemed little better than vagrants, dirty and ignorant. They were not the sort of people she usually dealt with—neither needy and dependent, nor wealthy and cultured.

But surely it was a matter of finding the right way to speak to them. The troupers Harry French had mentioned were standing in a group looking at the large tent, talking amongst themselves. Athena noticed the new look of the canvas, without so much as a scuff or tear. Many of the other tents had a worn appearance, as did the wagons.

"Miss Munroe," Harry said, waving her and Niall forward, "I am pleased to present to you my troupers, whom I feel I may boast are among the finest in our nation." He rocked back on his heels and swept out his arm in a grand gesture. "Caitlin Hughes, our graceful Lady Principal or equestrienne; Ulysses Marcus Aurelius Wakefield, also known as the Little Professor, genius and prognosticator; Tamar the Queen of the Snakes, and Morgan, our—"

"Very pleased to meet you, Miss Munroe." The girl French had introduced as Caitlin stepped forward, began to hold out her hand, and dropped it awkwardly. She was pretty in an unusual, impish way, very small in her circus costume of tights and short skirt. She glanced at Niall. "Harry told us that we'll be performing for the orphans you care for. It is very kind of you and Mr. Munroe to help children who don't have a home."

Athena smiled. The girl could not be very well educated, and certainly was not refined, but Athena warmed to her as quickly as she had to Harry French. "Good afternoon, Miss Hughes. I know that I will look forward to your performance."

Caitlin blushed as red as her hair and stepped back. The small man beside her bowed to Athena.

"Ulysses Wakefield, your most obedient servant," he

said with a soft Southern drawl. "I trust that you will find our humble company worthy of your highest expectations."

How strange it was to look upon another person who carried a physical burden so much greater than her own. Here was a gentleman, by his clothing, manner, and speech, yet though she was seated he could meet her gaze while standing straight on his own two, short legs. His face was handsome, and he carried himself as if he were of average height. But he, like Athena, must often face a world that could not understand.

She offered her hand. "I know I shall not be disappointed, Mr. Wakefield," she said. He kissed the air above her knuckles, leaving her feeling unaccountably flattered. She looked up at the third person and lost any sense of comfort.

Tamar was tall, voluptuous, and beautiful, but her black eyes were devoid of warmth. Her lips remained flat and unwelcoming. A darting, reptilian head thrust out from under her dark wrap.

"Miss Munroe," she said, her voice low and heavily accented. "I hope you do not find it inconvenient to come here."

"No. Not at all, thank you." Athena kept her hands folded in her lap and held Tamar's gaze, resolved not to let her unease show. It was clear she would receive no friendlier greeting from the Queen of the Snakes. But an even more disturbing sensation centered on her temple, seeming to emanate from the direction of the man Harry had not quite finished introducing.

She turned her head. Her eyes met those of the last man. She could have sworn that even her legs felt the impact of that golden gaze.

"Oh, yes," Harry said, bumbling up beside them. "How remiss of me. Miss Munroe, please meet Morgan Holt."

Chapter 5

So strong was the sense that they had met that Athena almost asked him where he had been and how he had fared over the years.

She caught herself before she made an embarrassing mistake. They had not met before. He was a stranger, though her heart insisted otherwise. A stranger who compelled her to stare in defiance of all good manners and propriety.

Morgan Holt was tall, though not quite so tall as Niall. He was broad through the shoulders and lean through the hip in the way of a natural athlete. While the others wore coats and wraps against the autumn wind, he was dressed in an open-necked cotton shirt and simple trousers, and his feet were bare.

But his face made such oddities insignificant. Oh, he was handsome enough—not in the conventional way preferred by the women in Denver society, but undeniably attractive. "Rugged" was the word that came to mind. He was clean-shaven, making no concession to the fashion for long side-whiskers and moustaches. His black hair fell to his shoulders, like an Indian's, and his brows were dark slashes above piercing golden eyes. Yet something in his face, in his expression, held a fascination for her that went far beyond looks.

Secrets. His face was full of secrets, a calm surface over hidden currents that bubbled and boiled. Utter fearlessness. Fierce independence. All the things she wished she possessed.

Morgan was a man who would never beg for a place in the world. Never have to prove anything. No one would pity him.

He blinked like a cat in the sun. She came to herself abruptly and realized that he was giving her the same methodical examination to which she had subjected him. His eyes grew hooded as they tracked from her face to her lower body and the chair with its special wheels. And then he met her gaze, and she saw what she had dreaded . . . and expected.

When men looked at her, they did not see a woman. They saw a cripple, a girl never permitted to grow up, a creature to be protected and pampered but never loved. Not as a man loved a woman, as her father had loved her mother.

Most of the time she was able to ignore masculine discomfort with her affliction. Most of the time she didn't allow herself to think of Niall's business partners, or her friends' brothers, as men at all. That entire part of her being remained safely locked away.

Until a man like this one came along. And suddenly, painfully, she was aware of his potent maleness and her own shortcomings as a woman.

"Miss Munroe," he said.

She started, hardly expecting him to speak. "I am pleased to make your acquaintance, Mr. Holt," she said, grasping at the rote phrase. "What is your area of expertise in the circus?" She smiled cautiously. "Are you the lion tamer, perhaps?"

He made a sound in his throat that she guessed was a laugh. "There are no lions here. No animals in cages, except for one. You could say that I tame him, as much as he can be tamed."

His voice was baritone, a little rough, without the accents of refinement that Mr. Wakefield's held, or the hint of a more advanced education that marked Harry French's speech. It had its own particular music, like the sighing of wind in mountain pines.

"And what sort of beast is it, Mr. Holt?" she asked.

"One you have never seen before."

"Rare and deadly, I suppose?"

"Yes." He stared at her face as if he could discern her thoughts through sheer determination. "What do you do, Miss Munroe? What is your . . . expertise? Or do you have one?"

He was mocking her. She prided herself on reading voice and expressions, and there was no doubt that Morgan Holt meant to provoke.

She glanced around to see if Niall was listening, but he was deep in conversation with Mr. French and Caitlin Hughes. Ulysses had gone, and only Tamar watched from a distance, her snakes coiling about her upper arm.

"You refer, perhaps, to this?" she said, gesturing at her lower body. "Do you judge that one in my situation is unable to do anything of worth? I assure you that neither my mind nor my heart are paralyzed, Mr. Holt."

As soon as the words left her mouth she wondered where they had come from, and why she had revealed so much to a hostile stranger. He did not know her, nor she him, yet already she felt as if they were at odds, engaged in a battle for which she did not understand the cause.

And that was ridiculous. If anything, he was an employee, part of a world separated from hers by class, money, and inclination.

"I am sorry," she said coolly. "I misunderstood your question."

"Harry says your family are important people in Colorado," he said. "Your brother hired the troupe knowing Harry had to accept his offer, whether he wanted to or not."

He scraped a hollow in the earth with his foot. "When you have money, anything is possible, isn't it?"

Now she understood his antagonism. He did not feel contempt for her disability, merely for her wealth. He resented what he and his people lacked, and what they owed Niall. Perhaps his own background was one of poverty.

That was no excuse for his discourtesy. "I think I see," she said. "You have decided that having money renders a person incapable of virtue or honest work. It is wealth that you object to, even when it provides you with employment. I am truly sorry that your life has been so difficult, Mr. Holt."

Ah. *That* penetrated his armor. "Very kind of you, Miss Munroe," he said with a curl of his lip. "I guess when you spend your life helping your inferiors, you don't notice what your own life is missing."

She did not allow him to see her flinch. Who in heaven's name did he think he was? He did not know her, or anything about her. She held on to her temper, bewildered by her growing anger. She had almost forgotten what real anger was. It distressed her far more than anything Morgan Holt had said.

"I can see that my activities would not interest you," she murmured. "I do not tame dangerous beasts, merely persuade reluctant ones."

"What would you call me?" he asked softly. "Dangerous, or reluctant?"

His questions made no sense except as another pointless provocation. That he could be dangerous she had little doubt . . . though not to her. How could he be? He was only a man—proud, rude, and difficult, but still a man. She could escape his company whenever she wished. And as for reluctant . . .

"You seem to like riddles, Mr. Holt," she said, "but I prefer to save such amusements for my friends."

They stared at each other. Athena felt increasingly uncomfortable, and the new, phantom tingling in her legs grew more pronounced. No, not in her legs . . . somewhat above and between them. Her mouth went dry. She thought about calling out to Niall and asking him to take her home, but her throat issued only a whisper.

This was quite ridiculous. Mr. Holt was a challenge, but she had faced such challenges before, from ruthless businessmen and distrustful poor alike. She felt sure that she could win, if not Morgan's liking, at least his respect. It seemed important that she do so, as long as she did not concede too much. It was necessary if she was to help him.

Help him? What had put such a thought into her head? He was neither destitute nor ill, merely ill-mannered.

"I did not mean to be discourteous," she said. "We simply do not understand one another. We are—"

"Too different." A strange expression passed over his face. Had she not known better, she might have thought it wistfulness. Loneliness. But then he laughed, shattering the illusion. "If I ever came to your world, Miss Munroe, you would have to keep me on a leash."

She knew better than to back down. There must be something truly wrong with him—a great bitterness, or some subtle disorder of the mind. And yet, even as she considered it, she knew the explanation was too simple. There was much more to Morgan Holt than met the eye.

His eyes. What was it about his eyes?

The uneasy silence came to a halt with a sudden commotion at the edge of the lot. A string of handsome carriages drew up behind Niall's, and Athena recognized them immediately. She sighed with mingled relief and apprehension. She didn't know who had told her friends about the circus, but she was glad enough of the distraction.

"If you will excuse me, Mr. Holt." She wheeled her chair about, intending to make her own way, but she found herself being propelled forward by strong, sure hands. She knew the touch was not Niall's. In spite of Morgan Holt's surliness, he pushed her chair with skill, avoiding stones and potholes as deftly as if he had been doing it all his life.

Perhaps it was a form of apology. She could scarcely object when her friends were already coming to greet her.

Cecily Hockensmith was in the lead, followed by several of the younger and more adventuresome ladies in Athena's circle. They advanced in a flock, exclaiming and staring at the astonishing sights and smells.

"My dear Athena!" Cecily said, holding out her hands. "We heard about this wonderful new scheme of your brother's, and just had to come and see for ourselves. How clever of him, to hire a circus just for the dear orphans. How very original!"

Suzanne Gottschalk, blond and beautiful, lifted her handkerchief to her nose. "How very . . . fragrant it is."

Millicent Osborn trilled a laugh. "Of course, silly. Have you never seen a circus before?" She nodded at Athena. "Do not pay any attention to Suzanne. We are all so impressed, are we not?"

"Indeed," Grace Renshaw said, sliding her spectacles up her nose. "Yet another feather in your charitable cap, so to speak. I do not know what the unfortunate of our city would do without you and Mr. Munroe."

Athena hid her pleasure and greeted them all with a smile. "You praise me far too highly. It was indeed my brother's idea, and quite unexpected. I have just arrived myself."

"Then we are not too late for a tour," Millicent said. "It must be terribly exotic. And, of course, we shall want to contribute to the performance—you must allow us to help!" She looked up over Athena's head. "Perhaps this . . . gentleman?"

Athena was keenly aware of Morgan behind her, of his earthy scent and masculine bulk. And the obvious fact that he was not a gentleman. He was more than likely prepared to insult her friends as he had tried to insult her. She could only pray that he did not.

"Ladies," she said, "may I present Mr. Morgan Holt, one of the performers of French's Fantastic Family Circus."

The ladies fell silent, gazing at Holt. Athena wondered if they were having the same reaction she had, or if they merely found him an uncouth curiosity. Most of her friends did not share her habit of going into the slums to distribute food and clothing. To them, he would not seem much different from the "lower elements" their fathers and brothers warned them about.

"I declare," Suzanne exclaimed. Millicent giggled, and Grace shushed her.

The back of Athena's neck continued to prickle. "I am sure that Mr. French will be pleased to show us the grounds, but Mr. Holt may have other engagements."

"What a pity," Cecily said with frosty emphasis. "We do not wish to keep you, Mr. Holt."

A gentleman would have taken Cecily's dismissal with good grace and beat a dignified retreat, but Morgan Holt did not move. Instead, it was Cecily who took a step back, bumping into Suzanne and causing a minor disturbance.

"I have no other . . . engagements," Holt said, faint mockery in his tone. "Should I show you the wolves first, Miss Munroe?"

Morgan stood still and let himself be stared at, as contemptuous as a raven surrounded by chattering sparrows. No, not sparrows, but extravagantly plumed parrots who had ventured from their cages for an afternoon.

The leader of the flock accepted their homage in regal majesty, prim and proper in her wheeled chair and only slightly less gaudy than the others. And he wondered, not for the first time, why he remained with her.

Their meeting had been less than cordial. Even had he not known her identity, he would have pegged her as the kind of woman—lady—who had existed only on the fringes of his life: an engraving in a tattered magazine; a beribboned mannequin on the arm of some overstuffed peacock parading down the dusty main street of a nameless town; a face from the box seats during a performance.

What else should she be? He knew what kind of people she and her brother were. His father had envied and aped them all his life. How many promises Aaron Holt had made, to his wife and children, always beginning and ending the same: "You'll lack for nothing once I make my strike," or "When I'm rich, in just another year or two . . ."

Athena Munroe came from a world Morgan touched only by rare chance, as alien to him as tea cakes to a timber wolf. The fabric of her gown alone might have seen a poor family through an entire winter. The pearls about her slender neck and in her ears were tasteful and even more costly. She wouldn't have looked at him twice if he hadn't spoken first.

And yet, within the space of a few minutes, he had said more to her than he generally did to his fellow troupers in a day.

And he was afraid.

He knew the reason, though it made no sense. When he had first seen Athena Munroe, when he had looked into her bright hazel eyes, he felt for an instant that he'd found the source of the voice. The voice, the call from the north, the one he had ignored and dismissed that last night in Colorado Springs.

The feeling persisted even when he realized the folly of such thoughts. It certainly was not her beauty that held him rooted to the spot, staring like a boy with his first woman.

Athena Munroe's face was pleasant and even of feature, with slightly full lips and high cheekbones. Her skin was clear, her jaw stubbornly firm. Her hair was an unremarkable brown. What figure he could see was slender. But her eyes . . .

Her eyes held unexpected depths. They shifted in color with every small motion, from brown to green and back again. They gazed at Morgan with a perplexing combination of vulnerability and defiance, and he had sensed that she was afraid—not of him, but of his pity.

She was a cripple. He could not imagine a fate more awful than to be trapped as she was, unable to run. That was the other, unlooked-for quality he'd seen in her eyes— the abiding sadness of permanent, devastating loss.

Loss he understood. Pity came, and with it the kind of emotion he despised. He had provoked and taunted her, hoping to shatter his unwilling sympathy, to chase her away or incite some pompous remark that would bolster his dislike of her kind.

But she had answered him with spirit, even attempted an apology, and he felt the stirrings of reluctant admiration at her courage. He had remained by her side to help her when he should have walked away. That had been a mistake.

She was not like him. She was a lady—spoiled, protected, used to having her way—and now that he saw her among her own people, he knew that his sympathy had been misplaced.

"Wolves, Mr. Holt?" she asked lightly, not bothering to turn toward him. "I thought you had said that there were no wild beasts in your circus."

He wheeled her chair around. "No beasts, Miss Munroe—only men who act like them."

"Of course. I have already seen an example. Would you not prefer to return to your friends?"

She, like the cold, black-haired beauty among the parrots, was trying to dismiss him. He smiled, showing his teeth. "I am all you have at the moment, Miss Munroe."

"Perhaps we ought to come at another time," the black-haired woman said.

"No," Athena replied. "If Mr. Holt is willing to guide us, then let us go ahead, by all means." She nodded to Morgan. "If you please."

So she turned her disadvantage around and kept her dignity, putting him in his place again. No, *she* didn't need his pity. He planted himself behind the chair and pushed her in the direction of the big tent, pursued by the clacking beaks of Athena's parrots.

He was debating how best to shock the silly creatures into flight when Athena's brother strode up to join them. He tipped his hat to the ladies, who simpered in return, and smiled down at his sister.

"Well? Are you pleased, my dear? I did warn you that these people are not what you are accustomed to, but—"

"It is lovely, Niall. Thank you." She half turned her head, as if she were trying to catch a glimpse of Morgan's face. "Have you met Mr. Holt? I believe he . . . handles the animals."

Niall glanced at Morgan with indifference, and then focused with a hard stare. It was obvious that he had not noticed who pushed Athena's chair. Morgan's instincts came fully awake, as they did in the presence of an enemy.

"We have not met," Niall said. "Mr. Holt, I will escort the ladies."

"Mr. Holt was about to take us on a tour—" Athena began.

"Mr. French has arranged one for a more appropriate time," Niall said. His gaze remained fixed on Morgan. "All of you ladies will be welcome, of course."

The black-haired woman pressed close to Munroe. "I was just telling Athena how very generous it is of you to provide such grand entertainment for the children."

"I fear that I cannot take credit, Miss Hockensmith. This was entirely Athena's idea."

"Niall—" Athena began.

"Please do not deny it," Miss Hockensmith said, covering Athena's hand on the chair arm. "You do so much, my dear. We can but admire your dedication."

Morgan studied the woman. His immediate dislike for her was almost as intense as it was for Niall. She hung on Munroe as if she claimed him for her mate, but his scent revealed no trace of interest.

Athena gently withdrew her hand. "You are too kind, as always."

"Not at all. But surely you tire yourself, dear Athena. We should all go back, as your brother has advised."

Morgan tightened his grip on the chair handles, recognizing what he was seeing. Athena was the lead female of her pack, and Hockensmith coveted her place. Among wolves such competition could lead to injury, even death. But these creatures were more likely to squabble and peck than rend and tear. He watched Athena to see how she would respond.

But he was denied the chance to find out, for Harry and Caitlin reappeared, Tamar a few yards behind. Caitlin stopped several feet away from the society ladies. She looked at Niall Munroe, and he looked back. The scent of attraction was unmistakable.

Munroe and Caitlin? As likely a pairing as himself and Munroe's sister. But he was not the only one to have noticed that mutual stare. Miss Hockensmith's dark eyes were narrowly centered on Caitlin. She all but snarled.

Harry bustled up to Athena's chair, a trio of rolled posters in his hands. "Ah, Mr. Munroe, Miss Munroe . . . ladies! I had thought them all burned in the fire, but I have managed to salvage several of our papers. You may find them amusing." He handed one to Niall, one to Athena, and the third to Miss Hockensmith. "We would normally have many more printed in advance when we are to play in a town, but since this is a performance for your children, Miss Munroe, that will not be necessary."

Niall Munroe tucked his poster under his arm without unrolling it, and Miss Hockensmith did likewise. Athena glanced at it and smiled up at Harry.

"I'm sure the children will enjoy seeing this. Thank you, Mr. French."

He nodded and glanced at Morgan. "Ah, Morgan, my lad. Perhaps Mr. Munroe has told you that we plan a tour and rehearsal for Miss Munroe and her friends in a few days' time. We wish to be at our best, do we not?"

Morgan understood the hint, if not Harry's reason for giving it. He stepped away from Athena's chair. Unexpectedly, Athena pivoted to face him and smiled as she had at Harry.

He forgot whatever had been in his mind. Speech failed him.

"Thank you, Mr. Holt, for offering to escort us," she said, extending her hand. "We shall meet again."

He took her hand without conscious thought. It was

small and warm in his, and her glove did not lessen the firmness of her grip. Why should a pampered rich girl be so strong?

"Would you like to see my little pet, Miss Munroe?" Tamar pushed between them, stretching one of her snakes toward Athena's face. The serpent probed the air, tongue flickering. Athena flinched and held very still.

"Tamar," Harry said, "I do not think that Miss Munroe—"

"Oh, do not worry. He is quite harmless." Tamar stroked the scaled head tenderly. "Harmless to *my* friends."

"*Tamar.*" Morgan grabbed her arm. "Take it away and leave her alone."

She let herself be pulled aside. "Of course, my darling wolf." She smiled at Athena. "I am certain that we will become better acquainted. I have many other little companions eager to meet you."

Niall took a step toward Tamar, looked at Morgan, and clenched his jaw. "Mr. French, I trust that you will make sure that no dangerous animals are allowed to run loose on these grounds." At Harry's hasty reassurance, he assumed his position behind his sister's chair. "Come, Athena. I'll take you back to the carriage. Miss Hockensmith, ladies."

He tipped his hat with one final, telltale glance at Caitlin and set off at a rapid stride before Athena could speak again. Most of her adoring flock went with them, and Tamar stalked away toward the tents.

Miss Hockensmith lingered. She dismissed Morgan with a glance and subjected Caitlin to a long, slow examination.

"Are you one of the performers, dear?" she asked. "What a very daring costume. If you go into the city, I do hope you will wear something less . . . provocative."

Caitlin glanced down at her tights and skirt. "I—"

Morgan saw with astonishment that Caitlin's sharp tongue had gone as mute as his own. He turned on Miss Hockensmith. "Caitlin has a reason for what she wears. You dress like that"—he indicated the woman's elaborate gown with a jerk of his chin—"to make males sniff after you."

She stared at Morgan, her lips parted in utter shock. "How dare you."

"He dares . . . quite a bit," Caitlin said, finding her voice. "I would not annoy him."

No insult quite fitting enough came to Miss Hockensmith. "I . . . I see that Mr. Munroe has been taken in by . . . by . . . I shall have to tell him—"

Morgan growled. Not a small growl from deep in the throat, but the kind he would use on a lesser wolf who came too near a challenge. Miss Hockensmith paled and took several hasty steps back, almost tripping on her ridiculously confining skirts. Without another word she spun around and hastened after the others.

Caitlin let out an explosive sigh. "That was not a good idea, Morgan."

"They are all alike, Firefly. Do not trust them."

"I don't think you follow your own advice."

"What?"

"I saw the way you looked at Athena Munroe."

For the second time in a handful of minutes she astounded him. "And how was that?"

"The way I've never seen you look at a woman before."

"You had better cut your hair, Firefly. It's getting in your eyes."

She shook her head. "You have a good poker face, Morgan, but you're a terrible liar. What was it about her? Her pretty voice? Her fine manners?" Caitlin's expression was uncommonly serious. "You have better taste than I thought. I liked her."

"And you never liked outsiders," he said harshly. "Until today."

"Niall Munroe is a gentleman. This is his doing, after all. He didn't have to be so generous."

"What is it about him, Firefly? His fine suit? The fancy way he talks? Most females would consider him handsome."

"The way his sister looked at you, she must think you're pretty handsome yourself."

The hair behind his ears bristled. "*I* am no gentleman."

"And I am no lady. Still—" She shrugged. "My feelings have been wrong before. Maybe they are this time."

He didn't ask her what particular "feelings" she referred to. If she chose to moon after the cold-blooded Niall Munroe, it was her privilege—so long as she did not expect others to have such feelings. Him least of all.

Caitlin yawned with exaggerated indifference. "Well, I am off to bed. It will be dawn soon. You should rest too— even wolves need sleep." She set off for her tent, and after a moment he headed for the one he shared with Ulysses.

The little man was lying on his cot, arms pillowing his head. He opened his eyes when Morgan walked in.

"Something is disturbing you," he observed. "I noted it when we met the Munroes."

"Everyone is interested in my feelings tonight," Morgan growled.

Ulysses rose on his elbows. "It is only that you so seldom reveal your inner thoughts, and it is rare that I am able to observe them."

"I should be honored that you find them entertaining."

"Nothing of the sort." Ulysses swung his short legs over the edge of the cot. "I am naturally concerned about the well-being of my fellow performers, especially when one of them has sacrificed much to remain among us."

Morgan poured water from a pitcher and drank several glasses in succession. "There is nothing wrong with me. I have no interest in this Athena Munroe."

"Ah."

"Sometimes, Wakefield, your brains get in the way of your sense."

"Perhaps. But your own objectivity is frequently in question, my friend."

"When have you seen me with a woman?"

"Never. But you are not like other men—except, I venture, in one essential manner. Neither man nor wolf is without certain instincts for the preservation of his kind."

"Including you?"

"It would be most inadvisable for me to father children," Ulysses said gravely. "But you have a gift worth preserving."

"I have met Miss Munroe once, and already you and Caitlin have decided that I want her." He laughed. "As if she would have me, crippled though she is. I am not human. Worry about Caitlin, not me."

Ulysses was silent for a time. "I feel that it is incumbent upon me to warn you that you talk in your sleep."

Morgan turned sharply to face him. "What?"

"You have spoken of things . . . deeply painful. I know you would not wish to share them with outsiders, but I am your friend, Morgan. I will listen, should you—"

"What did I say?"

Ulysses held his gaze without fear. "You spoke of your father. And of prison bars."

Morgan slammed his glass on the sawhorse that served as a table. "I am a convict. Does that change your friendship, Professor?"

"No. It only convinces me that you must speak of these things to someone if you are to put them behind you."

"As you've put your past behind you?" Morgan laughed. "I—"

The tent flap opened and Tamar eased inside. She glanced at Ulysses and ignored him, making straight for Morgan.

"I waited for you," she said.

Morgan eyed her coldly. "I was not aware we planned to meet."

"But you do not wish to spend this night alone."

"You make yourself foolish, Tamar," Ulysses said, the words clipped like a Yankee's.

"I do not care for your opinion, little man."

"Morgan wants no part of you."

"Oh, does the mannequin speak for you now, my wolf?"

She sat on the cot beside Morgan and breathed in his ear. "Is he your master? Or are you in love already with the little girl in the chair?"

Morgan stiffened. "If you want tender sentiments, look somewhere else."

"Ah, but I find love as tedious as you do. We have much in common, you and I. We share only what we wish to share, no more." Her long tongue curled about his earlobe. "Come. Come away, and let me show you."

Morgan's body had begun to throb in a way he had ignored one too many times. This was pain he didn't have to endure, especially when the cure was so free of consequences. He and Tamar could use each other without illusions or expectations.

Ulysses and Caitlin thought he was attracted to Athena Munroe. There was one way of making them see how wrong they were—and purging his own senses of Athena's unsettling effect.

He got up, pulling Tamar with him. "Very well," he said. "We'll give each other what we want. But don't expect a lover. I am in no mood for gentleness."

The pupils of her eyes were large with desire and excitement. "I do not want it." She darted forward and kissed him, pushing her tongue into his mouth. He responded with equal violence, despising himself. As she led him from the tent, she cast a final, triumphant glance at Ulysses.

Morgan did not look back.

Chapter 6

The streets of Denver's business district were everything Morgan hated. He stalked up Sixteenth Street, keeping his eyes fixed on his course, head down against the occasional stares and doing his best to ignore the cacophonous noise and overripe smells of horses, dung, spoiled food, smoke, unwashed human flesh, and the scent of many humans crowded together.

He would rather not have come here at all. The Munroes' boundless generosity had provided the circus's principal performers with lodgings at Denver's finest hotel, the Windsor. Morgan might have been included among those so favored, but he would sooner hang than stay in the city. Visiting it was bad enough.

So he remained on the lot with the roustabouts, crew, and lesser performers, watching the circus come to life again. At the end of the first few days in Denver, French's Fantastic Family Circus was back in trim, busy with practice and preparation for the orphans' performance to be held at the end of the week. Everyone had enough to eat, and new costumes were being constructed by the seamstress to replace those that had worn out or burned in the fire.

Harry supervised the improvements and restorations with even more joviality than before. Caitlin had groomed her horses to a satin sheen of renewed health, Florizel and his cohorts were perfecting a new clown act of which he was inordinately proud, and the jugglers, aerialists, acrobats, and dog trainers went about their tasks with cheerful absorption. Hope wafted in the air like a seductive perfume.

Morgan kept to himself. He did not visit Tamar again. His one night with her had been more than enough to purge him of any desire to share her bed a second time. She was easy to put from his thoughts.

The same could not be said of Athena Munroe. They hadn't met again, yet her eyes and her scent came back to him both waking and sleeping. There was no reason in it, and no sense. On the day that Miss Munroe and her society friends were to have their promised tour of the circus, he made an immediate decision to visit Ulysses at the Windsor and remain there. The only way to rid his thoughts of Athena Munroe was to avoid her as much as possible until the troupe left Denver.

It could not be soon enough for him. He walked in the street just off the plank sidewalks, preferring the feel of gravel to dead wood, and constant clouds of dust to human contact. He wore shoes, so as not to attract too much attention—that was one of his few concessions to civilization. And he would not embarrass Ulysses.

He slipped between carriages, drays, and wagons bearing every kind of freight. Water tank wagons sprayed the dirt in a vain effort to keep down the dust, and dirty water ran down the ditches on either side of the street. Fetid odors from the river and smelters hung in the still air. Bands of idle boys stood about and mocked passersby, though they left Morgan strictly alone.

He winced at the continual din of sawing and hammering as new construction went up throughout the district.

The tall brick and iron buildings on either side of the street seemed to draw inward a little more with each step he took, as if they intended to crush him. He passed numerous Chinese laundries squeezed between saloons and mercantiles, the Mint with its disintegrating bricks, and the vast Tabor block at the corner of Larimer.

The Windsor Hotel rose a full five stories at the busy intersection of Eighteenth and Larimer, ponderous in heavy gray stone. Morgan stared up at it, all the hairs on his body standing at attention. Men and women, most well-dressed and prosperous, went blithely in and out the door as if the sheer weight of the construction might not topple over upon them at any moment.

"Are you drunk?" someone shouted. "Get out of the way!"

He sprang to the side just as a heavily laden wagon bore down on the place he had been standing. His ears ached with the noise. He could run away from it—either back to the lot or into the hotel.

He stepped up onto the sidewalk and braved the doors. A pair of befrilled matrons, busy with their conversation, bumped into him coming out. They paused to gawk at him and then hurried on their way.

The lobby opened up around him, a glittering cavern of gilded ornamentation, wrought iron, and polished brass. Chairs and sofas with velvet cushions were arranged in groupings with potted plants. Laughter and conversation echoed. Morgan caught the smell of freshly cooked food from another entrance, which he guessed must lead to the Windsor's dining room.

He kept close to the edge of the vast space and worked his way to the desk where young male clerks waited on guests with their bags and bundles. Morgan stood to the side while the nearest clerk finished with the elderly couple at the desk, summoned a uniformed bellboy, and noticed Morgan.

"May I help you?" he asked, assessing Morgan with a practiced eye.

"Ulysses Wakefield," Morgan said. "His room."

The clerk consulted a ledger and nodded. "Yes, he is a guest with us. Mr. Wakefield is expecting you?"

"Tell me where he is, and I'll find him."

"I will send a boy to let him know you are here, Mr.—"

"Holt."

"Very good, Mr. Holt." He rang a bell. "Just a moment."

Morgan leaned against the counter, his ears pricking at every sound. Drifts of choking perfume streamed after fashionably gowned women like invisible trains. The artificial fragrances that human females used so freely almost succeeded in covering up their natural scents. Yet one such scent came to him, newly familiar, and he surveyed the room to find its source.

He picked her out from among yet another cluster of prattling females—one of the parrots who had come after Athena Munroe to see the circus. He quickly identified two more of the remaining three ladies as among those who had been with Athena on the lot. Only the black-haired one was missing.

Morgan stepped away from the registration desk to get a closer look. Athena was not among the women, but he heard the name "Munroe" rise above the general conversation.

"Sir?"

Ignoring the clerk's query, Morgan made a sudden decision and started after Athena's friends. No one noted his passage. He followed the women as far as the entrance to the dining room, where an officious-looking man directed them to a large table nearby. Morgan paused to study the room.

It was a much fancier place than any hash house or saloon Morgan had been in before his imprisonment, and there were many women as well as men eating and drinking at the white-linened tables. They sipped their wine and ate their steaks without a care in the world.

The attendant gave Morgan a dubious look, as if he

would have liked to direct Morgan to some less high-toned establishment. "Luncheon for one, sir?"

A small, unoccupied table stood fairly close to the ladies'. "Bring a steak to that table," he said. "Rare. And plain water." He showed his teeth. "Don't worry. I can pay for it."

The man opened and closed his mouth. "Very good, sir."

Morgan didn't wait to be shown to his place. He sat down on the upholstered chair, sifting through the interwoven conversations.

"Oh, but really, dear, you did not miss much. We were invited to view a rehearsal today, but I declined."

"And I. Once was quite enough."

The two voices belonged to Athena's friends. Morgan cocked his head without turning it.

"Was this Athena's idea?" a third woman asked.

"So her brother says. And isn't it just like her, bringing an entire circus to Denver for her orphans?"

"Really—it is too ridiculous. She cannot resist trying to surpass what anyone else does, and make herself look like a saint—Oh, I do apologize. I speak too freely."

"You know you are among friends here. And we all agree that Athena—well, how can we help but pity her? How can we but humor her projects, no matter how inconvenient?"

"You can say that, Marie, but you have not been called upon five times in the past month for some new scheme or other. I have had to miss a luncheon and two receptions because of her. And having to look at her, in that chair—"

"Poor thing. *She* will never be married."

"But she will never be one of us—how can she? If she hadn't been gallivanting about like a street urchin when she was younger, instead of learning proper behavior and decorum like the rest of us, she would not have been crippled. But her father spoiled her and let her run wild. Now she has nothing to do but make herself superior to everyone else."

"That is true, Suzanne. Those expensive French gowns are wasted on her. How can she display them properly when she cannot stand, let alone dance? And she is so *good*. I feel a positive ogre in her presence."

"She must try even harder to be perfect when she has such a very great . . . defect."

One of the women lowered her voice to a whisper. "Let us not forget the rumor that her mother . . ."

"Millicent! Remember where you are."

"Let us also not forget that her brother is a very important and eligible man in our city," said the first woman in a droll voice. "It would not be wise to snub his sister." She paused to sip at her drink. "We must face facts, my dears. Athena is *our* charity case, and we must accept that burden."

There was a murmur of agreement, and the discussion turned to the menu. Morgan stared at his hands, clenched on the table.

So these were Athena's friends. These were the ones who had seemed so deferential and filled with praise when they were with her, the companions Athena looked upon with obvious trust. They spoke of her as if she were an object of disdain, not admiration.

Morgan tried, and failed, to understand his seething emotions. Athena Munroe was not even present, and yet she created a storm in his belly and heart that would not let him rest. The pity he had felt the first time he saw her returned, triple what it had been before.

Why? Why should one brief meeting have done this to him? What power did she hold, she who lacked even the honest respect of her own packmates? All he knew of Athena was what he had observed and what her critics had said of her—and what he knew of people like her. This was not his world, nor these his kind. What they did among themselves was meaningless to him.

But over the past few months he had remembered what it was to have friends, to not be alone. He recognized a fellow outcast, no matter how different from him. And Athena did not know she was an outcast.

Every negative characteristic he had expected to find in Athena lay exposed in these women: arrogance, derision, the shallow desire for comfort and ease. Yet Athena was helping the unfortunate, whatever her motives, and these fine "ladies" mocked her efforts. If she was not one of them, what was she?

He got up and, remembering the steak, threw several coins onto the table. He did not go to find Ulysses. He walked past the officious man and out the door, across the lobby and into the afternoon sunshine. He had begun to see that it was pointless to question the impulse that drove him; it was instinct, to be obeyed as human reason could not.

Instinct had led him to the circus. It had given him friends when he had not wanted them. Now instinct pulled him back to the lot.

To Athena Munroe.

As undignified as it might seem, Athena could scarcely contain her excitement as Harry French welcomed her once more to French's Fantastic Family Circus.

He had taken charge of her chair right at the carriage, chattering all the while as he took her across the lot and pointed out the various features of the circus: the midway, with its sideshow and concessions, the cookhouse, the tent and wagon quarters of the crew and roustabouts who made the circus possible—and, of course, the "big top," bright and new. Every portion of the lot was filled with activity, as if the troupers expected a huge crowd of paying customers rather than an audience of orphans.

It was just as well that no other guests would be present at today's rehearsal to witness Athena's childish enthusiasm. Although she had invited her friends and fellow supporters of the orphanage, every one of them had offered some excuse or apology. Ordinarily Athena might have been troubled by so many refusals, but she was too flustered to dwell on them for long.

She had *not* intended to look for Morgan Holt. He had been undeniably rude during their one previous meeting; some might have said that he behaved in a positively unnerving manner, with his hard stares and utter lack of propriety. He, like the woman Tamar, had been the only circus trouper she had met who did not offer a genuine welcome.

But Athena had not been afraid—not of him. That was the strange part; if anything, she had sensed a need in him that spoke to her innermost heart.

What could such a man need, especially of her? He was neither an indigent, a drunkard, or an orphan. He seemed to resent the very idea that he or his friends might require the assistance of a patron, no matter how well-intentioned or what the cause. He had gone out of his way to show himself immune to human frailties.

Yes, that was it—he had needed to *prove* something. But why to her? Morgan Holt could not know very much about her, except by hearsay.

She recalled everything about *him,* in perfect detail: his eyes, the thick mane of black hair, the lean muscle and natural grace with which he moved. The warmth of his strong, bare hand, hot enough to set her gloves afire. The way he had stayed with her and pushed her chair, as if they had known each other for years rather than minutes.

And the way in which he had defended her against the snake charmer. Tamar was one of his own kind, yet he had warned her away with grim resolve. For just that moment, he had seemed as gallant as any gentleman protecting his lady.

What had put that thought into her head? She was not his lady. The mere notion was ridiculous.

She and Morgan Holt had nothing in common. Yet in spite of the huge differences that separated her from the circus folk, she liked Caitlin, Ulysses, and Harry French. Yes, she liked them very much.

"Here we are," Harry said, pausing at the entrance to

the big top. It was the size of a very large doorway, wide enough to admit several people abreast. "This is what we call the front door, Miss Athena. The performers usually come in the back door—that is the entrance from the back-yard, where our troupers prepare for their acts."

Athena smiled up at him. "All these interesting terms. I believe you could hold entire conversations amongst your-selves, and no one outside the circus would understand a word!"

Harry chuckled. "That is the idea." He drew himself up in sham pomposity. "You are greatly favored, my lady, to be privy to our secret language."

"Indeed" Athena said, surprising herself. "I feel most privileged."

Harry flushed, cleared his throat, and guided her into the tent. Immediately Athena felt the space all around her, smelled the sawdust and horses, heard the clipped words of performers calling to each other from high above. She fol-lowed the sounds to the tops of the platforms near the roof of the tent, where a man in tights executed a graceful som-ersault in midair and was caught by a second man.

"Two of our aerialists," Harry said. "They are nearly finished, but the clown and Caitlin's act come next. I have a place for you where you'll be able to observe everything closely."

He guided the chair down an aisle between rows of wooden risers that framed the front door, beneath a rope barrier, and to the very edge of the low-walled ring that en-circled the inside of the tent. He pulled up a chair beside her.

"The Giovanni Brothers are newcomers to our little group," he told her, pointing his chin at the men high above. "They joined our wire-walker, Regina. We were able to add their act when our fortunes took a turn for the better a few months ago. Thanks to you and your brother, Miss Athena, we will be able to keep them."

Athena pulled her gaze from the aerialists and glanced at the old gentleman. "Forgive me if I am too forward, but

my brother did mention a fire that destroyed your original
tent. Had you suffered many misfortunes?"

"Alas, such adversities can plague a small show like
ours. So much depends on elements like the weather, other
troupes in the vicinity, the prosperity of the towns we visit,
and the health of our animals." He shrugged. "The large
shows have begun to use locomotives to move from city to
city, and think the less of wagon shows like ours. Perhaps
we are not as competitive as we might be. But I would not
have it any other way."

"Because you are like a family," Athena murmured.

He looked at her in surprise. "Just so, my dear. A family. And like any family, we will do everything within our
power to help each other and stay together."

Athena felt a twinge of envy and quickly smothered it.
All that was left of her own family was her brother, and he
had so little time to spare for anything but business. Yet he
had brought the circus.

"That is why we are here on this earth—to help each
other," she said.

"And it was our good fortune that your brother came
when he did." He smiled, as if at a private memory. "Just
as fortunate as Morgan's coming."

"Morgan Holt?" She spoke before she realized how
quickly the name had come to her lips. "He has . . . he has
not been with you long?"

"Only a bit longer than our flying friends. It was because of him that we were able to hold our band together
through the summer."

Harry spoke with such warmth that Athena wondered
what Morgan had done to earn it. Harry was one of those
rare men who liked and trusted everyone, yet Athena recognized a deeper affection, almost fatherly. She had not
forgotten a father's love.

"I don't believe that you ever told us what he does, Mr.
French."

"What he does? Why . . ." He hesitated, floundering for
words. "He is currently—ah—creating a new act."

"I see." She glanced at him, wondering why he had been so ready to speak of Morgan a moment ago and then became so evasive. "Perhaps his act involves some special trade secrets?"

"Ah. Yes, exactly so." He patted her hand. "You are very kind in indulging an old man. We must keep our unique attractions from . . . from those who might try to duplicate them."

"I quite understand. I can see that whatever you choose to present, it will be wonderful."

Just as she finished speaking, the promised clowns arrived in the ring, accompanied by several dogs, a large ball, and objects as diverse as a trumpet and parasol. The leading clown, dressed in mismatched and exaggerated garments, had very white skin and hair that did not appear to be painted. He led the others in a series of tricks and pratfalls that had Athena laughing with far more abandon than she would have shown if her friends had been beside her.

The clowns bowed in Athena's direction when their performance was finished, and after a pause, several handsome gray horses were led into the ring. Running lightly after them was Caitlin, with her mop of red hair. She held no whip, yet as soon as she entered the ring the horses fell into order and watched her every move with pricked ears.

"Caitlin is our equestrienne—our Lady Principal—but she has more than one skill," Harry commented, beaming with pride. "She trains liberty horses and performs bareback riding. You will see an exhibition of her riding skills later. Such versatile performers are a great asset to a small troupe such as ours."

Athena nodded, but her attention was on Caitlin. The girl was grace itself. Her feet barely seemed to touch the ground as she stood at the center of the ring and gave brief commands to the caparisoned horses, which reared and danced and turned in an equine ballet.

Of all the things Athena might see in a circus, this was hardest. Once she had been as light on her feet as Caitlin.

Once she had ridden like the wind—and run faster. She felt her legs twitch, a moment of rare sensation, as they reacted in sympathy to the red-haired girl's fluid motions.

Athena rested her hands in her lap and clasped them tightly. It was good that she should remind herself of what she could not have again. Years ago she had abandoned unrealistic hope, but every so often the old longing returned. As it had done, however briefly, in Morgan Holt's company.

"She is truly amazing, Mr. French," she said. "I compliment you on . . ." She lost the thread of her thoughts. A familiar, imposing figure had appeared across the ring, staring in her direction.

Morgan. Her heart soared to the top of the tent, and she knew if she were not very careful it would likely plummet to the ground most painfully.

Harry saw Morgan as well. He shifted in his seat and glanced at Athena. "Please continue to enjoy the show, Miss Athena," he said. "If you will excuse me. . . ." He heaved up from his chair and set out along the sawdust path that skirted the outside of the ring.

Athena tried to concentrate on Caitlin's act, but her gaze sought Morgan across the ring as if some invisible wire connected them. She was hardly aware that one of Caitlin's horses had begun to buck and plunge, surging away from the others.

Someone screamed. Athena turned her head just as the animal leaped the ring and charged straight at her.

Seconds passed as if they were minutes. Athena grasped the wheels of her chair and tried to make them move. She was not afraid. She looked calmly across the ring to where Morgan had been standing.

He was not there. He was already running into the ring, leaving a trail of discarded clothing in his wake. In midstride his body was lost in a dark blur, and when he hit the ground again he was no longer a man. Four large paws threw up sawdust as a great black wolf dashed after the panicky horse.

Athena had the fascinating sensation of floating, as if she had become an aerialist herself. The wolf put on a burst of incredible speed, overtook the horse just a few feet from Athena's chair, and shouldered it aside. She could feel the rush of air as the wolf passed, hear its panting and the squeal of the horse.

Then she began to tremble. Raised voices faded in and out of her hearing. Only her vision remained sharp. With perfect clarity she saw Caitlin grab for the errant horse and take it in hand, watched the wolf skid to a stop and shake its dark coat. The unearthly mist surrounded it again, and when it cleared Morgan Holt stood in the wolf's place.

He was quite, quite naked. Magnificent. Athena bit down hard on her lower lip, struggling to escape the dreamlike unreality that had taken her mind captive. All her senses were working again, but her thoughts spun around and around in helpless circles.

She knew what she had seen. She *knew*.

Morgan took a step in Athena's direction. A trouper came up behind him and slung a heavy cape over his shoulders. Morgan fastened it and strode toward Athena, looking neither to the right nor left. Her view of him was blocked by the small crowd of circus folk who gathered about her. They seemed afraid to speak. Her own tongue was frozen.

"Miss Athena! Are you well?" Harry French's voice shook as he crouched beside her. "I have no words to express our—"

"Later, Harry." The crowd parted for Morgan, and he came to stand before her chair. His eyes—wolf's eyes—held hers. "Can't you see she needs quiet?"

Harry backed away. "Of course. Of course. Let her lie down somewhere. I—"

Without waiting for Harry to finish, Morgan swooped like a striking eagle and gathered Athena into his arms. She felt the thumping of his heart against her side, and his breath in her hair. His steps were so swift that she seemed to fly through the air on invisible wings.

No one had touched her this way except her brother, Romero, or Brinkley when they carried her to or from the carriage or from one chair to another. Those occasions had been impersonal, a matter of necessity. This was very different.

Morgan Holt *held* her. He could as easily have pushed her in the chair. She was not on the edge of death, no matter how shaken she was. But he carried her straight across the ring and through the rear entrance—the "back door," she incongruously recalled—to an antechamber furnished with chairs, a table, and a cot.

He laid her on the cot and settled her comfortably, smoothing her skirt without touching any higher than her knees. Lightning raced up and down her body, spiking below her waist. Phantom sensation—but oh, how wondrous!

Drunk. She felt as the inebriated must feel, though she had not touched a drop. Morgan produced a thin wool blanket and draped it over her. He dragged a chair beside the cot and sat down, wrapping the voluminous cape about him. She could not seem to forget that he was completely naked underneath it. His face was just a foot from hers, and she could see every detail of his features, so much more than she had remembered.

"Miss Munroe," he said. His voice was rough as gravel and filled with concern. Yes, concern, from Morgan Holt. "You are not hurt?"

"No." She smiled like a mooncalf. "I am quite all right."

He got up and stepped behind a blanket hung across one corner of the tent. He emerged a minute later in shirt and trousers, pausing to fill a mug with water from the pitcher on the small table. "Drink this," he said, pressing the edge of the mug to her lips.

The very mundane act of drinking restored her sense of reality. "I saw . . . what you did," she murmured. "I saw everything."

A muscle in his jaw tensed and relaxed. No denial came. He simply waited, staring into her eyes with all the grim patience of a natural predator. He looked ferocious enough to tear her limb from limb, but she was not afraid. Oh, nothing nearly so uncomplicated as fear.

It was not she who needed reassurance now.

She reached from under the blanket and touched his hand. He clenched it into a fist under hers.

"I understand why Harry would not tell me what you do in the circus," she said, gathering her words with care. "I am not shocked, or horrified. I know I am not mad." The shaking started again, a delayed reaction like the prickling that came to fingers warmed by the fireside after long exposure to bitter mountain winds. "I will not give your secret away. You see, I have one of my own." She took a long, deep breath. "I am like you. I am a werewolf."

Chapter 7

*C*ecily *Hockensmith gave her name to the secretary in* Niall's reception room and waited to be announced, gazing with appreciation at the tasteful appointments and the original Bierstadt on the immaculate wall of the office.

Niall had not designed the place, of course. He knew better than to entrust such matters to his own abilities, when his talents lay in other directions. But his had been the money behind everything she saw here, and in the house on Fourteenth Street. He owned the very building in which she stood, and many more in Denver besides. For all its rustic beginnings, this city might make an acceptable home for a lady who had been a leading light of New York's elite.

As long as that lady had the right husband, and all his considerable resources at her command. She had decided when she and her father had arrived, short on cash but long in ambition, that she would aim for the best. If she could not be comfortable in New York, she would be fabulously wealthy in Denver.

There was only one thing standing in her path.

She unrolled the poster halfway and looked in distaste

at the words and pictures. Her feelings in this matter were quite genuine, insofar as the circus people were concerned, and Niall would be as grateful for her efforts on Athena's behalf as he had been in the past. He was beginning to recognize that Athena needed something other than what he could provide. Something that might be found far away from Denver.

As long as Athena was the focus of Niall's life, neither one of them could be happy. Nor could Cecily Ethelinda Hockensmith.

The bronze Dore clock on the marble mantelpiece chimed the hour. Cecily knew where most of Athena's circle was at the moment—enjoying luncheon in the Windsor's dining room as they did every Thursday. Athena never joined them, and Cecily had not yet been invited into the sanctum of Denver's young female society.

That would come soon enough. Athena had welcomed her into her philanthropic sisterhood and to her home, but the unfortunate girl had less social influence than she believed. Cecily had eavesdropped on conversations not intended for her ears, or Athena's. She suspected that those haughty young ladies, who professed to be Athena's friends, needed only a nudge to look away from Miss Munroe and toward a more mature woman of greater sophistication.

"Miss Hockensmith? Mr. Munroe will see you now."

She nodded at the respectful secretary and followed him into Niall's office. It was not the first time she had been in the room, but it never failed to take her breath away. No similar office in New York was more impressive. Or more opulent.

She had learned that Niall did not keep such luxury for himself. He knew the value of impressing those who came to him seeking financial backing, or potential investors in his own enterprises. Money begat money. Niall Munroe had Midas's touch and utter indifference to his own personal comfort.

He rose from behind his leather-topped mahogany desk

and bowed slightly. "Miss Hockensmith. Charmed to see you." He gestured to one of the matched chairs across from the desk and remained standing where he was. "How may I be of service?"

Cecily took her seat, suppressing a frown. After months of acquaintance, he was still formal with her. She might even say aloof, but that was insupportable. She could be patient. And most devoted to her cause.

"I hope I have not inconvenienced you, Mr. Munroe," she said in her most melodious voice. "I would not have come if I hadn't felt a certain urgency in my errand. Indeed, I . . . considered carefully before coming to see you."

His gray gaze settled on her and slid past. "Please speak freely, Miss Hockensmith. I am happy to assist you in any way I can."

He was obviously impatient with her. She got in the way of his business. She knew how to trouble those still waters and make him take notice. She knew how to take a small, unimportant thing and make it seem of great consequence.

"Thank you, Mr. Munroe. If you will allow me . . ." She rose, taking care that her skirts fell just right, and moved with conscious grace to his desk. "I will be as brief as possible. A few days ago, while we were visiting Athena at the circus—you may recall?"

"Yes, Miss Hockensmith. It was kind of you to share Athena's enjoyment."

"It was my pleasure, of course. But while we were there, we received these posters from the proprietor—Mr. French, I believe? I confess that I had not thought to look at mine until some time had passed. I am not at all familiar with circuses and the people who inhabit them, so I had not thought it of importance."

Niall glanced at the rolled paper she had placed on the desk. "Ah, yes. I remember."

"You can imagine my distress when I saw the nature of the performance these circus people intended to give our orphans." She unrolled the poster and used a pair of weights on Niall's desk to hold down the ends, turning it toward him.

He barely glanced at it. "Miss Hockensmith, I understand the nature of the performance. I see nothing harmful in a circus."

Cecily held on to her temper. Men in general could be obtuse, but Niall Munroe was worst than most. He needed a little more encouragement. "Please read it, Mr. Munroe." She placed a gloved fingertip near the top of the sheet. "Only look at what they consider their greatest attraction!"

He looked. He frowned, and his brows drew down in a way that more than appeased Cecily's disquiet.

"The Wolf-Man," he murmured. Cecily watched his face as he examined the garish picture of a creature half-man and half-beast, fanged and slavering, its long nails raking at the bars of a flimsy-looking cage. " 'The only true beast-man in existence, certified by the experts in the greatest Halls of Science, acclaimed throughout the nation. Stand within inches of its ferocious claws. Hear its terrifying growls. See it with your own eyes . . .' " He looked up at Cecily. "I saw nothing of this when I was on the lot.

"I have always heard it said that these people excel at deception. This 'Wolf-Man' is not the only hideous attraction of which they boast. There is the snake woman and her poisonous serpents, and any number of freakish creatures unfit to be seen by young children who have no parents to guide them."

Niall continued to stare at her, the thoughts running swift behind his eyes. Cecily pressed her advantage.

"That is not my sole concern," she went on. "I realize that Athena hired these people without being fully aware of their natures. She has made the best of things and her desire to entertain the children is laudable, but Athena is much too warmhearted to judge with the cool reason we must sometimes employ to protect what we hold dear. I must say that I do not feel that circus people are appropriate company for either Athena or the children."

Niall locked his hand behind his back and half turned,

gazing at the velvet curtains drawn over the window. "They were to give only one performance."

"But what damage might be done while they are here? Athena is this very day observing a rehearsal." She leaned over the desk. "You must see, Mr. Munroe, that I speak only out of deepest regard for your sister. I have been in Denver a short while, but in that time I have observed that Athena's heart has complete control over her head. I fear for her."

Niall's shoulders hunched. She had scored a point in his most vulnerable region. "I had not known about this Wolf-Man—but the others . . ." His voice was as stiff as his posture. "I would not allow my sister to be in the company of anyone who might harm her. Of that you may be sure, Miss Hockensmith."

Ah. Of course he would be defensive. She must not let him think she found fault with his care of his beloved sister.

"Naturally you could not be aware of all this. You must concede, Mr. Munroe, that we women do understand each other better than even a brother could. You cannot be everywhere at once, nor think of every possibility. That is why I have taken it upon myself to help in any way I can."

At last he turned back to her. At last she had his full attention, even his appreciation. "I have not been unaware of your efforts, Miss Hockensmith. I have not disregarded your previous observations, and I realize that . . . even I cannot give Athena everything she may require."

"You are as fine a brother as any lady could wish. But Athena has no mother, no older sister to guide her. And though everyone in Denver society loves and admires your sister, Mr. Munroe, her very goodness may leave her defenseless against those who would take advantage of her. The uneducated and destitute, of any sort, are notorious for just such behavior."

He stared at the poster. "You once suggested that I send Athena away—to New York, perhaps. I did not see any benefit in it before. But we do have a second cousin there, in good society, who might provide companionship for her."

"And I know many in New York who would love her as much as we do." She clasped her hands eloquently. "It is only here that she is . . . bound by her past. She feels such a need to prove herself, and I see no evidence that she intends to moderate her activities."

"I have spoken to her on that subject."

"But has she listened? Some time away, in the company of well-bred and older advisers, would allow her to find a new perspective and realize how much more there is in the world to enjoy."

Niall subjected her to the same intense, piercing gaze that he had given the poster. "I am not yet convinced that she would be better off away from the only family she has. You do not know her as well as I, Miss Hockensmith."

Quickly she changed strategies and smiled gently. "Naturally not. You understand better than anyone how to care for Athena."

Her retreat softened his stance. "Nevertheless, you have valid points, Miss Hockensmith. I will consider them. As for the circus . . . there is no business here that cannot wait." He removed the weights and let the poster curl up. "I will see Athena at once. Would you be so kind as to accompany me?"

Her heart leaped. "Of course."

He smiled, a more genuine expression this time. "You are a lady of great generosity yourself, Miss Hockensmith. As generous as your father is astute. I believe he and I shall soon be sealing our partnership."

Elated, Cecily showed him only humble satisfaction. "That is wonderful news, Mr. Munroe."

"Athena and I will hope to see you and your father at dinner in the coming week," he said. "But for the moment—" He stepped around the desk, took his hat from the mahogany stand, and offered his arm to Cecily. "Shall we go, Miss Hockensmith?"

She took his elbow and walked with him to the door.

Let those overweening young ladies at the Windsor observe her now, and reconsider her worth. They had much to learn. Niall Munroe might be particularly unschooled where women were concerned, but he was still a man. And she was very much a woman.

Woman enough to rule all of Denver society.

"*I am a werewolf.*"
Morgan had never been one to question his senses. He had relied on their accuracy all his life, and he was not prepared to doubt them now. He had not misunderstood Athena Munroe's startling announcement.

Her gaze held his, steady and sane, though she shivered under the blanket and was not so well as she claimed. He would swear that she wasn't crazy. She'd have no cause to make up such a story, when most people would run screaming in terror after what she had witnessed.

But he would have known. Surely he would have *known.* Yet he had returned to the lot because of her, and just in time to save her from serious injury, if not death. Now they were connected more surely than by any tenuous sympathy. Now it was so much worse.

Fool.

"Have you . . . nothing to say?" she asked, a catch in her voice. "Perhaps you need proof of some kind. Unfortunately, I do not know how to give it."

She looked so small, so fragile without the armor of her chair, her legs like a rag doll's beneath her skirts. She had been a feather in his arms—no, not a feather, for a feather had no substance. She was altogether real, and warm, and female.

A female of his blood. He did not want it to be true. Oh, no. He wanted to prove her a liar.

"If you are what you claim," he said, "there are ways of showing it." He glanced around the tent. "Tell me what is in that chest."

She looked at the painted wooden trunk. "I don't—"

"Tell me what you smell."

Her eyes widened with comprehension. Not shock, or fear, or amazement, but recognition.

"A test," she murmured. "Very well." She closed her eyes again and breathed in deeply. Her brow puckered in a frown.

"There are a number of items in the chest," she said slowly. "Something . . . made of flowers. Dried flowers, and straw. A hat. Caitlin's." She breathed in again. "Yes, it belongs to Caitlin. And there is also a piece of leather— very worn—that is also Caitlin's, but it has been used with horses. Metal . . . a buckle, perhaps. A bit of harness. And . . . yes, the smell of an old book, one that has been damp too many times. Like an old, musty library. I think it is Ulysses's. And something of Harry's. Wool. Some article of clothing." She opened her eyes. "I hope you do not expect me to identify the specific garment?"

Morgan stared at her face. He knew she could not have seen the contents of the chest, yet she had described them accurately and without hesitation.

She had a werewolf's senses. If he bade her listen to some distant sound, report a fragment of conversation from the big top, he was sure she would oblige him. But if he asked her to stalk a buck in the deep wood, or run tirelessly for hours on end, or strip herself naked . . .

He worked his fingers into fists. "Impressive," he said. "But there is a surer form of proof. Change."

He might as well have struck her. She paled, and then the color returned in a rush. "You mean change into a wolf, as you did?"

She spoke as if the very idea was unthinkable. "What is wrong, Miss Munroe? Have you never done it before? Or is it that those who live as you do are above such things?"

"As I do?" She tried to push up on her elbows, thought better of it, and lay down again. "I do not understand you."

"Here, in the city. Among those people."

She was too practiced at the games of her kind to reveal any hurt, but he sensed it in her nonetheless. "*Those* people?" she said with a brittle smile. "You mean my friends? My brother? Those with orderly lives and assets and connections?"

"If you were anything like me," he said, "you could not deny your blood. And if you did not deny it, you could not tolerate the pretty cage you live in." He leaned forward, holding her gaze. "You know what I am. You must know others. Why did you choose *this* time to admit your nature if you prefer your safe and easy life? Why tell me at all?"

She let the blanket fall to her waist and made a Herculean effort to prop herself up. Morgan moved to help her, but her eyes flashed such proud disdain that he fell back.

"I confess that I know little of . . . our kind," she said. "I have only known of one other like me—"

"Your brother?"

"My mother. She . . . went away when I was born."

A peculiar feeling came over him, a desire to ease the sorrow he heard in her voice, to protect her from future unhappiness. Insane, unaccountable emotions.

But it was instinct—deep, reliable instinct—that told him to believe her words. To accept her claims.

To trust her.

"And your father?" he asked, more gently.

"He was not like my mother, but he knew what she was. When I was old enough to understand, he gave me a letter she had written before she . . . went away. It explained a few things, but so much was left unsaid. I was not even sure if there were others like us, or how many. Until now—"

"What about your brother?"

"He has a different mother—" She paused, weighing her words. "He knows what I am, but he is like Papa."

Human. Human father, human brother, absent mother. Raised in sheltered privilege in the heart of a human city. Alone.

Was that why she had come to him—for the answers her mother had not given her?

"Is that why you can't Change?" he asked. "You had no one to teach you?"

"But I did. I taught myself." Even in her awkward position she managed to square her shoulders and maintain her dignity. "I could do what you did, once. When I was younger. Before—" She made a brief, dismissive gesture toward her legs.

Pain. For a moment it was stark in her eyes, along with memories too agonizing to bear. His mind formed an image of himself crippled as she was, and flinched away from the horror. What had seemed an inconvenience for a human was worse than death to a werewolf.

"Your pity is quite unnecessary," she said, lifting her chin. "I accepted it long ago." Her eyes gave the lie to her words, but the deceptively tranquil cadence had returned to her voice. She might have been addressing her lady friends at tea.

If he'd been wise, he would have accepted her denial, told her whatever she wished to know, and sent her on her way. She believed she had come to terms with her affliction; who was he to suggest otherwise? If she had made a tolerable life for herself in the human world, that was her own affair.

But he remembered the small-minded conversation of the women she called "friends." Human friends. They could not know what she was, and still they branded her an outsider, an object of the pity she rejected.

He had been drawn to her by senses more profound than mere intellect. Drawn to protect her. And now that she had given him the secret that made her even more an outsider than before . . .

In all his wanderings, he had never met another of the wolf blood—not in the saloons or on the dusty roads, in ramshackle towns or mining camps. Now he found his mirror in a woman of wealth, education, and the position humans so valued. But there was no wildness in Athena Munroe. Spirit, perhaps, and courage, but no desperate yearning for the freedom beyond human walls.

We are nothing alike. We cannot be.

"I have tried to devote my time and resources to the

service of others," she said quietly. "I am quite content. I
have put that other life aside. But when I saw you . . .
change . . . I realized that there was still a small part of me
that was not yet laid to rest."

With an unwelcome jolt of insight, Morgan recognized
how great an admission she had made to him. Her physical disadvantages made her fight doubly hard to be competent and strong in every other part of her life. In one way
they *were* alike; they both did everything possible to avoid
needing. Athena helped others; they needed her, not the reverse.

There was little enough that *he* needed. But now Athena
needed him, and he did not know the extent of that need.
Did she expect him—him, of all people—to absolve her of
her werewolf nature?

He jumped up from the chair and paced out a circle in
the sawdust. "What do you want of me?"

Athena had managed to work her legs to the edge of the
cot, as if she might put her weight on her feet and walk
away. "If you would be so kind," she said, "I would like to
sit up. I am fully recovered."

He was certainly not. But he went to her and lifted her
again, carrying her to the chair. The contact was disturbing, and he was aware of her distinct female scent and the
acceleration of her heartbeat. Once she was settled he released her quickly and stepped away.

"Please forgive me, Mr. Holt," she said. "I realize that
you did not seek my confidences. I shall try not to impose
too much. If you can tell me—" She bit her lower lip. "Did
you ever meet a woman named Gwenyth Desbois?"

"Your mother?"

She nodded. Her eyes shone—with hope, perhaps. He
hated himself for having to shatter it.

"No. I knew only one other of wolf blood—my own
mother."

"I see." She gazed down at her hands. "I had thought
that you, having traveled so widely, might have known
more like us."

He shook his head, wishing he could lessen the sting. "I last saw my mother and sister when I was fourteen."

"So long ago? You were only a boy."

"I was not a boy for long."

"But you loved them. Something kept you apart from them. I know what it is to lose—" The corner of her mouth trembled. "I loved my father."

He did not pursue the path she offered. "They are gone," he said. "Life continues."

"Yes." After a time, she smiled. Always the smile, fore-bearing and generous, covering what she did not want the world to see. "I still have Niall, and my work."

Niall Munroe—arrogant, confident . . . and human. "Your brother knows what you are, and doesn't care?"

"As I said, he is my half brother. He has known since the first time I—for many years."

And he was undoubtedly glad that she kept her secret from anyone else. Few humans were so tolerant. "Your father was married twice?"

A faint blush came to her cheeks. "No."

So. Either she or her brother was what humans called a bastard—illegitimate, born to a mother without the status of a wife. Such things meant much in her world. When werewolves mated, it was for life . . . unless one of the pair was human.

"You have never tried to Change again?" he asked, eager to escape the subject.

"Not since the accident." Her smile was achingly brave and thoroughly fraudulent.

"Were you afraid?"

He had not meant the question to be so challenging. He did not expect an answer, but she gave it anyway. "I did not know what would happen if I tried to Change after I recovered from my injuries," she said. "It happened in the mountains, in wintertime. I was in wolf shape just before the accident happened, but I Changed back when my legs were hurt."

Then she *had* known what it was to run free. Once more

he was forced to amend his assumptions about her. From his own experience, Morgan knew that an injury was not always the same in both shapes. It was risky to Change when severely wounded, for the great effort could lead to death. But a minor injury could be healed by the Change itself. What crippled the woman might not cripple the wolf.

But he couldn't be sure. If she tried to Change and became a wolf with two useless legs . . .

That was what she feared. That was why she tried to forget her dual nature—until he reminded her of it. Better to live half a life than become a mockery of nature.

But she had said some part of herself could not forget.

"The past is the past," he said. "I can't help you, Miss Munroe."

She dropped her gaze, seemed about ready to reply, and gave her head a small shake. "You have been most helpful, Mr. Holt. You saved my life, and answered my questions willingly. I can ask no more. Now, if you would be so kind as to bring my chair . . ."

The courteous wall was back in place, vulnerability banished behind the boundaries of propriety and status. "You owe me nothing. But I do . . . ask . . . that you not blame Caitlin or the troupers for what happened. It was an accident."

"You do care about them, don't you?" she said softly. Her eyes warmed, and for an unbearable moment she looked as though she might reach out to him. She regained her senses quickly enough. "Never fear. I intend to go ahead with the performance. I am sure Miss Hughes will make sure the horses are safe for the children. Please thank Mr. French for a most enjoyable visit, and reassure him of my goodwill."

Morgan recognized the dismissal. She had spilled out her heart to him, purged herself of doubts, and now she was ready to return to her life. He could banish any thought of a mysterious bond between them.

"One last piece of advice, Miss Munroe," he said.

"Give your trust sparingly. Do not mistake enemies for allies."

He started for the exit before she could respond. Caitlin blocked the way just outside, pushing Athena's chair before her.

"Is she all right?" the girl asked, peering over his shoulder. "I was so worried, but I had to quiet the horses. . . . I can't believe that Pennyfarthing bolted like that. It is not like him, and he couldn't tell me what was wrong. Harry is beside himself, but he thought we ought to leave you two alone. She is all right, Morgan?"

"She isn't hurt."

"Was she terribly afraid of you?"

He wanted to laugh. "She accepted it quite . . . well."

"Then she didn't think she was going mad? She won't tell anyone?"

"I doubt it."

Her eyes narrowed. "Something else is wrong, then. Is she angry at us? Will she withdraw her support?"

"She said she wouldn't."

"Did you quarrel?"

"Strangers seldom quarrel."

"Especially when one stranger has saved the other's life, and reveals his deepest secret."

He avoided her too-knowing gaze. "See for yourself. You can show her to Harry and take her back to her carriage."

"That is all?"

"What more do you want, Firefly? Her pledge of undying devotion?"

"Has it gone so far already, Morgan?"

"The lady is waiting."

"But not forever. Don't make that mistake, my friend."

He growled at her and bolted. Her low, taunting chuckle chased him halfway across the lot.

Chapter 8

Athena Munroe was very quiet when Caitlin went to fetch her. She smiled at Caitlin graciously enough, but it was the sort of automatic smile that meant her mind was elsewhere.

Caitlin knew the name of that "elsewhere." Something was definitely going on between Morgan and Athena, only Morgan would probably rather die than admit it. Caitlin had a good idea that she wouldn't be any more successful prying information out of Athena.

Yet Athena had seen what Morgan truly was. He said she accepted it, but no one used to her sort of life would be so calm when all her illusions of reality were turned upside down. Townies often accused troupers of double-dealing, but the townies were just as good at playing false. Maybe better.

A very delicate situation, indeed. But Caitlin had never been the least bit delicate.

"I'm sorry for what happened in the ring," she said cautiously. "Pennyfarthing has never done anything like that before. If I'd a notion he would bolt, I wouldn't have used him today."

Athena blinked and looked at Caitlin as if recognizing her for the first time. "Please do not give it another thought, Miss Hughes. I believe that Pennyfarthing was more frightened than I was. As you can see, I am quite well."

Are you, then? "I am glad. Do you like horses, Miss Munroe?"

Athena's smile wavered ever so slightly. "Yes."

That simple answer said so much more than a speech. What must it be like, to be able to ride and run and walk and then have all that taken away from you?

"Then we're still to give the performance for the children," Caitlin said.

"I am sure that such an incident won't be repeated."

"I'll make certain it does not." Caitlin moved behind Athena's chair. "You'll want to go home, Miss Munroe, after all the excitement. Harry is that upset over what happened. He wants to apologize personally, if you'll see him."

"Of course. I—" She stopped, and Caitlin could feel the storm gathering. "May I ask a frank question, Miss Hughes?" Athena did not turn her head, but her shoulders were as tense as Regina's high wire. "Have you always known what he is?"

No need to ask who "he" was . . . and no point in pretending not to understand. "Since he first came to us."

"Then he will always have a place with you here."

Now *that* was an interesting remark. "If he wants it. We take care of our own." She crouched eye to eye with Athena. "What you saw today—not many townies would accept it as well as you have."

"Townies. Is that what you call us?"

"Troupers have learned not to trust too easily."

"Morgan warned me not to trust. I could not live that way, never trusting anyone."

"Here, we trust each other. And now we must trust you. For Morgan's sake."

"You are very fond of him, Miss Hughes."

"He is like a brother to me. A difficult brother."

"A difficult man."

"But he *is* a man, Miss Munroe."

Athena looked away. "You need have no fear. I will not reveal his secret."

On impulse, Caitlin touched her hand. The kid-gloved fingers were rigid with unexpressed agitation. "You are a very brave lady," she said

"For a towny, Miss Hughes?"

"You'd better call me Caitlin from now on. In a way, you are part of our family now."

Athena's fingers relaxed and curled about Caitlin's. Her smile became something more than just another gesture of impersonal benevolence. "Thank you, Caitlin. My name is Athena." She slipped her hand free. "As you said, we have had more than enough excitement for one day."

"Yes." Caitlin got up and took the handles of the chair. "If you'll just say a word or two to Harry—he's in the cookhouse, probably fretting himself to death." She hesitated. "Do you wish me to send for Mr. Munroe?"

"That will not be necessary. I can do a number of things without my brother's help."

Ah, a sore spot. Caitlin well remembered how masterful Niall Munroe was, and it was no wonder that he'd have a protective streak where his sister was involved. In his world, men expected obedience from their women—and Athena was less free than most. Did she chafe under her brother's rule?

There were some things even great wealth didn't buy— not freedom, not loyalty, and not love. Ulysses knew that only too well. And Caitlin was more grateful than ever that what she had didn't depend on the crutch of money.

As long as the troupe survived.

Caitlin wheeled the chair around and pushed it out into the backyard. "I think," she said softly, "that you can do anything you set your mind to."

Athena did not reply. Caitlin respected her silence. It was the beginning of a friendship that surprised her, and likely surprised Athena even more. Caitlin had a feeling that it was not the last wonder to come of today's events.

They were halfway to the cookhouse when her feeling was proven correct. A tall figure came striding across the lot with fell purpose in every step.

Niall Munroe. Caitlin pulled the chair to a stop and listened to her heart thunder like her horses' hooves. "I think your brother has come for you, Athena," she said.

Mr. Munroe was not a man to waste time on formalities. He looked at Caitlin—once, again—and then turned to his sister.

"Are you finished with your visit, Athena?" he asked.

"Quite finished. You did not have to fetch me. I was—"

"I would prefer you to go straight home. Miss Hockensmith is waiting at the carriage, and she will go with you."

"What is this about, Niall? Why—"

"It need not concern you. I will take you to the carriage."

Athena's mouth set in an obstinate line, so unlike its usual gentle curve. Caitlin looked from sister to brother. Oh, yes, there was rebellion here. "You didn't have to worry about your sister, Mr. Munroe," she said. "She has been quite safe with us."

His face reddened, a most unexpected sight on one so exalted. "I wish to speak to you, Miss Hughes. If you will kindly remain here until I return."

"Of course. I have nothing better to do."

He ignored her mockery and stepped into her place behind the chair. As he pushed his sister away, Athena glanced back at Caitlin. It was a look of hidden anger and an appeal Caitlin did not know how to answer.

She set her jaw and waited. She was under no man's orders, least of all Niall Munroe's, but he was paying the bills. And she was determined to find out more about the kind of man who acted as if he owned the world and everyone in it.

At the edge of the lot, Athena and Munroe met another woman—Miss Hockensmith, whom Caitlin remembered from Athena's first visit—and Niall lifted Athena into the waiting carriage which had been joined by a second, smaller vehicle. He and Miss Hockensmith held a brief conversation, and then he turned on his heel and started toward Caitlin. Miss Hockensmith stared after him.

Caitlin met him with a provoking smile. "Do you always treat your sister as if she were a servant, Mr. Munroe?"

"That is none of your affair, Miss Hughes."

"Then why do you want to speak with me? Surely I am too lowly for a fine gentleman to dally with."

That intriguing flush returned, playing up the sharp lines of his face. He pulled a rolled paper from his coat and held it out to her.

"I have only one question, Miss Hughes. What is this 'Wolf-Man?' "

She took a second look at the paper and realized that it was one of the posters that Harry had given to the visitors. She knew the design well, and what it advertised. Was it possible, even remotely possible, that Athena had broken her word and told her brother what she had seen today?

No. But if not, why should Munroe be so disturbed? "It is only one of our sideshow acts."

"And just what sort of act is it?"

"Every troupe has its secrets. The Wolf-Man is one of our special attractions. People come to be frightened and thrilled, and we try not to disappoint them."

The rolled paper began to buckle in his grip. "I saw no such person when I came to Colorado Springs. Does he hide from public view, Miss Hughes? Is he some sort of monster unfit for respectable society? What does he do— change into a wolf before the audience's eyes?"

She laughed. "Surely you do not believe in such things, Mr. Munroe. Not a smart, educated gentleman such as yourself."

He actually flinched. "I have a right to know what I have employed."

"You are a rather big man to be afraid of fairy tales. Your sister was not so alarmed."

All at once his hand shot out to grip her wrist. "Did she meet this . . . this 'fairy tale'?"

She stared at his hand. "Harry introduced her to everyone. Don't you think your sister would have told you if we presented a danger to her orphans . . . or to you?"

He let her go just as suddenly as he had grabbed her. "Miss Hockensmith was right," he said. "You are not fit company—"

"So you do let at least one woman rule you," she said sweetly. She waved to the vigilant figure standing beside the carriage, and watched with fascination as Munroe's formerly cool demeanor vanished in a cloud of wrath.

"I wish to see this man, Miss Munroe. At once."

"What are you so afraid of? Anyone who is not exactly like you?"

"I will not have . . . freaks on display for my sister or her dependents."

"In that case," she said, reaching up to her hair, "you should know exactly what you have bought." With swift, efficient motions she pulled the unruly mass behind her ears.

"My God," he said. "What happened to your ears?"

"I was born with them," she said, "just as you were born with your money and your pride. I am one of the freaks you so despise, Mr. Munroe. You may insult me as much as you wish, but not my friends. Any one of them is twice the man you will ever be."

He took a step back, still staring at the neat points on the tips of her ears. "Where is Mr. French?" he asked in a strangled voice.

She turned her back and marched across the lot, not waiting to see if he followed. With every step she cursed herself for her utter lack of sense.

Thanks to her outburst, the troupe might lose the patronage of the Munroes. And if they lost that, they lost the

money they so desperately needed to keep the family together.

She'd be damned if she'd let Munroe see her regret. She
led him to the cookhouse, where Harry was nursing a glass
of precious whiskey at one of the long plank tables, and
stood aside. Harry scrambled to his feet with a nervous
smile.

"Ah, Mr. Munroe! How delightful to see you. Your sister is most charming, most—"

"I must speak to you, Mr. French. Alone." He looked
pointedly at Caitlin.

Harry threw her a glance full of alarm. There was nothing she could do to comfort him—nothing but find a way
to hear what passed between him and Munroe. Her hearing
was keener than most, but not keen enough to catch the
conversation without blatant eavesdropping.

Morgan. She turned and went in search of him, hoping
he had not gone running as he often did when he was troubled. But luck was with her; she found him watching the
troupe's jugglers with tightly folded arms and a dark expression.

She grabbed his arm and pulled him away. It felt as if
she were dragging an angry tiger at the end of a silken
leash. "I need your help, Morgan. Niall Munroe is talking
to Harry, and I must know what they are saying."

One good thing to be said about Morgan was that he
never wasted time on useless questions. He went with her
to the cookhouse entrance and they stopped behind a shel-
tering tent pole. Harry and Niall were still talking—or at
least Niall was.

Morgan tilted his head. His eyes narrowed to slits, and
the corner of his mouth twitched.

"Munroe is trying to buy Harry off," he said. "He is
paying him to leave Denver at once, before the performance."

"How much is he offering?"

"Half of what he promised for the show." He lowered

his head, and she thought she could see the hair lift along his skull. "What is this about, Firefly?"

"He thinks he is protecting his sister," she said. "From the freaks, like us."

"He knew what he was getting when he hired the troupe." Gooseflesh rose on Caitlin's skin when he looked at her. "Or is it something else?"

She touched his arm. "He saw one of the posters. He didn't know about the Wolf-Man before, Morgan. I don't think he could guess the real truth even if he tried. But he—" She shook her head. "He is afraid of anyone who doesn't fit in his world."

"How do you know this?"

Morgan's voice had grown soft and dangerous. She shivered. "It was my fault. I said things I shouldn't. But he had already made up his mind before he came here. He has ordered Athena to leave. If it were up to her—"

"You like Athena."

"I believe she can be trusted. So do you."

He didn't deny it. "Munroe has no right—"

"He thinks he has every right."

He returned to Niall's conversation. "Harry is not giving an answer. He says that he doesn't want to disappoint Miss Athena. He is asking Munroe for a little time to talk to the troupers, and to prove that the circus is safe."

Bless him. Caitlin risked a peep into the cookhouse. She did not need Morgan's translation to see how Munroe reacted to Harry's evasion. He made a brief, final statement—loud enough for Caitlin to hear—and turned, his face thunderous.

"He said," Morgan finished, "that it would not be wise for Harry to remain in town—that it would be an unfortunate mistake." His lips lifted, baring his teeth. "Harry has one day to decide."

It was so much worse than Caitlin had expected. She ducked out of the entrance as Munroe charged toward it, prepared to pull Morgan aside with physical force if necessary. But Morgan behaved himself. He retreated—

"faded" was more the proper word—and Munroe shot out the door without seeing him.

"Do not waste your time on him, Firefly," Morgan said.

"What do you suggest? Will *you* talk to him? You're no better a diplomat than I am."

She set off after Munroe, running to match his long strides. She would apologize. She would beg, on her knees if necessary, for him to let the troupers remain long enough for the performance. Not only because of the money, but for Athena's sake.

Yes, for Athena. And maybe . . . just maybe for Morgan as well.

"Why the hurry, little fly? Do you have a new lover?"

Tamar could appear and disappear with the same disconcerting ease as Morgan. Caitlin slowed to a walk. "Not now, Tamar," she said. "I have important business."

"With him?" Tamar arched her long, elegant neck in the direction Niall had gone. "This should be most interesting."

Exasperated, Caitlin hurried on, hoping that Tamar would not interfere. She caught up with Niall just as he reached the waiting carriages.

"Mr. Munroe," she whispered, touching his arm. "I must talk to you."

His muscles were rigid under the fine wool of his coat. "I have nothing to say, Miss Hughes. My sister must return home."

"You are making a mistake," she said, pressing more firmly into his sleeve. "Please—"

He turned. Their gazes met, and locked. An incredible spark of . . . something . . . sizzled between them, forming a current that began at the eyes and rushed through Caitlin's body to the place where her hand touched his arm.

She could only guess what her own face must reveal, but Niall Munroe's might as well have served as a billboard. He leaned toward her—slightly, oh, so slightly—

and his lips parted. A glazed look came into his eyes. Caitlin sucked in her breath.

"Mr. Munroe. We really must be on our way!"

Miss Hockensmith's voice from the carriage window broke the current. Niall jerked back his hand. Without another word to Caitlin, he gave a terse command to the coachman and climbed into the driver's seat of the smaller carriage.

One glimpse of Athena's distressed face was all Caitlin saw before the carriages rattled into motion, rolling and bumping across the potholed ground.

"So sad," Tamar said behind her. "It was such a promising romance, was it not? But you will always lose to such a rich and beauteous lady." She blinked half-lidded eyes and stroked the head of one of her ever-present serpents. "Unless, of course, you make a gift of the one thing no man will refuse. Do you wish me to teach you how it is done, little fly?"

"Keep out of this, Tamar. It has nothing to do with you."

"Oh, no?" Tamar lifted her black, painted brows.

Caitlin strode past her and returned to the cookhouse, dreading what she would find.

Harry was still there, every bit as miserable as when she had left him. Morgan was with him, and Ulysses had arrived along with a dozen of the other troupers. They were talking amongst themselves, trying to decide what had happened.

Caitlin shook her head as she approached, and Harry sighed. "Ladies and gentleman," he said, "it seems that we have an important and unpleasant decision to make. Gather the others, and we shall meet in the big top within the next half hour."

Efficient as always in a time of crisis, the troupers were assembled and waiting in the big top well before the half hour was up. Ulysses and Morgan kept their places close to Harry, like grotesquely mismatched royal guards. Caitlin was grateful once more that Morgan had not gone after Niall Munroe. She half feared he might have devoured Athena's brother for supper.

"My friends, my children," Harry said in his most carrying voice, "circumstances have compelled me to call this meeting so that we may discuss our future."

A general murmur followed his words, but he raised his plump hands to quiet it. "As you know, in only a few days we were to give a charitable performance for the children of the orphanage patronized by Miss Athena Munroe and her brother. We were to be paid a most handsome sum for this privilege." He lowered his head. "Alas, complications have arisen."

In far less words than he usually employed, Harry explained what Niall had told him. There were cries of disgust, a handful of curses, and much shaking of heads.

"Never trust townies," someone shouted. "They'll always break their word."

"Why?" another man demanded. "What is all this about, Harry?"

Harry wrung his hands. "Well, you see . . . when he hired us, he did not know about our main sideshow attraction, our own Morgan. I confess that I do not quite understand his reasoning, but he has taken it into his head that our Wolf-Man may be dangerous to the children and his sister. It is entirely ridiculous, but . . ."

The troupers fell silent. As one they looked at Morgan. He bore their stares with cold indifference, a curiosity among curiosities.

"Munroe is afraid of freaks," Caitlin said loudly, stepping forward. "Any sort of freak. But his sister is not like him." She swept the crowd with her stare. "She is a good woman. She saw what Morgan is, and wasn't afraid. She wants to help us."

"Does she hold the purse strings?" Florizel the clown cried out.

"You said Munroe made a threat if we didn't get out of town," said one of the Flying Grassotti Brothers. "We have heard that he's a powerful man in this city. He has offered us money to leave—it's not worth the risk to stay and make him angry."

How could she counter that argument? Circus folk never stood up well against townies, let alone prominent ones. They knew the wisdom of strategic retreat when townies became hostile. She glanced at Harry, at Morgan, and last at Ulysses.

Ulysses moved only a little, but every eye focused on him when he did. "Harry formed this troupe," he said quietly. "Many of us had no homes, no employment, nothing at all before he took us in. His hearth has always been open to anyone in need—anyone who is different, regardless of the nature of that difference." He looked directly at Florizel. "Once you aspired to be a great thespian of the legitimate stage. But no one would employ you because of your appearance. Your talent meant nothing. You were lost in the throes of dipsomania when we found you, and Harry gave you a chance to play to the crowds."

He turned to Regina, whose tall, impossibly thin body towered over everyone else. "Your brother cast you out when you refused to marry a man who would not touch you if not for your family wealth. You would not easily have found a partner outside, but here . . ."

He didn't finish his sentence. Regina clasped her long, spidery fingers around the thick ones of her husband, Tor the strongman.

"There are countless other stories like these," Ulysses said. "It is clear to me—"

"Harry asked for our opinions," Giovanni said. "You don't want us to stay, do you, Harry?"

"It . . . well, it is true that Mr. Munroe wishes us to leave and will pay us half the promised sum if we do so. But Miss Munroe—she is so very set on our performance. She even wishes to keep us on for a second one."

"I still don't see how it's worth turning a man like Munroe against us," Giovanni said. "If we have enough to see us through winter—"

"Only if nothing else happens," Caitlin said. "If we have another fire, or any bad luck at all—"

"We'll get along. Let's pull out, Harry. We don't need to borrow more trouble."

"I also vote that we leave," Tamar said, slipping up to the front of the gathering. "What do we owe to this . . . Athena Munroe? To any of their kind?"

"That's right."

"Tamar speaks truth. As long as he pays, he doesn't matter what his sister—"

A deep, reverberating growl sliced through the strident words. Morgan fixed his potent stare on each of the speakers in turn. Every one of them stepped back into the safety of the crowd.

"Cowards," he said. He didn't have to raise his voice; every word rang like the clash of cymbals. "You pride yourselves on being different and better than townies. You say you are a family. Now one comes to you who needs what you can give, and you turn your back on her."

A chorus of protests. "You are not making any sense, Morgan," Giovanni said. "Athena Munroe is rich as Croesus. How can she need our help?"

"She is not like us," Florizel said, daring to step forward again. "In what manner is she a freak, as Caitlin so kindly refers to us? She is a cripple, that is all."

Morgan snarled. Florizel's face lost what little color it had.

"A cripple," Morgan said. "An outsider among her own kind, who helps strangers without asking anything in return. She saw me Change today, and she was not afraid. And she did not change her mind about us."

Caitlin stood at Morgan's shoulder. "What Morgan says is true. She may be a towny, but she knows what it's like to suffer."

"We gave our word to perform for her orphans," Morgan said. "I will go to Munroe. I'll tell him that I will leave Denver if he allows the performance."

"You'll do that just for this lady and her orphans?"

Florizel asked. "Have you been enjoying the lady's favors—what favors she has to bestow—and that is why her brother wants us gone?"

Caitlin had seldom seen Morgan make the actual Change into the "Wolf-Man," the creature he became in the sideshow. Now he began to transform, his body half-wreathed in black mist, fine dark hair flowing over his hands and feet and at the neckline of his shirt. His face remained almost untouched, but it was undeniably lupine. And deadly.

Harry intervened. "Morgan's honor and his word have been good from the first moment we met him," he said. "I trust his instincts, and Caitlin's. I think . . . I think they are right." He mopped at his face with a handkerchief. "I believe we should stay for the performance, and then leave."

"And what if Munroe refuses to pay anything?"

"Miss Munroe will see that you get your money," Morgan said. Between one heartbeat and the next, he was human again. "You decide whether or not you let a towny tell you where you can go and how you can live."

Harry coughed behind his hand. "I believe it is time for a vote. Will those who wish to leave say 'aye'?"

The few ayes were restrained and almost inaudible. When Harry asked for the nays, they rang out with conviction. Caitlin grinned at Morgan and Ulysses.

"This course does entail some risk," Ulysses said as the troupers began to disperse. "Munroe is a powerful man."

"I think you are underestimating Athena's strength of character," Caitlin said. "She wants us to stay, and I know she can stand up to her brother if she has to."

Harry blotted his face again. "I hope you are right, Caitlin. I do so wish to please the poor child. I confess that I have developed a certain . . . fondness for her."

"Calculated risks are occasionally necessary," Ulysses said, scrutinizing Morgan with interest, "if for no other reason than to preserve one's honor and keep one's word."

"Honor," Caitlin snorted. "When did honor ever get you anything, Uly? This is simply the right thing to do."

"Your reaction seems somewhat personal, Firefly."

"What's done is done," Harry said. "We've only to go ahead as best we can."

"And someone must explain to Athena what has happened," Caitlin added. "We will have to find an excuse to get her back to the lot. I'm certain her brother did not plan to tell her until we had left Denver."

"Maybe she won't defy him," Morgan said. "Her life depends on her brother's money. If he chooses, he could take away what freedom she has."

Caitlin stared at him in surprise. "It is true that he tries to protect her too much. I don't know what Niall Munroe is so afraid of, but he is not a —" She flushed and hurried on. "You spoke up for staying, Morgan. You want to help Athena—you even called her brave, yet you have no faith in her ability to fight for what she wants?"

She could see him withdrawing into himself again, denying the feelings that had prompted him to speak up for Athena with such uncharacteristic passion.

"What did you and Athena speak about in the backyard, Morgan?" Caitlin asked. "Are you testing her? Do you want her to fail, so that you'll have no reason to care?"

His head gave an almost imperceptible jerk. "Munroe thinks he can buy anything or anyone," he said through his teeth. "We are not his lapdogs."

"Neither is his sister. But if you're right, and Athena is willing to let us go—what then?"

"We must abide by her wishes, of course," Harry answered. "It is days like these when I wish I had retired years ago."

"Oh, Harry—" Caitlin paused when she realized that Morgan was halfway to the front door. "Where are you going?"

"To tell Miss Munroe," he said without breaking stride. "To find out what she wants."

Caitlin thought quickly. Who was better suited to deliver a clandestine message? *And who is more unpre-*

dictable when his heart is involved? "You can't just walk into her house. You do not even know where she lives."

"I'll find out."

"If Niall sees you—"

"He will not see me." As if to prove his point, he seemed to vanish even before he reached the door.

There's no turning back now, Caitlin thought, haunted by that sense of destiny that had first come with Morgan Holt and returned with Niall Munroe.

"This is a hazardous game, Firefly," Ulysses said, stepping up beside her. "Morgan is not one to be made a pawn of fate."

"I thought you didn't believe in fate."

"Only when it trifles with those I consider my friends."

She rested her hand on his shoulder. "Then, my friend, let me keep the faith for all of us."

Chapter 9

Athena had never longed quite so much for the ability to pace. Her body was racked with shivers born of conflicting emotions that sought to pull her one way and then the other. The walls of her peaceful, silent room seemed about to crush her like some medieval implement of torture.

If she had faced only a single quandary this evening, she might have dealt with it easily enough. But the incidents had come as thick and fast as snowflakes in a mountain blizzard—first the near escape in the big top, then Morgan's incredible exhibition . . . the disconcerting conversation that followed . . . and finally Niall's sudden appearance and irrational behavior.

She was still angry with Niall. It was easier to nurse anger than face the other feelings that pummeled her from every direction. But even the anger frightened her, for only in recent weeks had she allowed herself to become angry for any personal reason.

Anger on behalf of the downtrodden was useful, and justified; anger due to hurt pride, or resentment, was the worst sort of selfishness. Athena knew it, and yet the knowledge did not seem to help.

She rolled her chair to the window. Niall had escorted Miss Hockensmith home, but he had not yet returned.

The passage of hours had not helped Athena's mood. She continued to relive the moment when Niall had come for her at the lot—how he had barely looked at her, dismissed her like a child, and ordered her away. How he had spoken to Caitlin, with less courtesy than to a servant. And when they had reached the privacy of home, he had refused to give any explanation for his behavior.

She had felt humiliated, treated so by her own brother in front of a friend. For Caitlin had become a friend, despite all the differences between them.

In a strange way, Caitlin reminded Athena of herself when she was younger—rash, passionate, refusing any concession to femininity or propriety—quick to give her loyalty, and her heart. What must she think after the way Niall had acted? She would believe that Athena was under her brother's thumb.

Athena had done nothing to dispel that impression. She had let Niall bully her back to the carriage, endured Cecily Hockensmith's sympathetic looks, and tormented herself with speculation upon Niall's business with the troupe.

What had gotten into him?

She picked up a bit of needlework she had left on a side table and set it back down again a moment later. Surely Niall couldn't have guessed what Morgan really was. *She* had been the only one privileged with that secret. That amazing, wonderful secret.

I am not alone.

That single, foolish thought came to her again and again, beating out a rhythm as constant and indisputable as a heartbeat. *I am not alone.*

It was not that Morgan had welcomed her with open arms as a fellow werewolf. But she had seen his eyes widen and his guard drop for just an instant when she had told him what she was.

The man she had glimpsed behind the mask . . . oh, that unveiling was fully as powerful as learning his secret. He had claimed she could not be of his blood because she lived in a city and enjoyed a comfortable life. Yet when she had spoken of her mother, there was such understanding in his eyes, such compassion, that she could have wept.

That unexpected sympathy was the reason that she let self-pity slip its tight rein. She had said little of the accident, but it was so much more than she had ever told to anyone except Papa, just before he died. She had even admitted that her mother and father had not been married.

Thank heaven she had recovered before she could wallow in events long past and irreversible. She had been able to accept Morgan's final rebuff—and his touch on her body—without flinching. And she had seen that all the tough ferocity he exhibited covered a great vulnerability and the sorrow of profound loss.

Loss so similar to her own. And he was loyal to his fellow troupers, protective of them as any elder brother might be. Yet his last words to her held a cryptic warning: *"Do not mistake enemies for allies."*

What had he meant? Surely Morgan was not her enemy. She would have liked—even been grateful for—his friendship.

Friendship? Did you hope that he could share some great mystery that you never discovered? What kind of relationship can exist when you will likely never see him again once the circus has gone?

Had she not restored the boundaries between them—the high walls of money, temperament, and belief? Did those walls not reach far higher than even the strongest wolf, whole of limb, could leap?

And why should she think *he* would ever wish to scale such barriers? He wanted no part of them.

Yet . . . *You are not alone,* her heart insisted. *And neither is he.*

She rapped her hand on the arm of her chair and turned hard away from the window. Sleep was what she required.

A good night's rest cured so many ills, purged a multitude of unproductive thoughts. Most especially thoughts of what she should not want and could never have.

She bit her lip and frowned at the bed. Ordinarily she would call for Fran to assist her in moving from chair to bedstead, but it was pure selfishness to drag Fran out of her own cot at such an hour. Was it such an insurmountable gap, those few inches between her chair and the bed? Her arms were strong enough. The tiny ember of rebellion that had disturbed her of late, nursed along by the day's events, sparked into a flame.

Setting her jaw, she wheeled the chair as close to the bed as she could, aligning them side by side. She took a firm grip on the iron railing that ran the length of the bed, designed to keep her from falling out.

Perspiration broke out on her forehead, though the room was cool. The muscles in her arms already ached with the effort to come.

You can do this. You are strong enough. Alternately pushing and pulling, she began to transfer her weight from the chair to the bed rails. Her arms screamed in protest. She clenched her teeth and dragged herself up and over to the gap in the rail.

The chair rolled a few inches away. The space between it and the bed grew accordingly, widening into a chasm. The hem of her dressing gown caught on the arm of her chair. A stab of very real pain shot down her spine and lodged at its root.

She did not cry out. She would win, or they could find her on the floor in the morning. She made another laborious effort, and her dressing grown ripped and then slid from her shoulders.

For a moment she hung suspended between bed and chair, her upper half almost . . . almost . . . flat on the coverlet. Then some movement of her body shoved the chair another precious inch away. The dead weight of her lower half pulled her down, down, like grasping hands reaching from perdition.

She tumbled. Her elbow struck the bed railing as she fell, shooting pain into arm and shoulder. Far, far worse was the slow, ignominious slide to the floor.

She lay on the carpet, her nightdress bunched up about her useless knees and her elbow numb from the blow. Tears squeezed from the corners of her eyes. She let them fall. No one would see them tonight. But in the morning . . .

Rolling onto her stomach, she pushed up on her arms. It might take hours, but she could make it back to the chair or the bed. If one was not possible, the other must be. God forbid that Niall should find her like this.

A faint noise came from the direction of the stairs: footsteps ascending, so soft that she had to strain to hear them.

Morgan Holt had made her more aware of the keen senses she had always taken for granted. She knew the step of every member of the household, from Fran's light patter to Niall's purposeful thump. But this was not a tread she recognized.

Her skin began to prickle. Instinctively she reached for the hem of her nightdress and tried to tug it down over her knees. The movement set her off balance, and she fell back on her sore elbow just as the footsteps came to a halt outside her door.

It swung open. A familiar, disturbingly fascinating scent blew in with biting October air. The doorway filled with a lean and powerful figure.

Morgan Holt had come to return her call.

M organ knew, when he opened the door, that Athena Munroe's alluring scent had led him to the right room. But she was not where he expected her to be.

She lay on the floor beside the fancy four-poster, her awkwardly bent legs half-covered by her nightdress, her face pinched with a mighty effort to conceal shock and pain. He knew at once what she had been trying to do.

He closed the door behind him and knelt beside her. Her

shudder did not make him hesitate; he set his arms under her shoulders and knees and lifted her onto the bed. She brushed frantically at her gown, intent upon hiding her legs from his sight.

With an effort at detachment that should have come easily, he pulled the hem down to her ankles and drew the crumpled blankets to her waist. His fingertips brushed her calf; he snatched his hands away, but not before he felt the warmth of her damp skin and suffered a jolt of breathtaking arousal.

She flushed. "What are you doing here?"

His physical response to her left him so shaken that he could find no answer. Her emotions cascaded over him like a flash flood in the desert, and not a single one of his most impregnable defenses could hold them back.

Chagrin. Anger. Shame. All her self-contained pride was lost, for he had witnessed her failure. She recoiled from him, but it was not only because a man of her kind did not touch a woman so intimately unless he was her mate. She was ashamed because she was vulnerable, exposed—a wingless bird to be ridiculed, a rabbit to be devoured. She, who should have been strong and free.

His mind formed a picture of her rising stiffly from her chair, grimly bent on reaching her bed—her brave efforts to persevere even when her body betrayed her—her humiliating tumble to the floor. He knew what it was to regard a simple movement from chair to bed as if it were a leap across a hundred-foot chasm.

And how much courage it took to live with that insurmountable obstacle every day of her life.

Her gaze met his. He was the one, now, who recoiled at the assault upon his senses and his heart. It was as raw as an open wound, this terrible sharing. His skin seemed to take heat from hers, though they did not touch; he looked away only to discover the gentle swell of her breasts beneath the fine lawn of her nightdress, and the teasing disarray of her loose brown hair.

He crouched beside the bed, as much to protect himself

as to become less threatening in her eyes. He was the invader here. This was her place, her territory; she could order him to leave. He would be smart to obey and run before . . . before . . .

"How did you get in?" she demanded. Her voice had grown more sure, though it cracked in midsentence. "The servants—"

"Did not hear me. But you did."

"Yes." She sat up against a bolster of pillows, drawing the blanket with her. "That does not explain why you come in the middle of the night, break into our house, and walk right into my . . . my room as if you had a right . . ."

"No right, but a reason," he said quietly, balancing his arms across his knees. "I came to bring you a message. Your brother—"

"If my brother were here—"

"But he is not."

"Do you make a habit of trespassing like a thief, Mr. Holt, when there is no man to stop you?"

He could not help but admire the increasing steadiness of her voice and the directness of her gaze. Nor could he be angry with her after what he had witnessed. Here was not the nice, formally polite, and benevolent lady who had descended from on high to view her brother's surprise gift. This was the woman he had glimpsed briefly in the tent after the near-accident—the she-wolf reawakened—and he liked her the better for her honest annoyance.

Yes, he *liked* her. Even the word felt strange as he rolled it around in his mind, tasting and exploring it as if he were a cub with an intriguing bit of bone.

"I come and go where I wish," he said, "but not to do you harm."

"I do not suppose that your upbringing, whatever it was, taught you that it does considerable harm to enter a lady's room uninvited and unchaperoned. It is not only impolite—" She swallowed and gripped the edge of her blanket. "Among . . . townies, reputation is something of value. If anyone were to see you here, mine would be compromised."

"I know about your rules." He shifted, and her eyes flew to track his motion. "You and your friends waste too much time worrying about what isn't important."

"What do you mean by that?" She scooted higher on the pillows, forgetting to adjust her blanket upward. "What do you know of my friends, or any of the niceties of life?"

He dropped his chin onto his folded arms. Now was as good a time as any. He could tell her what he had overheard in the Windsor's restaurant. It might be a kindness to set her free from her illusions.

But he looked at her face and knew that the truth would destroy her. She was not strong enough. Perhaps she would never be. And when the circus left Denver—tomorrow, in a week, in a month—none of it would matter to him.

It shouldn't matter now. It shouldn't matter that her brother had her on a short leash and she chose not to see, or that she'd given up half of herself out of fear of losing what little she had.

What little she had. She would laugh at him if he said that, surrounded as she was with luxury and everything money could buy. All the things his family had done without, that his father had been so hungry for.

"You were right about my upbringing, Miss Munroe," he said. "We didn't have much. We lived in a small cabin in the mountains. One bed and a cot. Only the fire and candles for light. My parents—my ma hunted, and we fished and sold furs in town. We had books, but no schooling." Memories thick with the dust of years emerged from their hidden places, raising a fog in his mind. "We didn't need anything else, until Pa—"

Stop. He drove the memories back into oblivion and got to his feet. Where in hell had that come from? Why here, with her? She was no part of his past, or his future. And his future stretched no further than the next moment.

"Your parents," Athena said, her voice suddenly gentle. "You said that you hadn't seen your family since you were

a boy. To lose them at so young an age . . . I am sorry that
I spoke as I did."

He forced himself to look at her. Her face had resumed
that gracious, almost saintly expression, raising in him a
desire to snap and snarl until she lost it again. Deliberately
he raked his gaze from her eyes to her chin and lower,
where the high collar of her nightdress hugged the graceful arc of her neck.

Despite the lace and frills, the sheer fabric of the garment left little to the imagination. The pink tones of her
skin gave the white lawn a rosy tint, and where her breasts
lifted the cloth he could see the brown circles of her nipples. Each one formed a small, intriguing peak that grew
more pronounced as she noticed his stare.

Humans—or werewolves in human form—were much
like animals. Their bodies responded to instinct and desires
that had nothing to do with intellect. Morgan's body was
very much aware of Athena's.

He had not been oblivious to her during their previous
encounters. He had been conscious of her sex and tolerated
a certain attraction, even before he learned of her true nature. But the attraction had been only that, and easily set
aside.

No longer. Something had changed. It wasn't only his
respect for her courage in challenging the limitations of
her body and spirit, or that he had unwillingly shared her
emotions. It wasn't that he stood in her bedchamber, a
room humans regarded as the proper place for sex. Nor
was it that she wore a diaphanous nightdress instead of the
armor of corsets and layered skirts. He had seen many
women clothed in less, and regarded them as merely the
means to ease his body's needs.

Athena was not like those women. He understood the
difference between females raised as she had been, and
the worldly inhabitants of the circus or saloon. She had no
experience, of that he was certain, and no skill. Her allure
was completely unintentional.

She regarded mating as a wanton beast that could tear

her precious reputation to shreds, or worse—an enemy capable of making her remember what she had lost.

No matter how carefully she and her proper society friends tried to pretend otherwise, she knew why he looked at her and why she wanted to conceal herself from his gaze. Her skin flushed, color rising from under her collar and sweeping up to the roots of her hair. Her breathing quickened. He could hear the throb of her pulse under the soft flesh of her neck. Her scent had begun a subtle change as her body prepared itself for mating, and his nostrils flared to take in the fragrance of arousal.

She *wanted* him. And he wanted her. This girl, this haughty, naive woman in her cage of a chair—he wanted her as he had never wanted any woman in his life.

His feet moved of their own accord, carrying him toward her. His hands reached out to touch her, hold her, claim her.

Mine, the wolf howled. *Mine.*

"Stop," she whispered. "Morgan. Please."

He thought he had imagined the plea, but her hands fumbled at her blankets and her eyes begged for mercy. He stopped. Air flooded into his lungs. He shook his head to snap the spider-silk filaments of lust that bound him to Athena, and they released their tenacious grip.

But not entirely. His body still ached and cried out, refusing to be silenced. All he need do was breathe in her scent, and he was caught again. But he had come with a purpose, and he had yet to carry it out.

Niall Munroe had brought him here. He had betrayed Athena—his own, his family, his pack. And Athena was as ignorant of her brother's deception as she was of the hypocrisy of her society friends.

Morgan had intended to give Athena a chance to fight for herself. Until now, he hadn't questioned his motives. Physical attraction, the drive to help one of his own kind, dislike of Niall Munroe, pity . . . it all led to this room and this moment. This undeniable need.

He let out a long breath. "It is time I told you why I came—"

"Just go." Athena's blanket was up to her chin, framing her pale face. "If you don't leave at once, I will be forced to call my maid. It would be better if I did not, for both our sakes."

He gave his body a final shake and seized the chance for a safer kind of skirmish. "Call your maid, Athena—but I hope that she is a very brave woman. I would not want to frighten her."

"You enjoy that, don't you?" The defiant spark returned to her eyes. "You like to intimidate people just because you can. The feelings of others mean nothing to you. I would remove you myself if I were not . . ." She lifted her chin. "You are no gentleman, Mr. Holt, preying on unprotected women. If you thought—if you *ever* thought—that I had any interest in you beyond your part in the circus, you were sadly mistaken."

She had come too close to the truth. Morgan smiled. "Why do you think I am interested? Do you have so many men panting after you, Athena? Do you fight your suitors off with the edge of your tongue, or does your brother do it for you?"

He regretted his cruelty instantly. Her pupils constricted as if he had reached out and shaken her. Then the fierce light in her eyes went out, and she stared down at her hands upon the blanket.

"I have no suitors," she said. "You can see why I do not. I spoke . . . out of pride. You have a remarkable ability to turn me into a shrew. I forget my manners . . . I behave quite abominably unlike myself. But you saved my life, and I will not forget that."

Morgan felt about as tall as Ulysses, and much less honorable. "Athen—"

"No matter why you came, Morgan, it must be obvious that you and I are too different even to speak to each other in a calm and reasonable manner. Let us call a truce, and pretend this misunderstanding never happened."

Misunderstanding? He would have laughed if he hadn't become so keenly sensible of her fragility. A single tear would drive him to his knees.

"Morgan," he said.

She blinked. "I beg your pardon?"

"You called me Morgan."

"I am sorry. I did not mean—"

"No one calls me Mr. Holt," he said. "That is for gentlemen."

"I apologized for my rudeness—"

"Morgan."

She hesitated a long moment, worrying the blanket between her fingers. "Morgan."

"Good." He sank down where he was, not trusting himself to go closer to her. "I am not your enemy, Athena. I came here to warn you that your brother is working against you."

"Niall? I do not understand."

"He brought us—the troupe—to Denver to play for your orphans. Now he wants to buy us off before the performance, and I don't think he intends to tell you until we're gone."

"Buy you off?"

"I saw him offering Harry money if we would leave. The troupe wanted you to know, so you could decide."

"That is ridiculous. My brother brought you all the way to Denver. Why would he send you away now?"

"Do you want the truth?"

A door shut behind her eyes. "Of course. I still do not understand—"

"He found out about the Wolf-Man act. That was why he was so upset when he came to get you on the lot, and why he wanted you out of the way."

She paled. "He didn't know you were in the show? But you have been with the circus all along—"

"He didn't see me when he hired the troupe, and I don't think he knows that I am the Wolf-Man. It is the idea he hates. He told Caitlin he did not want the children to see something unfit for them, but she thinks he's afraid and hides it by claiming he's protecting you. He would have kept the troupe if it wasn't for me."

"Why should Niall be afraid?" The soft curve of her lips took a stubborn set. "If your act is too frightening for the children, we can leave it out. What you say of my brother—you must have misunderstood him."

He could have stopped there, told her what the troupe had decided, and left it in her hands. That would be the easiest way. Once he started saying what was in his mind, he'd only dig himself in deeper with her.

But wasn't he halfway to hell already?

"I did not misunderstand, Athena. If your brother were an ordinary human, he wouldn't believe my act was anything but a trick. He must suspect that the Wolf-Man is like you . . . and soon he may realize who and what I am."

"But I have told you that he understands—"

"Why does he fear it so much if he accepts what you are? Why does he want us gone before you see us again?"

Her mouth opened on a sharp intake of breath. "I know my own brother. There must be some other reason for his . . . acting so strangely."

For all the vehemence of her words, Morgan knew she was lying. Oh, not on purpose, and not to him, but to herself. There was something in this she didn't want to face.

"You said your brother always knew what you were. His mother was human, but your mother was one of us."

"Yes." Her face was pinched, as if she anticipated some terrible pain. "My father loved my mother. He accepted her completely."

"But did your brother? You ran as a wolf before the accident. Maybe he envied you."

"No," she said. "You are wrong." She looked quickly from side to side, like a cornered animal seeking escape. "Were both your parents werewolves?"

"My . . . father was human."

"And did he envy your mother?"

"I don't know." His throat thickened up, and he had to

swallow twice to clear it. "She loved him. He never raised a hand to her or said a harsh word, until he . . ."

She stared at him, waiting for him to finish. He couldn't. "We're talking about your brother, and why he is afraid," he said harshly. "Maybe he doesn't want you around another of your kind."

What is he protecting you from, Athena? Does he secretly hate what you are—what we are—the way humans hate what they don't understand? Or does he want you to forget what you were before your accident?

"My brother—" Athena began, struggling with her thoughts as he had with his. "You think he guesses, or will guess, what you are, and wants me away from you. But he has no reason to think you would harm me."

"I could never harm you, Athena."

He felt her reaction like a punch in the belly. "I know you would not," she said in a whisper. "Yet if Niall knew what you did tonight—"

"He doesn't know." He rose, stretching his spine until it cracked. "But you do not want him to find me here. I came to tell you that the troupe will stand by you. If you want us to stay, we will, no matter what your brother says."

Too much had shocked her, too much had been said to dismiss, but she gamely wrestled her bewilderment into submission and fought her way back to firmer ground. "Why would you defy Niall when he offered to pay you?"

"Maybe we don't like being ordered about by townies."

"That is not a good reason. Niall has much influence—"

"Harry knows what the performance means to you. He likes you. So does Caitlin."

"That is kind of them. And . . . and you?"

"I don't like your brother."

She gave a startled laugh. "You are very blunt."

"I don't like what he does to you."

"To me?"

"Controlling you. Making sure you stay the way you are."

Her eyes widened. "He doesn't try to keep me here . . .

this way. It cannot be helped." She shook her head, denying whatever unpleasant thoughts he had put in her mind. "Niall enables me to do what I can for the destitute and disadvantaged. He wants only what is best for me, to make me happy. He is a good man."

"He is human. You are not."

She was quiet for a long time. "You are a strange man, Morgan Holt. You hardly know me. Neither does Harry, or Caitlin. Yet you would do this for me."

"You help people you don't know. Why should the troupers be different? Or aren't we saintly enough?"

"I am not saint," she said softly. "What do you want me to do?"

"It is not my choice."

"Yet you came here, when you could have sent a message tomorrow."

"Are you afraid to stand up to your brother?" he demanded. "Caitlin said you wouldn't be. She said you had a will of your own. Do you, Athena? Is it easier to go along and pretend you agree with your brother so that you can forget what you gave up?"

She stared at him, stricken. Caitlin's words came back to Morgan as vividly as if she stood in the room beside him. *Are you testing her, Morgan? Do you want her to fail, so that you will have no reason to care?*

And he realized that he stood on the edge of a precipice, half longing for her to send them away, half hoping that she had the courage to be what her blood made her. Not this cripple in a chair, but a woman of spirit and strength. She was a prisoner who did not recognize her prison or the jailers she trusted. Her independence and social influence were illusions, her good works false consolation, her pride and acceptance of her fate only brittle paper masks that would crumple at a touch.

Yet if she decided to fight, if she dared to face the realities she so willfully ignored, then he was bound to her course. To *her*. For somewhere, sometime since their first meeting, he had taken Athena Munroe into his pack just as he had the troupers—reluctantly, hating himself for his weakness, but bound just as surely.

He had not wanted this responsibility for another person. He had meant to spend his life alone, unattached, unfeeling.

But the circus had changed him—Caitlin, Harry, Ulysses. He had begun to forget what it was like to live in chains, and what had put him there.

Athena's low sigh called him back from the past. "You asked for my decision," she said, meeting his gaze. "I want you to stay. The children are expecting a special treat, and I will not disappoint them. I will find a way to convince my brother, no matter what it takes."

Chapter 10

A *thena waited to see how Morgan would respond,*
profoundly grateful that she had managed to keep her
composure intact—just barely—during this harrowing
visit.

The facts that had been brought to light during their
conversation still rattled about in her mind, making it difficult to concentrate on any one disquieting revelation. She
was unable to decide which was worse: Morgan's untimely
intrusion, his witnessing her helplessness, or what he had
told her about Niall.

She believed Morgan, as painful as it was. Since that argument months ago when Niall had accused her of doing
too much, a part of her had been preparing for just such a
battle. She simply had not believed it would come so soon,
or in such unexpected form.

She had lied to Morgan when she told him that Niall accepted her inhuman nature; in her heart she knew that he
did not, not completely. It was a matter they had never discussed. But if Niall thought she might be reminded of her
mother's heritage, and how it had brought her to this life of
confinement . . .

How could she admit how much it hurt that Niall had schemed behind her back, all in the name of protecting her from herself?

Her reputation had become the least of her worries. Yet she could not ignore the effect Morgan had upon her, here in her own most private sanctuary. He was the wolf who spoke to the sleeping beast within her. The man who stared at her as if she were a desirable woman. Heaven help her, she had felt that stare like a touch whispering up and down her flesh, stirring sensations she had just begun to experience before the accident.

Why, oh why had Morgan come to waken them again? Why did he make her *feel* more than any man alive, more than any person had a right to?

And why was he so determined to protect her?

She held her head high and watched him weigh her answer as ruthlessly as he had judged her life. At last he cocked his head, and a smile tilted one corner of his mouth.

"Caitlin was right," he said. "You are brave enough."

"Thank you. And now you must leave. If my brother finds you here, nothing in the world will convince him to let the circus remain in Denver."

He inclined his head. "I will go."

Athena allowed herself to relax just a little, knowing there would be no further chance at sleep tonight. She would spend the wee hours concocting a way to broach the subject with Niall . . . while not revealing her source of information.

"Please convey my gratitude to Harry and the others," she said. "Ask them to wait until they hear from me. I will see that you get a message when I have spoken to Niall." Having a definite plan was comforting, however tenuous it was. "Regardless of Niall's response, I will make certain that the troupe receives the full payment they were promised."

"Even if you lose the fight?"

She shuddered inwardly at his insistence on using such violent terms. Perhaps he knew no other way.

If she pursued that line of thought, she would let herself be drawn to him, into his life, with the hope that somehow she might unravel the mystery of Morgan Holt. She wanted very badly to understand him, even though she knew such a course was dangerous beyond her wildest speculation.

The questions she might ask Morgan Holt would satisfy her curiosity, nothing more. The answers could not change what was.

"If I lose the battle," she said, "*you* will have lost nothing."

"And your brother will rule you for the rest of your life."

"You seem just as determined to 'rule' me as he is. Are all men as thoroughly vexing as the two of you?"

"Are all females as foolish as you and Caitlin?"

"You do not know—you, a man of the world? Have you not left a trail of broken hearts behind you?"

He twitched as if he would snap at her, and then his eyes kindled like golden lanterns. "Not yet. Should I begin now?"

Never in her life had Athena been so grateful for a distraction as she was when she heard the unmistakable sound of a slamming door downstairs.

"Niall is home," she whispered. "You must leave at once!"

He gave her a most wolfish smile. "What would happen if I didn't?"

"If you are quick, you can leave by the window. I am sure that climbing down from a second-story window is child's play for a man of your talents."

Stairs creaked below the landing. Athena gestured Morgan toward the window. He started in the right direction obediently enough, but at the last minute he turned and glided to her bedside.

Athena supposed that, somewhere deep inside, she was almost expecting what happened next. Morgan crouched beside her, his hands on the bed, and leaned very close. His heat washed over her like the summer sun. His thick, black, unfashionably long hair brushed the sheets, her pillow, her breasts.

And he kissed her. His mouth came down on hers, hard for only an instant before it gentled and began to caress. His weight pressed her back into the pillows. She might have felt smothered, terrified, but her senses had become so heightened that waves of pleasure pulsed all the way to her toes. One of her arms moved of its own accord to wrap about his shoulders. Firm muscle clenched under her palm.

"Athena," he murmured.

She caught her breath. Her lips throbbed. Her body throbbed. *"Morgan."*

A loose floorboard on the landing just outside her door groaned in warning. Morgan sprang back. He leaped for the window, threw it open and was gone. Cold air spilled through the curtains, making a vain attempt to cool Athena's heated skin. Hastily she rearranged her nightdress and scooted down under the blanket. There was no use in pretending that she hadn't been awake, not with the lamp still burning and the window wide open.

The door swung in. Niall entered the room and glanced about. His expression was, thank heaven, no more than slightly perplexed. He lacked the senses to know that someone else had been in the room.

"I saw the light on," he said. "Why aren't you asleep?" Before he could answer he noticed the billowing curtains and strode to the window to shut it. "You'll catch your death, Athena. Why is the window open?"

"I felt rather warm," she said meekly. "I could not sleep."

He frowned at her and stood by the bedside. "Are you feverish? Should I send for a doctor?"

"No. I am quite well . . . merely thinking."

He sat between the bars on the edge of the bed. "About what?"

Athena tried to remember how long it had been since she and Niall had had a heart-to-heart conversation that did not revolve around common courtesies or, more recently, arguments over her activities. "The circus," she answered honestly. "The performance for the children. It is only a few days away."

He had the grace to look uncomfortable. His fingers plucked at a bit of her blanket. "Would you be very disappointed . . . if the performance had to be cancelled?"

So he did feel obligated to say something, after all. She faced a clear choice: either pretend she knew nothing, using her supposed ignorance to undermine Niall's resolve, or confront him directly. She knew what she would have chosen yesterday.

Many things had been different yesterday. She would not have believed the time would come when she would be compelled to defy her brother. But then, she would not have believed the time would come when she was kissed in her own bed by a near stranger . . . least of all one like Morgan Holt.

"You plan to send the circus away," she said.

He looked at her sharply. "How did you know?"

"Something . . . something Cecily said today on the lot," she improvised. Cecily Hockensmith had acted rather strangely while she and Athena waited in the carriage for Niall's return, but Athena had been more concerned with her brother at the time. "I knew something was wrong by the way you behaved. It was not like you."

She drew a breath of relief when she saw that she had guessed correctly. "I discussed the matter briefly with Miss Hockensmith," Niall said, "and asked her to come with me when I went to the lot—"

"To ask the circus to leave Denver," she finished. "Why, Niall? They were a gift to me, to the children. Cecily said something about a bad influence, but surely—"

"I had hoped this would not come up until they were gone," Niall said, rising. "But since you have guessed, I see no reason to deny the truth." He strode across the room and addressed the wall, his hands clasped behind his back. "I made a mistake when I brought the circus to Denver. It is not a suitable entertainment for the children, nor are the performers fit company for you and the other young ladies."

"I see. And you discussed this with Cecily?"

"Miss Hockensmith agreed with me."

Athena bit her lip. It was difficult not to be a little upset with Cecily for taking her brother's side, but she knew that the other woman's motives were good even if her attitude was too severe. "What led you to make this decision, Niall?"

There. Either he would tell her the truth, or he would work his way around it as if it were a ticklish business deal.

He chose a middle path. "I received some new information that suggested it would be better if they did not remain. I offered them a substantial gratuity in compensation. They were happy enough to take it."

Now he was lying. "Were they? It's not really the children you wish to protect, is it, Niall? You are afraid for me."

He turned around and stared at her. "And if I am? You spend too much time with beggars and riffraff as it is. We discussed this before—"

"They are human beings, are they not? They are far more apt to be harmed than do harm themselves. The troupers are constantly on the verge of disaster, yet they are generous and warmhearted."

"You see? You already think of them as friends."

"We formed a contract with them, and you have always said that contracts must be honorably fulfilled. Even if you don't consider such a contract sacred, I do." She gathered her courage. "That is why you must agree to let them stay to complete the performance."

"I must? Did I hear you correctly, Athena?"

"Yes. I have asked very little of you in the past several years, except that you allow me to use my portion of the inheritance as I wish. Now I am asking for this."

He glowered and paced from one end of the room to the other. "I have already asked them to leave."

"Send a message and tell them that you have changed your mind. You need not give any explanation."

Now was the crucial moment. Either he must come up with a better argument than he had so far, or he would be forced to tell her his real reason for wanting the troupe—and most especially the "Wolf-Man"—out of her reach.

"If you do this, Niall," she said, "I'll stay away from the lot until the day of the performance."

"That is not enough. If I allow the circus to remain, you must promise to curtail some of your more intemperate activities."

Athena closed her eyes. She knew that he was using this as a means to do the very thing Morgan had accused him of—control her. "You ask a great deal," she said.

"So do you." The mattress creaked as he sat down again. "I am willing to compromise, but only if you will do the same."

Compromise? she thought with unaccustomed bitterness. *Negotiate is too nice a word. Manipulate is more accurate. You have all the advantages.*

"Very well," she said. "Will you send a message tomorrow morning?"

"Yes." He patted her hand. "It's for the best, my dear. The performance is to be on Sunday. I foresee no trouble as long as you remain at home until then."

Athena was very tempted to argue. She did not enjoy arguing, and she'd had her fill of it tonight with Morgan. But a kernel of anger lay hard and cold in her heart, threatening to grow into something larger and much more intractable. Something with claws and fangs and the tenacity to drive every obstacle from its path by any means.

Exactly like Morgan Holt.

She tucked her hand under the covers. "I am tired now. I think I would like to sleep."

"Good." He got up and went to turn off the lamp. "I'm

sure that you will have plenty to do until Sunday. I'll ask Miss Hockensmith to visit and bring your friends."

She didn't answer. After a while the light went out, and the door closed softly. Niall's footsteps retreated down the hall to his own room. Another door closed. All was silent save for the tapping of cottonwood branches on her window.

Athena lay cold and stiff under the blankets, fighting to control her unreasonable passions. Her stomach clenched and roiled as if she had digested every last shred of the contentment she had cultivated since the accident.

You lied to me, Niall. You treat me like a child, and I ceased being a child when you carried me out of that snowdrift.

A child. To Niall, she would always be that, dependent and unable to guide her own destiny.

Morgan Holt did not see her that way. She shivered, remembering the kiss, and the icy kernel in her heart was all but consumed in a blaze of sheer physical yearning.

Morgan Holt believed she was brave and capable. He saw her as a woman grown. He didn't give her pretty words. He was barely courteous. Yet his actions spoke more eloquently than the most cultured speech.

And he had kissed her.

She touched her lips. It was just as well that she must stay away until the performance. If she met him again in private, she didn't know what she would say or do. What *he* would say or do, when there was no future to be shared between them.

In dreams, she could walk, and run, and even Change again. In dreams, all the barriers between her and Morgan Holt dissolved like snow in a teakettle, and she forgot that her life was laid out now as it would always be.

She closed her eyes and willed the dreams to come.

Niall ushered Athena, Miss Hockensmith, and the few friends who had chosen to attend the performance to the special seats set aside for them at the very edge of the ring. Workers were busy making final adjustments to the props to be used by the performers—the high wire, the trampoline, the various balls and banners and hoops. Scaffolding for the aerialists hung overhead. An off-key trumpet sounded outside the trouper's entrance at the opposite side of the ring, and teachers from the orphanage herded the last of their charges in the common seating area, which the circus people called the "blues."

Children's voices rang and echoed under the artificial cave of the tent. Sounds of innocent, uncomplicated joy. Niall glanced at the happy, upturned faces, and was glad he had not begrudged the orphans this small pleasure. Athena had invited the residents of Denver's other orphanages in addition to her own; nearly a hundred youngsters filled the blues.

Athena had been true to her word. She'd kept quietly at home until this afternoon. If there had been a slight strain between him and his sister, Niall had dismissed it as minor pique on his sister's part. She would get over it—she always did. No one in the world was less apt to hold a grudge than Athena.

Niall knew that better than anyone.

As confirmation of his judgment, Athena beamed impartially at him and at anyone else who came in sight, including Harry French. The old man had personally attended them and arranged for refreshments to be provided, bobbing up and down the while with ingratiating humility. Fortunately, he had not found the temerity to ask Niall why he had changed his mind about allowing the performance, though Niall had made certain that the "Wolf-Man" stayed away. There was little risk that Athena would be reminded of things best left buried.

Cecily Hockensmith touched his arm. "Oh, Mr. Munroe, I am so glad that you found a way to permit the show in spite of our concerns," she said. "Athena looks so happy. You were very clever to find a solution that pleases everyone."

"I do not like making my sister unhappy," he said, sparing her a glance. "There is no reason why such matters cannot be settled in an equitable manner."

"Indeed. My father has often said how much he admires your skills of negotiation."

He murmured some rote courtesy and gazed about the ring. If not for Athena and her friends, he would have preferred to remain in the office at work, Sunday or not. But this was a moment of triumph for Athena, and he would not ruin her pleasure in it.

He didn't know why he continued to scan the tent while Cecily Hockensmith chattered away beside him. When Harry French, replete in bright coat and vest, entered the ring to announce the start of the show, he listened for a while and then let his mind wander to the latest reports from his mining investments and banking interests.

The performance began with the inevitable clowns. They gamboled about the ring, playing out skits and teasing children in the audience with their absurd antics. Niall watched the first act, decided that it was competent and quite harmless, and returned to his calculations of profit and loss. The laughter and cries of children, punctuated by the occasional gasp or comment from Miss Hockensmith, hardly disturbed his ruminations.

A blast of music from the small band marked the change to the next act, a motley pack of trained dogs. It flew by like the first. Niall made a few changes to a contract written in his mind. Another performance, by a trio of acrobats, followed the second, and he composed a letter to the manager of his smelting operation in Argo.

It was only when the fourth act began that he finally took notice, though he could not have said at first why he did so. A line of caparisoned gray horses trotted into the ring, necks arched and plumes waving proudly. Behind them, light as a fairy, bounded a girl in tights and short skirt, her red hair burning like a halo about her piquant face.

That was when he knew what he had been watching for.

Facts and figures vanished from his mind like chalk erased from a slate. Caitlin Hughes danced gracefully to the center of the ring, an ornamental whip in hand, and called out to her horses. They reared up in perfect formation, much to the delight of the children.

"I believe I recognize that girl," Miss Hockensmith said. "A tiny thing, is she not? I cannot imagine what sort of upbringing she must have had."

Niall barely heard her. He was remembering his last conversation—argument—with Miss Hughes, and how she had pulled back that remarkable hair to reveal her delicately pointed ears.

Ears like . . . like an elf out of legend. And she had been so defiant. Her eyes had flashed like the sapphire earrings Niall had given Athena two Christmases ago.

The girl was too far across the tent to see him now. His gaze followed her every motion as if she had cast a spell upon him. Once or twice Miss Hockensmith spoke, but he heard only her voice and not the words.

How remarkable Miss Hughes was. Niall tried to remember her coarse ways, her rudeness, and her physical oddity, but it grew increasingly difficult to do so. She handled the horses as if she spoke their language; they reared and bowed and frolicked at her slightest invitation.

All too quickly an assistant came to retrieve the horses, leaving one in the ring with her. She leaped up upon the animal's bare back and balanced there while her helpers positioned themselves at various points on the ring, suspending banners in the path she and her mount would follow around its circumference.

The horse began to trot and then broke into a canter. Caitlin might as well have been flying. As her mount approached a banner and ran underneath, she sprang straight up and over the stretched fabric, performing a double somersault and landing precisely on the animal's back. The ladies gasped and applauded.

Miss Hockensmith tugged at his sleeve. "Mr. Munroe—"
He pulled his arm away. Caitlin did a series of jumps

and acrobatic feats, each more perilous than the last. A second horse was brought out, and she leaped from one back to another as they ran, sometimes somersaulting between. Niall forgot to breathe. Caitlin followed the curve of the ring toward the seats and looked directly at him.

It was impossible, but he could have sworn that their eyes met and locked across that distance. Something snatched annoyingly at his sleeve. He disregarded it and held his breath as Caitlin smiled.

Canvas cracked loudly overhead, tossed by the wind. Caitlin's mount approached the next banner and plunged sharply to the left, its hoof striking the wooden ring. Caitlin lost her balance—only for a moment, but just long enough to leave her unprepared for the next banner.

Niall shot to his feet. Caitlin struck the banner at an awkward angle and flew in the opposite direction to her shying mount. She hit the ground hard.

"My God!" Athena cried. "Niall!"

He needed no further encouragement. Hopping over the low barrier between the seats and the ring, he dashed to Caitlin's sprawled form. If she had been hurt . . . if she were—

She opened her eyes. "Oh. It's you," she said, slurring her words. "I cannot understand it. Pennyfarthing has always been my best gelding."

"Don't try to speak," he commanded. He stripped off his coat and spread it across her. Others had come, forming a worried wall about them. Harry French pushed his way through.

"Firefly! Are you hurt?"

Caitlin grinned weakly. "I have been better."

Niall glanced up at Harry. "The children should not see this. Please ask the teachers to take them out, and be so good as to distract them in some way until . . . until this is resolved."

"Naturally, naturally, just as you say," Harry said, looking very near tears. "But we must get a doctor—"

"Of course. Niall, you should send for Dr. Brenner at once."

Athena. Niall cleared his mind enough to look for her, and found her reclining in the arms of the man he recognized as Morgan Holt. He stared into Niall's eyes with unmistakable challenge.

Holt. Niall remembered how the ruffian had remained close to Athena during her first visit, but now he began to wonder what interest Holt had in her. Who was he?

"Please, Niall," Athena said, all brisk purpose and unconcern for her compromising position. "We do not know how badly Caitlin is hurt."

She was right, and he had no time to worry about Morgan Holt at the moment. He turned back to Caitlin and tucked his coat more snugly under her chin. Her face was creased with pain.

"Lie quietly," he told her. "The rest of you, make sure she is kept warm and still. Her injuries may not be obvious to the eye."

The dwarf, Ulysses, stepped forward. "You need not worry, Mr. Munroe. We will take care of her until the doctor arrives."

Niall nodded. "I'll be back within the hour. Athena—"

"I will stay here, with Caitlin," she said. Her quiet conviction promised a lengthy argument if he protested.

"Mr. French, please get my sister her chair," he said. Belatedly he remembered Cecily Hockensmith and the other ladies. Miss Hockensmith stood safely beyond the ring of circus folk, her face set in a frown. The expression quickly transformed to one of worry when she caught his glance.

"Miss Hockensmith," he said, getting to his feet, "will you stay with Athena? I would be much obliged."

"Of course." She smiled tentatively as he made his way through the crowd. "I will do whatever I can."

"Thank you." He pressed her hand in passing and strode toward the tent's wide entrance. Once there he paused, half afraid that Caitlin would not be where he had left her.

But the crowd had dispersed enough to reveal her figure, covered now by a blanket as well as his coat. Harry French brought Athena's chair, and Holt settled her into it. Ulysses knelt beside Caitlin, speaking in his soft, pleasant Southern drawl.

Niall turned on his heel and headed for the carriage. The doctor would see to Caitlin. Now that the performance was effectively ended, time and distance would take care of Morgan Holt, whatever his interest in Athena, and dispose of the very unwelcome complication the circus had caused the Munroes.

He couldn't wait for life to return to normal again.

Chapter 11

Cecily stood with her hand resting on the back of Athena's chair and cursed Niall Munroe for the hundredth time.

Damn him. Damn him for giving in to his sister and her whims, damn him for making eyes at this crude snip of a girl, and damn him for leaving her here with these horrible people and their nauseating sentiments.

"Thank you for remaining," Athena said. "I know that this is not a pleasant situation, but I am grateful."

Cecily smiled. "You know that I would do anything for you and your brother, my dear," she said. She looked with distaste upon the red-haired devil's imp, whose flat chest seemed even less substantial when she lay on her back. What in heaven's name did Niall see in such a creature?

For he had seen something, of that she was sure. Her senses were remarkably keen where her own interests were concerned. She had noted how he ignored *her* while he watched the girl perform. He had failed to respond to several of her comments. He had left her sitting on the hard chair without a word of explanation and gone running off to be with his new flirt just because she had taken a little fall.

"There, now," the fat old man, Harry French, said to the girl. "It will be all right."

"Of course it will," Athena said. "Niall will get our own doctor. He is the best Denver has to offer."

Caitlin made much effort to return the smile, doubtless basking in the attention. "It is . . . very kind of you, Athena."

Athena. Cecily shuddered. How could Niall's sister allow the whore to call her by her Christian name? Cecily scowled and felt a prickle sweep up her spine.

Morgan Holt was watching her. He stood too close to Athena, on the other side of the chair, like some black-haired watchdog. It was if he could see right through Cecily and into her thoughts. She had disliked him instantly, but his low status made it possible to dismiss him. That was not so easy when he was a few feet away.

This was what came of Niall's permissiveness. She had thought that battle all but won. Now she must regroup, and consider new strategies to pave the way for Athena's departure from Denver.

She met Morgan Holt's stare and smiled with sure knowledge of her own superiority. So he found Athena attractive, did he? Niall must have observed the way he clung to Athena, and Cecily could easily make Holt's stubborn and inexplicable dedication to the girl sound much more ominous than it actually was.

And as for Miss Caitlin Hughes . . .

"You should go," Morgan Holt said.

Cecily started. "I beg your pardon?"

"Athena is with us. We don't need you."

Her amazement at his brazen command held her silent for several beats. Athena, talking to Caitlin, hadn't heard. Cecily curled her hand around Athena's shoulder. "I will do no such thing."

Incredibly, he bared his teeth at her. She managed to

keep herself from stumbling away to some illusory safety. "How dare you," she whispered.

He took a step toward her. She gasped and placed an equal distance between them.

All at once it seemed that every eye was upon her. The dwarf with his curling golden locks looked up as if he were her equal in height and every other way. One of the clowns leered, and the strong man in his animal skin tunic worked his fists. Hostile, alien gazes met hers everywhere she turned.

The walls of the tent threatened to collapse upon her if she remained another second inside it. She hurried toward the exit. Once outside she was able to breathe again. With safety came sense, and righteous anger.

Who did they think they were to send her scurrying away like a frightened rabbit? What must Athena be thinking at this moment . . . if she had even noticed?

Ignored. First Niall, and now Athena. It was insupportable. And yet, when she set her feet to return to the tent, she found them rooted to the ground.

Morgan Holt was a madman. There was no telling what he might do if provoked, and he had plainly taken as much dislike to her as she had him. It might be best to wait until Niall returned.

She looked about for a place to sit and, finding none, folded her arms and prepared to endure. After far too long, she glimpsed the welcome sight of Niall's carriage turning into the lot. The coachman drove it up the midway and stopped close to the big tent.

Niall jumped out of the carriage, followed more sedately by a bearded and white-haired gentleman. Cecily went to join the men at the fastest pace her dignity allowed.

"Oh, Mr. Munroe," she said. "I am so glad you have returned quickly."

"Why are you not inside with Athena?" Niall demanded, scarcely sparing her a glance. He urged the doctor along with a wave and headed at a blistering clip toward the tent.

Cecily could not keep up. She slowed and allowed the men to precede her. She would *not* be made a fool of or treated in such a way, not by the Munroes or anyone else. She ought to leave, now, without a backward glance.

And jeopardize your future here? All she need do was swallow her pride and the situation could yet be salvaged and turned to her advantage. Clenching her fists, she prepared to try once more.

"How sad a thing it is to lose a lover."

She spun about to face the one trouper she had not noticed among those hovering over Caitlin—the snake charmer, Tamar. Cecily recoiled. The woman had the usual snakes draped about her shoulders like some grotesque necklace, but it was not that which alarmed Cecily. There was something inhuman about her dark, slanted eyes.

"I . . . I do not know what you mean," Cecily stammered.

"Oh, but you do." The snake woman smiled. Her teeth were white and slightly pointed at the tips. "This man you want, this Niall Munroe, is slipping through your fingers."

"What do you know of me or Mr. Munroe?"

"I have eyes." Tamar tickled the underside of one serpent's satin jaw with a red-nailed fingertip. "I know that you want this Niall Munroe. I know that our Caitlin also wants him, though she does not admit it. And I have seen how he looks at her and does not look at you."

Hearing her own thoughts laid out so plainly was a considerable shock. This woman, a stranger, had seen the sordid attraction between Niall and the little slut. She might not be the only one.

"Why do you tell me this?" Cecily demanded. "What possible reason—"

"You wish to be rid of your rival, do you not?" Tamar blinked, and Cecily realized with a chill that she had not seen the woman do so since the conversation began.

"Maybe there is something that I also wish. Maybe we can help each other."

"You must be joking." Cecily glanced with disgust at the snake charmer's patently false hair, the garish cosmetics, the gown that concealed so little of her generous figure. "How could *you* possibly help me?"

"You dislike me, no? Maybe you think I am too low for you, like my snakes?" She smiled. "Never mind. You will agree, because you want the circus gone, as I do. And if Athena Munroe gets her wish, the circus will not go away for a very long time."

"What do you mean? You are to leave Denver now that the performance is over."

"I think not. Because our Caitlin was hurt, your friend Athena has said that she will ask her brother if the troupe may stay at his ranch in the mountains until she is well again. And that may take all winter, no?"

"Preposterous. Niall would never agree."

"Would he not?" Tamar shrugged. "He looks at our Caitlin as if he has never seen a woman before. Do you think that he will let her go so easily?"

The swift and obvious answer died on Cecily's tongue. She became as cold as Tamar and her snakes, examining all the possibilities with calm rationality.

As repulsive as she found the circus folk, and this creature in particular, Cecily had no allies against Caitlin and her tawdry charms. Tamar had presented herself as a fellow conspirator, with keen powers of observation and a cool sense of purpose. She would make a daunting enemy. She doubtless had resources Cecily could not hope to duplicate . . . if she could be trusted. And if she did not demand too high a price for her services.

"You said you can help me," Cecily said. "What do you propose?"

Tamar licked her lips with a flicker of her tongue. "I know the circus as you cannot. I can hear what is said, and tell you as I have told you of Athena's plans. There are many ways that I can . . . make difficulties for your lover and our Caitlin when they wish to be together."

Cecily had little doubt of that. "And what do you want in return? You said you wish the circus gone. Why?"

"I, too, have a lover," Tamar said, her eyes growing as cloudy as those of a snake about to shed its skin. "There is one not of our troupe who casts a spell on him, as the girl bewitches your man."

Thinking quickly, Cecily cast through her memory for characters who might fit such a vague description. Who on earth would take such a creature as Tamar for a lover? Whom would she pursue?

Who but one equally as bizarre? Not the dwarf, surely. The albino clown, perhaps—

No. The answer was evident. Which trouper had taken such a strangely personal interest in Athena that first day on the lot? Who had been standing so close, so protectively, to Athena's chair as if he had some special right?

"Morgan Holt," she said. "It is him, isn't it?"

Tamar hissed. "He is my wolf. Mine alone. She will not have him."

Her wolf? *Of course. The Wolf-Man. Morgan Holt is the Wolf-Man!*

And he had set his sights on Athena.

Cecily smiled. "Let me be sure that we understand one another. You will act on my behalf to keep the girl away from Mr. Munroe, and I will do what I can—within reason, of course—to do the same with Athena and Morgan Holt."

"Then we understand each other." Tamar glanced toward the tent. "Use what I have told you. You will tell me where to send messages when I learn that which is of interest to us both. And you will help me when the time is right."

"Unless, of course, I persuade Mr. Munroe to do as he originally intended, and send your circus away. Then we shall both have what we want with no further trouble."

Tamar inclined her head. "I shall be most curious to see if you succeed."

Cecily found a bit of paper and a pencil in her chatelaine bag and wrote out her address. A definite risk to trust this creature, but she was confident that she could control their partnership. If not, she might as well pack her bags and leave Denver tomorrow.

She passed the folded paper to Tamar and quickly withdrew her hand. "Send a message to me if you learn anything more of use, but be discreet. If you cause me embarrassment, I can assure you that it will become most unpleasant."

"Threats?" Tamar laughed, a husky rattle from deep in her throat, like scales against stone. "I, too, can make threats. But it is better not to be enemies, no? Go to your fine lover before it is too late."

She turned and, with a swing of her hips, left Cecily alone to consider the wisdom of pacts with the devil.

The white-haired doctor put his implements, bottles, and bandages away in his bag and shook his head. Morgan knew that no one else was meant to see the gesture; he glanced at Athena in the chair beside him. She had missed it. Caitlin had not.

"It is so bad then, Doctor?" the equestrienne said, grinning crookedly. "Must I start planning my funeral?"

The old man glanced at Niall Munroe, who crouched at Caitlin's other side. He had hovered over the girl ever since his return with the physician, as possessive as a puma with a fresh kill. Munroe probably didn't think anyone noticed that, either.

"Perhaps we should speak in private, Miss Hughes," the doctor said.

"These are my friends," Caitlin said, bravely ignoring her pain. "I am not afraid for them to hear."

The doctor sighed. "Very well. As I told you before, your leg is broken. I have done what I can to set and stabilize it with a plaster of Paris cast, but time must do the healing. It is my considered opinion that you must have several months of complete bed rest if you ever wish to walk again. If you do not, I fear that you will be permanently—" He hesitated, looking from Niall to Athena.

"Please speak frankly, Dr. Brenner," Athena said. "I am not afraid to hear the truth." She reached down and squeezed Caitlin's finger. "Dr. Brenner has been our physician for many years. I trust his judgment completely. That is why you must do exactly as he says and have rest in a quiet place where you can be properly cared for."

An expectant hush fell over the group. Morgan stared at Niall, bracing for his reaction when Athena proposed her scheme for Caitlin's recovery. He moved an inch or two closer to Athena, his hip against her chair. Not quite touching *her,* oh, no; if he were to touch her now, after what had happened in her bedroom, he didn't know what he might do.

Carry her off and ravish her? he mocked himself. *It was a kiss. That is all.* And Athena showed no signs of being either flustered or disturbed in his presence.

She had probably dismissed the kiss, just as he had—an impulsive act swiftly explained as a momentary madness. Better this way. Better that whatever lay between them begin and end with that kiss. Even so, he could not bring himself to leave her side.

"Niall," Athena began. Morgan could feel her body tense, hear the swift intake of her breath. He tightened his grip on the back of her chair.

"Niall, I have been thinking . . . about how we might help Caitlin." She glanced, once, at Morgan's face, and he smiled at her in encouragement.

Smiled at her. The expression felt strange on his face. But she seemed to take courage from it and faced her brother again.

"The doctor has said that Caitlin must have complete rest. It is obvious that she cannot travel far under these conditions, and a tent is not adequate accommodation for an invalid."

Niall stood up and brushed off his trousers. "Of course not. Miss Hughes may remain in the hotel until she is—"

"Not the hotel, either." Having dared to interrupt her brother, Athena forged ahead. "There is a much better place where she can be cared for and remain with her friends. Very little goes on at Long Park this time of year—why can we not allow the circus to winter there, while Caitlin recovers?"

"The ranch?"

"Yes. Of course there will be snow and cold temperatures, but Long Park is sheltered from the worst weather, and there is plenty of room. The second barn hasn't been used in years. It could hold the circus livestock, and between the bunkhouse and the main house, surely there would be enough beds or cots for everyone. I have already discussed this with Mr. French, and he has agreed that in return for winter quarters he and the troupe will give two charity performances in the spring—"

Niall held up his hand, silencing her. Morgan stiffened.

"If you will excuse us," he said brusquely to the doctor, "I must speak to my sister." He stepped around Caitlin, shouldered Morgan aside, and took the handles of Athena's chair.

"It's all right," Athena said in a whisper meant only for Morgan. He stepped back, and Niall took her away from the group and to a place of relative privacy across the tent.

The conversation that followed was both quiet and vehement. Morgan ignored the murmurs of the troupers and watched Athena and Niall, listening to the debate progress. Keeping her calm, Athena presented her argument. Her brother, as expected, was furious, though he made some effort to hide his anger from the unwelcome witnesses. She had put him in an awkward position by asking his cooperation in public.

But Athena did not back down. Her voice remained firm and full of conviction, even when Niall loomed over her and looked as if he would have liked to give her a good spanking.

God help him if he did.

"Morgan?"

He glanced down at Caitlin. She was white about the mouth and her eyes revealed great pain, in spite of the doctor's efforts.

"You should be moved to a bed, Miss Hughes," Dr. Brenner said. He followed her gaze up to Morgan. "Can you carry her?"

Caitlin gave a husky laugh. "I think . . . Morgan is up to the task. I will be all right. Thank you, Doctor."

He nodded and packed up his bag. "Mr. French, if I may have a few words?" With a wary glance toward the Munroes, he walked off with Harry.

"What are they saying—Athena and Niall?" Caitlin asked.

Morgan crouched beside her. "Athena is telling him what she told us. Munroe is against it."

Caitlin wrinkled her nose. "I could guess that. What else?"

"Munroe says that they have no responsibility for what happened, and he and Athena had agreed that the circus would leave right after the performance. He isn't saying it, but he does not want her around us."

"I know that, too." Caitlin sighed. "I tried to tell Athena that it was not a good idea."

"But she isn't giving in to him. She is telling him that whether or not they have responsibility for what happened to you, providing you with a place to recover is the right thing to do. It is . . . 'common decency.' "

"To her it would be. But Niall—"

"He says it would be too expensive to keep the troupe fed for the whole winter. She says that the cost is nothing to the Munroe fortune, and the charity performances in spring will more than make up for it."

"Go on."

"He tells her that she had no right to make such promises without consulting him, and she asks him what he's so afraid of."

"*That* will make him angry."

"Yes. But she . . ." He lost his train of thought as he watched Athena, the proud lift of her head and the set of her shoulders. Niall ranted and bullied, but she did not buckle.

"You're proud of her, aren't you?" Caitlin asked.

Proud? He began to deny it, but the word rang true. Yes, he was proud. She had stood up to her brother not once, but twice—both times for the sake of people she hardly knew.

Would she do the same for herself alone?

"She says," he continued, "that if he cares anything about you being able to walk or ride again—" He met Caitlin's eyes. "She asks how much he is willing to do to make sure that what happened to her does not happen to you."

Caitlin closed her eyes. "I never asked Athena what made her—"

"An accident. That is all I know." He looked at Niall's face. "Munroe is wavering."

"Because she compared herself to me. I wonder . . . He is so protective. Maybe it's more than just the duty of looking after a crippled sister."

Her statement caught Morgan's interest. Was there more to it? Was Niall's vigilance driven by something other than brotherly devotion? When the opportunity arose, he would ask Athena . . .

No. He didn't want more details of her life, poignant little facts that would work their way deeper into his heart. "Do you want to go to their ranch, Firefly?"

Caitlin shifted her body and winced. "I dread the thought of staying in bed for months."

"It is not likely to be months, is it?" Morgan had learned soon after he joined the circus that Caitlin had an ability to heal almost as strong as his own.

"Niall doesn't have to know how quickly I can be on my feet again." She smiled slyly. "What about you?"

Morgan had deliberately avoided imagining what it would be like to stay at a snowbound ranch through a long winter, idle and restless, with Athena in reach. Had she thought of that? Had she even considered what would happen if she and Morgan were thrown together time and time again?

"If you go to the ranch," he said, "I may not stay."

"Because of Athena?"

"You will not need me anymore."

"You are avoiding the obvious, Morgan. It's Athena you are afraid of."

"As you are 'afraid' of Munroe, Firefly?"

"Maybe I am."

They fell silent. Morgan saw that the troupers, satisfied with Caitlin's care, had dispersed. The doctor had left the tent; Ulysses and Harry stood talking a few feet away. The Munroes had finished their debate and Niall was pushing his sister's chair in Harry's direction. Nothing in either face suggested who had won the skirmish.

Miss Hockensmith chose that moment to return. She minced her way up to Munroe's side and bent an apologetic smile upon Athena. Words were exchanged, with a certain coldness on Munroe's part and a plaintive question by Miss Hockensmith.

"Please do go speak to Miss Hockensmith, Niall," Athena said. "I would like to say good-bye to Mr. French."

Niall's expression was as stormy as an August sky. "Very well. I will come back for you in a few minutes." He glanced at Caitlin and allowed Miss Hockensmith to lead him out of the tent.

Athena was already wheeling herself toward Caitlin and Morgan. Harry and Ulysses joined them—Harry, as usual, torn between worry and apology.

"Mr. French," Athena said, holding out her hands to him as if the past hour had been perfectly pleasant and unremarkable. "I must go now. The children have had a rather exciting day, and I wish to make sure that they return to the orphanage in good order."

"I quite understand, Miss Athena. Quite. We are all most grateful for your kind care of our Caitlin."

"It is nothing." She paused and looked at each of them turn. "As for that other matter . . . Niall has agreed."

Harry grinned. "Wonderful. Most wonderful. Yet another debt we owe you, my dear."

"I will not be seeing . . . a great deal of you over the winter. I promised my brother that I would remain in Denver while the troupe is at Long Park. I know you can be comfortable there. I will make sure of it, even if I cannot be present."

So that was how she'd sealed the bargain—with a promise to stay apart from the people her brother did not trust. It was no more than Morgan had expected.

Why, then, did he feel like tearing the tent apart with his bare fingers?

"It was the only way," she said, meeting his stare. "Caitlin will have plenty of rest among her friends, and she will be as good as new by spring."

"He'll let you come to see us later," Caitlin said. "I know he will."

"Perhaps." Athena continued to gaze at Morgan. Her lips parted, full and moist. His body remembered, vividly, how they had tasted. How they had responded.

Harry cleared his throat. "Perhaps you had better take Caitlin to my tent, Morgan, until we can get her to the hotel."

"I will arrange transportation," Athena said. Her tongue darted out to wet her lower lip. "Everything will be made ready at Long Park, and you'll have a guide through the pass. There may be some snow, but the weather should not be too severe."

Morgan broke the almost painful connection between them and knelt to gather Caitlin in his arms. She sucked in her breath at the motion, but her gaze darted from Athena to Morgan with avid attention. Athena noticed and turned quickly to Harry.

"Good-bye, Mr. French. Mr. Wakefield, Caitlin . . . Morgan."

"Good-bye for the time being," Harry said. "Thank you, my dear."

Morgan didn't remain for the end of the scene. He carried Caitlin out the back door and to Harry's tent.

"It's that bad, is it?" Caitlin murmured.

He grunted and laid her on Harry's cot. "Worry about your leg, not me."

"I worry about you denying what anyone can see."

The cold, relentless stare that Morgan frequently used to great effect did not work with Caitlin. "And what is that?"

For once her expression was perfectly sober, and not just because of the pain.

"Why, my friend," she said, "only that you're in love with Athena Munroe."

Chapter 12

M organ seldom laughed. He did so now, a bark that sounded half cough and half growl. He could not have confirmed Caitlin's diagnosis more completely.

She had seen it coming, of course. At first the sparks between him and Athena had seemed mere attraction, the kind of curiosity a person might have about someone the very opposite of oneself. *Like me and Niall Munroe.*

But somewhere along the way curiosity and attraction had turned into something far more serious. Serious enough to frighten both of them. Badly.

As it frightened Niall.

"You are making this much more difficult than it needs to be," she said, trying to settle her aching leg more comfortably. "For once in your life you had better be willing to take advice. I understand Athena as you cannot. I am a woman too, you know."

"So Munroe has observed." He glared at her. "Are you in love with him?"

"That is foolish," she said lightly. "And even if I were, he'd have nothing to do with me."

"No? The way he stayed close to you, when you were hurt. . . ."

"Means nothing." She shrugged. "And we are talking about you, so don't try to change the subject."

"You are wasting your breath. Athena will not be coming to the ranch."

Caitlin chuckled, though the motion jarred her leg. "I have a feeling that she'll find a way."

Morgan muttered under his breath and paced up and down the short length of the tent. "You are her friend," he said. "If you speak to her again, tell her not to come."

"Why? She likes the troupe, and we like her. I have no right to even suggest it—unless you have a very good reason for me to give her."

He paused in midstride and fisted his hands behind his back. "It would be better if we never met again."

"Better for her, or for you?" She tried to sit up, but the pain was too intense. Damn the inconvenience of being so . . . so helpless, even if it was only for a little while. "I do not believe that you think less of her because of her affliction. I know you don't care for townies. You two are very different in many ways. But that isn't why you want her to stay in Denver." She took a deep breath. "You want to protect her from yourself. You don't think you're good enough for her, and it has nothing to do with money or position or any of those things. What happened to you that made you so sure she's better off without you?"

She had pushed too far and too fast. He swung to face her, head lowered and teeth bared.

"Enough," he said. "Do not speak of this again, Firefly."

"I'm not afraid of you, Morgan. I know you too well. You bluster and bully, but you wouldn't hurt me. Or her."

Never had a man looked more like an affronted and very hungry beast. But Morgan closed his mouth and backed toward the door, prepared to retreat where he could not win.

"I'm sorry," she said. "I have no right to judge you. But

whatever you did in your past—whoever you were before you came to us—I know you are a good man. You've proved that to all of us. And as for Athena—"

A tall shadow loomed against the outer tent wall. Niall Munroe ducked his head into the tent and nearly bumped into Morgan. He scowled, caught sight of Caitlin, and quickly smoothed his expression.

"Miss Hughes" he said. "I beg your pardon. I would like to have a word with Mr. Holt."

Morgan bristled. "You'd better leave, Munroe."

"Not until you hear what I have to say. Privately."

Without a word, Morgan shoved past Niall and left the tent. Niall followed.

If her leg had hurt only a little less, Caitlin would have hobbled her way to the door and listened for all she was worth. As it was, she heard only the rumble of deep voices, rising in pitch and hostility as the minutes ticked by. Niall did most of the talking—or ordering, for Caitlin had a very good idea what he said. Morgan's replies were brief and edged like a knife thrower's blades. When it was over, only one man returned to the tent.

Niall Munroe paused momentarily at the entrance and then came inside, bending his long body awkwardly.

"Where is Morgan?" Caitlin demanded. "What did you say to him?"

Perhaps he had expected a kinder welcome. He straightened and removed his hat. His brown hair was mussed underneath, though the recent duel had been made with words and not fists.

"That need be no concern of yours, Miss Hughes," he said stiffly.

"Morgan is my friend," she said. "What concerns my friends also concerns me."

"Very well." He set his hat down on a stool beside the cot and folded his hands behind his back. "I asked him to stay away from my sister."

Gritting her teeth against the discomfort, she rose up on her elbows. "Did you, then? Why, pray tell?"

He held her gaze without apology. "It has been brought to my attention that he is showing a certain . . . interest in her, and that she has not been entirely indifferent."

Brought to his attention. Then it was not he who had observed the attraction, but someone else. And Caitlin had a very good notion of who that someone might be—the officious, pinch-faced, and resentful Cecily Hockensmith.

"I can assure you that nothing improper has gone on between Morgan and Athena," Caitlin said. "Harry wouldn't allow it, and neither would I."

"What you consider proper—" He thought better of what he'd been about to say and began again. "I was not mistaken, then, in believing that my sister is keeping company with Holt."

How much to admit, when his mind was already so set against Morgan? "They like each other," she said. "Why is that so terrible?"

"Because Athena is still very much a child in many ways, and has no experience with men. She is far too openhearted, and Holt is—" He paused again, setting his jaw. "My sister is dependent upon me, and upon my judgment. Your 'Wolf-Man' is not fit company for a lady."

So Munroe had discovered the nature of Morgan's circus act. Doubtless that was also Miss Hockensmith's doing.

"I am surprised you deigned to visit me," Caitlin said, "for surely I'm no better company for so fine a gentleman as yourself. Will you tell your sister to avoid what you will not?"

He could have left then, and escaped her insulting questions entirely. But he lingered, staring about the tent as if it were filled with valuable and fascinating treasures rather than the flotsam and jetsam of circus life.

"I know the world as Athena does not," he said. "She is the one thing in my life with which I will take no risks and no chances."

"I see. And what did Morgan say to your kind request?"

His gaze jerked back to her. "He denies any interest in my sister."

Liar. Either you or Morgan is a liar of the worst sort, because you're lying to yourself. "Then you have nothing to worry about. I understand that Athena has promised to stay away from the ranch while we are there. You have arranged everything just as you want it." She eased back on to the cot. "You had better not waste any more of your valuable time, Mr. Munroe."

He swept his hat off the stool and sat down, straddling it with legs spread wide. "Is it not enough that we are giving you a place to stay for the winter, Miss Hughes? Have we not demonstrated our goodwill?"

"Troupers are not fond of unwilling charity."

"It's not unwilling, damn it—I beg your pardon." He swiped his hand across his brow, further ruffling his hair. "You must understand that—"

"That charity is all right from such as you to the likes of us, but not friendship?"

He blew out a sigh. "Miss Hughes—Caitlin—"

"Only friends should call each other by their Christian names, Mr. Munroe."

"What proof of friendship do you wish of me?" he roared.

She stared at him. He subsided into something like meekness. "I apologize. It is just that I—" His curse was not quite low enough to escape her notice. "I consider myself your friend . . . Caitlin. And I hope you will consider yourself mine."

Well, well, well. "Indeed? That *is* generous of you . . . Niall."

He didn't balk at the familiarity, so she was compelled to grant his sincerity. Still, he was far too high-and-mighty for his own good.

"Since we have become such bosom friends," she said, "you must explain to me why Athena and Morgan cannot be friends as well."

"It is different—"

"Just how is it different? I have little education myself, no name or money. I'm no better than Morgan."

He frowned. He brooded. He turned about on the stool so that he faced away from her, lost in his own thoughts. At last he seemed to reach a decision and met her gaze.

"My sister . . ." he began, "Athena is not like you. She has lost the kind of freedom you enjoy, and the ability to protect herself. She is vulnerable in body and in spirit. And she is that way because of me."

"What do you mean, because of you?"

"She was in an accident." He lowered his eyes, scuffing at the straw with the heels of his boots. "It happened in the mountains, during winter. We were at Long Park, and I— In those days, I had a tendency to be foolish. Reckless." He sighed. "I got myself into trouble. Athena believed she could save me. She was caught in an avalanche that did severe damage to her legs. The doctor told us she would never walk again."

Caitlin bit her lip. This man who spoke with such regret and shame was not the same whose arrogance had annoyed her and infuriated Morgan. She could scarcely believe that he had confided so much to her, of all people. Or was it *because* she was so different, so far outside the boundaries of his rarified circle, that she was a safe recipient for such a confession?

Guilt could drive a man to horrible acts. It certainly gave Niall reason to regard his sister as a fragile China doll, an heirloom kept high on a shelf, admired but never touched.

And perhaps it even explained why he had been moved to agree to Athena's scheme, and came to see Caitlin now. Her injury reminded him too much of his sister's, but this time he had a chance to make it come out right.

Caitlin had a very strong desire to reach out and touch him. She knew it would be a mistake. Pity, even sympathy, he would tolerate no better than Morgan. Were they so much alike, after all?

What sort of guilt made Morgan doubt his own worth, and drove him away from Athena?

"I am sorry," she said, meaning it. "But Athena is stronger than you know. She does not blame you, I am certain of it."

"Her heart is generous by nature. And that is why she is in that chair." Niall snatched up his hat and got to his feet. "Now you understand why Morgan Holt must stay away from her."

No, I do not understand, she thought. *There is something you are leaving out, my friend. Something more you will not admit.*

"I think you're wrong," she said. "I know you are."

He pushed his hat onto his head with unnecessary force. "The decision has been made. You and the circus will go to Long Park, and Athena will remain here. She has plenty to keep her busy all winter."

"And you?"

He glanced back at her from the tent door. "I will see that you have everything you require. Good-bye, Miss Hughes."

Caitlin closed her eyes and listened to him stride away. Well, now it was in the open. Her feelings had proven correct once again—about Morgan, and Athena, and Niall Munroe.

The only opinion she had not yet heard was Athena's. And that wouldn't be easy, if Niall resolved to keep his sister in Denver.

If there was one thing Caitlin loved dearly, it was a challenge. Niall was the biggest challenge she had ever faced. Doubtless he was rich because he was ruthless, and seldom failed to get his way. He was the kind of man who wouldn't hesitate to crush a rival.

But he was only human. He had weaknesses. And Caitlin Hughes, once her mind was made up, could be a very formidable opponent.

I give you fair warning, my stubborn friend. This is a game I intend to win.

• • •

The next five weeks were the longest of Athena's life.
It should have been a busy time, far too busy to
allow for loneliness or daydreaming. The Winter Ball was
drawing closer, and she was bound and determined that
this second annual ball would be the finest and most well-
attended of any in Denver that year.

Athena had frequently seen Cecily Hockensmith, but a
good deal less of her own brother. Niall was constantly off
on some business or other; currently he was in Chicago
and had telegraphed to say that he expected to remain there
through the end of the month. Caitlin's prediction that he
would relent and allow Athena to visit the ranch did not
come true.

Nevertheless, she took advantage of his absence by
throwing herself with even more energy into the work he
had disapproved: visiting the slums and tenements with
clothing and coal, personally speaking to the forgotten
girls with their fatherless babes, purchasing beds and
school supplies for the orphans, and devising new charitable schemes that would reach far into the future. She drove
the other ladies of her several philanthropic organizations
almost as ruthlessly as she did herself.

It was never quite enough. Any stray, quiet moment,
and her thoughts fled across the Front Range and to the
ranch where she had spent every summer as a girl. Before
she fell asleep each night, the image of a certain face
seemed to shimmer in the air above her: thick black hair,
golden eyes that sang to her of wild dashes by moonlight,
a sensuous mouth promising more forbidden kisses.

At such times, she felt strange, phantom sensations
below her waist, just as she had when Morgan visited her
room. But she always managed to banish such fantasies,
and remind herself that she missed all of the troupers:
Harry, Caitlin, Ulysses, even those men and women she
hardly knew. Morgan had no solitary claim on her affection.

Yet Morgan had smiled at her. That dreadful day of the performance, when everything had fallen apart, he had granted her courage with that simple expression and the unexpected warmth of his gaze.

Now he was thirty miles to the west, behind a wall of hills and mountains. Those mountains were already coated with snow, and soon the pass to Long Park would be all but impenetrable for the winter.

Ensconced in her sitting room late on a late November evening, wrapped in a woolen shawl against a chill that even the bountiful fire could not dispel, Athena eagerly unfolded the letter she had saved to read at the end of the day. It, like the others that came faithfully twice a week, was from Harry French.

Harry had made himself chief chronicler of all the events at Long Park, of Caitlin's condition, and of the doings of the troupers. Each time Athena opened one of his missives, she forced herself to read through slowly, refusing to jump ahead. She did the same tonight.

My Dear Miss Athena, the letter began,

You will be delighted to know that because of your brother's munificence and your own great kindness, we are all prospering at Long Park. As I wrote previously, the animals are well settled in the barn, which your brother had prepared for us; the rooms in the main house, and the accommodations in the bunkhouse, are indeed most praiseworthy. We could not ask for better.

Our small performance for the ranch workers met with great approval by your men, who at first seemed somewhat suspicious of us; they have since gone out of their ways to make us feel welcome. The victuals are plentiful, the fires blazing, and the mood merry. We lack only one thing—your own dear presence.

Caitlin asks after you constantly. She is very brave and does not admit any pain, but I must be frank and confess that I fear for her; there are times when the look in her eye does not bode well for her future. I wonder if she has not

already given up hope of resuming her former activities.
They have always been so important to her.

Athena dropped the letter in her lap. This was not good
news. Not good at all. Harry had only hinted at a certain
resignation in Caitlin's aspect, but until now had not said
that the equestrienne might be abandoning hope.

Heaven forbid that should happen. Caitlin could not,
must not lose what Athena had lost.

However, I beg you not to worry, dear Patroness. We
will stand by her as we have always done, and refuse to
grant her surrender. Either I, Ulysses, or Morgan—

Morgan. Athena swallowed and paused to catch her
breath before resuming.

or Morgan are with her at every hour and keep her
mind from such unproductive musings. We follow the doc-
tor's instructions precisely. We have taken advantage of
your kindness and read to her from books in your library,
and Morgan brings her small gifts from outdoors: withered
leaves and evergreen boughs or colored stones from the
stream. Caitlin seems to enjoy them, and they lift her
melancholy for a short while.

Gifts from Morgan. Athena smiled, recognizing in such
simple gestures his reluctant generosity. Morgan cared for
Caitlin as he would for a sister. He guarded her from every
harm. How much more would he do for a woman he chose
as his . . .

Quiet, she commanded her heart. *Be quiet.*

Morgan spends a great deal of time roaming the park,
even in the most inclement weather. You know, of course,
that such small inconveniences as bitter temperatures have
little effect upon him. He is careful to conceal his dual na-
ture from the ranch hands, but when he is not with Caitlin
his restlessness is almost alarming. We have on occasion
feared that he might leave and not return. He has repaid
any debt he ever owed us, but we have continued to hope
that he will choose to remain as one of our family.

As if the piercing mountain winds had reached across
the miles and into her home, Athena pulled her shawl

closer and rang the bell on the small table beside her. Brinkley appeared, and at her request he sent for a chambermaid to add more coal to the fire in the grate. Even after the flames leaped up with renewed vigor, Athena took no comfort in them.

Harry would not speak of Morgan leaving unless he felt it was a very real possibility. Surely Morgan would stay until Caitlin was on her feet again; surely he would inform Athena of such an intention, if only to say good-bye.

It was too much to hope that he would write as Harry did. Too much to ask that he send some personal message to her, when there was nothing tangible between them save for a shared secret and a stolen kiss.

Athena scanned the rest of the letter, barely registering the words, and tucked the folded paper inside her shawl. For a while she laid her head back against the chair and let the emotions rush through her, tumbling like a spring-swollen creek that carried rock and branch and earth inexorably before it.

When the deluge was over, only one consideration remained in her heart. Whatever Morgan might do, however he chose to regard her, he was not her principal concern. Caitlin was. Caitlin, on the brink of surrendering to the despair that had once nearly claimed Athena's spirit.

If there was a single action Athena could take to prevent that from happening, she must attempt it. Even if it meant breaking her word, defying Niall, and leaving last-minute particulars of the Winter Ball undone for several days. No one else could understand Caitlin's situation better than she. No one else could advise, coax, and bully with greater authority.

Cecily Hockensmith had been unstinting with her company and assistance with the ball. She could be entrusted with any details that must be addressed during Athena's absence.

Once the idea coalesced in Athena's mind, the practical impediments presented themselves in swift succession. As much as she liked and trusted Brinkley, Fran, Romero, and the others, she did not wish to involve the servants in her insubordination; she must make preparations and arrange transportation to Long Park without alerting them beforehand. Fortunately, her dealings with the charities gave her ideas about where she might discreetly employ a sturdy wagon and skilled driver.

However, she would require Fran's help with dressing and getting downstairs. Athena had not been forbidden to leave the house, and Fran wouldn't question her if she pretended to be going on another clandestine excursion to the tenements. If she lied to Fran, the maid would have an excuse for unwittingly assisting in her escape.

Athena was forced to admit that she was a little bit afraid of where this open defiance might lead. Niall had made his position very clear. But she had succeeded in winning him over before, and could do so again.

Cecily might help her in that as well. With the deed a fait accompli and Cecily taking Athena's part, Niall could not be entirely unreasonable.

This is for Caitlin. Niall's anger is a small price to pay for her recovery.

And Morgan Holt had absolutely nothing to do with it.

She consulted her watch and saw that it was not yet too late to send a message to Cecily, asking her to come first thing in the morning. Just as she rang for Brinkley, he stepped into the room poised to make an announcement.

"Miss Hockensmith has called, Miss Munroe," he said. "I told her I would inquire if you were at home."

"Yes. Yes indeed, please show her in directly."

He bowed and went to do her bidding. Regretting the rather shabby nature of the old shawl, Athena pushed it farther down her shoulders and assumed a welcoming smile. Cecily glided into the room, brushing a bit of snow from her coat, and came to take Athena's hand.

"Ah, Athena. What miserable weather! I fear that winter has come." She allowed Brinkley to remove her coat. "I realize that it is late, but I so regretted not being able to see you today. You know how very dull Mrs. Coghill's dinners are, but I could not refuse her invitation."

"Of course not," Athena said. "Will you not sit down? Some tea, perhaps?"

"I do not believe that I could swallow another drop," Cecily said, sinking gracefully into a chair. "And how are you today, my dear girl? You have not worked too hard, I hope?"

Athena was in no mood for small talk when her mind was thrumming with plans. She dismissed Brinkley and waited until he had shut the sitting room door behind him. "Cecily . . . I have a great favor to ask of you."

"Indeed?" Cecily leaned forward. "Pray, tell me."

"I have decided to take a short excursion to the mountains. While I am gone, I would be most honored if you would assume final preparations for the Winter Ball."

"An excursion?" A faint shadow marred Cecily's alabaster brow. "Why would you wish to visit the mountains at such a—" Her expression cleared. "Athena, you cannot mean to go to the ranch."

"Yes. I have received correspondence from Harry French which suggests that Miss Hughes is not recovering as swiftly as we might wish. I feel that I must offer my friendship and every encouragement at this crucial time, which I cannot do here." She met Cecily's stare without apology. "I am aware that Niall does not wish me to go, but Miss Hughes's condition outweighs such personal considerations. I am sure you understand."

Cecily tugged at the fingertips of her white kid gloves. "I am afraid that I must advise against it, my dear. Not only is it likely to upset your brother, but this is hardly the time of year for such travel. And how would you go? You cannot drive yourself."

"I don't intend to. I can arrange everything, if you will agree not to speak of this to my brother until I am back in Denver."

"Isn't Mr. Munroe in Chicago?"

"Yes, and he is not to return until the day of the ball. I

will be safely home in good time." Athena clenched her hands in her lap. "I know that you are very fond of my brother, Cecily. It is possible that you may hear from him. That is why I request that you say nothing of this beforehand. No harm will be done by it."

Cecily sighed and took on a pensive air. "You know that I am your friend, dear Athena, but I do not feel quite comfortable in deceiving your brother. And I must be concerned for you, as well. Even if you take your maid—"

"I will be going alone. I do not wish to involve the servants, though of course they will know where I am."

"I see."

It was obviously time to bargain. Athena had some familiarity with the method, for she had used persuasion many times when soliciting the sometimes reluctant contributions of the lions—and lionesses—of Denver society. She was sorry for the need to manipulate Cecily, but what she intended to say was not very far from the truth.

"It is a great deal to ask," she admitted, "and I abhor deception just as much as you do. But in many ways I have come to think of you as a sister. I consider it an excellent sign that my brother is not so much alone as he has been in the past."

Her gentle hint did not go unnoticed. Cecily straightened, and her eyes took on a certain gleam.

"I am flattered that you think so, Athena." She lowered her gaze. "I . . . I fear I have not been particularly successful in concealing my affection for Mr. Munroe."

Athena relaxed. "My brother can be quite stubborn, but he is blessed with many fine qualities. I will keep your assistance in this matter between the two of us, and Niall will know only of your tireless work for charity and the constancy of your friendship."

Cecily was quiet for several minutes, and Athena wondered if perhaps she had gone too far in suggesting the bribe of her influence with Niall. He had shown more attention to Cecily than he did most women, and a good word or two on Athena's part might make the difference.

Athena wondered why she had not more actively encouraged Niall to consider Cecily as a wife. She had recognized the possibility of it from the beginning of her acquaintance with the older woman—she had seen Cecily's strong interest in Niall—yet she hadn't pursued the scheme in spite of the advantages.

Niall could not be driven, in any case, and heaven help the woman who tried. The girl he chose to love must be far stronger than his sister was.

"Are you quite sure that you feel comfortable leaving the ball in my hands?"

Cecily's voice startled Athena back to attention. "I have no doubts whatsoever. Your taste and experience are impeccable."

"But if there are sudden changes—if alterations must be made—"

"Then I know that you will do just the right thing." Athena glanced at the clock on the mantel, impatient to have this over and done with so that she could begin planning for the trip.

"When did you intend to depart?" Cecily asked.

"The day after tomorrow, at dawn," she said, making a quick decision. "Will you help me, Cecily?"

"I will do all that I can." Cecily rose and shook out her skirts. "My carriage is waiting. I must be getting home."

"Of course." Athena released a quiet breath. "Is there anything you need to know about the ball? I will inform the necessary parties that you have complete authority, and additional expenses can be deferred until my return, but if there is anything else . . ."

The older woman smiled. "I have observed your work carefully for the past few months, my dear. I believe I can act as your deputy with all due efficiency." She paused at the door. "Take great care. I would never forgive myself if anything were to happen to you."

"You are a true friend, Cecily."

"And I hope one day to be much more—to you, and to Mr. Munroe. Good-night, Athena."

"Good-night."

Athena listened for Brinkley's steps and the sound of the front door closing on a gust of wind. She tugged the shawl back over her shoulders and wheeled her chair to the secretary. She chewed on the tip of her pen, considering the letters to be written, and began the first of them while sleet rattled against the windowpanes.

Tomorrow she would see the letters delivered. And in a few days, she'd be at Caitlin's bedside, among the people who had come to mean as much to her as any of her Denver friends.

Perhaps Morgan would smile at her again. She did not expect it, let alone anything more. If she could see Caitlin through her most difficult time, it was enough.

It would have to be.

Chapter 13

The necessities of business had never seemed so interminable or the conversation so dull as they had been for the past five weeks. Niall leaned his head against the seat of the Pullman Palace car on the railroad heading west from Kansas City, profoundly grateful to be going home.

Or was he? When he walked in the door of the house on Fourteenth Street, he would have to face Athena—and he knew the awkwardness that had grown between them would not have vanished so quickly.

It wasn't that he expected Athena to defy him. In matters of importance, she had always deferred to him no matter how stubborn she might appear. That was how it ought to be. And Miss Hockensmith—Cecily—was looking after her. In fact, he had felt relieved at the prospect of getting away, allowing Athena a chance to reconsider her foolishness and return to her normal routine.

But the niggling little worry remained: Athena was infatuated with the circus—worse, with Morgan Holt—and those people were a mere thirty miles away in the mountains. God only knew what they were doing at the ranch. And the girl—

He loosened his collar and tried to relax, though he had neither slept nor eaten well since he had left Denver. That girl—Caitlin—he had thought of her far too many times in Chicago, in the loneliness of his hotel room with the empty commotion going on in the street below. He had remembered her smile, the halo of red hair, her courage in the face of a serious injury.

The doctor had said she would recover with proper rest. That was the only reason she and the others were at Long Park. Apart from his providing them winter quarters, he was not responsible for what happened to Caitlin Hughes.

Yet he thought of her. He imagined her like Athena, confined to a chair, her vibrant spirit stilled forever. And the sickness of guilt welled up in his chest, reminding him that he was as much a cripple as his sister.

Athena had used their shared memories against him— he was too skilled a negotiator not to recognize that. Without directly calling upon the great debt he owed her, she had forced him to acknowledge the necessity of keeping Caitlin from the fate she had suffered.

It will not *happen to Caitlin.* He had made sure of that. He had behaved correctly, honorably. Athena was grateful.

But none of these truths comforted him. The closer the train drew to Denver, the more certain he was that he must see for himself how matters went at the ranch. He could speak to Mr. Durant and the foreman, make certain that the circus people were not taking too much advantage of their free accommodations. And while he was there, he would look in on Caitlin and carry a report back to his sister.

Yes. I will go to Long Park. Only a brief stop in Denver, and then I will be on my way.

The moment he made the decision, the tightness in his chest eased and his mind was clear again. He closed his eyes. The train's rocking became a soothing motion, and he no longer noticed the smoke or the discomfort of the long journey. For the first time in a month, he slept through the night.

• • •

For three whole days, Cecily kept her fingers crossed and prayed for just a little bit of luck. Athena had left Denver early yesterday morning; a mere day and a half later, Cecily had achieved more than she had any right to expect.

At first she had resented the position Athena had put her in. After all, the last thing she wanted to do was lie to Niall should he ask how his sister was faring—though, thank goodness, he had done so only once during his sojourn to Chicago. But Cecily had found it impossible to turn down the opportunity Athena unwittingly offered: that of making the Winter Ball her own.

True, there were relatively few details left to attend in the week and a half remaining before the event, but those could be made quite important with the right emphasis. The usual guests had already been invited, and the catering arranged, but Cecily had been doing her own investigating while she helped Athena. She knew that the grand ballroom at the Windsor was available the night of the ball. And she had decided, immediately upon Athena's departure, to change the venue from the Munroes' private ballroom to the public setting.

That, of course, meant more decorations, more hothouse flowers, and many other alterations. Cecily knew that Athena preferred intimacy and the same familiar circle of acquaintances to crowds and public display. With a complete lack of imagination, she chose guests who were generous with donations, not those who made fascinating company or offered new social or business opportunities.

Cecily had no interest in charity beyond what it could do for her social progress. She knew of several dignitaries and businessmen from other states or cities, and even outside the country—including a prince of some small European nation and at least one English earl—who were currently in town; she sent invitations to them and a number of other useful personages who had been left off the guest list for want of space.

After that, it was necessary to order additional food-stuffs, suitable for such elegant attendees. By the time the day of the ball arrived, the affair would bear little resemblance to the one Athena had planned.

And Athena, bless her naïveté, would remember that she had given Cecily carte blanche to do as she saw fit. She would seem both foolish and selfish if she protested the changes. Indeed, if the girl were gone only the few days she had proposed, Cecily would be most surprised. By the time she came back, it would be too late to return to the previous arrangements.

Cecily sighed with airy regret and stepped down from her carriage, glad to be home after a long day of shopping. The price of this deception might very well be the loss of Athena's trust and friendship. But Cecily had grown more and more confident of Niall's attachment to her; in fact, she had prepared several stories to explain Athena's absence should he return to Denver before his sister. Every one of them would reflect badly on Athena and leave Cecily the injured party.

That was a risk, too, of course. Niall might decide to believe his sister instead, if she chose to brand Cecily a liar. But whom would Niall trust when his sister had so blatantly broken her word?

The door to the Hockensmith house on Welton swung open as she reached it. The new butler, one of several servants recently employed thanks to Mr. Hockensmith's profitable partnership with Niall Munroe, bowed and took her coat.

"Miss Hockensmith," he said with just the right note of deference, "there is a gentleman waiting to see you."

"A gentleman?" She was both intrigued and annoyed; the man should know better than to admit a visitor when she was absent. "Who might that be?"

"Mr. Munroe. He arrived only a moment ago, and is waiting in the parlor."

Fear and excitement swallowed up Cecily's irritation. Niall had returned early, and might already know that

Athena was gone—but Cecily was prepared for that very contingency.

"Very well, Parton. Please inform him that I will be with him directly." She hastened up the stairs to her room and made the necessary adjustments to hair and clothing, rehearsing her story as she did so.

She was quite clear-headed when she entered the parlor. Niall was on his feet, but he did not look particularly upset. Cecily released her breath and put on a look of grave concern.

"Mr. Munroe! I am so glad you have returned."

He swung about to face her, and his neutral expression changed into a frown. "Miss Hockensmith? What is the matter?"

So. He could not have been home, or he would know. The servants would have told him at once. "Have you come directly from the station?" she asked, urging him to sit.

"Yes. I will not be in Denver long. I came only to ask—" His frown deepened. "Why? Is it Athena?"

"Oh, dear. I had so hoped to reach your hotel before you left Chicago, but the telegraph must not have been delivered. Naturally, as soon as I learned—"

"Learned what? Where is Athena?"

"She has gone to the ranch." There. If he admired directness, he would appreciate hers more than ever now. "It is all my fault. Things had been going so well—Athena seemed quite settled and I was helping her with the ball. Then, three days ago, she made some remark about wishing to visit her friends from the circus, in spite of your instructions to the contrary."

"She has gone to the ranch?" Niall repeated, as if he did not quite believe it. "How?"

Cecily composed her face into a mask of contrition and embarrassment. "I . . . I fear that she has hired some conveyance to take her there. She did not notify me or the servants—I only learned of this yesterday when your butler sent a message to inform me of her absence and the note she had left." That, at least, was very close to the truth. She had played ignorant with the servants as well.

"I was so very sure I had talked her out of such an intemperate scheme," she continued. "I used every method of persuasion, you can be sure. It simply did not occur to me that I should mistrust her when she said she felt overtired and preferred to spend the next few days in seclusion. She seems so fragile, and she has been working so hard that I feared for her health. I even offered to send the doctor, but she refused. Apparently she lied to her maid about where she was going." She lifted her gaze in earnest appeal. "Oh, Mr. Munroe. I pray you can forgive me my terrible mistake."

Her gamble paid off. If Niall had been prepared to blame her for dereliction, her stream of explanations and apologies had taken the first edge off his anger.

"No," he said. "It is not your fault, Miss Hockensmith. I should not have expected you to succeed where I have failed." He strode to the window and twitched back the curtains. "I should have anticipated this all along. My sister has changed greatly in the past few months, and I have refused to see it. She has become adept at deceit and manipulation."

"But surely you are being too harsh—"

"There is no need for you to lessen the blow," he said. He turned back to her, all traces of anger hidden by a mask as expert as hers. "We were both taken in by her apparent innocence."

Cecily rose. It was time to give him a few pushes in the right direction, and let him think the solution was his all along. "Perhaps she has simply gone to look after the injured girl."

"You know that is not the reason. I may have been blind to the attraction before, but you were right. She has developed an inappropriate liking for Holt, and that is the true reason she has disobeyed me."

Cecily dared to touch his arm in sympathy. "Whatever you may fear, Mr. Munroe, I am certain that Athena is not lost to all common sense. She may be driven by feelings she does not understand—so many young girls are—and her judgment is flawed. She has lived too sheltered a life in Denver, and at the same time she has a child's confidence in her own invulnerability. When you bring her back, you will have a chance to set things right again."

"Set things right." A muscle in his jaw flexed. "I have not always listened to your advice in the past, Miss Hockensmith, but now I see that I must take direct action. Athena has grown to consider her position in Denver as unassailable. Her chair makes her safe from all censure. She does not believe that anything can change her world, even a flirtation with a scoundrel like Holt, and that is a conceit she cannot afford." He bent his head. "I have let her have her own way too often, and yet I have tried to protect her by keeping her close. Sending her away may be precisely what she requires."

Cecily gave a silent crow of triumph. "Indeed. I cannot disagree with you, Mr. Munroe." She hesitated for a calculated moment. "You did say that you have cousins in New York. If I may be so bold—perhaps it might be best if you send her directly there rather than bring her back to Denver. Any rumors will be extinguished quickly, and she will be well out of reach of temptation. I will be able to complete preparations for the ball, so Athena's efforts need not be undermined. I realize that it is very sudden—"

"No. Not at all." He met her gaze with grim approval. "I will leave for Long Park as soon as possible—if the weather holds, on a good horse I can reach it by tomorrow morning. I will begin making arrangements immediately for Athena's departure for New York." He took her hand. "I know that I may continue to count on your help, Miss Hockensmith."

"Always." She poured her heart into her eyes. "I will make inquiries of my own and be ready when you call upon me."

He lifted her hand as if he might kiss it. "You have been invaluable . . . Cecily. I will not forget."

His use of her name was the crowning touch on her victory. "We understand each other so well . . . Niall."

He smiled, but his thoughts were clearly focused on his imminent journey. "I will take my leave of you, for the time being." He strode into the hall and took his hat and coat from the butler. "Good afternoon, Miss Hockensmith. I will send word when I have Athena in my care."

After he was gone, Cecily sank onto a chair and caught her breath. Her good fortune had not only held, but doubled. Niall had already been prepared to think the worst of Athena. No matter what his sister might say now, he wasn't likely to believe her.

And Athena wouldn't be coming back to Denver. One major obstacle removed with little effort on Cecily's part—and the remaining impediments in her climb to the top of society would fall, one by one, when the Winter Ball proved a grand success. All the snobbish, insular doyennes of Denver would flock to her door once they realized just what Cecily was capable of.

Especially after she became Mrs. Niall Munroe.

Cecily stretched out her legs, licked her lips, and began to count her wedding presents.

*I*t had been a day like this one—*crisp, cold, and ready* with a gentle gift of new snow—when Morgan had gone to the wolves and left the bitterness of his old life behind.

Once more he stood on such a threshold. Once more he considered casting off his previous existence just as he shook the snowflakes from his fur. But this change was not so easy.

This change was terrifying.

He crossed the open meadow at a fast lope, paws striking the ground noiselessly as he pursued the hare. Sharp air pierced the insides of his nostrils and whistled past his ears. Scents were always more acute at this time of year, and he knew, as he passed, where the bear had chosen her den, the bobcat had made his most recent kill, and the squirrel had stored her winter provisions.

Windswept leaves and moist earth, the dry stalks of tender plants, and brittle twigs brushed his pads and the short fur that fringed his feet. Most of the last week's snow had melted, for the days were not yet cold enough to maintain it. *But soon,* the wind promised. *Soon,* the pines whispered. *Soon it will be winter again, and you must choose.*

The hare dodged abruptly to the left, hoping to evade its deadly pursuer. But Morgan was more than wolf, just as he was more than man. He spun in midair and cut directly across the hare's path. It skidded to a stop no more than a foot from his lowered head. He could hear its stuttering heartbeat as it flattened to the ground and waited in silent, terrified resignation.

Morgan touched the trembling body with the tips of his toes. Years ago, he would not have paused as he did now. A wolf did not contemplate the feelings of his victims. He thought of his empty belly and the hard winter ahead.

Sentimental fool. Morgan backed away, shaking his head in disgust. The hare remained still. Morgan bared his teeth and snapped at the air. The hare leaped straight up and was off before the mist of Morgan's breath ebbed away.

Was this inexplicable urge for mercy not proof? Proof that, even if he wished, he could not go back to the wolves?

He heard them often, singing in the mountains. They stayed away from the ranch, but they were there. A new pack, one that would accept his presence just like the first. Until, one by one, they were killed by men or driven deeper into the wilderness.

Driven. Instinct and need drove the wolf. The thing that drove Morgan was a far more brutal master. It collared him with new memories and hopes, yanked and tugged him again and again toward those who had claimed his loyalty. Toward the ranch, and to the east and the city where

Athena Munroe lived out her life of rules, rank, and restrictions.

She would not come here. She would be a fool to do so, and Athena was no fool. Yet each time Morgan ranged a little farther to the edge of the long park, gazed up at the hills and dreamed of escape, he turned and went back.

Just as he did today.

The slow-witted cattle that browsed on the brittle grass blinked at him as he gave them wide berth. Munroe's ranch hands, who answered to the foreman and seldom saw their employer, were not even aware that a wolf roamed the park. Morgan was careful to choose paths that concealed his tracks. The last thing he wanted was a pack of men up in arms over the presence of a lone wolf among their precious livestock.

The afternoon sky had taken on the flat gray patina of imminent snowfall, darkened with vertical drifts of smoke from the ranch's many chimneys. Morgan circled the out-buildings and the two bunkhouses, one reserved for the ranch hands and one for the troupers. He trotted out to the barn where the troupe's horses were stabled, nudged open the door, and jumped up into the hayloft where he kept his clothing.

He dressed and walked among the horses, making note of their condition. They were growing lazy and complacent here, just as he was.

Still, he walked a little faster as he approached the main house with its imposing stone exterior and sprawling, baronial magnificence. Long Park might run cattle, but at its center was a mansion a foreign prince might envy. Niall Munroe was not one to accept less than the best for himself or his sister. Athena would be as comfortable here as in her own home on Fourteenth Street.

And there was always the chance, however small, that she had come.

He entered the house by a side door reserved for the servants and followed the narrow hall to the ground floor guest rooms that had been reserved for Harry, Caitlin,

Ulysses, and a few of the others. Since Morgan slept in the barn, Harry and Ulysses shared a room, while Caitlin had one to herself.

The door to Harry's room was open, releasing the smell of pipe smoke into the hall. Caitlin's door also stood ajar.

". . . can think of no reason why Harry writes so incessantly unless he hopes to effect a particular response from Miss Munroe," Ulysses's voice said. "I know he is fond of the young lady, but he has never been an admirable correspondent. I am bound to conclude that you have had some influence upon him, Caitlin."

"Me? What a suspicious mind you have, Uly. Naturally Harry wants to keep her informed of—"

"The gravity of your condition? His deep concern about your state of mind and indefinite prospects for recovery?"

"Can I help it if Harry exaggerates?"

"He knows as well as I that your injury is almost healed."

"But Athena heard the doctor say it was serious. She had no reason to believe I would recover so quickly."

Morgan folded his arms and leaned against the wall just outside the room. Ulysses coughed discreetly.

"Miss Munroe is of a naturally altruistic and accommodating nature and is apt to consider the welfare of others before her own. She made certain promises to her brother as a condition of our remaining here for the winter. Have you weighed the practical consequence of fomenting domestic rebellion?"

"If you mean that Niall Munroe might not get his own way for once—"

"You may grant, Firefly, that my preference for reason over passion has given me reliable powers of observation. It is my judgement that Mr. Munroe may only be pushed so far before he pushes back."

"And it is mine that Niall is not nearly as heartless as he thinks he is."

"Your heart tells you this because you believe that you are in love with him."

Caitlin burst out laughing. "Your almighty powers of observation, Uly? When were you ever in love?"

Ulysses was silent just a beat too long. "A man of my nature—and stature—is wisest to avoid the tender emotions and the complications that result therefrom. But I am human. I can recognize infatuation when I see it."

Morgan waited for Caitlin to deny it. When she did not, he let his hands fall to his sides and took an involuntary step toward the open door.

"I don't know," Caitlin whispered. "He and I—we have nothing in common. I'm no innocent, Uly. I am much older than I look. I know that Niall Munroe is a man—only a man—and I will not let him destroy the lives of the people I care about."

"Athena and Morgan."

"And you, and Harry, and the others. All we need do is get through this winter, and our luck will change for good. I know it."

Ulysses sighed, and his feet rapped on the floor as he hopped from his seat. "I have no right to tell you what you should or should not do," he said. "It is even possible that your faith and loyalty will prove more formidable than the untrammeled wealth and power of a man like Munroe. But be careful. Devotion exacts a heavy price."

Morgan stepped aside as Ulysses walked through the door. The dwarf paused, looked up at Morgan, and gently closed the door behind him.

"I will not ask if you overheard our discussion," he said.

"What is this about letters to Athena?" Morgan demanded.

"That you must ask Caitlin. I see that you have decided to remain with us another day."

"What makes you think I was planning to leave?"

"It has never been a question of if you would go, but when. It is not loyalty to the troupe that keeps you here."

"You shouldn't listen to Caitlin's wild fancies."

"Are they so improbable?" Ulysses glanced toward the closed door. "Miss Munroe did not seem, at first glance, to match Caitlin's strength of will. It has been brought to my attention that first impressions are deceiving." He turned toward the room he shared with Harry. "Do not be too severe upon the girl. If you find yourself with a desire for rational conversation, you know where to find me."

Unmollified, Morgan strode into Caitlin's room. She looked unsurprised to see him. Her lids fell halfway over her eyes.

"Hello, Morgan," she said weakly. "How was your run?"

"Are you in love with Munroe?"

"We've had this conversation before. I could ask the same—"

"I do *not* love Athena Munroe!"

His roar bounced about the room. The corners of Caitlin's lips curled up in satisfaction.

"Then why don't you leave?" she asked. "Athena may arrive any time."

"She is not coming here."

"Are you so sure?"

"What have you and Harry been doing?"

Caitlin examined her nails. "Oh, nothing. Athena has been worried about me, so we've been—"

"Lying. Telling her you're worse than you are. Caitlin—"

"You had better not growl at Athena the way you do at me. She's likely to growl back."

Morgan froze. "What do you mean by that?"

"Women in love can be very fierce creatures."

"She is not—"

"I know, I know. She is not in love with you." She rolled her eyes. "And you haven't been stomping about the place like a bilious bull because Athena is out of your reach."

Morgan stepped back from the bed. "Do you think she binds me here, Firefly? Do you think I couldn't leave now and never look back?"

"I think you could try. But I hope you will not, my friend."

As she had done many times before—as only she and

Athena, had the power to do—she left him silent. Caitlin was like the hare that he had neatly caught and released out of maudlin sentimentality. Like a lesser wolf in the pack whom he had failed to teach its place. She and Athena could twist him round and round their fingers, spinning him this way and that until he didn't know east from west or sky from earth.

Athena. When she looked into his eyes with that slight lift of her chin and that warmth in her hazel eyes, he almost forgot why he wanted to run.

"After all these months," Caitlin said softly, "I still don't know where you come from, or why you were hiding as a wolf in the wilderness. I know you were hiding— we all are, one way or another."

"You are wrong. I was free. The only kind of freedom worth having."

"Free from ties to other people. That is it, isn't it? It's what you've always been most afraid of. Owing us for saving your life. Making friends even when you didn't want to. Athena increases your dilemma a thousandfold."

"I choose my own path."

"I wonder if any of us do." She frowned at the bare toes that protruded from the cast on her leg. "Something happened to you, Morgan. Something bad enough that you never wanted to risk it happening again. People you cared about—they got hurt, or they hurt you. Ulysses's own family drove him out because he couldn't possibly be a true Wakefield looking the way he does. But he still writes to them, hoping to be reconciled." She looked up. "I know it's difficult to keep hoping when you don't want to. Love is the worst of all, because it's like a lantern shining on everything you don't want to see. Or remember."

Morgan clenched his fist around the top of the bedpost. "I don't like you as a philosopher, Firefly."

"I don't think I do, either." She laughed. "That's what happens when you are stuck in a bed listening to Ulysses read from musty old books written by dead Greeks and Romans."

The room around Morgan changed, its cheerful yellow walls closing in to become a gray, crumbling cell. "The dead should be forgotten."

"No one should be forgotten."

"You live in a dream, Firefly."

"And you, Morgan? Have you forgotten what it is to dream?"

Morgan released his aching fingers from the bedpost. "Men dream. Wolves do not. I know which is better off."

"We fool ourselves," she said. "I pretend just as much as you do that nothing really matters. At least I know I'm pretending."

"Then you know that Niall Munroe cares nothing for you," Morgan said cruelly. "He may take your body if you offer it, as he would from any whore."

"Perhaps I'll choose to give it to him. Have you forgotten the pleasures of the body, Morgan? Oh, no—I do remember you have enjoyed Tamar's company from time to time. She must be very skilled, and she knows exactly what she wants. Athena is only half a woman, isn't she?"

Her words slashed at Morgan from heart to belly. "Athena—" he began, choking, "Athena is . . . more than a woman. More than you can—" He broke off, breathing hard. Caitlin stared at him, her freckles as lurid as wagon paint.

A light tap came on the door. Harry stepped in, oblivious, filling the room with his voluble and sunny presence.

"Ah, Morgan, my boy. Ulysses said I would find you here. Caitlin, how are you on this very fine afternoon?"

"Isn't it snowing outside?" Caitlin asked, craning her head toward the lace-curtained window.

"So it is, so it is. But that should not dampen our pleasure in a most unexpected visit. One of the ranch hands just came to report a wagon coming up the lane. Some hired conveyance and driver, no doubt, for these mountain passes." He rubbed his hands. "Is it not wonderful news, Morgan? Our very own Miss Athena has come at last."

Chapter 14

Morgan stood toe to toe with Harry, looking down a full foot at the older man. "You brought her here," he accused. "You and Caitlin."

Harry's brows arched toward the ceiling. "Why, my boy, this is her property, after all!"

Morgan growled and walked around him. His heart sent jolts of lightning up and down his body with every beat. Had he not been waiting every day for this? Had he not sensed, deep in his soul, that she could not stay away any more than he could stop thinking about her?

But Harry and Caitlin had arranged this between them, played with his life and Athena's as if they were ivory pieces on Harry's chessboard. Morgan wouldn't have been astonished if Caitlin had planned her own injury, just to push him and Athena together.

But he could refuse to play by the rules they had set.

A cool, supple body blocked his path. If he had not been so preoccupied, he would have smelled Tamar a mile away, and avoided her.

"My wolf," she said. "What makes you frown so? Have the hunters set one too many traps for your liking?" She smiled, and he was driven back to the memory of kissing those lips, holding that willing body against him in the night.

He could have had her a thousand times since, if he had so much as looked at her. But he had kissed Athena. One kiss, lacking even the most basic intimacies of the flesh, and he was ruined for the taste of another mouth.

Tamar could have taken any number of lovers in the troupe, for all her strangeness. Instead, she chose to pursue him. She had schemed her way into one of the rooms in the main house, and had become impossible to avoid completely. Morgan had finally realized that she believed she had some claim on him because of their brief liaison.

Why, he did not understand. He had offered her nothing. Whatever ambition lay behind her calculating eyes, he could not fulfill it. Her beauty was like a jungle flower he had heard of, intoxicating to look at but thick with the smell of rotten meat.

"Yes," he said. "Too many traps." He tried to pass, but she held out an arm to stop him. She had great strength for a woman, coiled and always lying in wait.

"You will never have her," she said. The very calmness of her voice set his hair on end. "She would spit on you, my wolf, like all *gadje*."

"Do not speak of her, Tamar."

"Ah, the fierce growl." She laughed softly. "Why should I not speak of her? The others do. They all *love* her, the little helpless one." She drew her long nail down his cheek. "Do you love her, too? Do you dream of her useless legs coming to life and wrapping around you in the night? Do you imagine living in her big house in the city, with a fine lady's golden collar about your neck, or do you think she will follow you to rut in the woods like a beast?"

He grasped her wrist and pulled it away. "No."

"Men are children," she said in that same calm, passionless voice. "They want only what they cannot have or what will make them sick in the belly. She will make you sick. And when you have need of the cure, come to me."

She left him, gliding away without a single seductive glance. And a strange sensation washed through him, startling in its truth.

He was sorry for Tamar. He pitied her and her inexplicable obsession with him. He wondered what had made her what she was, and why she saw in him, of all men, a cure for her private pain.

Was this what humans called compassion? Had Athena taught him its meaning?

He wanted no part of it. He began to walk again, hardly knowing which direction he was headed. Tamar was just like the others, aiming to bend him to her desires.

He found himself at the end of the hall, where it opened up into the great parlor. The place echoed with emptiness, not quite as grand as the public rooms of Athena's Denver home, but large enough to hold a pair of average cabins or an ordinary farmhouse within its high walls. The wooden floor and rustic embellishments did little to make it seem less palatial. Padded and polished furniture was grouped around sumptuous woven carpets and a thick bearskin rug. The hearth was immense, its perpetual blaze constantly fed with the trunks of small trees.

The parlor's door stood open to the entrance hall. Snow blew in from the outer doors. Athena wheeled in, one of the ranch hands behind her with a pair of carpetbags.

Athena loosened the collar of her thick wool coat. "Please set the bags down anywhere, Sterling," she said to the hand. "I would appreciate it if you will make sure that my driver is given a meal and a bed for the night."

"I'll do my best, Miss Athena," Sterling said, dropping the bags onto the floor, "but it's mighty crowded here what with the circus folk and all. The foreman ain't none too happy with the tight quarters at the bunkhouse and them trick horses in the barn, and I hear Mr. Durant is thinking of quitting—begging your pardon, ma'am."

Athena smiled, tugging at her gloves. "Poor Mr. Durant. For many years all he has done is keep the house in readiness for guests that seldom arrive. I will be certain to tell him and the foreman that they will be very well compensa—"

She saw Morgan and stopped. Morgan was vaguely aware that Sterling had vacated the room, leaving them alone. Athena continued to stare, her lips slightly parted, and Morgan felt as if he had been shot, skinned, and hung on the wall for a trophy.

He had told Caitlin that he could leave any time and never look back. He had lied. He could not make himself move a single step away from the woman across the room.

"Morgan," she whispered.

Absence makes the heart grow fonder, the old saw proclaimed. Now Athena understood exactly what it meant. One look at Morgan, standing so still by the hall, and she knew her coming had been inevitable. One breath of the air he breathed, and she wondered how her heart had continued to beat in the cold void of their separation.

A thrill of almost painful sensation shot up her legs from heel to hip. Morgan's eyes burned, compelling her. Commanding.

Come. Come to me.

It was as if he had been calling every moment of the past five weeks, and only now did she truly hear him. Her fingers clutched at the arms of her chair. The muscles in her legs, so long dormant, began to quiver and twitch.

Come. He smiled, lifting the burden of her fear. He held out his hand.

Come.

Athena pressed all of her weight onto her arms and pushed up. Her feet touched the floor. Her knees quivered, but only for a moment. Then they locked, steadying her, and she rose. Slowly, carefully she stood up, the chair at her back, and swayed from the dizzying height of her own five and a half feet.

She had no time to contemplate the miracle. Morgan summoned her, his eyes ever more demanding, his fingers curled to beckon. She slid one foot along the smooth wooden floor. The second followed the first.

One step taken. Another. A third. She dared to look up from the ground again. Morgan's eyes flashed triumph and pride—for her. But he waited—waited until she had taken all the steps between them and only one more led directly into his arms.

She made it. She reached up and wrapped her arms about his shoulders—not for support, not out of need, but because she wanted him. With her own strength she drew his face to hers. She opened her mouth and inhaled the warmth of his breath.

And she kissed him. She kissed *him*, free to make that choice as she was free to stand and walk and feel again.

Morgan's mouth opened over hers, seizing what she offered. Some great mystery waited to be revealed in his embrace, a tale only he could illustrate with his lips and his tongue. She felt its erotic promise all the way down to her toes.

Let it not end too quickly. Let it never end. . . .

"Athena."

Something was wrong with Morgan's voice. She opened her eyes, and the shock of reality flung her back into her chair.

The chair she had never left. She was not on her feet, not in Morgan's arms. She remained exactly where Sterling had left her, and Morgan still waited by the hall.

All a dream. All a cruel, treacherous fantasy concocted by her addled mind. She could have wept, but many years of practice had taught her how to swallow the tears.

You forgot why you are here. You saw Morgan, and everything else disappeared, even Caitlin. This is your rightful punishment for such base selfishness.

Punishment, and a stark reminder that Morgan was not what her childish dreams made of him.

"Athena," he said. His eyes were not welcoming, but wary. "Are you ill?"

"No." She managed a smile. "I am quite well. How is Caitlin? I have come to make sure she is recovering as she should."

"You came here without your brother's permission?"

She couldn't tell if it was censure or admiration she heard in his voice. Hadn't he encouraged her to defy her brother in the past? "Niall is away on business." She lifted her chin. "Will you show me to Caitlin's room?"

He took half a step toward her, stopped, and made a strange, almost helpless gesture. "Athena. You should not have—" He shook his head, grim about the mouth. "I will take you to her."

"Miss Athena!"

Harry swept out of the hall, barely pausing to step around Morgan, and greeted Athena with a warm smile. "Welcome, welcome! Of course I have no right whatsoever to welcome you to your own home, but we are all so glad you have come. Caitlin will be pleased—"

"How is she?"

The sparkle in his eyes dimmed. "I have been worried about her, as you know, but—" He cast a wary glance back at Morgan. "Now you are here, she will surely make progress. Morgan, would you be so good as to take Miss Athena's bags to her room? Mr. Durant was quite plain that he was saving your chamber for you, my dear, as well as Mr. Munroe's, in case you should come—just as he ought, of course. Not that any of us would dream of appropriating it!" He took the handles of Athena's chair. "I confess that I feel some pity for Mr. Durant's situation. He was not at all prepared for us, even with the addition of the extra staff your good brother hired. I understand that Mr. Durant has been caretaker here for years . . . but even though most of the troupers are in the bunkhouse, the poor fellow has clearly not had to deal with so many guests. In spite of our efforts to help he seems . . . quite annoyed."

Athena remembered Mr. Durant as a nervous, efficient, but generally kind older man who had competently handled the large parties her father had given when she was a child. Prominent men and women had come from Denver to talk business or simply relax away from the city's summer heat, but that had been many years ago. Evidently Mr. Durant was out of practice.

"Don't worry, Harry. I will speak to him myself this evening."

"I am sure that he will be quite upset to have missed you—I believe he is consulting with the foreman about a shortage of provisions." Harry pushed her chair away from the door, and Athena was very much aware of Morgan gathering up the baggage and trailing along behind.

"You did not bring your maid, my dear?" Harry went on. "I know there are several young women here to clean and cook and whatnot. Perhaps one of them might attend you—"

"That will not be necessary," Athena said, wishing that she had eyes in the back of her head. "I should be staying for just a few days, and I will need only occasional assistance."

"Quite so, quite so. Nevertheless, I will see if I can locate a girl for you so that you may refresh yourself. Caitlin is sleeping at the moment, but when she wakes—" He paused halfway across the room and gazed at the great oak staircase in dismay. "Oh dear. How extraordinarily foolish of me. Your rooms are on the second floor, are they not?"

"I haven't been to Long Park many times in the past several years. Niall had meant to have an elevator installed, but it seemed unnecessary . . ." *And he always carried me. But he isn't here. Mr. Durant isn't strong enough, and neither is Harry. That leaves—*

"Morgan, if I may impose upon you once again," Harry said.

Athena held her breath. Morgan stalked up beside them, bent over Athena, and lifted her into his arms. It was not the first time he had held her so, but since the kiss—since her fantasy of walking—the act was charged with almost unbearable excitement.

And shame for her pitiful expectations.

Morgan mounted the stairs, unspeaking, while Harry puffed along at a much slower pace. "To the right," she whispered when they reached the landing. Morgan carried her to the room she indicated, balanced her weight on one arm, and used his free hand to open the door.

The room's furnishings and decorations were the frothy, unsophisticated selections of a young girl, unchanged since before the accident. Morgan hesitated when he saw the white, lace-canopied bed, and then gently set her down upon it.

She stared up at him. He stared back. The room grew very warm despite the empty fireplace. Huffing like a bellows, Harry appeared in the doorway.

"Morgan," he said between breaths. "The bags—"

Morgan backed away and fled the room. Athena pressed her hands to her face, wishing for a handful of snow to cool her flush.

"There, there, my dear girl. What is the matter?"

She tried to gather herself into a more dignified position on the bed and smiled at Harry, inviting him to sit in the delicate wicker chair at her dressing table. He closed the door, gave the chair a dubious glance and sat down cautiously. The chair creaked, but held.

"I suppose I am tired, that is all," she said. "The driver I hired was quite competent, but the wagon was not comfortable, I fear."

"Your brother does not know you have come."

"No. He's away, and I made the decision on my own." Best not to elaborate on that point; sharing such worries with Harry did neither of them any good. And there was something else that she could no longer keep to herself. "Harry . . . is Morgan . . . is he upset that I have come?"

Harry leaned forward, eliciting a groan from the chair, and clasped his hands between his knees. "My dear child," he said with uncharacteristic gravity, "How can you ask such a question?"

"He . . . I . . ." She turned her face aside. "I have never spoken of this to anyone. It feels very strange . . . wrong—"

"No, no. Never say so." Harry placed his hand over his heart. "I am honored beyond words that you choose to speak to me as you would to your own father. You see, I have regarded you as something of my daughter from the day we met. And Morgan is like the son I never had."

Casting discretion to the snow-laden wind, Athena met his gaze. "I loved my father very much," she said. "I still miss him dreadfully. But if I could have a second one, I would choose you."

"Thank you, my dear. Thank you." He reached into his pocket for a handkerchief. "I have seen much in my time. Very little surprises me. Nothing you may say will disturb me, I assure you."

Athena swallowed. "I hardly know how to begin. Ever since I met you . . . the circus . . . I have felt as if you are a second family."

"As we have felt of you."

"And . . . and—" Oh, why did all eloquence desert her at times like this? Yet how often had she spoken with real intimacy to anyone, discussed anything but charitable work, social affairs, fashion, or household management? Among all the women she considered her friends, why would she never dream of confiding in them as she did this garrulous and good-hearted old man?

Because she trusted him—trusted Harry, and Caitlin, even Morgan more than she did her own kind, the very people whom she regarded as her peers.

And she was not ashamed.

"Tell me what you know of Morgan," she said in a rush. "Where he comes from, who his people were. Please, Harry. I must know."

"I have been waiting for you to ask that for quite some time, my dear. I will tell you what I know, though in many ways Morgan is as much an enigma to me as to you."

Athena hugged herself. "I know what he is. It doesn't shock me—"

"And that is why I find it so easy to love you."

The lump in Athena's throat had doubled in size. She tried, and failed, to remember when she had heard such tender words from anyone since Papa's death. "It is as if he doesn't wish to speak of his past—not his family or what he wants from life. Why, Harry? What happened to him?"

"No one knows. He came to us as a wolf pursued by hunters, and changed into a man before our eyes. Our troupe has always been a home for those who have no place in the outside world, so naturally we took him in. He felt he owed us a debt, and though he did so reluctantly, he repaid us by becoming our 'Wolf-Man' act. He was so successful in drawing audiences that he was almost entirely responsible for saving us from certain ruin. He could have left us many times, and seemed to wish to—and yet he has remained."

"He cares about you."

"Yes, though he will not willingly admit it."

"How did he live before he came to you?"

"That I know. He spent many years as a wolf, among the beasts—deliberately avoiding the haunts of men. But his reasons I cannot tell you. There is great bitterness in him, a desire to see only the worst in mankind."

"And you always see the best."

"I try." He studied his plump, interlaced fingers. "He will not speak of his family, except to say that he lost his parents and sister before he fled to the woods. I suspect some dark tragedy, and that he blames himself. They say there is a boy in every man, and the boy that Morgan was came to manhood in sorrow." He gave her a sad smile. "Yet there is something in him that allows one to forgive his rough nature. At heart, he is deeply generous and protects those he considers friends, even though he would deny he has any friends at all."

"And you want to help him," Athena murmured. "You want to find out why he suffers, and mend it somehow. . . ."

"I am certain that there is only one person in the world who can bring about such healing," Harry said quietly. "The one he does not believe exists."

Athena was afraid to decipher his words. "He has never tried to talk to you, as I do now?"

"Never. But in my heart of hearts, I dare to think that he sees me, just a little, as his foster-father."

"Thank you, Harry." Despite the brevity of their conversation, Athena felt both drained and exhilarated. Harry loved Morgan. So did Caitlin. What *she* felt could not be so unthinkable.

But what did she feel?

"You must rest now, my dear," Harry said, rising to his feet. "I will find a maid to attend you, and inform you as soon as Caitlin is awake." He cupped the side of her face. "Sleep well, my child. And have faith."

She covered his hand with hers. "Thank you, Harry."

He opened the door and nearly tripped over the bags Morgan had left just outside. With a brief shake of his head, he lifted them one by one and set them in the room.

The ache in Athena's chest continued long after he was gone. A maid arrived within the hour to bring water for washing and help her unpack the bags. Mr. Durant, too, found time to come to her, apologetic for having neglected her but clearly overwhelmed by his additional responsibilities.

She absolved him of any need to personally look after her and arranged to have the hired girl within calling distance. She remained on the bed rather than ask Durant or some stranger to lift her in and out of her chair. Harry failed to return, and Morgan stayed away. At last she grew too sleepy to wait. The maid helped her into her nightdress, and she buried herself beneath the quilted coverlet.

Exhaustion overcame worry, and she closed her eyes. Out of the mist of half-sleep, she woke to an intense pain in her legs, so sharp and sudden that she cried aloud.

Pain in her legs. She reached down to touch them, certain she must still be dreaming. She closed her eyes again, willing herself back to sleep—but instead, she plunged into another dream, this one even more fantastic.

For she was running. Running, not on two legs, but four—running as a wolf, jaws wide to catch the falling snow. And at her side . . .

At her side was Morgan. Morgan as a magnificent black wolf, dwarfing her with his size and power. Yet for all his strength, she matched his blistering pace; her paws were like snowshoes, skimming over the soft quilt of fresh snow. The cold did not reach through the lush density of her coat, and her nostrils were filled with smells as rich and subtle as the colors on an artist's canvas.

They raced the wind itself, she and Morgan. And he looked sideways at her, yellow eyes brilliant with pain, and laughed. With a burst of speed, he lunged ahead of her.

She faltered. For an instant, she knew that this could not be happening, that she had no hope of catching up to him.

But Harry's gentle voice was there, inside her: *"I am certain that there is only one person in the world who can bring about such healing."* And she understood that she must help Morgan, though she did not know how or why; she must heal him, and heal herself as well.

Heal myself? The sheer incongruity of the thought hurled her forward, and at the same time she could feel the snowy world dissolving around her, replaced with hard-edged shadows and woven carpet.

Carpet firm and warm beneath her feet. Two feet. She could see her toes in the darkness, very white at the end of a long column of fabric. They wiggled at her.

Another cruel, intolerable jest at her expense. She looked for her bed, determined to end it.

The bed was several feet away. She would have to walk to reach it. Walking meant standing.

She was standing. Her legs hurt, oh, they hurt most terribly, the way her hands felt when they had been exposed to the cold and then held before a fire.

This was no dream.

She put her hands to her cheeks. Not a dream. Not the pain, and not the fact that her muscles were far too weak to hold her up much longer.

Impossible, her heart told her as she turned carefully toward the bed. *Impossible,* echoed her mind as she measured out the distance she must cover—the same distance she had traveled unconsciously only moments ago.

She began to tremble. Not only her legs, overtaxed as they were, but her entire body. It was joy. She gulped on laughter and tasted saltiness on her lips.

I can stand. I can walk. I am free.

It seemed only natural that Morgan should come then, to share her triumph. Completely right that he should walk up to her—his feet bare, trousers half-buttoned and shirt open at the neck—and kiss her.

This time . . . oh, yes. This time it was real.

Morgan *had carried the memory of their one previous* kiss for weeks, obsessed with an impulsive act he should have dismissed a moment after it was done.

Now he knew why he had been unable to forget it. Her mouth opened under his so sweetly, with such trust, that he knew she had been thinking of it, too. Wanting it as much as he did.

But it hadn't been mere desire that had driven him that final step. He had been running . . . running as he always did when the company of others became unbearable. Especially the company of this woman. He had found little peace in the outing, for he had not been alone.

Somehow *she* had followed him. He had become aware of her presence as the first hint of false dawn seared the edge of the sky, outlining the jagged, snow-topped profiles of the mountains. The silence had been absolute. One minute he ran alone, and the next he felt her by his side, a ghost-wolf, racing him as he raced his own fears.

He had known it was impossible. She was not really there. But her spirit had come to him, as the Indians said sometimes happened in the night. She had challenged him on his own ground, unafraid. And he had sensed that there was more to this vision than a dream they both shared.

As the stars faded overhead, he doubled back on his tracks and loped to the ranch, not knowing what he might find. No one stirred on the grounds or in the house when he entered it. Up the stairs he had run, soundless, to the door of Athena's room.

And there she stood—*stood,* in the center of the carpet, on her two legs. Her face bore the look of a startled deer. Then she began to shake, and Morgan felt the mingled fear and triumph as if it were his own.

Triumph, and pride. Pride in her, in the achievement she had made against all the odds. Deep and unexpected joy that she could be whole, and free.

He did not question. He went to her, took her in his arms, and kissed her.

This was a kiss as the other had not been—lingering, ardent, and shared with equal fervor. In it Morgan poured all the desire he had kept so tightly sealed away, unfettered by Athena's new strength.

She could do more than stand. Her arms were strong and sure about his neck. The she-wolf who had run beside him was present in full measure, and her teeth locked on his lower lip with a ferocity for which he was unprepared.

The wolf in him cried out for conquest. He explored the velvet interior of her mouth with flickers of his tongue, and then deeper thrusts. She seemed ready to devour him. If she had never kissed a man before that night in her bedchamber, she learned very quickly.

It was as much the werewolf blood that sang in her heart as it did in his own. Powerful, undeniable attraction. The wolf she could not be while bound to her chair had awakened to all the possibilities of liberation.

He gathered her thick, loose hair in his fists and pulled her head back, kissing and nipping her bared neck. She hissed with pleasure. A distant part of him wondered at so vast a change in her, and cast the thought aside.

Take her, the wolf demanded. *She wants you. You want her. Nothing else matters.*

No one would see. No one need know. A single frenzied coupling, and he would be gone again with none the wiser.

Gone? Did he think he could run from such a binding? Once it was done . . .

As if they were truly of one mind, they drew apart at the same moment. Athena was panting and flushed, her lips slightly swollen, her eyes vivid, more golden than green or brown. She swayed. He caught her again and carried her to the bed.

She lay back without protest. He could see how her legs trembled, pushed to the very edge of their strength. It was remarkable that they had supported her so long. Surely they would not have done so had she been of pure human blood.

"Morgan," she whispered. "I did it. I . . . stood up."

Already the kiss was relegated to the back of her thoughts. He could not blame her. He should be relieved, though his body ached and cursed him for his cowardice.

"Yes," he said. He considered the edge of the bed and chose to crouch beside it instead. "How did it happen?"

"I don't know. One moment I was dreaming, and the next—" She ran her tongue over her lower lip. Morgan winced. "I dreamed that I was running as a wolf. With you."

"I felt it," he said. "I saw you, in my mind."

"You did?" She smiled, as if she had just discovered that there was a joy greater than recovering the use of her legs. "It wasn't only a dream?"

He began to understand. She had dreamed of running, of her wolf blood carrying her to freedom, and her body had acted. It had defied the doctors and naysayers who had declared that she would never walk again . . . including herself. He should have sensed from the beginning that her paralysis was made up of denials and assumptions, not of a ruined body. That was why he had kissed her the first time, goaded her to defy her brother, allowed himself to get so close. . . .

When did you become so wise?

"If you can walk," he said, avoiding her question, "your injuries must be healed."

"Healed." She breathed the word, exhaled it, savoring a taste she had not expected to sample again. "Is it possible?"

"Your legs held you up. Your muscles must be weak and thin, but they work. Can you feel them?"

"Yes." Wonder in her eyes, she ran her hands down her body from waist to thigh. Her nightdress molded to the shape beneath, and Morgan clenched his teeth. "I *can*. It hurts."

The pain must be great, but she bore it without complaint. Pride swelled his heart to uncomfortable proportions. "I only know a little about such injuries, but I have seen men who have not used arms or legs for many months, and they can get well if they do not give up. It will continue to hurt, after so long. The wolf will help. It was the wolf that healed you."

She met his gaze. "But I . . . I haven't Changed in years."

"Your body doesn't forget. Just as your muscles don't forget how to stand. They will learn to walk and then run again." He stared into her eyes. "You are brave enough to do it, Athena. You always have been."

She pulled herself up to lean on the pillows, carefully flexing her knees. "But if all it needed was courage, then why did it take me so many years to find it?"

Ask Ulysses, he wanted to tell her. *He is the philosopher—he and Caitlin.* "What were you afraid of?" he asked.

"I—" She closed her eyes, and he could feel her traveling back over the years, to that snowy mountainside long ago. "I don't know. I believed the doctors. I believed Niall."

Niall. Morgan bit back a snarl. "He kept you in that chair."

"No! No." She shook her head, refusing to hear anything against her brother. "Nothing is that simple. He did everything for me."

"He did not understand the wolf," Morgan said. "Neither did you."

The confusion in her eyes cleared, and a new energy coursed through her. Morgan could see it, radiating from her body. "I believed the wolf was gone forever. I made myself believe it." She looked at him in such a way that his throat closed up and he couldn't have spoken had he wished to.

"It wasn't only the wolf inside me that made this happen," she said softly. "It wasn't a miracle. It was you. Your inspiration, your belief in me . . . even your bullying. You were an example I had never found anywhere else."

He jumped to his feet. "You give me too much credit."

"I don't think I do. You are so much more than you know, Morgan."

"And you know *nothing* of me."

"Then tell me." She leaned forward, deliberately working the muscles of her legs. "If you have suffered . . . I want to help you as you have helped me. I owe you so much. Let me repay at least a little."

He started for the door, and stopped. Every nerve burned with conflicting urges. *Run. Stay. Avoid her at all costs. Take her. Possess her. Make her yours forever.*

"There are many who care about you, Morgan," she said behind him. "You do not want to owe anyone . . . and you don't want anyone owing you. Do you think I have not seen that time and again in my work?"

"Among your charity cases?" he snapped. "Those who are too weak to survive on their own, and too proud to admit it?"

"The circus needed your help, and you gave it. You could have left, but you stayed. You had no reason to encourage me, yet you did. I cannot understand you, Morgan . . . and yet, somehow, I do."

"You are a child."

"I had a father who loved me, and a brother who protects me even when he is too diligent. Perhaps I let myself be protected. But who protected you?"

"I don't need protection."

She paused, and he thought he had driven her from the subject. But she was not finished.

"You lost your family when you were young," she said. "But you have a new family now. Caitlin, and Ulysses, everyone in the circus. They are all your friends. And Harry regards you as a son."

He couldn't bear it. The bit of conversation he had heard between her and Harry, when he had left the bags by the door—that had been more than he wanted to know. And yet he had envied their easy intimacy, the affection between parent and child. His last conversation with Aaron Holt had been . . . best forgotten.

"What was your father like?" she asked.

He turned on her. "He was a dreamer, a wastrel, a man who could not care for his family." He closed his eyes, seeing the haggard, agonized, pleading face that bore so little resemblance to the man he had known in boyhood. "He left my mother . . ."

Too hard. Too much. "I went looking for him," he said. "To bring him home."

"Did you find him?"

She seemed to sense the enormity of what she asked, for her voice had grown very small. He smiled brutally. "I found him."

"You hated him," she whispered. "Oh, Morgan—"

Was that pity in her eyes, her voice? Was she reaching out, her fingers poised to stroke his cheek, pat his hair as if he were a disconsolate child—one of her precious, pitiful orphans?

He moved faster than human eyes could see and grasped her about the wrist.

"Don't pity me," he growled. "Don't you dare pity me."

He crouched over her, his legs to either side of her hips, pinning her arms to the bed. Athena understood, oh, yes, she knew—but she was calm, unafraid.

He did not want her fear. He wanted . . . he wanted . . .

"Morgan—"

He silenced her once more with his lips.

Chapter 15

Athena knew better than to show fear. The wolf was in Morgan's eyes, in his need, and she knew she had pressed too quickly.

But she needed, too. She needed to understand him, and now—as he kissed her with a harshness that swiftly transformed into a hungry caress—she realized she needed something far more physical.

The very physical desires she had denied herself, knowing that no man would be able to satisfy them even should he wish to bother with a cripple. The entirely selfish fulfillment that benefited no one but herself.

Now she had begun to *want*—not dream, not wish, but actively seek what had not been within her grasp until this moment.

That frightened her as Morgan himself could not. Her legs had begun to waken from their long sleep, but she hadn't reckoned how every other part of her would so brilliantly come alive at his touch.

It had happened before, with him, but not like this. His fingers tangled in her loosened hair, fiercely holding her still as he kissed her with all the thoroughness she had imagined in her waking dream downstairs.

But his anger, his seeming ferocity, was as much a facade as his ordinary human shape. Even now his hold on her was tender as that of a she-wolf carrying her pup in jaws that could crush bone.

His mouth formed her name against her lips, and he released her arms. She left them where they were, though she felt far from passive. Her instinct was to reach for him and pull him down, down, into herself.

But *he* must feel in control. She sensed that the way she sensed the crushing sorrows of young, unwed mothers or the anger of men who could not find work to feed their families. In such cases she knew how to respond—how to give, heal, mend—but now she must find her way like one blind.

One blind who had just begun to see.

Morgan nuzzled her ear, hot breath sizzling against the cool flesh at her hairline, and did something indescribable with his tongue. She gave a brief cry of surprise. He kissed her again, first on the lips and then on her forehead, her eyelids, her nose, her chin. Each kiss was little more than a breath, yet charged with such potency that she could not mistake it for anything like a brotherly salute.

No sooner had she recognized the utterly erotic nature of the caresses than he surprised her again. His tongue swept down the angle of her jaw, from earlobe to chin. It was as if he were sampling her before beginning his feast, a promise of more to come.

More than what had transpired in her bedroom, or even in her dream. It could go so much further, if she dared let it. All she need do to stop it was tell him "no."

He pressed his mouth to the underside of her jaw, where the pulse beat very fast, where she was most defenseless. She bent her head back and closed her eyes. He nipped her here, there . . . love-bites that she vaguely thought must be common among his kind. *Their* kind.

Then he began to unbutton the top of her nightdress.

She held her breath. One button undone: he peeled back the two seams and kissed the space between. One more: another kiss. The third button lay nestled in a valley of flesh. The last ended just where her breasts pushed up so shamelessly against the sheer linen.

Needles of sensation prickled in her belly and nipples. When he got below the buttons, he wouldn't be doing what an importunate suitor might have done, if she had suitors. She had no illusions about his intention.

Why? her much-abused common sense cried. *Why here, now?*

Why not? Did you expect avowals of love, a slow and formal courtship that any normal woman might prefer? Are you normal? Is he?

Might this not be your only chance to know what it is to be loved?

He laced his fingers through hers and pulled her arms above her head. He did not hold her there. Instead, he let his hand slide down her body, grazing shoulder and breast and hip without lingering, coming at last to rest on the juncture of her legs.

Her legs, which were no longer dead weights but strange appendages not yet sure how they belonged to the rest of her. They would not yet obey her, but they could *feel*.

She *felt* the heat of his palm through the lawn of her gown. She *felt* him begin to slide the fabric up her thighs, inch by inch, from the middle of her calf and higher. She *felt* the draft of cool air lick at her bared skin as his tongue had licked at her ear and chin.

Then his hand was on her, nothing between.

He brought his face close to hers. His lungs worked like those of a man who had been running many miles without rest. Her nostrils drew in scents that belonged only to him, unique and intoxicating, wolf and human. Damp, heavy locks of his hair curled under her jaw and into the cleft between her breasts.

"You feel so much for others," he whispered hoarsely in her ear. "But do you feel for yourself, Athena?"

He moved his hand under the bunched cloth of her nightdress. His fingertip just barely—or so she thought—brushed the small, tight curls at the tops of her thighs.

She had read of electric shocks and had imagined what they must be like. But that was scarcely an adequate comparison when he touched the most private place beneath that downy shield.

He had asked if she felt for herself. No answer was necessary. Pleasure like pain danced and burned with each small rotation of his finger, wringing gasps from deep in her chest. Standing on her own feet, walking, running again . . . all that was nothing compared to the ecstasy that reached into the very center of all she was or could ever be.

Was this it, the thing women spoke of in veiled allusions and whispers when men were safely out of hearing? The thing that made sharing a man's bed more than a duty and a way of making children?

Morgan. He touched her again, and her voice lost its way somewhere between throat and tongue.

To feel . . . to feel so gloriously was worth any price. To feel *this* at Morgan's hands, with his body stretched out above her was a miracle she did not deserve.

But what did Morgan get for himself? He had started this to silence her—to prove something to her, to himself, that he was master of his own fate and hardened against any sentiment she could offer. Yet his attempt at mastery had become a giving—of pleasure, of new feelings and wonder such as Athena had never known.

Did he realize what he did to her? Was it part of his game? Or was it as real and sincere as the renewed wholeness of her body?

He was no fool, and neither was she. The exact nature of the physical consummation between man and woman was but a vague idea in Athena's mind, but it must be connected to the way he touched her, the way her body responded and grew moist and warm and wanting. She could understand, now, how women bore children outside the bonds of marriage.

But Morgan's skilled fingers were not the organs capable of planting new life in a woman's body. Children— good heavens, children—she had dismissed that future as completely as she had one that freed her from the chair.

Children, marriage, physical love. Suddenly all three had become solid and tangible, vivid landscapes she could see through an open window instead of hazy specters glimpsed in a fog of resignation.

Morgan had made them all possible. He alone. He gave and gave, without knowing how much, and now he gave again. She knew in her heart that he wouldn't force himself upon her, risk getting her with child. God forbid that he should create such an unbreakable tie between them.

But if he thought of her—of her reputation, which he had seemed to ignore in Denver—and of the future he would alter forever if he continued—then how could she accuse him of such a sensible selfishness?

No. If he had meant to prove his independence, his indifference to human tenderness, he had chosen the wrong way. He gave unstintingly, denying himself the kind of fulfillment men must derive from such a joining. And she could not bear the thought that he had nothing but the dubious comfort of knowing he could make her *feel*.

That was when she realized she had fallen in love with him.

The notion was so blindingly obvious that she was briefly numb to sensation. Everything froze—lungs, heart, even her ability to hear and see.

She *loved* Morgan Holt. It wasn't mere attraction for one like herself, one who could understand. It wasn't some sort of rebellion against the life she thought she had chosen after the accident. It wasn't even this, this marvelous thing he did with his lips and his hands.

And it was not at all what she expected love to be. She had thought it beyond her reach, an emotion connected with gallant, handsome, courteous men who had wealth and presence and would never look twice at a woman in a invalid's chair. Men like her brother and his associates, the husbands and fathers of her society friends.

Morgan was not gallant, or courteous, or even handsome in the way of those men. He was bad-tempered, gruff, impolite, indifferent to propriety, and far too plainspoken. It was rare that he considered the feelings of others as he ought . . . as she tried to do.

But his was a breadth of soul, a tormented devotion, a passionate loyalty that could not be bought but, once given, was eternal. He had decided soon after their first meeting that she belonged to his small circle of family and friends. She knew he would never let harm come to her, and that he would fight to the death on her behalf.

All *that* he gave, having nothing but himself. But he felt. He felt as deeply as anyone she had ever known.

How could she make sense of this emotion, this knowledge of what he meant to her? She saw how much she had taken from him, and was ashamed. She did not take without giving back.

She must *give* to Morgan—help, and succor, and healing, if she could. Even love, if there was any chance in the world that he might accept it. But there was a more immediate gift within her power to bestow. A small, temporary gift that mattered less to her than to her society, but might begin to repay the debt she owed him.

If she had the courage.

Morgan stroked her with gentle pulses, and she momentarily lost the power to consider such abstracts as courage and selfishness. Light-headed, she arched up, up, her spine curving as if to bring every inch of her body into contact with his. Higher, higher, unfurling wings to carry them both into the heavens.

It was coming, the moment of perfect freedom. No more chair, no more waiting, no bondage even to the earth. Just one more stroke, one more caress, and she would prove . . . prove to herself, and everyone . . .

Morgan stopped. Athena opened her eyes with a wordless protest, but the look on his face kept her silent. She heard the thump of footfalls running up the stairs a second after he did.

Niall. She barely had time to pull her nightdress over her knees before he burst through the door.

"My God," he said hoarsely. "Athena." His gaze fixed on Morgan. "You damned bastard—"

"Niall!"

Athena's cry might as well have been a whisper. It did not penetrate Niall's rage. He could see nothing but the man who had despoiled his sister.

Morgan Holt. The cur crouched over her on the bed— *her* bed—an ugly snarl on his face as if he would defend her against her own brother. *Defend* her, by God, when he had stolen what little of value she had left.

Niall clenched his fist and dove at his enemy. Morgan sprang up and met him in midstride. Niall felt his fist connect with flesh and bone, heard the satisfying grunt of pain as Morgan staggered and fell to his knees with the force of the blow.

But he did not remain down. He stood again, shaking blood from his split lip, and braced his legs apart. Niall obliged him with a second strike directly to the jaw. Morgan's head snapped to one side.

"Niall, stop it!"

He was aware of the motion at the edge of his sight, a figure in pale linen lurching toward him with an awkward gait. Confusion stopped him from hitting again, though Morgan remained stubbornly on his feet. If one of the whoreson's circus friends had come to help him . . .

A hand caught at his arm. Athena's face swam into focus.

"Niall!"

Athena. He blinked. She could not be here. She was on the bed. But the bed was empty, coverlet and sheets rumpled but unstained. The hand that gripped his arm with such frantic strength was slender and feminine.

She was standing—leaning her weight against him, but

on her own two feet. Shock reverberated through Niall. He had come into the room expecting the worst, and finding it . . . but he had not been prepared for this. Not Athena able to stand, to walk, to participate willingly in her own ruination.

He met her gaze, a strange, cold calm muting his rage to a dull throb behind his eyes. "How long?" he asked in a soft, reasonable voice. "How long have you been lying to me, Athena?"

A vise made of five steel fingers caught him about the throat. He clawed at an arm roped with muscle, implacable in its grip. Vision narrowed to a pair of slitted amber eyes and a mouth full of bared white teeth.

Then the grip relaxed, and he caught himself as he fell, scrambling out of reach while he labored to fill his lungs with precious air. His back hit the wall, and he let it hold him up until he could see clearly again.

They stood together, not touching but close, the bastard and Niall's shameless, half-human sister. Athena's hair was half loose about her shoulders like that of a cheap Cherry Creek slut, her lips bruised with kissing. Morgan . . .

Morgan stood in front of her, head lowered, shoulders hunched like a bear ready to charge. Coarse black hair fell in his eyes, giving him the look of a madman. His lip and nose bled where Niall had struck true, but he hardly seemed aware of the injuries. An almost inaudible growl rumbled from his throat.

He was an animal. Worse than an animal. Niall thought of the rifle downstairs—his father's, hung on the wall when Walter Munroe first took up with Gwenyth Desbois, and never used again. Father had abandoned hunting for pleasure because of that woman. But the rifle was still there.

The door was close. All he had to do was avoid provoking an attack. He took a step backward.

"Niall," Athena said. She moved one of her feet, sliding

it across the floor. "It isn't what you think. Please, listen to me!"

He looked at her in such a way that she faltered, folding her arms across her chest as if she could ward off the contempt in his gaze.

"I am no more blind than you are lame," he said. "You are a whore, just like your mother."

He wasn't quite sure what happened then, or how it started. Morgan's teeth were the first to change. They began to lengthen, became more pointed, the incisors graced with a cutting edge like miniature daggers. Then the face . . . subtly, slowly, so gradually that Niall could not have said exactly how the transformation progressed. His stomach roiled with horror at the sight of something that God and Nature had never intended.

Skin stubbled with a day's growth of beard darkened further, taking on the rough texture of short fur. Nose blended into upper lip. Ears shifted, lengthened. The body took on proportions that mocked the human shape, pushing and pulling at the seams of Morgan's clothing.

And through it all, the eyes barely changed. They focused on Niall with all the single-minded purpose of a starving predator in sight of an easy meal.

The face of Morgan Holt was no longer that of a man. Nor was it a beast, though it most closely resembled a wolf. A wolf . . . the Wolf-Man. A legend made to frighten children and entertain jaded audiences. A creature like Athena's mother. Like Athena.

Morgan Holt's circus act was no act at all. And Niall understood everything.

In such moments—as if he were in the middle of a crucial business negotiation—Niall's mind became as sharp as the Wolf-Man's fangs. He knew that Morgan had the strength to tear him apart with little effort, and that for some reason he had not done so. He saw that Athena was moving, hobbling, setting herself between the two men as if her slight body could hold them apart.

"I will not let you hurt each other," she cried. Her voice

trembled, but it did not fail. "Now you know what Morgan is. I broke my word by coming here, but I did not lie to you. I couldn't risk telling you the full truth."

"Because I would stop you from seeing him again? From going to your . . . what is he? Your mate?" Niall laughed. "Have you been waiting for another like you to come along and take you away? Will you be the bitch to his dog, Athena?"

Morgan lunged. Athena interposed herself, almost falling, and Morgan stopped to catch her. Niall noted with icy curiosity that each of Morgan's fingers was tipped by a curved black nail, and wondered if he could speak in a human tongue.

"She has done nothing," Morgan said in a rasping voice, answering his question. "If you do not leave her alone, I will—"

"Now isn't it just like men to grunt and squabble like pigs over slops."

The voice was a little breathless, but Niall would have recognized it in a shout or a whisper. He spun toward the door. Caitlin stood at the entrance, with Harry French supporting her on one side and Ulysses Wakefield on the other. Lines of strain framed her eyes, but she was perfectly capable of impaling Niall with a look of utter scorn.

"The gallant white knight, charging up to save a lady's honor," she said, looking past him at Morgan without batting an eyelash at his grotesque appearance. "You're no better, Morgan Holt." Her eyes lit with pleasure as they found Athena. "And you. Look at you!"

"Caitlin!" Athena exclaimed. "You should not be out of bed. I . . . I am quite well. Everything is all right."

Everything was clearly not all right, but Niall knew the most dangerous moment had passed. "This is none of your business," he said, addressing French. "Get out."

Athena pulled halfway from Morgan's grip. "Harry, take her back—"

"And miss all the fun?" Caitlin leaned forward, almost

dragging the two men with her. "I think this should become one of our regular acts, don't you, Harry?"

The old man glanced in an agony of worry from one face to another. "Oh, dear. I did not know . . . I did not realize that Mr. Munroe had arrived until we heard the shouting, and Caitlin insisted—"

"It was very kind of you to come visit us," Caitlin said to Niall, smiling sweetly. "I am sorry you are so put out, Mr. Munroe, but if you insist on entering private rooms unannounced, you are bound to see things you don't like."

Niall opened his mouth to answer and was held mute by the sparkle in Caitlin's blue eyes. Dammit, how could he be thinking of her eyes at a time like this? She had always approved of Athena's attraction to Holt. Good God, *she* had probably urged Athena to abandon her principles and humanity for a night of passion in this monster's arms.

"You . . . you defend my sister giving herself to this . . ." He waved toward Morgan, sick in his gut. "You knew what he was, you and your circus freaks. And you let Athena get near him—"

"I think you'll find she has a mind of her own. Athena has known what he is since he saved her life from a runaway horse in the big top." Caitlin cocked her head. "You didn't want her near Morgan because of his act. But you couldn't have known it wasn't an act at all. You don't look like a man who's shocked by something he's never seen before."

"He isn't," Athena said quietly. She stepped away from Morgan's support and stood free on unsteady legs. "He isn't shocked because Morgan and I share the same nature. My mother . . . she was a werewolf, too."

Caitlin's eyes widened. "Of course. It explains so much—why you reacted so calmly when you saw Morgan change, and why you have been drawn to each other." She looked at Niall. "But that means that you must also be—"

"I am not," he snapped. "My mother was a normal woman. She was Walter Munroe's *wife*."

"Ah. I see." Caitlin's stare was so bleak that Niall had

difficulty in meeting it. "Athena's mother was his mistress, then."

Her frankness should not have surprised him at this late date. "It doesn't matter. She is my sister, and I promised to protect her from harm."

"And a fine job you make of it."

Seldom had Niall felt such anger. It was as if his skull were an overheated boiler, blackening his vision with scalding steam. When he looked at Caitlin, he dared not loose his rage. But Athena, and Morgan, were another matter entirely.

"I thought she needed protecting," he said, turning on his sister. "Look at her! She has been deceiving everyone, pretending helplessness to win sympathy and support for her charities . . . and for herself." He ignored Athena's horrified protest. "Did you think you could make me dance to your tune by playing the cripple, Athena? Has that been your game all along, just like . . . just like pretending you aren't exactly the same as your mother?"

Morgan snarled. Caitlin hopped forward on one leg. "And who do you take after, Niall Munroe?" she demanded. "You've never been driven by fear for your sister, have you? It's hatred—hatred of anyone different, hatred and guilt, eating you up inside because you helped put Athena in that chair. Controlling her and calling it protection is the only way to salve your guilt and cage what you don't understand!"

Her words echoed in the total silence that followed. Niall heard the accusation over and over, hating Caitlin for revealing his shame, sickened by the truth.

And she knew only half of it.

He had to get out, before he disgraced himself further. But he'd be damned if he'd leave Athena in the hands of these people, no matter what Caitlin claimed as his motive. He had never retreated from a fight without some plan for ultimate victory.

Caitlin provided the distraction he needed. As if she had used up all her strength in castigating him, she gave a soft moan and stumbled sideways. Niall stepped in and caught her before anyone else moved, steadied her, and handed her over to Holt. Morgan took her reflexively, leaving Niall free to grab Athena.

She felt almost boneless as he lifted her, and he was certain when he held her in his arms that her legs were not those of a healthy woman. They were too thin, lacking the full development of muscle. She might be able to stand, even hobble, but she was by no means recovered. Perhaps her deception hadn't been quite as heinous as he had believed.

Niall shouldered his way past Harry and the dwarf and paused in the doorway, Athena rigid in his hold. Caitlin's presence prevented Holt from following. His yellow eyes tracked Niall with an unspoken vow that the battle was far from over. The world narrowed down to the two of them, a long, red tunnel of hatred that connected them as surely as Athena bore her mother's bestial blood.

"Listen well, Morgan Holt," Niall said. "I make you a solemn promise. If you ever touch my sister again, I will kill you."

Almost tenderly, Morgan passed the half-conscious Caitlin to Harry French and started toward Niall. Athena pushed against Niall's chest, and her eyes locked with Holt's.

Niall had no explanation for what followed. Woman and beast-man gazed at each other, and it was as if yet another tunnel linked them, excluding everyone else—a tunnel made of light instead of hate. Athena smiled. She held out her hand, stopping Holt with a gesture as graceful as a dancer's.

"Please stay, Morgan," she said. "Look after Caitlin. She needs you now."

Holt blinked slowly, and the bizarre transformation that had taken him before began to reverse itself. When it was done he was human again, though the shadows under his cheekbones seemed more pronounced and pain pinched the corners of his mouth. Niall hoped that the Change had been excruciating.

He turned his back on Holt, on all of them, and carried his sister out of the jaws of hell.

Chapter 16

At *times like these, Athena thought, it would have* made perfect sense to weep. But her eyes remained stubbornly dry, though the twisting pain in her legs was a constant reminder that the worst was yet to come.

Niall all but ran down the stairs, charging blindly away from the terrible danger that existed in his mind. At the foot of the stairs he paused, irresolute, and carried her down the hall to the door of Walter Munroe's study.

The room had been closed up ever since Papa had died. It was dark inside, and smelled of mildew and old books. Athena's throat ached with the memories stacked on the shelves and in every corner.

Niall deposited her on the dusty leather-padded chair behind Papa's desk and stood back as if she might somehow corrupt him if he touched her any longer than necessary. That hurt, too, but all the hurts had blended together so that it was difficult to tell one from another.

If she had been able, she would have stood up and marched right back up the stairs to Morgan. But her legs had been pressed beyond their limits, the atrophied muscles seized with spasms, and they would not have carried her as far as the door.

"Are you happy now?" Niall demanded.

He looked drained, ill—not the vital, confident man she knew, but a stranger more terrifying than Morgan in his half-wolf shape. He had threatened to kill Morgan, and Athena believed him. He would try, at the risk of his own life, if Morgan came near her again.

Unless she could make him understand.

"I didn't lie to you about my legs, Niall," she began, gathering the words slowly. "I only just learned that I was able to stand. I didn't think it was possible. I believed the doctors, just as you did."

He flung back his head and gave a harsh laugh. "A miracle, is that it? A miracle that just happens to come when you lie with Morgan Holt?"

She let the cutting remark pass. "I know that you have felt responsible all these years. I didn't want you to. That was why I tried to make a life for myself, as much as I could, and a place in society that wasn't dependent upon you. I succeeded, Niall. But you never saw it as success."

"Is this success, Athena?" he asked. "Choosing these . . . people over the life our father worked to build for the family? Animal instinct instead of the civilized behavior my mother tried to teach you? Instinct to follow after your own kind?"

"It's what you were afraid of, wasn't it? When you learned of Morgan's act—"

"I didn't guess what he was. I only thought he would remind you of what you should forget. I hoped and prayed that your confinement and your social activities would make you give up any idea of ever . . . changing again."

"Then Caitlin was right," she said. "It was fear that made you try to protect me from the world. Fear, and guilt." She swallowed. "Did you ever love me, Niall? Or have you always hated?"

"I hated what you were. I hated Gwenyth Desbois, because of what she did to Mother."

Athena closed her eyes. "I always suspected, but . . . I tried not to believe it."

He leaned over the desk. "Do you know what life was like before that whore seduced Father . . . before she convinced him that rutting with an animal was better than staying faithful to his wife?"

"My mother . . . Morgan is not an animal," she whispered.

"I hoped you would be different. I did my best to make it so." His face was the color of chalk, or the gently falling snow beyond the windows. "I was glad when you were hurt. Glad, Athena. I could have not asked for a better way to . . . keep you from turning into something like her. But I wasn't careful enough."

She stared at him, filled with such anger and pity that no answer would come. He pushed away from the desk and walked about the study, aimlessly touching the spine of one book and then another without seeing the titles.

"You can't fight what you are," he said in a dull voice. "There is too much of that animal in you, Athena. And it's because I love you that I can't let you give in to it."

"Because you love me, or hated my mother? I know your mother was hurt, Niall. I am sorry for that. But she never loved me, either. I always sensed her resentment, even though she didn't let our father see how she felt. If Papa hadn't insisted that you and I be treated the same, I don't know what—"

"Our father." He snorted. "He doted on you. You were always special. After the whore was gone, you reminded him of her. He would have given you anything."

Athena fell back, remembering something Morgan had said not so long ago. "Did you envy me, Niall? Were you jealous that Papa could love me? Or was it because I could do things that no ordinary person could? Did you want to be like me?"

He laughed. "The very idea disgusts me. I could never understand how our father could touch that woman. But I thought you should be considered innocent of her stain, because you didn't choose to be born. Now you have to choose." He faced her again, haggard and wan. "You boasted of the life you've made, all the people you have helped. Everyone in society respects you. That life must be important to you, Athena. Now you will have to decide how important it is."

A dreadful foreboding spilled like acid into Athena's stomach. Cramps seized her thighs, and she fought down a cry. She could not be weak, not now.

"You pride yourself on being unselfish, don't you?" he said, taunting her like the cruel stranger he had become. "Athena Munroe never thinks of herself. She is the most generous, the most noble lady in Denver. So noble that she will sacrifice what she wants for the sake of others." He sat on the edge of the desk, one leg swinging as if they were having a friendly chat. "I have a proposition for you, dear sister. I could send the circus away, as soon as the weather clears—pay them for the one performance and nothing more. Your Caitlin seems able to walk, so there's no further need to pamper her."

"Caitlin—"

"Be quiet, unless you wish me to throw them all out in the snow right now." He studied his manicured fingers. "I can make them leave, and I can tell the sheriff that they've abused our hospitality and stolen property from Long Park—you can be sure I'd be believed where people like them are concerned. Just as decent folk will believe that you were seduced by the confidence games of Harry French and his followers."

"You would lie—"

"I'd do more than lie. I learned many tricks running our father's businesses. It would be easy to make sure the circus can never return to Colorado. They might have to travel some distance to find winter quarters, with the weather getting bad."

Athena shook her head, but he went on relentlessly. "That's not all, Athena. I still have control of your bank accounts. Our father left it to my judgment when I should let you have charge of them. I don't think you'll ever be ready to manage your own inheritance . . . unless you prove to me that you can live the quiet, reasonable life of any decent woman."

Athena saw where he was leading. "Niall, you can't punish innocent people because of what I—"

"So many depend on your charities," he went on, ignoring her. "All those young mothers. The orphans. The unemployed men. What would they do if your contributions were suddenly cut off? Oh, you've talked plenty of others into giving, but a word in the ears of husbands and fathers would stop up that source as well. You know the women, but I know the men. They'd be glad not to have the burden of philanthropic obligations." He sighed. "And then there's your famous Winter Ball. Less than two weeks away now, isn't it? Everyone will be there, ready to compliment you on your fine work. It would be a shame if you were unable to continue with it, and someone else took the credit."

The ball, which Athena had left in Cecily's hands, expecting to return well before the date. The ball that she had schemed and struggled to make the finest charity event of the year, the pinnacle of all her efforts, the defining element of her place in Denver society.

And Niall meant to take it from her. She did not doubt that he could. Cecily was enamored of him; if it came down to it, wouldn't Cecily choose obedience to his will over friendship for Athena?

A small, cold hand gripped her heart. How had Niall known to come here? It was no accident. Athena had trusted Cecily to keep her secret, but she had expected to return to Denver before Niall did. If Niall had discovered his sister's absence and confronted Cecily, how would it benefit her to defy the man she wanted? And she had not *promised* to help. She had said she would "do all I can."

Niall knew exactly how to strike at his sister. All these years Athena had thought him oblivious to her work, but now she saw her error. Either he or someone else had been watching very carefully.

"Miss Hockensmith—Cecily—warned me months ago that you were taking on too much," Niall said. "It is perfectly natural that you should be relieved of your burdens and given a chance to . . . recuperate in another city, perhaps with our cousins in New York. As for Holt—I meant what I said. If he comes near you again, I will kill him. Even creatures like him can be killed, one way or another."

The full weight of Niall's threats pushed Athena deep into the chair, paralyzing her will as the accident had stilled her legs. She could see no way out. If she defied Niall, she would lose everything—all she had worked for, the funding for her charities, the ball, her place in Denver . . . and Morgan's life as well.

"You think you would be happy with Holt," Niall said. "You must decide whether you'll be happier with him, living as a vagabond and an animal, or among civilized people in your family home, surrounded by your friends and equals and able to help the less fortunate to your heart's content."

He was silent after that. Athena could hear the ticking of a clock somewhere in the house, the creak of footfalls upstairs, whispered voices in the hall, but Morgan's voice was not among them.

She let out a shuddering breath. "I need time . . . time to think about what you have said," she whispered. "Niall, if you would only listen—"

"I've done enough of that. You lied to me, Athena, when you promised to remain in Denver if the circus came to the ranch. I can't trust you again. If you expect to keep anything of the life you made in Denver—if you have your friends' welfare at heart—you will have to submit yourself to me and do exactly as I tell you. Any deviation—" He shrugged. "I can impose punishment at any time."

Which meant that she would live with an impediment more sure than the one that had immobilized her legs for so many years. He could command her life completely, and she had no means of stopping him. Even if she found the courage to Change again, it would be at too great a cost.

"Now you can play the martyr with true sincerity," he said, driving the nails deeper. "Your wicked half brother will keep you prisoner in the dark castle. But you will still have everything you always did, Athena—and you'll be safe."

She had enough determination left to sit up straight and look him in the eye. "Let me be sure that we understand one another. In exchange for my . . . cooperation . . . you will allow the circus to remain for the winter, unmolested, only to depart when the passes clear in spring. You will not interfere, in any way, with my charities, and will continue to provide the funds I require to properly maintain them. You will leave Morgan alone."

"If you never contact him, and he stays away."

Why was it that Niall's betrayal struck most piercingly in that personal case, instead of in the matter of the charities and the circus quarters? Was she truly as selfish as he implied, to consider her happiness . . . this fragile new happiness she had hardly dared to imagine . . . over the welfare of others?

But she had presumed too much without consulting Morgan. Perhaps he would not regard this as a sacrifice at all. She had decided, in a moment of passion, that she loved Morgan Holt. But he, and his deepest desires, remained a mystery.

Niall assumed she wanted a life with Morgan. A *life*. What did that mean? What would Morgan say if she were to propose such a thing, out of the blue, without a single sensible plan? Would the future she envisioned have anything to do with the one he saw for himself?

Would you ever be brave enough to ask him? Would he ever ask you?

"I agree," she said, letting the words tear out of her in a rush before she could consider the damage they did. "I accept your conditions."

"I knew you had not lost all your sense, Athena, or your pride." Niall hesitated. "Did Holt . . . did he—"

"He did not ruin me, Niall. But it wouldn't matter if he did, because I will not be saving myself for anyone else, will I?"

He had no answer for her bitterness. Now that he had won, he almost seemed ashamed. But the moment passed. He got up from the desk.

"I'll have one of the maids see to your things. You will sleep in my room tonight, and I'll stay in the parlor. We will return to Denver as soon as possible." He left the room for a moment, doubtless to make sure the way was clear, and returned to lift her up again. She lay passively in his arms while he carried her back upstairs and left her on the plain, masculine bed in his room, locking the door behind him.

The day dragged by. A muffling snow fell outside, creating a womb of white that cast unreality on everything that had happened. Athena tried not to hear the sounds around the house, or listen for Morgan's voice. No one came to see her save a maid, with her bags and fresh linens and water. The maid helped her dress—a belated attempt to restore her dignity—and then Athena sat in the plain oak chair in a corner and let her mind go blank.

Night fell. The maid brought her dinner on a tray, and she ignored it. After ten, she heard the unmistakable wail of a wolf's howl within the ranch boundaries. Her heart clenched.

Morgan. Was he trying to speak to her? Thank heaven he hadn't come to her. Maybe she had been right. Maybe he was relieved at the separation, or the others had wisely talked him out of further confrontation.

She wished she had the ability to howl back with the eloquence of his powerful voice.

Stay away, Morgan. Please, stay away.

She drifted into a half sleep. Her chin bounced on her chest, and she woke with a start. Someone was outside the window. Her senses told her that it was after midnight.

Knowing what she would find, she gritted her teeth and planted her feet on the floor. Pain spiked from heel to knee. She hobbled to the window and pushed back the curtains.

A black wolf stood hock-deep in snow, gazing up at the window. Frosted breath rose in a cloud from his muzzle. She had seen him as a wolf twice before . . . when he had saved her, and in her dream . . . but now she realized the full measure of his magnificence. No ordinary wolf had ever been so big, so thick of coat, so brilliant of eye. Love became a knot in her chest, struggling to untwine.

He loped toward the wall. Athena lifted the sash on the window. She lost her balance, grabbed at the nearest furniture, and made her way to the chair. Even if her legs had been whole and strong, they would not have held her now.

Morgan made no sound as he scaled the wall. A silhouette darkened the gray square of moonlight. Athena felt a chill of memory, as if she were reliving the past a second time—the night that Morgan had come to her room in the Denver mansion. Once more he had found his way to her in spite of all obstacles.

And she had nothing to give him.

The window creaked as it opened wider, just big enough to admit a man. Morgan's dark, human head appeared in the room, framed by his mane of damp hair. He balanced on the sill and leaped to the floor.

It took her an instant to realize that he was naked. He straightened. She stared. She wished she had drunk some of the water the maid had brought, for her mouth was dry as cotton.

She had seen him naked before, in the big top, but not so close. Every proportion, every line of his body was perfect—not too large or muscle-bound, not too slight, but ideally suited for a life of running and hunting, jumping and adapting to the wild in all its harshness and beauty. Comparing him to a statue was far too inadequate. His chest was lightly dusted with dark hair that ran in an arrow to the base of his stomach. She dared not look there. Yet.

"How . . . how is Caitlin?" she asked.

"Resting." He shook his head, as if to cast off all outside distractions. "Did Niall hurt you?"

In his voice was a promise of what he would do if she answered in the affirmative. "He is my brother," she whispered. "He does . . . what he thinks is best for me."

"Do you still believe that?"

The clean, snow-kissed, masculine scent of him displaced all the air in the room. She could hear the sound of his pulse, just below the skin at the base of his neck where it met his broad shoulders. And below . . . all the way past the slender firmness of his waist and hips . . . he was vibrantly alive. Alive and wanting her.

"Niall is human," she said, listening to the sound of her voice as if it belonged to another woman. "How can he understand?"

"Understand what? That you cannot be collared like a dog? That he does not own you?"

His contempt might as well have been aimed at her. He expected her to spurn the world she had always known, pretend it didn't matter. In that she had failed. Failed his expectation, failed herself, and failed him.

She would have preferred any other way, any other time and place, to tell him. But there was no escaping it. He would stand there, naked to her eyes, his body fluent as his tongue was not, and hear her make her choice.

Feel nothing. Cut off your senses. Pretend you have no need, no wanting, no heart.

"Morgan," she said, "I am going with Niall, back to Denver. I will never see you again."

Morgan heard the words. They were clear, precise, dispassionate, as if Athena were reciting a lesson from the *McGuffey's Reader* Morgan remembered from childhood.

He heard the words, but they made no sense. The only thing that did was the clamoring of his body, the hot yearning for Athena, the need to finish what he had begun in her room. Finish it completely, and to hell with Niall Munroe and all the scruples of human society.

She sat there, so prim in her gown buttoned up to the

neck, hands clasped in her lap. He might have been a supplicant before a queen, as he had once thought of the society women who fluttered about her chair.

But she had not been a queen when he had caressed her. She had been helpless with need, prepared to surrender everything . . . yes, even the maidenhood her kind valued so highly. If he had chosen to take it. But he had been undecided, torn between his desire and freedom, between the life he thought he wanted and the bonds her surrender would wind about his neck.

If he listened to his body now, the decision was simple. If Athena made a single welcoming gesture, gave him one sweet look of yearning . . .

"I am going with Niall," she had said. *"I will never see you again."*

Stupid words. Meaningless, born of habitual fear of her brother, the habit of obedience. And fear, too, of him and what he made her become.

Very well. *He* would decide, here and now. Every instant they had spent together, every memory of her when they were apart, led to this.

He held out his hand. "Come," he said. "We will leave now. Tonight. Your brother will never find us."

She stared at his hand. "What?"

"Put away your fear." He took a step toward her. "You are not a human. You will heal quickly, now that you know your injuries are in your mind and not your body. Soon you will be able to run. And before that—now—you can Change."

Stark terror crossed her face. "Change . . . I . . . No, Morgan. It's been too long—"

"Stop." He stared down at her, willing her all the courage he knew she had. "Stop believing what you can't do. Believe in what you are. Take off your clothes and come with me."

As quickly as it had come, her fear was gone. "Come where, Morgan?"

Her question sent ice trickling down the length of his

spine. He had asked her to come with him. To become—yes, to become his mate, to remain with him until death. He had offered to another person the thing he had thought long dead in himself. And she asked "where."

"With me," he said. "Into the woods. The mountains. We'll run, you and I, as we did in dreams. We will hunt and breathe clean air and drink water that has never tasted the metal of man. You will be free, Athena."

"Free?" She dropped her head, and her shoulders rose and fell in a shudder. "What is freedom?"

He heard the tears in her voice and closed the space between them, reached for her, clasped her shoulder and felt it tense in his gentle grip.

"You created your own cage, and let your brother make the bars too strong to break," he said. "But I can break them. I will teach you everything you need to know. I will protect you until you can protect yourself. I will never leave your side."

He lifted her chin. Tears hung like stars on her cheeks. He bent and kissed them, one side and then the other, tasting the salt and Athena. Then he crouched, took her face between his hands, and kissed her lips.

She responded as she had in her room, passionately, with a new edge of violence that excited and almost frightened him. It was the she-wolf in her, coming alive at his touch, waiting for a final word to burst forth and make her all she was meant to be. Her fingers caught in his hair, pulled and wound about, crushing him against her.

Then she pushed him away and let her arms fall limp. "I cannot come with you."

He heard her this time, but he refused to believe. "Athena—"

"I can't, Morgan. I can't live in the way you want, in the wild, apart from people and society." There were no tears now, no passion. "I am not like you. I have become . . . used to my life. I have responsibilities. I try to help people, and if I were to vanish . . . who would help them in my place?"

He stepped back, searching her eyes. The she-wolf had disappeared. This was the haughty, closed-in woman he had first met on the circus lot, the one who had been so scrupulously fair and polite to her inferiors. To him.

"You think they need you," he said, cruel in his anger. "They need your money. How many others in your city have money to give?"

"You don't understand. Not everyone is generous—"

"As fine and generous as you?"

"No." She warded him away, turning her face. "But I have the time and the inclination to work. I have . . . a place, a role that others accept. Others who might not give if I were not there to ask."

"Even though you are no longer a cripple?"

"I am the same, inside. The things that mattered to me . . . before . . . they still matter now. My friends are still my friends."

"And Caitlin? Harry, Ulysses? They are not?"

She stared fixedly at the far wall. "I care for them. For . . . But they are part of a different world, as I am a part of mine. And yours is different from both. Too different, Morgan. Can't you see that . . . we are simply . . . too different?"

"That is not the reason," he said. He grasped the top of the chair and pulled it around, forcing her to look at him. "It's still your fear. You do not want to give up the fancy house and the fine clothes and the people who lick your jaw like hungry pups, because that is all you know how to be. You like the power of giving people what they need when they have nothing. Making them beg—"

"*No.* I have never made anyone beg, for anything."

"Haven't you? What do those poor folk see when they look at you with your fine ways, and know that you can give or take what they need? Do they hate you while they pretend to offer their throats? All those fine ladies who follow you—what do you give them, Athena? A reason to think they are fine and noble people because they help the poor crippled girl help the ones they never see?"

The stark pain in her eyes stopped him cold. He knew he had hurt her, that he had come very close to a truth he hardly fathomed himself.

"Athena," he groaned. "I do not want to . . . Damn you, listen to me. You have a chance to be strong, not to need anyone." He fumbled to put his confused feelings into words. "When you don't need, you can give freely. When you don't care what those others think of you, you can make your own place. Your real place. Don't you understand?"

She stared at him, and he thought he saw the beginnings of comprehension before she shut him out again.

"Do you know your own place, Morgan?" she said. "Do you know what you want out of life? Have you ever thought beyond the next hour?" She smiled with weary resignation. "You can cast off all your ties. I can't. I can't. But—" She closed her eyes. "You . . . you could come with me."

He held very still. "With you?"

"To Denver. Not right away. After . . . after I've had time to make Niall understand, when he has overcome his anger."

She did not elaborate. She didn't have to. He saw what she meant in those few words, and terror clawed its way up from his belly to fill his mouth and his brain.

"Come with you?" he said in a mocking echo. "Join you in your cage? Live in your fine house and wear your fine clothes and become a lapdog for your ladies?"

"Isn't it what you asked me to do . . . give up everything?" She didn't look at him. He was cold, bitterly cold, though the winter wind should not have affected him at all. Athena was sucking all the heat from his body, all the tenuous hopes from his heart, all the foolish dreams from the future he had never considered.

Just like before. Just as it always was and would ever be.

He backed toward the window. "I ask you for nothing," he said. "I want nothing from you, or anyone."

She made no attempt to stop him as he reached the window and gathered his muscles to jump. The eagerness of his body had drowned in sorrow and rage and bewilderment; he could look at her and see a stranger, an enemy, and not the woman he had asked to become the mate of his life.

Let her look at him, one last time. Let her know what she had rejected. Let her feel what he felt.

"Go," he said. "Go with your brother. Cripple yourself again, and pray that all your fine things will make you forget what you have thrown away."

Her eyes met his, moist and expressionless. He leaped up and back, balanced on the sill, and let himself fall from the window.

Snow cushioned his landing, but he welcomed the jarring blow that rattled his bones and shook the despair loose from his head. Barely pausing, he Changed and began to run as hard and as fast as he could, away from the room and the ranch and Athena.

It was a strange thing, that he returned. He dragged himself back to the barn to dress just before dawn, aware that the snow had started again and boded a storm for the day ahead. A storm that might trap anyone—any human—who desired to leave the mountains.

A wolf could leave any time. That was what kept Morgan circling the house like a whipped cur, until Harry stepped out one of the side doors shortly after sunrise and blew a puff of pipe smoke into the expectant air.

Harry was looking for something. Someone. Morgan knew what he hoped to see, and what the others must think. He would make sure they knew how wrong they were.

Morgan Changed in the barn, pulled on his clothes and stalked up to the porch. Harry started slightly when he saw Morgan, and then his shoulders fell.

"It looks like snow," he remarked as Morgan joined him. "Bad weather. I feel it in my bones."

"A storm." Morgan willed the hair to lie flat against his neck. "You don't have to worry. You are safe here."

"Are we staying?"

"Athena would not let Munroe drive you out," he said bitterly. "She cares too much about . . . helping."

Harry glanced at him. "Morgan, I am sorry. I wish I could have done something to intervene. We all do. We've known . . . almost from the beginning how the girl felt about you, and you her." He coughed behind his hand. "I'm a meddling old fool. I made her come here, with my letters, when I should have stayed out of your business. But all we want . . . all *I* want, is your happiness. Yours and Athena's." He blinked several times. "I know you well enough—I presume to know—that what you want to do now is run off. Permanently. But—"

He took a long breath and faced Morgan. "I ask you to trust me, Morgan. Trust me, as you would your own kin. You're like a son to me, even though . . . though I'm a poor excuse for a father. Even so, as a father I advise you to wait. Be patient. Stay a little longer. Whatever obstacles may stand before you now, they can be overcome."

Morgan swallowed and looked toward the mountains. Harry reached out a hand, hesitated, and let it come to rest on Morgan's shoulder. It felt curious, that touch, after Athena's. Too close, too intimate, like that of kin. Family.

A father's touch.

"You do not want to be my father," he said, holding absolutely still, afraid of his own terror. "Do you know what happened to my real father, Harry?" He lifted his hands. "I killed him. I killed him with these two hands."

Chapter 17

"I don't believe it," Caitlin said. "Not for a moment."
Ulysses looked at her gravely and met Harry's gaze.
They sat, the three of them, in Caitlin's room while the
storm raged through its third day outside the sturdy walls
of the ranch house. The wind howled no more fiercely than
Morgan had done every night since Niall's arrival. No one
had seen Morgan since Harry's brief conversation with
him, but he had not gone. The howls proved as much.

Caitlin knew that Harry had waited to tell her and
Ulysses Morgan's terrible revelation, working himself into
a dither over how much to share. In the end, he had been
unable to keep it to himself. It was not in his nature to suffer alone, or let others suffer likewise. His heart was too
big to hide in a corner.

All the troupers had been hiding, in one way or another,
while Niall remained at Long Park. He avoided them, and
Athena kept to her room—Niall's room, given to her after
the incident with Morgan—but the atmosphere felt as poisonous as the smoke belching from one of those horrid
Denver smelters. Ulysses had learned, from listening to
maids who hardly noticed his existence, that Athena was to

return to Denver with Niall as soon as the weather permitted. She was not to see Morgan again, and she was to keep apart from the circus folk.

A devil's bargain, Caitlin thought. Niall had demanded her obedience in exchange for the safety of the circus—and perhaps of the man she loved. That she loved Morgan, Caitlin had no doubt. Just as she knew Morgan could not live without her.

"No," she repeated firmly. "Morgan could not have killed his own father. Didn't he say anything else, Harry?"

The old man's face sagged as if he had lost several pounds in as many days. "No. He left me with that, and walked away. As if he . . . wanted me to think the worst."

"He lives under the weight of an intolerable burden," Ulysses said quietly. "Intolerable enough to make him avoid the company of other people—as you observed yourself many times, Firefly. He punishes himself."

"For murder?" Caitlin snorted. "No. There must be much more to the story. Did he talk to you, Uly? You must tell us."

Ulysses only looked away, avoiding the question. Caitlin longed to shake him. "You're hiding something, I know it. But I also know Morgan is not a killer. I would feel it if he were."

"There are times when feelings are inadequate."

"And sometimes they are all we have," Harry said. "If he had something to do with his father's death, there must have been a very good reason."

"I agree," Uly said. "But I am at a loss as to how to assist him."

"The help he needs most is with Athena—and Niall," Caitlin said.

"Interference now might make matters worse," Uly said. "Morgan must recognize the danger of confronting Munroe directly."

"And what of you, Firefly?" Harry asked gently.

She knew what he was asking but chose to pretend otherwise. "I know there must be a way of thwarting Niall," she said. "He needs to be distracted until Athena finds a means of outwitting him. With a little encouragement . . ."

"I don't like the look on your face, Firefly," Harry said.

"Niall is as dangerous as Morgan," Ulysses cautioned. "You have seen that for yourself."

"And you've repeatedly warned me to take care, like an old grandmother," Caitlin said with a laugh. "Did you think I really swooned up in Athena's room?"

Ulysses and Morgan exchanged glances. Harry assumed a stern expression ill-suited to his jolly St. Nicholas features.

"We are here on Munroe's sufferance," he said. "Athena would never allow any harm to come to us, but if she chooses to defy her brother, he may eject us forthwith." He met Caitlin's eyes. "I won't see us cast out, Firefly, as long as we are capable of leaving of our own free will. Nor will I allow you to place yourself in jeopardy, of body or of soul. I will give orders for the troupers to prepare to depart as soon as the storm passes."

"You don't mean it, Harry. It's almost winter. We can't travel now—and you want to see Athena and Morgan together just as much as I do."

"Yes. But I have witnessed the consequences of our meddling, and I feel—" He blinked, giving the impression of a slightly befuddled owl. "I feel in my bones that we must go."

"Is this because of what Morgan said?"

"I fear what he will do if he is driven too far," Harry admitted. "I'll try to persuade him to come with us. Then, when everything is calm again, he may return."

Caitlin studied Harry with growing trepidation. She had never seen him look so grave, or so determined. Did he truly believe that she would get herself, or the troupe, into a predicament she couldn't climb out of?

"You're wrong, Harry," she said. "No good will come of running away now."

"I have made my decision." He got to his feet and started toward the door. "I shall tell the others to begin preparations, and we will leave at the first sign of clear weather."

When Harry was gone, Caitlin looked at Ulysses. "You agree with him, don't you?"

"I would make any personal sacrifice on Morgan's behalf," he said. "I would assist Miss Munroe if I were able. But it is my considered judgment that the welfare of the troupe must take precedence over that of Athena and Morgan. They must make their own choices." He paused. "I am sorry, Caitlin."

She saw that arguing with him was as futile as it would have been with Harry. Men could be so stubborn once they had an idea in their heads, no matter how wrong it was. She'd thought that Harry followed his heart more than most, but even he fell prey to the idea that money meant power, and women had to be protected from their own foolish notions.

She lay in bed, fuming silently, for a good hour after Ulysses left. The troupe must not leave until the business with Athena and Morgan was resolved. She had taken great pains to throw them together, and she'd be damned if she'd let Niall Munroe ruin her plans.

The storm might pass at any moment, but it would take several days for the troupe to prepare to move. Even in fair weather, the snow would impede progress and make the pass difficult to negotiate. That gave her a little more time.

If Harry and Ulysses feared some rash action on her part . . . well, she would make very certain not to disappoint them.

"A letter has just arrived, Miss Hockensmith," Parton said, presenting the paper on a silver tray with a little bow. "It was marked urgent."

Cecily paused to accept the envelope, listening to make sure that the ladies assembled in her parlor were still engaged in conversation. When Parton had gone to retrieve more refreshments for her influential guests, she examined the return address with an eager smile.

It was marked from Yankee Gulch, the only substantial town nearest Niall's ranch. Her hope that the letter might be from Niall was all too quickly dashed. The spidery writing was definitely not his, nor did it belong to Athena.

Niall had been gone several days, doubtless due to the bad weather blanketing the mountains. She had been glad for the respite. With the Winter Ball only days away, nothing could interfere with the social coup she was about to achieve.

She frowned at the envelope and turned it over in her hands. If it was not from Niall or Athena . . .

She began to read, wrinkling her nose at the highly spiced scent of the paper, and nearly dropped it.

You promised to help me, it became without salutation, *if I aided you in keeping Munroe and our Caitlin apart. I gave you information that you were to use to control the girl and influence your lover. But now you must know that he is here, with Caitlin, as Athena is with my wolf.*

Cecily held the letter by her fingertips, wishing she could burn it immediately. She did not have to read the scrawled name at the bottom of the letter to know who had sent it.

Tamar. Tamar, that horrid snake-woman with her veiled threats and promises, whom Cecily had hoped she would never hear from again. She had not even guessed the gypsy could read, let alone write.

Your brother intends to make Athena return to Denver, the letter went on, *but Morgan remains under her spell. She is now able to stand and walk, which removes an obstacle between them. Morgan may attempt to follow. I have spoken to Harry French and convinced him that our Caitlin will put herself in danger by pursuing your brother and trying to meddle in Athena's affairs. He has agreed that we must leave this place. We will be departing when weather permits. But if Morgan does not come with us, you must make sure that Athena is made to wish never to see him again.*

I know that Morgan was sent to prison for the crime of killing his own father. You must learn the truth of these matters swiftly, so that when Athena returns you may tell her what breed of man her lover is. When she turns against him, he will come to me. Do not fail.

Cecily crumpled the paper in her fist, her mind racing with the information Tamar had imparted. So Niall had seen Caitlin, had he? And the girl was still pursuing him, in spite of her supposed injury?

And Morgan Holt was a convict. A patricide. Cecily smiled with satisfaction. She was not surprised, for it fully justified her complete dislike of the man and his cohorts. A crime of that kind could not easily be forgiven. Even Athena would quail and shudder at such knowledge, especially when she had so adored her own father.

And she was able to walk! Cecily's smile soured. It had occurred to her, once or twice, that Athena's lameness might be a ploy to win the sympathy of society and support for her causes. Certainly many of the ladies would not have been so generous had she not been a cripple, and thus worthy of pity herself.

Had "love" transformed Athena, or had she decided she wanted something more than what had contented her in the past? Niall would not be so cursed protective if his sister could walk. But the girl might prove much more troublesome and difficult to influence. She might even fight for the position Cecily was stealing from her.

Cecily shoved the letter into a fold of her skirt and walked slowly toward the parlor. Tamar claimed that Cecily owed her, but Cecily recognized no such debt. Indeed, if she chose she could simply ignore the information about Morgan and allow matters to take whatever course fate decreed. If the foolish child fell into the hands of a convicted murderer and ran off with him, why that was of no consequence as long as Cecily had Niall's devotion and he did not suspect her of any personal involvement. Why should he? Athena would be out of the way once and for all, ruined in society.

On the other hand, if Cecily were to confirm Tamar's information and report it to Niall, he would have even more reason to be grateful to her for alerting him.

Yes. Cecily paused at the doorway to the parlor, listening to Mrs. Merriwether's lavish expressions of anticipation for the ball to come. She would take great personal delight in exposing Morgan Holt to Niall, Athena, and the world. That would put an end to his contemptuous looks and loutish disrespect for his betters. All she need do was make a few discreet inquiries—her father certainly knew the right people, now that he was in partnership with Niall—and she could learn everything necessary to shatter Athena's puerile hopes of romance.

Smoothing her skirts, Cecily sailed into the parlor and graciously accepted the homage of her new and most devoted courtiers.

F*our days after Niall's disastrous arrival, the snow* stopped falling. That same morning, just after dawn, he bundled Athena into the ranch's heavy drag and ordered the driver to take them to Denver.

Athena had nothing to say to Niall, and he maintained the same grim silence. She stared out the window and looked for Morgan, tormenting herself with the thought that she would never see him again. Once, near the edge of the park, she heard a wolf howl. That was all.

She had known that Morgan would refuse her invitation to return with her. She had known that she risked nothing in asking him, that there was no question of breaking her bargain with Niall.

She could have told him all her reasons for declining his offer to take her with him. But when he had made his accusations, pride had left her mute. Let him believe such things of her. Let him go back to his wild life and freedom.

She did not let Niall see her weep.

Passage through the mountains was difficult because of the depth of the snow, and they stopped to change horses and stay overnight in a hotel in Golden. By the time they reached Denver on the evening of the second day, Athena had made herself numb to all feeling.

Cecily was at the house to greet them as if she had known exactly when they would arrive, and instructed Brinkley to see to their comfort with presumptuous confidence. Once they were settled in the sitting room, she fawned over Niall—elegantly, of course—and acknowledged Athena with a brief nod. She did not mention the ball, though it was only four days away.

Athena hadn't the heart to ask. For the first time she saw something in the older woman she neither liked nor understood. She had assumed that Cecily was her friend and confidante, but Niall had said she'd warned him about Athena "taking on too much" some time before. How long had Cecily been talking behind her back? Did she see Athena as a hindrance to her social ambitions—the crippled sister who would only be in the way?

Athena had misjudged so many people. Could she have been so wrong about Cecily's friendship? And if she had been wrong about that, how much else had she also misjudged? How would her society friends respond to her ability to walk again? Would they be happy for her? Would they welcome her as an active, mobile member of their elite circle?

She had always been safe in the assumption that she was one of them, regardless of her inability to shop or take luncheon at the Windsor or waltz at a dance. Not merely one of them, but a leader, an impeccable hostess able to persuade the wealthiest Denverites to attend her gatherings, join her charitable societies, and donate liberally to her causes.

She should have been eager to resume her work and her place as founder of one the grandest balls of the year. Yet all the things that had once seemed so important had become more duty than pleasure, responsibilities that must be seen to no matter how much she wished she could crawl into a cave and hibernate until the heartache had passed.

Morgan had become a part of her. It was more than love, more than any longing she had ever suffered. She could almost feel him across the miles, sense his anger and confusion and pain, as if their very emotions had merged into one. One heart, one being, one soul. A soul denied any hope of solace.

Niall's raised voice drew her out of the pit into which she had fallen. He was still speaking to Cecily, and his expression told Athena that he had heard some news he did not like. He looked up and stared at her as if she were Morgan himself.

"Niall? What is it?"

He jerked his head aside and gave Cecily a terse command. She nodded, glanced at Athena with a too-blank expression, and left the room.

"I am returning to Long Park at once," he said, as soon as they were alone. "You will remain here in Cecily's care. I have asked her to make certain that you are confined to the house this time, and will instruct the servants accordingly. Remember that if you break your promise—"

"Returning?" She gripped the armrests of her chair so hard that her fingers ached. "Why? I have done what you asked—"

"You do not need to know my reasons. Do as Miss Hockensmith tells you—she has the wisdom and experience you so obviously lack—and I may explain when I come back to Denver."

"No." She tensed the muscles in her legs, preparing to face him on her feet. "That is not good enough, Niall. Your reasons may have bearing on our agreement, and that gives me the right to know."

Never before had he looked so ready to strike her. She refused to retreat. After a moment he drew back, fists balled at his sides.

"I will leave it to Miss Hockensmith to explain," he

said. "Perhaps you will hear from her what you would not accept from me."

Before she could protest, he turned on his heel and strode into the hall. Brinkley appeared with a tray of hot tea, set it down on the table beside her, and gave her a glance of such sympathy that she wondered what he knew. But he, too, fled just as she gathered the words to ask. She was forced to wait, needles of pain stabbing into her legs, while Niall made preparations to leave and Cecily spoke to him in the hall.

An hour before midnight, just as the long-case clock struck like a portent of doom, Niall put on his coat and left the house. Only something terrible would drive him out at such an hour, when the darkness would impede travel into the mountains. What could be so urgent?

Cecily knew. She had been harbinger of the mysterious bad tidings. She had broken Athena's confidence. She was to be Athena's official jailer, at Niall's behest. Athena meant to get an explanation, even if it meant assuming that Cecily was her adversary . . . or her enemy.

Gritting her teeth against the discomfort, Athena pushed herself up and focused her attention on getting to the sitting room door, one shuffling step at a time. Once there, she caught her breath, renewed her courage, and compelled her trembling legs to bear her just a little farther.

Brinkley caught sight of her at the end of the hall, stopped in amazement, and rushed up to support her. She leaned on his arm with some gratitude. If it was not her imagination, her legs were getting stronger . . . but they were not yet strong enough for the tasks she might have to ask of them.

"Thank you, Brinkley," she said. "Please take me to Miss Hockensmith."

His usually stolid face showed a flicker of emotion, and she knew she had not misinterpreted it. "You don't like Miss Hockensmith, Brinkley?"

"I beg your pardon, Miss Munroe. It isn't my place to like or dislike the lady."

"But you do have an opinion."

He assumed a carefully neutral expression and guided her down the hall toward the library. "Miss Hockensmith seems very free about the house, Miss Munroe. I think—" He hesitated.

"Go on." She pulled him to a stop. "I need to know what I am up against, and you may be able to tell me."

His mouth tightened. "I believe Miss Hockensmith sees herself as mistress here, very soon."

Well, that was certainly no surprise. Athena started to move again, anger lending new energy to her muscles. "Thank you for being frank, Brinkley. Will you speak honestly to me if I ask again?"

He looked down at her gravely. "Miss Munroe—we—the staff hope the best for you. Now that you can walk . . . perhaps things will be different."

Different. How had the servants perceived life in the Munroe house? Had they considered it a burden to wait upon her? She had tried to be fair in her running of the household, but Niall was, at best, brusque with the staff and treated them rather like machines. Brinkley's admission made clear that he did not want Cecily Hockensmith as mistress of the house.

But she would be that, if she married Niall. And suddenly Athena recognized what she had so avoided acknowledging until now—that the life she had returned to would be forever changed if Cecily became Mrs. Munroe. Cecily would arrange the house as she saw fit, give the orders, and take her place above Athena in the scheme of home life.

A great chasm seemed to open under Athena's unsteady feet. Of course she should have known that everything must alter when Niall married. She had wanted him to concentrate on someone other than herself. She wanted him to be happy. But his happiness meant that she must either live as a dependent in the house she had managed, or strike out on her own.

That had ceased to be impossible. She could walk. She

was getting stronger. But this was the home she had loved, had made the perfect refuge from the world outside. Every detail had been refined to her specifications. It was her sanctuary, and she had seldom felt any desire to leave it.

Yet, when she had gone to Long Park, it had been a break with the past she had not recognized for the profound event it had become. She had ventured far, not only in miles but in spirit. She had not returned unchanged.

The Athena-that-was and the Athena of today were sisters, but they were no longer identical. One had been content in a life of service, of holding a secure place in society, even if that place was one of confinement and few surprises. She had believed that correcting social injustice was the only worthy undertaking for one such as herself. One who had nothing else to contribute.

The new Athena had lost that contentment and sense of purpose. She didn't know who she was, or what she was capable of. But the wolf could not go back in her cage.

Heaven help her. It was the wolf who hated Niall and suspected Cecily of the basest duplicity. It was the wolf who made her question all the truths she had lived by, who spurned the sacrifices she had made, who tore her apart inside with claws of steel.

And it was the wolf who howled that she would always be alone.

Alone. It is Morgan or nothing. There will be no other.

"Miss Munroe? Are you ill?"

She opened her eyes at Brinkley's voice and saw that they had somehow reached the end of the hall. "I am sorry, Brinkley. Is Miss Hockensmith in the library?"

"Yes. Do you wish me to remain nearby, Miss Munroe?"

"I'll be all right. Thank you, Brinkley."

He escorted her to the library door, and she released his arm to demonstrate that she could negotiate the short remaining distance on her own. He lingered until she had stepped into the room, and quietly shut the door behind her.

Cecily was seated in Niall's substantial leather chair behind his mahogany desk, leaning back in a most unladylike pose as if she had a perfect right to claim anything that was his.

"It is time you told me why Niall left so quickly after you spoke to him," Athena said.

Cecily bolted upright in the chair and looked genuinely astonished, as if she had expected Athena to remain meekly in the sitting room until the servants escorted her upstairs to bed. Had Niall not told her she could walk?

"Athena!" she said, putting a hand to her throat. "You startled me. I had thought you would be much too tired to stay up late after your long journey." Her gaze swept the length of Athena's body. "My dear, how very wonderful! How long have you been able to walk?"

Athena had no intention of allowing Cecily to escape the question. All of her senses boiled with anger and distrust. She chose, against the habit of many years, to listen to what they told her.

"Niall is returning to the ranch," she said. "He made clear that you were to be my caretaker in his absence, and prevent me from leaving the house without your chaperonage. I presume that is why you are still here."

Cecily's expression changed from one of feigned pleasure to a much more honest wariness. "Your brother is concerned for your welfare, as I am. It is unfortunate—"

"Yes. Something is most unfortunate if he felt the need to leave almost as soon as we arrived . . . but it was also unfortunate that you told him where I had gone when I trusted you to keep my secret."

"Why, my dear . . ." Cecily rose and walked around the desk, brushing her fingertips along the burnished wood. "I had no choice but to tell him where you had gone when he asked me. I did not wish to break your confidence, but your brother is not easily denied."

"No, he is not. But because you prefer his regard to my friendship, I find myself a prisoner in my own home. And you have not suffered by it, have you?"

Cecily's eyes sparked with affront. "I beg your pardon. I have always wanted only what is best for you. I have the experience that you do not, and that is why Mr. Munroe trusts me to look after you while he is gone."

"And why has he gone, Cecily? You haven't answered my question." She took a step forward, careful not to grab for the doorframe. "Kindly tell me the truth."

The pleasant curve of Cecily's lips grew thin and hard. "Is it the truth you really want, my dear? The truth of what I think of you, and of your lover?"

Athena braced herself against the blows to come. "Yes."

"Very well." Cecily smiled, a look as cold and calculating as it was triumphant. "But first you must sit down, dear child, or you may fall down. I do not believe you are quite steady on your feet."

"I prefer to stand."

Cecily leaned against the desk and folded her arms across her chest. "Yes, I informed your brother of your location when he arrived earlier than you had estimated. He would have discovered your absence soon enough." She sighed and shook her head. "You will recall that I made you no promises—quite deliberately. I prefer not to break my word if it can be helped."

"What else did you tell him?" Athena demanded when she fell silent.

"Why, merely that your judgment was not sound, and that you should perhaps live elsewhere for a time to gain much-needed experience and become detached from your various . . . obsessions. I am happy to say that your brother agreed with my judgment."

"Obsessions?"

"Your charitable causes, of course, which drive you to such excess. And also your infatuation with Holt—for is he not the real reason you went to the ranch? To be with your wild-man lover?"

A week ago she could have answered in the negative with complete sincerity. Then she had told herself that

Caitlin's welfare was her sole reason for the unprecedented journey. That willful naïveté was dead.

"Morgan is not my lover," she said calmly. "But I love him. He has an honesty you would never understand."

Cecily laughed. "Indeed. Is he the knight in shining armor come to rescue you from life as a cripple?"

"It is because of him that I can walk," she said. "He gave me the courage to challenge the things I had always believed without question . . . about the world, and myself."

"And now you see the truth?" She continued to chuckle unpleasantly. "How amusing. Since you are so devoted to complete honesty, you will be most unhappy to learn that your Morgan Holt is less than the noble savage you believe."

"What do you mean?"

"Why, have you never asked him about his past? Have you so little interest in the honor and good name of your brother and the respect of your friends?"

Cecily knew nothing of Morgan's true nature, or of Athena's. Her insinuations bore on some other secret, one that Cecily plainly considered most detestable. And she was right . . . what did Athena know of his past, except that he had suffered?

"I know that Morgan is a good man," she said. "What he did before—"

"Is far worse than your imagination can conceive. You take such pride in helping the destitute and ignorant, the great and needy unwashed, and yet you remain so sadly callow." She put on an air of mock regret. "My dear Athena, it is indeed time that you knew the truth. Your lover is far worse than an uncouth boor who should not be allowed among civilized people. He is a murderer—a convict who spent years in prison. And you, child, are simply another one of his victims."

Chapter 18

Athena was hardly aware that she was moving until her back struck the wall. For a moment her thoughts were in chaos, and then she knew exactly how to respond.

"You are a liar," she said. "You would say anything to further your own cause . . . whatever that may be. If you think that you can win my brother by tricks and stratagems such as this, you are the one who is sadly mistaken. Once I tell him how far you will go to become his wife—"

"Do you think that is all I want?" Cecily's lids dropped over her eyes, as lazily vicious as a panther's. "Oh, yes, I do intend to marry your brother. And I do want you out of the way . . . which will be so much easier now that you must no longer be carried to and fro like a spoiled princess." She laughed again. "No, not a princess. A goddess. The goddess Athena, always ready to condescend to the unfortunate of any rank, and bestow her vast wisdom and generosity upon an unenlightened world. Yet all the time you perched so high upon your throne, you have had no idea how society regards you."

"But you will tell me, won't you, Cecily?"

"As your friend, I have no choice." Cecily toyed with

the cuff of her sleeve. "You fancy yourself a leader of Denver society, and I suppose you are—if only because your brother is one of the most important, influential, and wealthiest men in the West. No one wishes to offend him by offending you. But when the ladies come to your house for meetings and bully their husbands and brothers and fathers into making donations . . . do you think they do it out of sheer admiration and devotion? Oh, no. They pity you, Athena . . . and they have come to resent what you force them to do with your 'gentle' persuasion. You make them suffer guilt for not feeling as you do. And so they allow you to rule them in small ways—and go about the rest of their lives without you quite happily."

All the breath squeezed from Athena's lungs. "You are new to Denver society. You cannot know—"

"I am not such a newcomer anymore, dear girl. You have helped with introductions, and your brother's partnership with my father has done wonders for my position here. The crowning touch was in giving me control of the Winter Ball which I have perfected in ways your dull sensibilities would fail to grasp. It will be a triumph, I will take the credit, and Denver will have a new princess to adore."

Athena's legs had gone beyond the point of mere pain and felt like blocks of ice. "I do have friends in Denver. They will come to realize what you are, and so will my brother."

"Will they?" She clucked sadly. "Your brother is already convinced that I have been right all along in my warnings about you. He has had the evidence that you cannot be trusted to run your own life, especially not in Denver among so many unprofitable memories. I always knew that having a cripple underfoot would be annoying, but you have a will strong enough to oppose mine. Soon you will be gone to New York, and Niall will ask me to marry him. And as for your lover . . . I doubt that you need be troubled by him ever again."

The doorframe bit into Athena's palm. "Why did Niall return to Long Park?"

"It should be obvious. Once I told him what Holt is, he knew he must personally see to it that such a foul criminal—a man who killed his own father—is driven from Colorado. Permanently."

Athena allowed her weight to sag against the wall. Morgan had killed his own father? It was unthinkable, inconceivable. One might as well accuse Niall of killing his beloved mother.

And yet Morgan was a werewolf. He was impelled by urges an ordinary man could not understand. Was it so impossible that a man with a wolf's nature might kill more easily than one fully human, could lose control to the beast within him?

She shook her head violently, sickened by her doubts. Morgan was no murderer . . . and even to consider that he had committed patricide was absurd. Ludicrous.

Niall had gone after Morgan, believing such stories, already driven by rage. It would not be a simple matter of protecting Athena or society from a supposed murderer. Oh, no. This would be personal. How much of an excuse would he need for his hatred to become lethal? And how much would it take for Morgan to strike back with the same fell purpose?

"Do you know what you have done?" Athena whispered. "You've not only endangered Morgan but my brother as well."

"Come, now. Do you have so little faith in your brother?"

Think, Athena. "Who told you? Who passed on these lies about Morgan?"

"They are not lies, I assure you. I have had the information from very reliable sources. As for who alerted me to the grave danger Holt presents . . . you remember that horrid snake-woman from the circus? It seems she has no more love for you than I have for that red-haired hussy who set her cap for Niall. We found ways to be useful to one another."

Red-haired hussy. Who could she mean but Caitlin? Athena thought back on the times she had seen her brother and Caitlin together. If there had been an attraction there, she had been too caught up in her own problems to see it. But Cecily had not been so oblivious.

Niall and Caitlin. It was almost as mad a notion as branding Morgan a killer. And Tamar . . . she had always seemed to resent Athena, but why would she betray Morgan? What did she know about his hidden past?

Cecily was right about one thing: Athena could not trust her own judgment, which had been so horribly flawed from the beginning. She had put her faith in false friends, underestimated her brother's guilt and resentment, and complacently believed herself to be a respected and useful member of society. Cecily might exaggerate the opinions of the women of Denver, but there was a grain of truth in that particular claim that Athena couldn't ignore.

I wanted to see, in myself and everyone else, only what made me feel important and needed.

She met Cecily's eyes. "You have taught me a valuable lesson, Cecily. From this moment on, I will not unquestioningly accept what others tell me. I will discover the truth for myself, with my eyes open. Morgan will give me the truth, and Niall will listen to what I have to say."

"Even if he would—which I strongly doubt—you will not have the opportunity to speak to him, my dear. You are to remain here, safe and sound. Remember?"

Cecily's smile filled Athena with such rage that she hardly perceived the emotion for what it was. "How do you intend to stop me?"

The older woman's mouth dropped open, as if she had seen a wolf rise up on its hind legs and speak.

"Do I shock you?" Athena asked. "Perhaps you do not know me as well as you think you do."

Cecily's mouth closed with a snap. "You will remain here as your brother ordered, or . . ."

"Or you will . . . what will you do, Cecily? Are you prepared to restrain me yourself?"

"The servants. Niall left strict orders—"

"You assume that all the servants will obey without question."

Cecily took a step back, her gaze flashing to the door behind Athena and then to the bellpull in the corner of the room. She rushed around the desk to yank the cord.

Brinkley stepped into the room so quickly that Athena knew he must have been waiting very nearby. "Miss Munroe," he said, "how may I be of assistance?"

"*I* called you here," Cecily said sharply. "Mr. Munroe left clear instructions that Miss Munroe is not to leave the house unchaperoned. Miss Munroe may not be inclined to cooperate. Please escort her to her room, and lock the door."

"Do I understand that you wish me to imprison Miss Munroe?"

"Do not presume to question my instructions, or those of your employer! If you do not feel capable of controlling one half-lame girl—"

"It is all right, Brinkley," Athena said. "I don't expect you to defy my brother."

The butler raised a well-shaped brow. "Why, Miss Munroe, I do not recall any such orders."

"You—you heard him as clearly as I did!" Cecily cried. "I warn you, my man, if you continue in this way—"

"I have been considering a return to England," Brinkley said to Athena. "Perhaps this would be a convenient time to give my notice."

Athena could have hugged him. "You can go if you wish, Brinkley, but I am sure you can find excellent employment here in Denver if you must leave us."

"Perhaps. I fear that the other staff may also wish to give notice, if "—he looked down his nose at Cecily— "they are compelled to take instruction from Miss Hockensmith."

"How dare you!" Cecily started toward him, stopped,

and glared at Athena. "You will not get away with this, either of you."

"Don't worry, Cecily. You can tell Niall that I forced you to let me go."

"You . . . you can't! You can barely walk. How do you intend to—"

"I did it before, remember? And this time I can drive myself. If I leave at dawn, I should be able to reach Long Park not too long after Niall."

"You are mad! If you drive into the mountains alone you will surely meet with disaster!"

"It is kind of you to be so concerned, Cecily, but I have resources you know nothing of."

Cecily's face hardened. "I will not let you go, servants or no servants." She gestured to Brinkley. "Get out."

The butler looked at Athena. She nodded. "This is between Miss Hockensmith and me. I will not be requiring your services tonight. You may tell Fran that she may also retire."

"You need only call, Miss Munroe." He left without a backward glance at Cecily.

The moment the door was closed, Cecily advanced on Athena. Her fists were clenched, and for all her fine garments and meticulous coiffure, she looked like nothing so much as a fishwife.

"Make no mistake," she hissed, "I will stop you." She reached for Athena's arm. Athena batted her hand away. Cecily gasped and fell back a step.

"Good Lord," she said. "You are brazen! I will advise your brother to send you to a madhouse!"

"In that case, let me give you a good reason for the recommendation." Athena smiled, and the wolf crouched on its haunches and prepared to spring. Cecily struck again, bent upon knocking her off balance. Athena twisted to the side, allowing Cecily to strike the wall, and pulled the older woman's arm behind her back.

Cecily shrieked. Athena kept her grip with surprising

ease, reaching deep within for the strength of the wolf, the strength she had known and embraced before the accident.

"You might as well give up," she said. "You cannot hurt me, but I might hurt you if you struggle."

All the fight went out of Cecily, and Athena began to relax. She saw the flash of light on metal an instant before the hairpin plunged toward her shoulder.

Deftly she spun Cecily about and dodged the makeshift weapon. The silver hairpin scraped across the door and fell to the carpet. Athena growled.

She growled, just as Morgan did, teeth bared. Cecily forgot to cry out in pain and shrank away from her in horror.

"I warned you," Athena said. "You had better leave this house at once." She released Cecily, who stumbled away, clutching her wrist.

"What are you?" she whispered.

"You may pray that you never find out." She stepped aside, leaving the doorway clear. Cecily did not need further encouragement. She rushed past Athena and scurried into the hall, her dark hair falling loose about her shoulders.

The front door slammed. Athena leaned against the door and felt her body's reaction to what she had done. Her legs no longer cramped and trembled, but they would not hold her up much longer. She was living on energy borrowed from the very wolf she had only begun to acknowledge.

She knew she had to act before that energy gave out. There was no leisure to contemplate how dramatically she had changed, or how close she had come to real violence. No time for regrets or second thoughts. By the time the sun rose, she would be well on her way toward the mountains. And Morgan.

Bracing herself against any surface within reach, she made her way out of the library, into the hall, and back to the sitting room. Brinkley came to her before she had the chance to call.

"Miss Hockensmith has left us," she said, finding a seat on the nearest chair. "I don't believe she will be back. I would appreciate your help, if you still feel able to give it."

"I do, Miss Munroe. And so do the others. Your maid is prepared to resign with the rest of us, if necessary."

Athena closed her eyes and leaned her head against the back of the chair. "Thank you, but I think I am capable of doing this alone."

"Shall I ask Romero to prepare a carriage, Miss Munroe?"

Would Brinkley be so cooperative if he knew she intended to ride rather than take a carriage? "I will speak to him later. For the moment, I would like to go up to my room."

Brinkley offered his assistance, and she permitted herself the luxury of riding up in the elevator rather than taking the stairs. Once in her room, she shut the door and leaned against it, well aware that her plans were pitifully tenuous.

The boy's trousers and oversized flannel shirt were still in the chest where she had packed them away years ago. The trousers were too large, but with the help of a pair of her brother's suspenders they fit well enough. She had Brinkley retrieve her shearling jacket from the storage closet and asked Monsieur Savard to pack a meal to carry with her on the road.

At dawn she crept out of the house and to the stable without alerting Brinkley, dodged Romero, who had fallen asleep in the carriage house waiting for her, and selected the sturdiest riding horse. Her legs had received enough rest that they held her up with relatively little pain as she saddled and bridled her mount. After several tries, she made it into the saddle.

It felt strange to hold the reins again, to feel the power of a horse at her command. Her legs were by no means back to normal, but they seemed more capable with every passing hour, and she had little fear that they would betray her when she needed them most.

They, like the servants, like the circus folk, could be trusted. As she knew she could trust her own heart.

Before sunrise she left the house and all her doubts behind. For the first time in her life, she wondered if she would ever return.

I am coming, Morgan. You will not face my brother alone. And when we meet again, the whole truth will finally be spoken.

Niall pushed his exhausted horse a few more paces and then reined it in, looking down on tree and meadow from the rocky escarpment that bordered the southern end of the park.

The weather had been clear all during his journey into the mountains. Driven by rage and little else, he had made it halfway to the ranch before he realized that he and his mount needed a few hours of rest and sleep.

Even so, it had taken him only a few hours longer than usual to cover the distance from Denver, and it was just midday. His anger had been muted by weariness, but the sight of the ranch sprawled out below, and the numerous figures scurrying among the buildings, rekindled his determination.

Before the sun set, he'd have it out with Morgan Holt once and for all.

He clucked to the horse and guided it down the steep pack trail into the valley, a much more difficult and direct route than the road through the pass. Oddly enough, it was not thoughts of Morgan that accompanied him. The face he saw in his mind's eye belonged to someone else entirely— mocking and impish and topped by a tangle of curling red hair.

Caitlin. She was down there, as unsuspecting as the rest that he was on his way. What would she think if she knew he was coming? Would she mock him and spit in his eye the way she had done when she'd defended Morgan and Athena? Or would she . . . might she possibly . . .

His mouth curled in disgust. She had deceived him just as much as the others. She'd led him to think that she risked permanent crippling if she didn't have proper rest and quiet.

The doctor said as much, he reminded himself. *You had no reason not to believe him.*

Yet that same doctor had predicted that Athena would never walk again. So much for the opinions of doctors. Caitlin was strong enough to stand between him and something he wanted. His sister had turned from an obedient, well-bred, and quiet young lady to a willful, defiant hussy. It was no coincidence that she had become so only after close association with the circus.

And with the former convict Morgan Holt.

Niall gritted his teeth and felt the horse let out a great breath as it reached level ground. Little eddies of snow whirled about its hooves. No one else had come this way in some time . . . nothing human, at any rate. The air was brisk and cold, with a stillness that suggested bad weather to come.

Sensing food and refuge very near, the horse picked up its pace and set off across the park at a trot. Niall didn't mind the jarring. Physical discomfort drove the image of Caitlin from his mind. A man couldn't think of a woman when his legs ached and his fingers were numb.

Unless he began to picture a fire, a tumbler of whiskey, and a warm bed already occupied by a supple, naked, and very female body . . .

The horse snorted as he jerked on the reins. *Damn it.* He'd see the witch soon enough, and the reality would abolish these ridiculous fancies. Lust for one such as Caitlin Hughes? It embarrassed him. Yet when he tried to imagine Cecily Hockensmith sharing his bed, he shuddered with something far worse than embarrassment.

He kicked his horse into a brief but satisfying canter that carried him to the farthest outbuilding. Smoke rose in dark plumes from several chimneys, and he noted that there was considerably more activity among the circus

people than he had seen before. People and animals moved
to and fro. Wagons stood in the half shelter of buildings,
and men were loading the vehicles in preparation for a
journey.

Niall could not mistake what he saw. The circus was
getting ready to leave the ranch, livestock, tents, and all.
Was Harry French mad, or simply an idiot?

Or had he guessed that the troupers wouldn't be welcome at Long Park after the display in Athena's bedroom?
In that, at least, he wasn't wrong. Niall had been too angry
at Cecily's revelation to consider what he would tell
French when he arrived. He might have decided to let the
circus stay—except for Morgan Holt.

But if they had already chosen to run, well . . .

His horse attempted to head for the barn, and Niall
pulled it about toward the main house. He dismounted at
the steps to the wide, snow-blanketed veranda. A ranch
hand conveniently appeared to take the animal to a stall,
and Niall ran up the stairs and through the front door with
hardly a pause to kick the snow from his boots.

After the noise and bustle outside, the house was very
quiet. Niall paused in the parlor to consider his course of
action. Morgan might be here, or he might already be
gone. Harry French wasn't likely to reveal the truth either
way.

Nor was Caitlin. Yet his feet inevitably carried him
down the hall as if she had lifted her voice in a siren's call,
summoning him to destruction.

He opened the door to her room as silently as he could.
She was there, in her bed. He had half expected to find her
on her feet, no longer compelled to keep up the pretense of
serious injury. But she was quite alone, plucking at the
edge of her blanket with nimble, nervous fingers. *Worried,*
he thought. *Worried about my sister—and Holt.*

He slammed the door shut. Caitlin jerked and turned
to stare at him, and he noticed for the thousandth time
the way her freckles only added to her allure instead of
decreasing it. The way her hair seemed to blaze in any

kind of light, as if illuminated from within. The way her eyes . . .

"What are you doing here?" she demanded. "Where is Athena?"

He laughed. It was no better a welcome than he had expected.

"Athena is safely at home," he said, walking toward the bed. "Where she will remain. I am . . . grateful to see you looking so well, Miss Hughes."

"*You* do not look well at all," she said, studying him with a frown. "You must have left Denver almost as soon as you got back. Did you ride all night?"

Was that worry in her voice? "Aren't you interested in the reason I returned so quickly?"

She settled back on her mounded pillows with a false air of nonchalance. "I do not even try to guess what may be passing through your mind, Niall Munroe."

"And you are a liar." He found a chair and pulled it alongside the bed. "But I'll tell you anyway. Where is Morgan Holt?"

She showed no surprise at his question, and he wondered how much she really knew. "I have no idea. We haven't seen him since you left. You should be glad that he's gone—" She narrowed her eyes. "Or aren't you?"

"It depends upon whether or not I wish to see a killer run loose."

That caught her attention. She straightened, holding his gaze with eyes as frank and fearless as a child's. But this was no child . . . far, far from it. "Are you calling Morgan a killer, even though he had the chance to hurt you and didn't?"

"I'm calling him what he is," Niall snapped. "I'm surprised you are so sanguine about having such a creature in your midst, you and French . . . and yet you defended him. Encouraged him—"

"Even though he is not quite human?" She smiled, and her eyes crinkled at the edges. "I sometimes think he is more human than anyone I know."

"And how well do you know him, Caitlin? Did you know that he was in prison for years after murdering his own father?"

"In prison?"

She hadn't known. It was a small but important point in her favor. "I only just discovered it myself. But it explains a great deal about Holt and his behavior . . . his dishonorable treatment of my sister, and his propensity for violence. That is why I have returned, Caitlin—to make sure he can't harm anyone else."

She considered his statement in silence. He sensed that his revelation hadn't been a complete shock to her, any more than Cecily's had been to him.

"Well?" he demanded. "Do you still consider Holt your friend? Would you defend him now?"

"Even if what you claim is true . . . and I'm not saying it is . . . what do you think you can do about it?"

Niall had played out several scenarios in his mind during the ride from Denver, and every one of them had ended with Holt in a whimpering, bloody puddle at his feet. Beyond that . . .

"Do you truly believe," Caitlin said, "that you can simply walk up to him and . . . what? Make him turn himself in to the authorities?"

"I do not fear him."

"Then you are a fool. A wise man would be afraid. But you have no right to do anything to him. He has not hurt anyone in all the time I've known him. You cannot ruin his life, and Athena's, simply because you hate what you cannot understand."

"If I hated everything I did not understand," he said, "I would hate you."

She caught her lower lip between her teeth. "You might as well hate me if you intend harm to my friends."

He smiled bitterly. "I'm only interested in finding Morgan Holt. The rest of you . . . You are leaving, are you not?"

"Within the hour. Harry decided that it would be the

right thing to do. It was obvious that you would want us gone. You need not worry that we'll cause you any more trouble, Mr. Munroe."

"It's too late to worry about that, Miss Hughes."

"You have had your way. Isn't that enough?"

He jumped to his feet. "No. It's far from enough." He crossed to the bed in two strides, gripped Caitlin's shoulders, and kissed her.

She did not even bother to resist. The temporary stiffness came from shock, but an instant later she was pliable and willing in his arms. Her mouth opened to his with all the enthusiastic skill of an experienced whore.

Oh, yes, she wanted him, just as he wanted her. No sentimentality or inconvenient expectations, not even the benefit of love or even real liking—simply raw, unbridled lust. And Caitlin was not ashamed. No, not in the least.

He ended the kiss and pushed her away. She leaned back, neither offended nor outraged by his liberties. Her freckles were very prominent.

"What was that for?" she said, catching her breath.

"You know." He turned his back on her so that he wouldn't see her lips and the frank desire in her eyes. "You've known since the day we met."

"That you want me? That I want you?" She laughed softly. "What a relief it is to say it aloud and stop pretending. I was never very good at pretending."

"No." He folded his arms across his chest and stared at the wall. "Ordinarily I am very good at it. One must be, in my type of work. But I seem to have lost my abilities where you are concerned."

"And that troubles you?"

"Why should it trouble me, that I am infatuated with a girl of no parentage, dubious morals, and interests that directly conflict with my own?"

"And what sweet, loverlike words they are," Caitlin said as if to herself. "No woman could wish for a more devoted suitor."

Niall turned on her. "How many have you had, Caitlin?

Scores, I should think. Hundreds. Am I just another conquest, or am I a particular prize?"

"What arrogance. You think the worst of me for having taken other lovers, but I'm sure you feel no qualms about the women you've had. Oh, no. All your remorse is for wanting me."

He was torn between the desire to strike her and kiss her again until she was incapable of speech. "I allowed the circus to stay on the ranch for your sake, and yours alone. You've repaid me by taking Athena's part against her own brother, and against what is best for her. Holt is a convict, a murderer, and I will not allow him to remain where he has any chance of contacting my sister again."

The change of subject steered the conversation back where he wanted it, but he could not concentrate. Caitlin's eyes continued to laugh at him, though he could have sworn he saw hurt under the humor. Could a woman like Caitlin be hurt, truly hurt, by a man?

"I see," she said at last. "Well, I cannot help you. I do not know where Morgan is, and I wouldn't tell you if I did. I may want you, Niall Munroe, but not at any price."

"Not even the price of wealth beyond your imagining?"

"I will not betray my friends for money—"

"I do not speak of betrayal." He took a step toward her and stopped, unable to think of what to do with his hands. "I speak of . . . you and me, Caitlin. Of what we might have together."

"Can I believe what I just heard?" She closed her eyes. "Are you offering me—"

"Everything." He perched on the edge of the chair, fighting the absurd urge to go down on his knees. "Security, fine clothing, carriages, jewelry, all the things you have never had. A real home to live in, Caitlin, not a tent. No need to endanger your life ever again."

"You wish me to leave the circus? To abandon all my friends, the life I have always known, to become your . . ." Slowly her mouth relaxed, and she met his gaze. "To become your mistress. That is what you are offering, isn't it?"

Heat rose in his face. Damn her, the woman could make him feel like a little boy who had just been caught with his fingers in the pie. How could he let her have such power over him?

"Yes," he said coldly. "That is exactly what I am offering. But the mistress of Niall Munroe would lack nothing, I assure you." He looked toward the window, feeling a cold rush of air against his cheek even though the sash was closed. "I have never taken a mistress. I have never believed I wanted one, until now. I want you, Caitlin. I admit it. And I am willing to pay whatever you ask."

The look on her face was so gentle that he could have wept. "There is only one problem, my friend. I'm used to freedom. I come and go and behave exactly as I wish, and no man tells me what I must or must not do. Your society would never allow that, not even in a great man's mistress. And I don't care to be owned. Not even by you."

He stared at her blankly until he realized exactly what she had said.

She'd turned him down. Turned *him* down, whom very few ever refused without profound regret. She, who had nothing, who lived from day to day with no guarantee of the next night's dinner, shunned by all decent folk, refused a life of ease and luxury. And him.

"I have seldom in my life asked anything twice," he said. "I am accustomed to getting what I want. But I will offer once more. Come to Denver with me. Live in a fine house that you may call your own, where you may do whatever you please within its walls. I do not expect you to move in society or become like other women. I do not ask that you change yourself. I demand only that you and I enjoy each other as we wish, in all the freedom you desire."

"But don't you see? I would change myself if I did what you ask. The woman you want now would cease to exist, and you would grow to despise what you admire in me. As

I would grow to despise you." She sighed. "I'm sorry, Niall. There is only one reason that would compel me to accept, and that is if you give up this persecution of Morgan and Athena." She held out her hand. "Let them live their own lives, Niall, and I will share yours."

He backed away from the bed, averting his eyes from her appeal. So she could be bought, after all . . . at a price he refused to pay.

Damn her.

"Very well," he said. "You have made your position clear. But understand me, Caitlin—my offer has no bearing on my intentions toward Morgan or my desire to protect my sister. I will do whatever is necessary, with or without your help." He bowed stiffly. "If you will forgive me, I have a murderer to find."

Caitlin's hand hovered in midair, fingers curled in supplication, even as he shut the door on impossible dreams.

Chapter 19

It is too risky. We ought to delay departure for at least another day," Ulysses said, studying the sky as if it were a dangerous and unpredictable beast.

Which, Caitlin thought, was precisely the truth. And she would rather face that dangerous beast than spend a single night under the same roof as Niall Munroe.

There was no sign of the noonday sun behind the flat gray canopy of clouds. She, Harry, and Ulysses stood near the barn, where the entire circus caravan was assembled and ready to make the journey east through the pass—a dozen wagons, fifty horses and ponies including Caitlin's, and the much-prized calliope. Niall, thank heaven, had not emerged from the house.

Caitlin balanced her weight on a pair of makeshift crutches, aware of the stiffness in her leg but no longer in pain. If her injury couldn't stop her from leaving the place, no human being was going to do so. Not even a well-meaning friend.

"You are as unlike your namesake as any man could be, Ulysses Wakefield," she chided. "Where is your sense of adventure? Your trouper's spirit? Or, for that matter, your pride?"

"I have never been one for suicidal acts," Ulysses said. "Nor do I wish to see the troupe caught in a snowstorm. My desire to leave does not seem quite as urgent as yours, Firefly."

Caitlin had told no one about Niall's offer. Despite Uly's misgivings, Harry was obviously as eager to leave as she was. It was difficult to say whether he worried more for her or Morgan—who was still in the vicinity, to judge by the wolf tracks that appeared every night near the house. He could not quite break his final ties to the troupe. Or to Athena, though he hadn't gone after her.

How can men be such fools?

"We are ready to go," Harry said, tugging his worn scarf more snugly about his neck. "Everything is in order, and I do not relish the prospect of remaining here with Munroe hovering over us like a starving buzzard."

"I have spoken with many of the others, and they all agree," Caitlin added. "We will have to get through the pass while the weather is clear. If we don't do it now, we may not get another chance before winter's end." With an unreadable glance at Caitlin, Harry hurried off to consult with the boss hostler. Horses stamped, dogs barked, and troupers waited impatiently for the order to move.

The order came at last, and the caravan lurched into motion with much cracking of whips, groaning of harness, and hails passed down the line of wagons. Billows of vapor rose from the horses' mouths. The hazy light could not dim the bright colors of wagons and props, or the resplendent patchwork of apparel worn by the troupers. But there was no fanfare, and the circus folks were subdued as they trampled a path through the snow past the outbuildings and into the park. The ranch hands paused in their work to see them off, a few tipping their hats, and Mr. Durant came out onto the veranda, undoubtedly glad to see the last of his unwanted guests.

Caitlin sat beside Harry in the office wagon, her injured

leg propped out straight before her, and refused to look back. Niall had no reason to pursue them. He, like Durant, would be happy to see them gone. His only remaining interest in the troupers lay in what they knew of Morgan, and no one had answers that satisfied him.

Inching along the half-covered dirt road all too slowly, the caravan passed through the gate that marked the boundary of the inner pastures. Before them stretched a blanket of white punctuated by the bare limbs of leafless shrubs, and the deeper green of fir and spruce. Ruts and furrows marked where ranch hands and their cattle had passed. Soon even those signs disappeared, replaced by the subtler tracks of fox, rabbit, and deer.

When the last wagon had crossed the point halfway to the pass, a light snow began to fall. Caitlin sneezed and readjusted her blankets. A little snow couldn't hurt them, surely.

But soon even she wasn't able to pretend that all was well. The drizzle of snowflakes transformed into dense clumps that settled on every surface not warm enough to melt it. Soon the snow fell so thickly that Caitlin could not see any farther back than the next two wagons in line, and the trees beside the meadow became unidentifiable shadows. The mountains had entirely vanished.

"Oh, dear," Harry murmured, his gloved hands very tight on the ribbons. "This does not look good. Not good at all." He clucked to the horses, but they were already struggling to break a trail through the ever-deepening snow. Their ears lay flat against their heads in eloquent protest.

Caitlin closed her eyes and whispered an almost-forgotten prayer. "Ulysses was right," she said. "We must go back."

"I agree. The road has disappeared. I cannot see how to find the pass, even if we could cross it. But there is a small difficulty. I am not sure how to get back to the ranch."

"But surely we can retrace our steps—"

"We can but try." Only his worried eyes were visible between hat and scarf as he turned the ponderous wagon about. The horses heaved and plunged sideways through the unbroken snow. The wagon's wheels caught on some buried obstruction, but with many pleas and promises, Harry got the horses to pull them free.

Gradually the other wagons followed Harry's example, each driver taking his cue from the one ahead of him. Visibility had declined to the length of a single wagon. Harry drove back the way they had come, using the caravan itself as his guide. Disembodied voices cried out questions and instructions. Caitlin caught a glimpse of Ulysses, but he was soon lost in the blizzard.

It seemed hours before Harry reached the end of the line of wagons. Then there was nothing ahead but a wall of white, blending earth and sky together in a featureless void. Even the tracks left by the caravan were rapidly filling, as if Nature resented the blemish the intruders had made on her chaste perfection.

"I do not know where to go," Harry said, his voice sunk to a whisper. "Every direction looks the same."

"The boss hostler has a compass," Caitlin said. "Go find him, Harry, and I'll wait here."

He sighed and passed the ribbons to her. With a grunt he eased himself down from the high, narrow driver's seat, landing awkwardly in the knee-deep snow. He trudged back toward the nearest wagon, no more than a smudge in the distance. His breath trailed skyward in steam-train puffs with every step.

As long as he keeps close to the wagons, he can't lose his way, Caitlin reminded herself as the minutes passed. The wagon behind was invisible now, and no others had come nearer. It was difficult to believe anyone else existed in this bizarre world of nothingness. Even sound had become muffled, and she doubted that she could have heard a shout from a few feet away.

After an hour, she began to be afraid. If Harry had gotten himself lost, she would have to find him. The crutches were useless in snow. Unhitching one of the horses and riding it bareback was hardly a better option. But if she did

not try, some roving cowhand looking for stray cattle after
the storm would find them frozen to death only a few miles
from safety.

Niall, she thought, grasping at the name as if it were a
magical incantation. *If you ever cared for me, even a little,
come and find us. Help us.*

But it was not Niall who answered her silent call. At
first she thought the dark shape emerging from the haze
was Harry, safe and sound, and she laughed in relief. But
the figure was too low to the ground to be human.

Morgan. She sat up, ignoring the gale that tore at her
clothing, and squinted against the snow. "Morgan!"

He glided toward her like a dark angel borne on imperceptible wings, his coat repelling the snow as if it were the
gentlest of spring showers. He stopped well distant from
the nervous horses and made a low, questioning sound between a bark and a growl.

"Thank God you're here," she shouted into the wind.
"We're lost! Harry is back there somewhere, and I'm
afraid—you must find him!"

Morgan lowered his muzzle in a wolfish nod and turned
gracefully on his hind legs, bounding off with ears pricked
toward sounds only he could hear. Caitlin slumped on the
seat and dared to breathe again. Strange how she had
prayed for Niall when Morgan was by far the better choice
to save them. Niall, after all, was only a man.

Yet she continued to imagine, with absurd persistence,
that Niall was even now on his way. When Harry and Morgan returned to the wagon, the old gentleman clutching
Morgan's fur and stumbling along in the path he had made,
she cursed herself for wishing Niall out in this nightmare.

Perhaps Niall was lost as Harry had been. Perhaps he
would die proving false all the terrible judgments she had
made of him out of anger and hurt.

At the end of his strength, Harry climbed onto the
wagon's seat, and Caitlin covered him with her own blanket. He tried to speak, teeth chattering each time he opened
his mouth. His ice-rimed moustache was stiff as a board.

"Don't try to talk," she said. "Morgan?"

The wolf appeared beside her, his immense paws resting on the side of the wagon. His slanted eyes met hers, and he Changed.

As remarkable as it was to see a naked man standing thigh-deep in snow and unaffected by the cold, Caitlin was in no mood to marvel. "We have to get back to the ranch," she said. "Can you lead us?"

"Yes." He glanced the way he and Harry had come. "I'll take word to the rest of the caravan and gather the wagons." He paused, frowning at Harry. "He will be all right, Firefly. Keep him warm. I'll be back as soon as I can."

"Morgan . . . Did you . . . did you by any chance see Niall on your way to us?"

His eyes were hard as topaz. "No. No one could follow you in this, even if he wished." He turned and leaped into the snow, moving twice as fast as any human. Caitlin inured herself to another wait, warming Harry with the heat of her body and their shared blankets.

A horse's urgent whinny was the first indication that Morgan had succeeded in reaching the others. Soon another wagon pulled alongside Harry's, Ulysses at the reins. He nodded to her calmly, but his eyes told a different tale.

"Is everyone all right?" Caitlin called.

"Well enough. It is fortunate that Morgan arrived when he did." He gestured behind him, and Caitlin saw the shadows of other wagons drawing near. Morgan ran among them, human and then, in a heartbeat, wolf again.

It was as a wolf that he took the lead and guided the troupers to shelter. The going was difficult, far more so than it had been in the other direction, but Morgan was endlessly patient and resourceful in keeping the caravan together, providing encouragement to the weary horses, and pulling wagons out of snowdrifts.

Riders met them when they reached the outskirts of the ranch. Morgan scrambled into the back of the wagon while Caitlin pulled up at the ranch hand's signal.

"Miss Hughes?" the leader said, his face obscured

under layers of scarfs and bandannas. "We thought you wouldn't make it back. We were just headed out to look for you."

"We are all right," she said, glancing at Harry. "Please tell . . . tell everyone that we're safe."

The rider shook his head. "Mr. Munroe set out after you when the storm began. Some of the men went with him, but they got separated. They came back, but he hasn't. Did you see him, miss?"

Her heart plummeted to the heels of her boots. "He . . . Mr. Munroe went looking for us?"

"Yes, miss. As soon as the snow lets up, we'll be going ourselves. Mr. Munroe ain't used to this kind of weather."

The men saluted and rode off. Morgan jumped down from the rear of the wagon and ran alongside, keeping the vehicle between himself and the riders.

Sick to her stomach, Caitlin guided the wagon toward the barn, only half-aware of the other wagons rolling up behind. Several hands were there to help her and Harry to the bunkhouse. Shivering, miserable teamsters unharnessed the horses and secured them in the barn.

Caitlin did not see Morgan again. She sat on the edge of a cot, rocking back and forth while constant noise and movement swirled around her. Someone threw another blanket over her shoulders, and Harry came by, much improved, to ask her a question she didn't quite hear.

She looked up. Harry and Ulysses stood side by side, stout old man and handsome dwarf, gazing at her as if they had grim news to impart. Caitlin prepared herself for pain.

"You're worried about Munroe, aren't you?" Harry asked softly. "You needn't worry any longer."

Hope seeped into the shriveled husk of her heart. "Is he here?"

"He is still missing," Ulysses said. "But we came to tell you that Morgan has volunteered to search for him. If any man—any creature upon this earth—has the skill to locate him, it is he."

"Morgan . . . volunteered?" Morgan, who hated Niall

and was hated in return? Why should he wish to save his enemy from almost certain death?

Because, like it or not, he had an unbreakable tie to Niall Munroe. Caitlin didn't imagine that Morgan did it for her sake. Niall was Athena's sister, and she knew that Morgan would risk anything to spare her the sorrow of losing the last member of her family.

So much for indifference. So much for freedom and breaking all bonds of love or friendship.

Now all she had to do was pray—pray, not only that Morgan found Niall, but that they didn't kill each other when he did.

"*You'd be crazy to go on in this storm, miss,*" the innkeeper said, shaking his finger at Athena. "They say it'll be the worst of the season. Can't figure how you made it this far."

Athena stood in the doorway of the livery stable and gazed out at the blowing snow. Even after a long stop in Golden, it did indeed seem something of a miracle that she'd come all the way from Denver in increasingly bad weather. Though she scarcely felt the cold, the journey had been far from pleasant. Her legs had gone well past the point of pain, numb appendages useful only for gripping the belly of her horse.

The gelding had shown great spirit in carrying her so far into the mountains, to this small mining town with its narrow street of saloons, shops, and the single hotel and stable. Dandy certainly deserved a warm stall, an ample portion of oats, and a good night's sleep.

But Yankee Gulch was still miles away from where she wanted to go. Where she *must* go.

"I can't let you take one of my horses out tonight," the innkeeper said fretfully. "There's only another hour of daylight. It'd be the same as murder—you and the horse, both."

He was right about the horse, and hers certainly could

not go any farther. She faced the unpalatable choice of staying the night, knowing that Niall must already be at Long Park, or risking the life of some innocent beast.

That she could not do. But the third alternative filled her with such terror that she felt a coldness far more savage than anything nature could provide.

She sighed and turned to the innkeeper. "You said that you have a room," she said. "I will take it for the night, and leave in the morning."

The grizzled man relaxed and scratched under the brim of his stained hat. "Good. Now let's get out of this cold, and I'll make sure your horse is well taken care of tonight. The rooms ain't fancy, but on a night like this—" He shrugged and gestured toward the door of the adjoining hotel.

The room was every bit as plain as the innkeeper had warned, and only marginally clean. It stank of a previous tenant's stale sweat and cigar smoke, fouling each breath she took.

Athena swallowed her distaste and set her small pack on the uneven floor. The sheets on the bed, while much mended, appeared reasonably tidy. Not that she expected to get much sleep.

She pulled the single, rickety wooden chair up to the window and watched the snow cover the street, the cheaply constructed buildings and the handful of wagons tied up in front of the general store. The few pedestrians moved hastily, anonymous figures with lowered heads and white-caked boots. Denver, and the comforts of home, seemed a million miles away.

Going back was another possibility she did not consider. The tightness in her stomach told her that her instincts were correct. She must get to the ranch. The two men she loved most in the world were in horrible danger.

In spite of her conviction that sleep was out of the question, her chin began to nod on her chest. She tried to eat a little of the bread Monsieur Savard had packed for the journey, but it was as dry and tasteless as sand. The small room felt like a cage—the kind of cage Morgan had described when he had spoken of her life—and the unthinkable idea she had rejected began to seem inviting. Only that final, lingering fear held her back.

She dozed fitfully in the chair. Out of the maelstrom of her imagination, a picture formed in stark black and white. At first all she could see was snow: snow on the ground, among the trees, in the sky, painting everything one sullen, lifeless hue.

Then she saw the black shape, lying in the snow—black fur, black tail, black muzzle. The eyes were open, but they did not see. The body lay perfectly still. No breath plumed from the open jaws. But there was one other color present in this ashen world . . . one vivid shade that wept in the snow beside the great wolf's head.

Scarlet. The color of fresh, bright blood.

Athena sat up in the chair, choking on a scream.

Only a dream, she told herself. But that was a lie. She had "dreamed" of running with Morgan as a wolf, sharing what he felt as he ran alone. Part of it had been real. What if this apparition, too, were real . . . or soon to be?

All her choices were gone. Morgan needed her, now, and there was but one way she could face the storm and make it through alive.

Shaking with reaction, she kicked her bag under the bed and pulled a wad of banknotes from her pocket, leaving them where they would be found by the innkeeper. The sun had gone down; few if any people would be on the street to see her leave or try to stop her.

She crept down the stairs, willing the other guests to remain in their rooms. The smell of greasy cooking hung in her nostrils, but the innkeeper was busy elsewhere, and she passed through the lobby unseen.

The snow continued to fall as heavily as before. Athena ran to the stable and made sure that Dandy had his blanket and oats. She had only one more favor to ask of him.

Hiding behind his sturdy bulk, she quickly stripped out of her clothing. First came the coat, and then the two layers of shirts, and then the cinched trousers. Icy wind whistled through chinks in the stable walls, curling around her bare flesh. But the cold was unimportant, as easily shrugged off as the shirts and trousers and boots.

She stood naked at Dandy's head, stroking his muzzle as much to comfort herself as him. He could rest at his ease, his care assured by the generous payment she'd left in her room. But *she* had a long way to go.

And that journey must begin with an act of courage she was not sure she possessed. Nor could she take that first step among the horses. Making a quick search of the stable, she discovered a small loft where she concealed her bundled clothing—no need to give the poor innkeeper more concern than he would already face when he found her gone.

Straw crackled under her bare feet as she crept to the stable door. She had no need to worry for the sake of modesty, or of being dragged away to an asylum for the insane. The street was empty of man or beast. Even the most recent wagon tracks had been erased. Yankee Gulch was dark save for one or two lights shining in windows, but her wolfish night vision made it seem almost as bright as day.

Wading through the snow, she circled the stable to the alley beside it. It was as good a place as any to attempt the impossible.

Not impossible. You did it once, easily. When you were hardly more than a girl, you couldn't imagine a life without it. Or a life without the use of your legs.

Now you have your legs again. Claim the rest of yourself, Athena. For Morgan's sake.

She closed her eyes and *willed.*

Nothing happened. She stood on two weak legs, her loosened hair lashing about her face. It would be so easy to give up and admit defeat.

I cannot. It has been too long. My body does not know how.

She sat down in the alley, burying her face in her hands. Better to just lie here and let the snow cover her up. How could she help Morgan—she, who had lived a soft and easy life, believed herself so important, and yet had no real courage to face a true challenge when it came?

Who was she, to think she had the power to save him?

She flung her head up and stared at the falling snow. That same snow fell on him now, in a place where he might lie dying and alone.

She clenched her fists and pushed to her feet. She remembered what it had been like when Changing required no more than a thought. She remembered racing through the forest up at the ranch, borne to ecstasy on a hundred smells and sounds even her superior human senses could not detect.

Above all, she remembered running beside Morgan, wolf with wolf, utterly free.

A peculiar frisson swept through her body. It was as if every muscle, every bone, every nerve twisted inside out, yet there was no pain. A mist rose about her like a silken veil, untroubled by the wind.

She threw up her arms and gave herself to the Change. Life flowed and shifted. Her sight altered, taking in the world from a vantage much closer to earth. Scents and sounds burst in upon her senses like a tidal wave.

For a moment all she could do was breathe, struggling to manage the overwhelming assault. Gradually what seemed so alien became familiar, as natural as walking had been before the accident. She took a step on four wide paws. Her hind legs trembled, the lingering remnant of her lameness, but they carried her out of the alley, first at a walk and then a trot and a gallop.

She ran down the deserted street and to the shacks at the outskirts of town, past the mine and the tailings and waste of man's grubbing in the earth. The forest called to her, and the mountains, with songs only one of her blood could hear.

Instinct pointed the way to Long Park when no trail remained for a human being to follow. Instinct, and a very human emotion called love.

Athena howled defiance into the blizzard and ran as she had never run before.

*N*iall had come this way. Morgan sniffed at the ground, detecting the odors buried under a layer of newfallen snow. Any tracks Munroe had made were long gone; if he were not dead already, no human born could find him.

But a werewolf could. And Morgan planned to do so, setting aside his hatred of the man he hunted. For Athena's sake.

He almost felt Athena beside him, bounding over frozen creeks and through thickets of serviceberry shrubs. But she was in Denver now, safe and warm where she ought to be.

He sat on his haunches and chocked on a howl. The last words he had spoken to her had been filled with cruelty and bitterness. That was her final memory of him—angry, hating, blaming her for being what she was instead of what he wished her to be.

She had not made the same mistake. She had understood that he wouldn't go with her. Perhaps that was why she had asked.

Damn you, Athena Munroe. I will find your precious brother. And then you must let me go. Let me go, do you hear?

His growls flew away in the wind. Tensing his muscles, he leaped up and over a snowbank and followed the trail of scent. No other animals were foolish enough to be abroad; the forest and park looked as they must have done before the first intruding human had walked in these mountains. Peaceful. Still as death, or forgetfulness. A sweet offer of ending he could not accept.

A few hours before dawn, he found his quarry. Niall crouched in the partial shelter of a fallen tree, his coat drawn up over his head. There was no sign of his mount. Morgan smelled the ash where he had tried to start a fire, but no flame could survive this gale.

Morgan stalked closer, ears flat to his head. He heard

the ragged sound of Niall's breathing, felt the warmth of body heat—alive, then. He shook off savage regret and drew closer.

Niall's head jerked up. His brows were frosted with rime, his skin nearly blue. He tried to move, feeling in his pocket.

Morgan dashed in and seized Niall's wrist between his teeth, tasting leather and sheepskin. Munroe's smell was rank with fear and exhaustion. He met Morgan's gaze, and the last spark of fight went out of him.

He had one more shock to face. Morgan released him and backed way, shaking the foul scents from his coat. It was almost a relief to Change and find his senses dulled, as they always were in human shape.

Munroe exhaled a great cloud of steam and tried to sit up. "You," he said hoarsely.

"Yes." Morgan crouched on his heels. "I've come to take you back to the ranch."

Munroe laughed. "You have come to . . . save me?"

"I would just as soon let you die here. But there are two who care for you, and it is for their sakes that I came tonight."

"Two?" He shivered and tried to adjust his collar with frozen fingers.

"Your sister, and Caitlin."

"Caitlin." He shifted again and fell back. "Is she all right?"

"She and the others are safe."

Niall closed his eyes. "You found them?"

"Yes. Your men said that you went out to look for them after the storm began. That earns you the right to live."

"The right to live," he echoed. "And what gives you the right to judge me, Holt? You, who murdered your own father?"

Morgan felt no surprise. He'd lived too long among men to keep such secrets indefinitely, and no one had better motive to uncover those secrets than Niall Munroe.

But Munroe's accusation did not touch him. It was as if

Athena's brother spoke of another man, summoned memories of another life.

"You do not deny it," Munroe said. He sat up, emboldened by Morgan's silence. "Not that it would do you any good. I blame myself for not having discovered it long ago. The only thing I don't understand is why you were not hanged."

"Then there is something about me you don't know."

"That you claim justification for patricide?" He laughed again, teeth chattering. "A man capable of that could do anything. But you are not a man, are you? You're a beast that thinks nothing of killing."

"A beast like your sister."

"No!" Munroe scrambled to his feet and leaned on the fallen tree. "My sister cannot help what she is. I will not let her give in to the monstrous heritage her mother imposed upon her." His eyes glazed. "I knew she was evil the first time I saw her in my father's bed."

Morgan became aware of his body again. "She?"

"Gwenyth Desbois. The bitch who seduced my father and stole his love for my mother." Munroe's teeth flashed white in the rigid oval of his face. "I saw her Change long before Athena learned how to twist her body into an animal's. And my father knew. He *knew* what she was, and wanted her anyway. He forced my mother to raise Athena as her own—"

"And you hate Athena for that. You've hated her since she was born."

"Shut up! You know nothing about it, what it was like to know what she was. I would have kept it from her, let her live an ordinary life. But our father told her everything when he thought she was old enough to understand. He ruined her." He slammed his fist against the tree, shaking snow from the dead branches. "And you—you will destroy her completely. That's why I must stop you just as I stopped her mother."

Morgan cocked his head. "What happened to Athena's mother?" he asked softly.

"I was eight when I first saw them together. My mother didn't know. She didn't find out for years. And I was too young to do anything then. But when I was twelve, I got rid of the bitch, and Father never knew."

Twelve. Two years younger than Morgan had been when he'd left home forever, vowing to find his own father and bring him back to California. He had abandoned his childhood by the time he was fifteen.

At eight years of age, Munroe had seen his father in bed with his mistress. Four years later, he had gotten rid of her. The ugly pictures that formed in Morgan's mind came from the darkest of places within himself: images of a boy with a revolver, a woman begging for mercy, the terrible finality of a gunshot.

A gun, a knife, poison—it didn't matter. Niall was too clever to implicate himself in Gwenyth Desbois's death. It wasn't easy to kill a werewolf, but it could be achieved by someone with knowledge, resolve, and sufficient hatred.

"I had to do it," Niall said. "I had to set my father free and restore my mother's honor. It was the only way."

Hatred was a ruthless master. It could make a boy, or a man, believe that whatever he did was justified. It could convince him that his reasons were pure and good and unselfish.

The boy had stood there with the gun and listened to the pleas. He had seen the upraised hands, the hollow eyes, the quiver of the lips. He had aimed, so carefully. One shot was all it took.

"You see why I must stop you," Niall said, his voice very far away. "There is just enough human left in Athena to be worth saving."

Morgan saw the gun in Niall's hand. He knew what it meant, and what it would take to stop his enemy. A gathering of muscle and sinew, a leap, a single blow, a clean snapping of the bones in a human neck.

Another murder.

Niall fired. The bullet seared Morgan's side, a startling instant of pain that seemed less real than the calm indifference of his thoughts. He staggered. A second bullet grazed Morgan's temple.

For Athena.

He fell. Blood steamed in the snow. Morgan felt his body laboring to heal the wounds, but he let the blood flow and the pain wash over him. He willed his heartbeat to slow, his lungs to cease their struggle for air. He closed his eyes.

Niall's presence was a faint warmth above him. He waited for a third shot, but it didn't come. His body absorbed Niall's kick without reacting. Cold metal pressed into his jaw. He stopped his heart just as Niall's fingers sought the pulse at the base of his neck.

"So easy," Niall murmured. "You didn't even fight, you bastard. Why?" He lurched up and away, his movements receding with Morgan's awareness. "Damn you. Damn you to hell."

Chapter 20

A thena knew the way. *As a woman she might have be-*
come lost, but the wolf could not be confused or mis-
led by distorted senses. She ran without pause through the
storm, and at the coming of dawn she knew she had
reached Munroe land.

She could not have said what made her stop so close to
her goal, with the scents of woodsmoke and horses and humanity thick in her nostrils. The place was very much like
any other in the park, where evergreens grew thick at the
edge of a meadow. No animal or bird broke the silence.
But she stopped, her fur bristling and her ears tilted to
catch the sound of a voice.

Morgan's voice. And she realized what it was that had
halted her. The wind had gone still; the cacophony of a
thousand scents, tangled by the storm, had settled back
into a gentler song. And one subtle note rang sweet and
beloved among all the others.

Morgan. She turned her muzzle toward the scent, all her
weariness dropping away. Morgan was here, very close,
perhaps behind the next stand of firs.

She raced across the meadow, leaving a deep gully in

the snow behind her. Halfway across she slowed, and her hind legs began to cramp and seize up with pain that shouted in her body like a warning of doom.

Wrong. Morgan's scent was wrong. What had seemed a pure, sweet melody was tainted. Mingled with Morgan's scent was another she knew as well as her own, and a third she recognized and feared above all others.

Niall had been here, or very close. And either he, or Morgan, had shed blood.

Not even the pain in her legs could slow her now. She forced her muscles to obey and leaped up, broke the surface of snow in her descent and leaped again. The edge of the meadow loomed ahead. She clawed her way onto a jutting boulder and entered the cover of the trees.

The smell of blood grew thicker, Morgan's scent stronger as Niall's faded. Athena's paws hardly touched the ground. In a small clearing, protected from the worst of the storm, she found him.

He lay on his back in snow melted by his own blood, limbs twisted and dark hair thick across his face. The ground all around him had been trampled by booted feet. Niall's boots.

Niall had been here. The sharp tang of metal and gunpowder played counterpoint to the stench of blood. No mist of breath rose from Morgan's parted lips.

Athena covered the remaining distance in a single jump. She lost her balance, fell to her side, and scrambled the last few feet on shaking legs.

Morgan lay unmoving. Athena nudged his chin with her muzzle and snarled in his face. His skin was cold. She clawed at him frantically, heedless of the scratches she left on his bare skin. His chest didn't move. She grabbed his arm between her teeth and tugged him this way and that with small, despairing whimpers.

Only then, when every attempt had failed, did she sit back on her haunches and howl. Wolves could not weep. But she was also human, and humans possessed a strange and foolish quality called hope.

Hope gave her the strength to Change. Hope kept her heart beating as she lay atop him, spreading her arms and legs over him like a living blanket. Hope warmed her breath as she kissed his unyielding lips.

"Be alive," she whispered. "Damn you, Morgan, be alive." She pushed her fingers into his hair and lifted his head as if he could see the determination in her eyes. "Are you going to give up, after fighting the world with every breath? Is this how it ends? Well, you've underestimated me for the last time, Morgan Holt."

She kissed him again, bruisingly, biting into his lower lip until she tasted blood. Hating him, and loving him more than life itself.

He gasped. His chest arched up as if pulled by invisible cords, and he sucked in a lungful of air. Bright, fresh blood welled from the wounds in his side and temple.

"Morgan!" she cried, searching for something to stanch the flow. But he didn't hear her. His eyes remained closed. Dark mist formed over his body, the telltale sign of impending Change.

She slid away from him just as the transformation began. It was neither swift nor smooth; midway through the Change, he hovered between wolf and man just as he had in her bedroom at Long Park. Only this time it was not by choice. His body could not complete the Change in its weakened state, so near to death. Blood continued to stain the snow.

Athena caught at his fur-mantled shoulders and shook him. "Decide, Morgan!" she shouted. "Live or die. Wolf or man. But if you choose death, I'll know you were a coward!"

His eyelids fluttered, revealing the alien yellow of a wolf's eyes. He shuddered violently, and the mist became like a choking cloud. The shape under Athena's hands finished its transition. The black wolf lay on its side, barely breathing.

She buried her hands in Morgan's fur, feeling for the wounds. Her fingers came away dry. No more blood. Bone and muscle felt firm and whole. His heart beat strongly under his ribs.

Without questioning the miracle, Athena let herself go limp and rested her head on his flank. She knew she had slept when she felt hands—human hands—in her hair, stroking it away from her face.

She blinked and sat up. Morgan lay beside her, his bare skin unmarked and his eyes free of pain. He let his hand fall and gazed up at her, waiting for her questions.

"I'm not dreaming?" she whispered.

"No." He smiled—that faint, almost imperceptible smile she had finally learned to recognize. "And neither am I."

She reached out, touching any part of him that she could reach. It was not her imagination. The wounds that had bled so freely were gone as if they had never existed. At first she thought even the blood-stained snow had vanished, but then she saw the dark blotch several feet away and realized that Morgan had moved both of them to clean ground.

It was daylight now, and the storm had passed, but the temperature remained below freezing. Athena felt as warm as if she and Morgan lay wrapped in blankets before a crackling fire.

"You healed yourself," she said in wonder. "How?"

"It is a dangerous thing," he said. "A great risk to take when there is no other choice. One of us who is injured badly—if we Change, we either die or heal ourselves."

"I thought you were dead." Her eyes welled with belated tears. "You weren't breathing."

"But I heard you." He caught a tendril of her hair and tucked it behind her ear. "You called me a coward."

Her fist bunched with the savage desire to strike the gentle mockery from his face. "Did you find that amusing? Did you enjoy making me think you were dead?"

"No. I had to convince Niall that I was."

Niall. Athena closed her eyes, and the tears spilled over. "He thought he'd killed you," she said. "When he said he was returning to Long Park, I knew something was wrong. I left Denver as soon as I guessed what he intended."

"You risked everything," he said. "You Changed, Athena. You brought me back."

Somehow that victory seemed hollow. Whatever Morgan said, she had not saved him. The admiration in his eyes, the pride in his voice made the coming trial that much more unbearable.

"Yes," she said. "I Changed."

"Because you feared for me. But you must have known it was Niall who was in danger."

She met his gaze, and she knew. She knew that Morgan understood the reason Niall had come back to kill him. Cecily's accusations hung between them, unspoken but impossible to ignore. Even now, after his miraculous reprieve from death.

Especially now.

"I will believe you, Morgan," she said. "Whatever you tell me, I will believe."

He looked away. "My great secret," he said. "It would not have mattered if I had remained among the wolves. But Harry and his people drew me back to men, where the past is never forgotten. Not even by the ones who lived it."

Then it was true. The horrible things she had refused to accept . . . some part of them must be true. But the question she knew she must ask froze on her tongue.

"I was in prison," he said, his voice without expression. "Niall discovered it. That was why he came back. To protect you."

Athena sat very still, afraid that if she moved her entire body might shatter like a figure sculpted of ice. "Cecily told me," she said. "She was the one who told Niall."

"About me. About what I am." He made a harsh sound under his breath. "It is true." At last he looked at her. "You didn't believe it until now. You had *faith* in me."

How bitterly he mocked himself. She recognized the contempt, the unrelenting self-judgment. Whatever he had done, his punishment had never stopped. He carried it with him always.

He would tell her everything if she asked. Every ugly detail of his crime and imprisonment, anything she might possibly wish to know. And he would hope, as he told her, that she would turn from him in disgust and horror.

"You should not have come back, Athena," he said. "Your brother would have been safe."

He spoke with such reluctance, as if he were revealing a great weakness—as if sparing a life were more shameful than taking one. In spite of what he had said earlier, he assumed she'd escaped Denver to protect Niall. And hadn't she? Hadn't she been equally afraid for both men, knowing that Niall didn't have a chance against a werewolf?

But she knew her brother. His ruthlessness, and his tenacity. He would have been prepared to face a werewolf . . . or a murderer.

"A man who killed his own father." Those had been Cecily's words. And Morgan admitted it. But he had not hurt Niall. Her heart filled with the conviction that he had deliberately allowed Niall to attack and leave him for dead, so that he would not be compelled to kill her brother.

She could think of only one reason he would risk his own life to spare Niall's.

"If you are a murderer," she said, "it would be easy to kill a man you hate."

He stared at her, stubbornly mute. He would force her to draw her own conclusions rather than do anything to clear his name, or his worth in her eyes.

So it was up to her. She must decide: whether to believe Cecily and Niall and Morgan himself, or look beyond the cold facts to the man behind them. The man whose goodness shone like the biblical light under a bushel. The man she loved.

Words were inadequate. Here, in the wilderness, the two of them sat in the snow unaware of the cold or the nakedness that would have killed a normal man or woman.

Here, human language had no power to express the feelings that crowded her chest and seared her throat.

But there was another kind of communication far more eloquent. Suddenly and most acutely she was aware of her nakedness in a new and tantalizing way—hers, and Morgan's.

Morgan seemed to read her thoughts. He tensed his muscles and tried to stand, but his knee buckled. He caught himself against a fir and leaned there, breathing hard. Athena bit back a cry of alarm.

"We are both weary," she said. "We need rest before . . . before anything else."

"Are you ill? Your legs . . ."

Naturally he would worry about her and not himself. "I am tired. My legs hurt, and we need time to recover." *And to decide what to do.* She left those words unspoken, but he heard them.

"I'll take you to the ranch."

So that Niall has another chance to kill you? So you can run away for the last time?

"No. Not yet." She kept her voice tranquil, her expression calm. "I just need to rest. Somewhere quiet. Please, Morgan."

The muscles in his jaw flexed. "There is a cave not far from here. It isn't much better—"

"It will do" She started to rise and Morgan rushed in to support her. She felt the vibration of muscles under his skin as he tried to lift her. "I can walk," she insisted. "Take me to the cave, Morgan."

He withdrew instantly, and she realized he believed that she didn't want him to touch her. The thought sickened her, but she swallowed her protest and let him move ahead, forging through the snow at a pace too rapid for a weakened man to sustain. Even so, he glanced back at her every few steps to make sure she followed.

They hadn't far to go. His path led through the trees and to a granite escarpment that formed a stairstep of ledges up the hill, ending in an overhang crusted with icicles. Beneath was the dark mouth of a cave. Morgan entered, moved around inside, and emerged a few minutes later.

"It's safe," he said, addressing the air over her head. refusing to look at her body or into her eyes. "A bear denned here once, but not for a long time."

She nodded and stepped over the lip of the entrance. Morgan pressed himself against a rock so that she would not touch him by accident. Her feet shuffled among dried leaves and pine needles, redolent of several former inhabitants. It was a soft, warm, and comforting scent, like that of a well-worn nursery blanket. The roof of the cave just cleared the top of her head.

This would be the place. Here Athena Sophia Munroe would do something her former self could not have dreamed of, just as she had never dreamed of walking again.

She knelt on the mat of leaves and watched Morgan come in, hesitate, and settle against the curved stone wall near the entrance. "I can make a fire," he offered.

I'm not cold, she almost said, and realized her mistake. She needed to draw him close, but he was staying as far away as he could.

Was his self-contempt so powerful? Was it that he didn't trust himself with her? Did he no longer want her?

No. Not unless his body acted independently of his mind. She knew what she saw, what he tried to hide. *He thinks you don't want* him. *Maybe he hasn't enough strength. Maybe this is wrong.*

Wrong, yes, by the rules that governed people like Cecily Hockensmith. But not wrong for them. This was not only right, but necessary.

All the questions were silenced. She stood and walked toward him, each step taken with great care. He looked up and flinched as if she confronted him with a loaded rifle and death in her eyes.

She dropped to her knees before he could move. "Morgan," she said, and touched his arm. "I don't hate you. I could never hate you."

He didn't respond. She brushed his face with her finger-tips. Every muscle in his body tightened.

"Whatever you may have done, Morgan . . . whoever you were in the past . . . it is not who you are now. I *know* you. Did you think I would stand as your judge, like Niall, and condemn you?"

His laugh was barbed like the new wire fences being strung across the prairie. "The saintly Miss Munroe, al-ways so generous to the wretched."

The insult had no power to wound. She understood its source.

"Would a saint do this?" she whispered. She took his face between her hands and kissed him. His lips, firm and set, resisted for the space of a second. Then he groaned deep in his chest and pulled her into his arms.

Victory was sweet, but Athena knew at once that the sa-voring must come later. Morgan's kiss was urgent, almost ferocious, brimming with needs she could not expect him to control. Didn't wish him to. Not when she had the power to ease his pain for this little while.

She allowed her body to melt into his. He raised up onto his knees, taking her with him, so that their bodies touched along nearly every point: breast to breast, hip to hip, thigh to thigh. He was burning as if with fever. She felt the stiff fullness of him pressed to her belly and went hot and cold by turns.

Not fear. There was no room for fear. But this was the next great Change, the one that followed the transforma-tion of her heart and her human body. This was the thresh-old from which she could not return to what she had been.

Morgan must not sense any hesitation or doubt. This was for him. Just for him. He'd have no cause to rue what they did together now, no matter how many other things in his past he regretted. This was their chance to make one perfect memory to last a lifetime.

Athena was prepared to accept Morgan into her body even without the sweet persuasion of kisses and caresses.

She almost wished him to pull her down and consummate
the hunger they shared.

But he anointed the corner of her mouth with a whispered kiss, his tongue darting out to touch the rim of her
lips. Its very delicacy was arousing. She opened her
mouth, needing to feel some part of him inside her. He ignored the invitation and gently closed his teeth over her
lower lip.

The sensation of his suckling was exquisite, tugging at
nerves that reached deep into her belly. She closed her eyes
and stopped resisting. When he had carefully explored
every line and curve of her mouth, he bent his head to her
shoulder and grazed his teeth across the sensitive skin at
the juncture of her neck. There was no pain, only delight,
but he soothed each nip with his tongue. His breath sizzled
in her ear.

"Morgan," she sighed. "It is—"

He pressed his finger to her mouth and shook his head.
She understood. There were to be no words, nothing of the
human world to invade this oasis in the snow. Morgan
lifted her against him and pulled her down again, warm
skin on skin. Her breasts came to rest in the hollow of his
shoulders. Effortlessly he positioned her, hands about her
waist, until her nipples brushed his chin and then his lips.

Once before he had touched her there. What he had
done in her room at the ranch was nothing compared to
this. The very tip of his tongue teased her nipples to throb-
bing peaks, and then he took her into his mouth.

Athena had learned, long ago, that women's breasts
were made to feed and nurture infants. Now she discovered that they held secrets of pleasure only a man could un-
lock. Morgan suckled her, kneading her flesh between his
hands. He drew tiny circles with his tongue and drew his
teeth to the very tip before filling his mouth with her.
Athena let her head fall back, revelling in the body Morgan so adored.

This body, this woman's body so perfectly designed to
fit his. And Morgan was determined to make himself ac-

quainted with every part of it. Athena was not sure she could stand the wait.

He gave her no choice. His was a gentle tyranny of pleasure. When he had finished with one breast he moved to the other and gave it equal attention, drinking in her moans with quick kisses.

Then he slid her down, her thighs parted to either side of his hips. She did not quite dare to look between them. The sleek hardness of his erection pushed against her, the hot tip very near to the place that had become so wet and swollen. Already her body knew what it would feel like, how the delicious agony would be soothed only when he filled the hollow ache inside.

But his fingers found her instead, skimming between her legs until they found the hidden nub. His thumb stroked in a rhythmic motion while his other arm supported her even when her legs could no longer hold her up.

A little more, just a little more, and she would find her way to paradise. But it was too soon. This time, when it happened, she wanted him with her in every way. Blindly she reached for any part of him that she could touch and found the warm, ridged plane of his belly.

He caught her wrist and pressed her hand to his chest. He bent her back, and her newly supple body arched to lift her hips over Morgan's thighs, her knees to either side of his, her hair spread across the cave floor.

She was utterly exposed. Helpless, yes, but not in the way she had been in her chair. This was willing surrender, excitement, anticipation of inconceivable joys ahead.

It was not long in coming. Something slipped inside her, past the yielding gateway so open to Morgan's touch. She gasped in surprise.

He leaned over her and kissed her brow. "I am making you ready," he said. And she knew it was fingers that had found their way inside, preparing her, making her mad for a bolder penetration.

"You're so wet," he whispered, brushing her ear with his lips. "So eager to take me inside you."

The human words he had foresworn held an unbearable magic. Yes, she was wet, and ready, and eager with wanting him. But her mouth would not form the sounds to make him obey. She closed her eyes and endured with mingled pain and pleasure, and when the heat of his mouth replaced his fingers, she knew how naive she truly was.

His tongue followed the same burning path as his hands had done, teasing and suckling her, lapping up her wetness, thrusting deep only to withdraw again. Her body climbed to the precipice, leaving her mind still bound to the dull earth.

"No," she gasped. "Morgan, I want . . . both of us. Together."

The heat of his breath left her, and for a moment she was cold and bereft. Then his strong hands were parting her thighs, lifting her bottom, drawing her onto him. Poised, at last, to finish what he had begun.

"When I go inside you," he whispered, "there is no turning back."

She lifted her hand to cover his mouth as he had done hers, silencing him, feeling her wetness on his lips. Then he was inside her, as she had imagined, only a thousand times better. There was no pain, only the fullness of him stretching, filling, completing.

Morgan had known, the moment he had held Athena naked in his arms, the moment he had tasted her, that their joining would be unlike any he had felt before. It wasn't only the many years of enforced celibacy. It wasn't that his one time with Tamar had been so cold and bereft of emotion. No, it was so much more than that, more even than the desire he had felt for Athena almost from the day they had met.

Athena was his. He would be the first to possess her, to take the virginity she willingly conceded to him. She gave herself without reluctance or false modesty. The scent of wanting wreathed the cave, and the intoxicating flavor of his desire still lingered on his tongue.

He knew that this act of love was a gift of the moment.

After it was over, the questions would still be there—the questions and the doubts and the fears. And he didn't care. For now there was only one reality, and both wolf and man cried out to seize it for the first and last time. For a while he and Athena would grasp salvation in both hands.

Yet when he entered her, holding himself back and desperate not to hurt her, he knew how pitiful had been his greatest expectations.

She was slick, hot, and tight around him, and as he moved deeper she pushed her fingers into the carpet of leaves under her back and moaned sweetly. The small barrier gave easily, and still he held back until she reached up and grasped his shoulders in urgent demand.

With a groan of relief he thrust hard and true. It was like coming back to a home long lost. She arched into him, lifting her hips, drawing him deeper still. He cupped her firm buttocks in his hands to hold her steady as he withdrew and thrust again more swiftly. Her gasps came in time to his movements, the very beat of life itself.

But she was too far away. He drew her up so that she straddled his lap and her nipples pressed into his ribs. Her eyes were closed, her skin flushed, her lips parted in an expression of ecstasy.

He wanted to see her eyes, watch them looking into his as he rocked her again and again.

"Look at me," he demanded. "Look at me, Athena."

She did as he commanded. Her lashes fluttered open, revealing changeable eyes almost swallowed up by the black of her pupils. Her gaze held his as if they could join minds as well as bodies, and he remembered the time in Denver when he had felt her all the way to her soul.

She gave her soul to him now, holding his gaze as he carried her to completion. Her little gasps became a long sigh of wonder. He had a moment to savor his triumph, and then he was borne away to that same perfect place.

Athena fell against him, panting, and he held her trembling body close. They were still as one in every way. But separation would come, as inevitable as sunrise, and all he would have was the memory of her silken heat and the rapture in her eyes.

Silence claimed the cave, but it was not the peaceful quiet of rest after vigorous loving. Morgan had no hope for such a reward, and he felt, in Athena's stubborn grip on his body, that she had not found it either. The one thing he could give her had lasted but a few, mindless moments.

Yet when she finally withdrew, it was all he could do to keep from pulling her back and beginning again. His body should not be capable of wanting her, but it did. *He* did. He leaned his head back on the cool stone wall and closed his eyes.

Go, he wished her. *For your sake, Athena. Go.*

He cursed when he felt her breath on his cheek, but even curses deserted him as her hands moved to cup him below. So slight a touch made him full and firm as if he hadn't just taken her.

"This is so new to me," she murmured. Her fingers traced up and down his length, lingering at the velvet tip. "You don't mind?"

He groaned. "Mind? Athena—"

"What you did . . . was so wonderful. I want to do the same for you."

The same? He had never imagined she might touch him, explore him the way he had done with her. She was a sheltered lady, ignorant of the ways of the flesh until he had taught her. But her hands moved again, and he was compelled to admit that she had learned very quickly indeed.

But that was not the final surprise. Just as he had resigned himself to suffering the exquisite torture of her caresses, her hands left him, and her mouth continued the work they had begun. He held on to sanity with fraying resolve. She wanted to give, unselfishly as always, but he would not be in her debt. Not even in this.

With implacable gentleness he grasped her shoulders and pulled her up. Her eyes reflected puzzlement, even hurt. He kissed her mouth and lay back on the blanket of leaves, stretching her out across the length of his body. He eased her legs on either side of his hips to straddle him.

She looked down at him and understood. He gave her control, mastery over what they did together—*together,* sharing pleasure and fulfillment. Morgan became her willing prisoner, and she did not fail to accept his invitation.

Tiny movements of her thighs and hips teased and tormented him as she found just the right position. She eased down, down, taking him in, and then finished with a heady plunge. It was she who controlled the rhythm, who smiled with amazed satisfaction as he became helpless in her power. Her hair swept across his chest in time to her motions. Her small, even teeth nipped at his shoulders.

Neither of them could control the inevitable finish. Morgan was as inept as a boy with his first woman. And yet, by some marvel of the magic they made together, they found the heavens in flawless harmony.

Athena lay with her head tucked beneath his chin, her heartbeat slowing with his. Morgan closed his eyes. If she remained here long enough, her flesh would become his flesh, her bones his bones, her very being an inseparable part of him. But he held her there until she slept and the sun's steep angle cast the cave into twilight.

Darkness let him conceal the thing he could admit in his heart but would never speak.

I love you, he whispered into the fragrance of her hair. *I love you. But love is never enough.*

Chapter 21

The sun was a copper ball in a clear blue sky when
Niall reached the ranch. He saw the circus wagons
massed at the side of the second barn, half buried in snow
that glistened like bright new trappings.

Morgan had told the truth. Caitlin was safe.

Niall dragged his feet the last few steps to the house, up
the stairs and onto the veranda. He had long since ceased
to notice his weariness. His heart had dissolved a little
more with each step away from the murder, melting like an
ice block to pool in his legs and freeze anew.

Many other feet had trod this way in the past few hours.
Caitlin would be with the others. Her friends, her family,
the people she trusted. They would all hear what he had to
say. It didn't matter what they thought of him. No one
else's judgment could affect him now.

He didn't bother to wipe his boots as he entered the hall.
A blast of warmth buffeted his face, sending rivulets of
water from his hat and his snow-crusted clothing.

The hearth in the parlor blazed with an immense fire,
hungrily consuming the heavy branches upon which it fed.
To one side stood a table laid out with the remains of a

meal and several steaming pots of coffee. The space in front of the fire was crowded with people, among them many faces Niall had come to know well: Harry French, the dwarf Ulysses, Tamar the snake charmer . . . and Caitlin. Caitlin, who looked up as he paused on the threshold.

"Niall!" she cried. She started toward him. Her gaze fastened on the closed door at his back and returned to his face. Her footsteps slowed and stopped.

"Morgan went out to find you," she said. "Where is he?"

So that was to be his greeting. Did she know he had been the first to go after her and her companions? Did she care that he had returned unharmed?

If she did not, it was no more than he deserved.

All of them were staring at him now. Their faces told him what they expected to hear.

He pulled off his gloves and let them fall to the floor. "I heard that you tried to leave in the storm. I am . . . glad that you returned safely." Taking his time, he went to the table and poured himself a mug of coffee. It was still hot, and very bitter.

"Where is Morgan?" That was Ulysses, the dwarf, behaving as if he were three times his height. Niall saw something of the old Southern aristocracy in his face, the indomitable stubborn will that could not be entirely broken by any misfortune.

Harry French gripped the back of an armchair and gazed at him through watery blue eyes. The snake charmer glared. The other circus folk, the ones he had never bothered to identify, held an unnatural silence.

Niall set down the mug. "Morgan Holt is dead. I killed him."

The long-case clock at the other end of the room tripped out its steady, imperturbable beat. No one spoke. Ulysses clenched his fists and started toward Niall. Harry held him back.

Caitlin only stared.

Niall turned to French. "You may remain at Long Park as long as necessary—all winter, if you choose." He flexed his fingers. They were coming back to life, as his heart was not. "I will not be here to disturb you."

Harry shook his head. A tear tracked its way down one seamed cheek. Ulysses rested his small hand on the old man's arm.

There was no warning of the attack when it came. Tamar burst out from among the other troupers and charged at Niall, her mouth open on a wordless scream. He put up his hands to stop her, but she carried him back with the weight of her body and sent them both tumbling to the floor.

Niall felt her nails score her cheek and her poisonous breath in his face. His own body was paralyzed. Disembodied voices cried alarm, and hands reached down to restrain his assailant. She struggled, not like a wild cat with tooth and claw, but like a serpent, hissing and darting her head from side to side.

"Murderer," she whispered as troupers pulled her away from him. "I curse you!"

Two brawny men carried Tamar away. The others fled the room as if they could not bear to breathe the same air as the cursed Niall Munroe. Even Harry French left, and Ulysses.

Only Caitlin remained. She had not spoken another word.

This was to be his just punishment.

"It is true, Caitlin," he said. "I killed him."

She swayed, and he had to lock the muscles in his legs to prevent them from carrying him to her side.

"Are you going to tell me . . . that you had no choice?" she whispered. "When he went to save you?"

"No." He stared into the black, round pit of coffee in the mug on the table, imagining it the gateway to hell. "I did it to save my sister." With an effort he met her gaze. "It's not the first time I have done something like this. You should know the whole truth."

"You have—" She choked, swallowed. "Murdered before?"

He picked up the mug and drained the lukewarm coffee. "When I was twelve years old, I drove Athena's mother away. She stole my father from my mother and made Athena what she is. A beast, like Holt. She never came back. She chose her own life over her daughter and the man she claimed to love." He held the mug to his lips long after it was empty. "I did it for my family. I don't regret it."

They said that confession was good for the soul, but his felt no less black. "I don't ask you to understand. As I said, I will not be troubling you further. I'm returning to Athena immediately. She will be leaving for New York as soon as I can arrange it."

"So that she can forget?"

Niall set down the mug so sharply that it cracked, and a last drop of dark liquid leaked onto the table. "Yes."

"And what if Morgan isn't dead?"

Her words cut through his calm facade. "What?"

"He is not an ordinary man. Did you make quite sure that you'd killed him?"

The thought struck him hard between the eyes. "He was dead. I shot him twice."

"He once told me that his kind heal very fast. Didn't you ever notice that about your sister? The way she was able to walk so quickly after she began to try again?"

He had noticed. But he had chosen to ignore what Athena's rapid progress might mean. If Caitlin was correct . . .

Tears flooded his eyes. It was a shameful thing for a man to weep, worse still when he did not comprehend the reasons: anger and frustration that he might not have succeeded. Relief that he had not become a murderer himself. And fear—that worst of all.

He prayed that Caitlin hadn't seen his weakness. "You should not have suggested that possibility," he said harshly. "Now I will have to find him and make certain."

"You're crazy!" She limped forward, forcing him to

avert his face. "I refuse to believe that you would hunt him down again, when you have a chance to atone for your mistake!"

"By giving my sister to him? You have no right to ask that of me. No right."

"But I do." Her silence compelled him to look up. She had stopped a few feet away, skin flushed and eyes very bright. "You gave me that right. Damn you, Niall Munroe, is it that you cannot see what love is?" She lifted one small, graceful hand. "Or can it be that you don't believe yourself worthy of love and forgiveness?"

"I ask no forgiveness."

"But you want it, just the same." She came closer, lips parted. "Maybe my forgiveness doesn't matter much, but I forgive you, Niall. You have not lost all your chances. You can choose to let Athena make her own life. You can change yours."

He laughed bitterly. "For the sake of love?"

"I have faith in you. You wanted me once, as your mistress. If you still do . . . it is not too late for us."

His legs had become paralyzed with more than cold and weariness. They kept him still as she put her roughened fingertips to his face, holding him prisoner with eyes incapable of deception.

"I will go with you, Niall—wherever and however you wish." She lifted her face to his and kissed him.

Need surged within him, scattering every other thought. He lifted her supple weight in his arms and returned the kiss with interest, devouring that full, tender mouth with all the violence of unrequited lust. She did not recoil. In her little body was a whirlwind of passion every bit a match for his. She leaned into him, small breasts tucked into the hollow of his shoulders. Her warmth dissipated the last of the cold, a source of heat more effective than any fire could have been.

Heat, and desire. His body hungered for her the way a man near death hungered for life. She *was* life. If he took what she offered, he would choose a path he had never considered before, one that led to beginnings and not endings. He would not be weak, but strong—everything a man was meant to be.

A few steps up the stairs and they'd be at his bedchamber. Already the wiry muscles in her thighs clasped him about the hips, inviting him inside. He knew he could take her again and again and never be satisfied. She'd buck and writhe beneath him, astride him, in every imaginable way a woman could accept a man. Her eyes told him that no pleasure, no erotic wish, was to be denied.

Breathing hard, he clasped her to him and carried her to his bed. Already she was undoing the hooks and buttons of her bodice, baring the light chemise that was her only concession to modesty. He could not shed the layers of his clothing swiftly enough. In frenzied impatience she helped him, tearing at fastenings and pulling sleeves.

She was the first to be naked, her petite form unmarred save for a few small bruises. Her cast had been removed, and her leg seemed whole and sound save for her slight limp. *She* was not like Athena, and yet . . .

Before he could complete the thought, her hands were upon his trousers, tugging and caressing at the same time. The torment was almost intolerable. Somehow she came to be astride him, her clever fingers teasing him free of all restraint. A whisper touch danced over his hot, aching flesh.

"Ah," she whispered. "What a grand mount it is. Let me ride, my stallion. Let me ride as I've never ridden before."

Niall stood at the center of one last moment of sanity, one final chance to take control. *Must get back to Denver,* the cold part of his brain muttered. *If Morgan isn't dead . . . if Athena . . .*

Then rational thought ceased, because he was being enveloped in heat and warmth, and Caitlin's mouth was on his. She rode just as she had promised, fulfilling the wildest fantasies he had ever entertained as boy or man. He thrust hard, and she fell upon him with cries and groans, her head flung back and her hair aglow as if from a thousand tiny sparks.

He came as quickly as an untried boy. Caitlin collapsed across his chest, refusing to set him free. And he found, much to his amazement, that his body was not finished with her. Not nearly finished.

She gave a little cry as he rolled her beneath him. He held himself above her, gazing into her heavy-lidded eyes.

"Do you think you've won?" he asked softly. "Do you think you've had the better of me, Caitlin?" He cupped her cheek in his palm, the first gentle caress he had given her since their joining. "No woman masters me. Not even you."

She squirmed, the motions of her body arousing him all over again. "Niall, it isn't what you—"

He thrust his tongue into her mouth, absorbing her protest. In a heartbeat her arms were linked behind his neck. He reached back and caught her wrists, pulled them one by one to the pillow above her head.

"Now it is my turn," he said, and held her hands trapped with one of his while his other slid between her thighs. He sought and found the moist, sensitive part of her that had clasped him so boldly and stroked with a fingertip. She released a low, satisfying moan.

He took his time with her, as he never had with the easy women he'd known in the past—teasing, caressing, watching her face as it altered from surprise to pleasure to mindless ecstasy. So she didn't think he could be a lover, to give as well as take?

Let her realize just how wrong she was. Keeping his own lust in check, he kissed her from forehead to the tips of her toes, lingering at her breasts, finely formed and winsome—those he'd once considered so small—and the intimate place he had made ready with his touch. She tasted of sunshine and exotic spices, simple and complex all at once.

Caitlin Hughes was no virgin. She was a sorceress of ancient carnal rites made to entrap a man—innocent and wanton, sweet and sinful, naive and wise beyond her years. Yet now she was his, and he possessed her as fully as she had seduced him. Her thighs were already parted for his entrance. As he thrust inside her, he began to understand why reasonable men would risk everything, give up the world itself, for the sake of a woman.

"Caitlin," he whispered. "Damn you, Caitlin."

She only locked her ankles behind his waist and pulled him deeper. This time she was the one who reached the peak first, shuddering with rhythmic pulses of abandoned joy. He followed a moment later and felt his seed pour into her body.

He should have slept then, or left the room without a backward glance as he had done with the other nameless women who had given themselves for something far more concrete than love. But Caitlin looked up at him with gentle wisdom, inviting him into a place that went beyond mere bodies and brushed the soul with velvet wings.

She had opened the gates too wide, and through them he saw terrible visions of all he had been and done. The sheets upon which Caitlin lay were stained with blood. Morgan's blood. And beside the bed, looking on with mocking eyes, was Gwenyth Desbois.

You will never be free of us, she whispered. *Never.*

Niall pushed away from Caitlin and jumped to the floor. Morgan and Desbois vanished. Caitlin sat up, reaching after him. Beckoning him to return to the bed he had made for himself.

"Niall?"

He snatched up his shirt and trousers. "I must go to Denver."

He expected her to make some claim upon him, subtle feminine blackmail for the privilege of enjoying her favors, or a storm of tears to awaken his guilt. He should have known better. She swung her legs over the bed and stood before him, hands on hips as if they had never shared a lovers' bed.

"Don't be a fool," she said. "There are things more powerful than all your wealth and influence. This is a battle you cannot win."

He turned his back on her and buttoned his shirt with shaking fingers. "You should not stand against me, Caitlin. I would very much regret it should any harm come to you."

She laughed. "Is that your fine declaration of love, Niall Munroe?"

"Love?" He faced her again, ignoring the blatant lure of her body. "Is that what you thought we shared? I am sorry to disappoint you, but I trust you will accept reimbursement for your time, even if it is only in the paltry form of money."

She caught her breath. He saw how well he had struck, and hated himself for it. Hated her more for having made him feel guilt, and tenderness, and shame. For having made him *feel*.

"Damn you," he said. "Damn you and all your kind—"

An explosion of pain ended his curse. Fireworks burst in his head, and then he was falling, falling endlessly into the pit reserved especially for men destroyed by love.

"*What have you done?*"
Caitlin snatched the branch from Tamar and tossed it aside. It thudded against the wall and came to lie at the foot of the bed that she and Niall had so recently shared.

She dropped to her knees beside Niall and touched his forehead. Her fingers came away bloody. She pressed her ear to his chest, numb with terror, and heard the muted beat of his heart. His breaths were shallow but steady.

Still alive. Thank the gods, still alive.

Working quickly, she snatched a pillow from the bed and gently rested Niall's head upon it. She dipped a towel in water from the washbasin and dabbed at the wound. It was not a large cut, though the swelling had already begun. She devised a makeshift bandage of pieces torn from the bedsheet and wrapped it about Niall's head. Knowing she hadn't the strength to lift him, she covered him with a blanket and tucked it close.

Only then, when her ministrations were complete, did she turn on the snake charmer with all the fury at her command.

"Why?" she demanded. "Why, Tamar?"

"You ask why?" Tamar showed her small, slightly pointed teeth in an unrepentant smile. "He killed my Morgan. He deserves to die."

Caitlin closed her eyes and prayed for fortitude. "You are an idiot, Tamar."

"And you are a traitor and a whore to lie with him who murdered my love!"

Caitlin became aware of her nakedness and draped herself in the torn sheet. "Morgan was never your love," she said, forcing herself to calm. "And he is not dead. I was making sure that he had a chance to recover and get away before Niall realized that fact."

Tamar's vicious mask crumbled into bewilderment. "How is he not dead? Tell me!"

"I think that is something we would all like to know."

Harry and Ulysses walked into the room, eyes carefully avoiding the disheveled bed and Caitlin's state of undress. Ulysses crouched beside Niall, and Harry took Tamar's arm in a firm grip.

"Munroe said he had shot Morgan," Ulysses said, inspecting Caitlin's bandage. "Do you believe that he was lying?"

"No." Caitlin shivered and sat on the edge of the bed, watching Niall's quiet face. It was the first time she had ever seen him at peace, even for a moment. "Will Niall be all right?"

Ulysses sighed and sat back on his heels. "A man who remains unconscious too long may not recover. You must hope that he wakes soon."

How coldly he spoke, as if Niall's life or death didn't matter. But he still regarded Niall as the man who had murdered his friend.

"Morgan is not dead," she said, putting her conviction into every word. "Think, Uly. He could have killed Niall if he chose. But other things are important to him now. He must have known that his best chance of keeping himself and Niall alive would be to use Niall's ignorance and feign death."

"You assume a great deal, Firefly."

"I don't assume. I believe. Morgan has a reason to want to live. If he has any strength at all, he is on his way to Denver at this very moment."

Ulysses and Harry exchanged glances. Harry fished in his pocket for a handkerchief. After a moment he composed himself and straightened, casting Tamar a stark glance that failed to cover his relief.

"Caitlin is right," he said. "Morgan does have a reason to live. And if he is alive, he will go to Athena."

"As Niall would have, once he realized there was a chance that Morgan survived." She took Ulysses's place beside Niall, stroking bloodstained hair away from his pale forehead. "I could have let him go on believing that Morgan was dead, but he had already begun to torment himself over what he had done. He is not an evil man. I had to give him a little hope of redemption. But I also had to stop him from going after Morgan again."

Ulysses's glance at the bed was evidence enough that he understood. Harry blushed. Tamar took advantage of the moment and pulled free.

"If my wolf is alive, I must go to him at once," she said.

Caitlin jumped to her feet. "*You* are not going anywhere. You've brought only pain to everything you touch."

"And who are you to stop me?"

Tamar's hateful face blurred in Caitlin's vision. She knew then that she was prepared to do anything, even kill, to protect Morgan and Athena. And Niall, who needed everything she had to give. "If he dies—"

"I fear that Caitlin is correct, Tamar," Ulysses said, stepping between them. In his hand was a tiny pearl-handled derringer. "We cannot let you leave."

Tamar stared down at him with unconcealed contempt. "Will you shoot me, little man?"

"If I must. But I think that you also wish to live."

She spat at him. Ulysses stood unwavering, his gaze fixed to Tamar's face. "Morgan cannot love you, Tamar. His heart is bestowed upon another, and his kind mate for life."

Her eyes widened. "And do you think I would turn to you if I cannot have him?"

Caitlin watched with growing bafflement. For Ulysses to threaten violence was unthinkable. But something in his face, the stoic pain of a man pushed beyond his endurance, told a tale that shocked her more than the pistol in his hand.

"No," Ulysses said quietly. "I do not believe that. But you have done enough mischief, and it must stop."

"You cannot get to Denver alone," Harry added, making a last attempt to reason with her. "Ulysses and I will leave immediately and make sure that Morgan is all right. It is better this way, Tamar."

She answered by turning quickly toward the door. Ulysses raised the derringer and fired. The bullet pierced the doorjamb a few inches to the left of Tamar's shoulder.

Caitlin had never seen Tamar blanch, but she did so now, staggering back into Harry's arms. Harry forced her hands behind her back, hardly less pale than she.

Ulysses lowered the pistol. His hand was shaking. Caitlin knew that he had not missed due to lack of skill, or even nerves. In his face she read the conviction that he could never hurt Tamar, no matter what the provocation.

"I know there is one thing you truly love, Tamar," he said. "Since I knew you were apt to cause further difficulties, I took the liberty of commandeering your serpents and securing them in a safe but hidden location where you are unlikely to find them. They require warmth, and they will continue to receive it as long as you comport yourself reasonably. I trust I have made myself understood."

Tamar's mouth fell open. Ulysses had, indeed, found the one weak spot in the snake charmer's arsenal.

"I will have my vengeance," she hissed.

Ulysses shrugged and glanced at Harry. "Lock her in one of the rooms," he said. "She will not try to escape as long as her snakes are in custody."

Shaking his head sadly, Harry hustled Tamar out of Niall's room. Caitlin checked to make sure that Niall was still breathing steadily and touched Ulysses's shoulder.

"You and Harry must go right away," she said. "Morgan and Athena will need all the help they can get if he's made it back to Denver."

"And you?"

She ached for the sadness in his eyes. "I must remain here with Niall until he wakes up."

"Yes." Ulysses frowned at Niall. "You may not have to wait too long. I believe he is stirring. I would definitely prefer to be well gone before he regains full consciousness."

Caitlin gazed at Niall's face and saw the faint twitch of his lips, the flutter of an eyelid. Thank the ancient ones.

Harry appeared at the door. "It's done," he said. "I think you were right about the snakes, Uly. But how shall we get to Denver? The wagons are far too slow."

"There are several more practical conveyances in the carriage house. Mr. Munroe is in no position to object if we borrow one, and the horses to draw it. We will enlist our fellow troupers to create a distraction in the event that any of the ranch laborers attempt to interfere."

Harry nodded. Caitlin left Niall's side long enough to hug the old man and plant a kiss on the top of Ulysses's golden curls.

"Good luck," she said. "Do everything you can to help Morgan and Athena. They were meant to be together."

"We will find a way," Harry said. He nodded at Niall. "Firefly, are you sure?"

"Yes." She smiled wryly. "But the mad are always certain."

Ulysses took her hand and placed the pistol in it. "Keep this, just in case."

She wanted nothing more than to fling it across the

room, but she placed it on the bed instead. "You had better go."

With a final, worried look, Harry followed Ulysses from the room.

Caitlin took up her vigil at Niall's side, noting each sign of returning consciousness. They came with increasing frequency, and at last he opened his eyes, blinked, and tried to focus on her face.

"What?" he murmured. His hand flailed toward his head and the large lump that had formed there. "Caitlin?"

"It's all right." She checked the bandage and stroked his cheek. "You must rest."

"Something is—" He tried to sit up, gasped, and subsided back to the floor. Caitlin tucked the blankets about him, prepared to sit on top of him if necessary.

Fortunately, his body seemed to realize what his will did not. He closed his eyes again and fell into what Caitlin prayed was an ordinary, healing sleep. An hour passed, and then another. He woke and asked for water; she poured from the pitcher and held the glass to his lips. Day became night; he slept fitfully, waking often with vague questions and requests for water. By the time dawn came with its false promise of peace, she knew he would not remain still much longer.

His features frozen in concentration, Niall rose onto his elbows. He felt the lump on his head and met Caitlin's gaze.

"How?" he asked hoarsely. "Someone . . . hit me."

"Yes." There was no point in lying. "Tamar struck you from behind."

"Tamar." He tried to gather his feet under his body and reached out for Caitlin's support. She helped him rise and cross to the bed, remembering at the last instant to cover the pistol with a corner of the coverlet.

"She was very angry, but she can't hurt anyone now," Caitlin said, easing him down. "It was a bad blow. You must be careful, Niall."

"Holt . . . might still be alive. I must get to Denver."

The blow had obviously not dulled his memory in the slightest. "I wish Tamar had managed to knock some sense into that thick skull of yours," she said. "If you try to ride now, you will suffer for it. I doubt you can even drive a wagon."

He pushed her away. "I warned you before, Caitlin. Don't . . . try to stop me."

She thought of the pistol at the end of the bed, and of how far she'd be willing to go to protect him and the others she loved. Uly hadn't been able to shoot Tamar. Could she so much as threaten Niall? Would he believe such a threat?

Simple persuasion, even of the sexual variety, would not work on him now. And that left but one option.

"If I don't try to stop you," she said, "then I am coming with you."

"No." The word was instant, sharp, and lucid. "I don't want you involved in what I must do."

"But I am involved. And there is nothing you can do to change that." She gripped his arm, compelling him to look at her. "You have suffered a blow to the head. What if you fall unconscious again? What if you cannot drive or ride? You would be foolish to go alone." She smiled grimly. "And even if you keep me from accompanying you, I will follow."

He stared at her, weighing her words. Would he dismiss her, as he would most anyone who made a similar promise . . . or would he realize she meant exactly what she said?

"You damned, stubborn wench. You would get yourself killed." He gathered his weight onto his feet and tried to stand. His body tilted dangerously. "I can't stop you . . . now. But you will do as I say and not interfere. Do you hear me?" He grabbed her shoulders, pressing a little too heavily. "Do you, Caitlin Hughes?"

"I hear you." *But do not ask me to promise anything. Do not ask me to choose between you and my dearest friends.*

"Then—" He gritted his teeth. "Help me dress. We must go."

How he hated asking for her help. Meekly she collected his clothing and assisted him with the lightest touch possible, as if she were a servant and not a lover who had seen his every vulnerability. When they were both bundled up and Niall had collected two saddlebags' worth of provisions, he led her out to the barn and met one of the ranch hands walking hurriedly toward the house.

"Mr. Munroe," the man said, taken aback. He shot a glance at Caitlin. "I was just comin' to find you. Them circus folk—they stole one of the buggies. Chuck says they must a' left a few hours before sunset last night."

Niall swore. "No one stopped them?"

"Some of their friends played a trick to get us away. Said they'd seen a wolf after the cattle, so we all went out . . ." He ducked his head. "I'm sorry, Mr. Munroe."

Niall swung on Caitlin. "Did you know about this?"

"Yes. Harry and Ulysses were worried about Morgan, as I was."

"The old man and the midget? Even with the night's travel, they can't be that far ahead." Niall turned back to the ranch hand. "Saddle two of the fastest horses, and do it quickly."

The man hastened to obey. Soon he was leading out two horses, both fine mounts to Caitlin's experienced eye. Before Niall or the hand could offer help, she leaped onto the smaller horse's back and caught up the reins. Niall followed, gingerly, wincing at the pain in his skull.

He would not want her solicitude now. All she could hope was that she had some small influence upon him when the time came to face the battle that lay ahead.

Chapter 22

Dawn crept into the cave on velvet feet, so soft that neither human eyes nor ears could detect it.

Athena heard. She kept her eyes squeezed shut and begged the light to retreat, to let night come again. Endless night, untroubled by future or past. A night made only for loving and being loved.

Morgan's chest rose and fell beneath her cheek, and his arm held its protective curve about her waist, loose but undeniably possessive.

As merciless as the passing of time, the light teased its way beneath her lids. She opened them slowly. Her first sight was of Morgan's broad chest, the fine, dark mantle of hair, the slope of his hard belly. She checked herself before her gazed strayed lower.

There was no going back to last night's joyful interlude. She clung desperately to the last threads of it, as she'd once done when she woke from a dream of running on crippled legs. But like all dreams, this too must come to an end.

Moving by the tiniest increments, she leaned back to study Morgan's face. It had not yet taken on the harsh lines and wariness it usually wore by daylight, nor did his features reflect the surrender and abandon of their love-making. Jaw, lips, eyes, forehead, all were relaxed. Waiting. Holding fast to the peace he so seldom allowed himself.

She ached to touch him. But if he still slept, she couldn't rob him of these moments. She wished she could sleep again and find herself in a new dream, one in which she and Morgan were together with no thought of the vast gulf that lay between them.

A raven croaked harshly among the pines outside. Morgan opened one eye and muttered an inaudible curse. His arm tightened about her as if he expected her to flee.

"Good morning," she whispered. She kissed his cheek, challenging him to reject that homely intimacy. His jaw flexed and released. "Did you sleep well?"

He might have thought her mad for indulging in such banal civilities, as if they were an ordinary newlywed couple the first morning after their marriage—a little shy, a little awkward, still aglow with sensual discoveries and looking forward to many more such adventures to come.

But he turned his head to look at her, and all the tenderness he found so difficult to show lay raw and exposed in his eyes. "Did you?"

"Very well." She tucked her head on his shoulder and laced her fingers through his. "I only wish . . ."

He stiffened. "What do you wish?"

She threw caution to the winds. "I wish that you and I could make this moment last forever."

He sat up, taking care to let her down gently as he changed position. Athena swallowed the sudden thickness of tears and drew her knees to her chest. *You have ruined it. Words . . . words only frighten him away.*

Morgan sat with his back to the sloping cave wall just as he had last night before the loving, as unapproachable as a heathen idol carved of stone. She knew the nature of the heart that beat within his broad chest, the gentleness of which he was capable, the stubborn loyalty that belied his judgment of himself. But he wanted to pretend she did not understand.

"It's no use, Morgan," she said. "We cannot go back."

He stared fiercely at the opposite wall. A gust of cold air blew in the cave mouth, lifting long black strands of hair across his face and shoulders. He made no attempt to brush them away.

"No," he said. "You cannot go back to what you were."

It was not what she had meant. "An invalid? Living in denial of half of myself? You're right, Morgan. I can only go forward, as you must."

He said nothing. She wanted to scream and jump up and down, if only to make him look at her. The closeness of their joining had been as fragile as a snowflake, evaporated in an instant of heat and passion. How could everything they had built last night have vanished so completely?

With an effort she composed herself. Violent emotion would only drive him further away. The wrong words might frighten him, but they were all she had.

"We never finished our discussion," she said. "There is still time for you to tell me everything, Morgan. I said I would listen, and not judge. I meant it. And whether you like it or not, you can't shut me out so easily. You see . . . I love you."

The cave reverberated with her calm declaration. Her heart tripped out a frantic tattoo. Morgan blinked, once, the only sign that he had heard and understood.

"There," she said with false lightness. "I have given you my greatest secret. I doubt that yours is any more terrifying."

Slowly he looked at her, expressionless to any eyes but hers. "What do you want of me?"

No tears, she commanded. *It is his way. It is always his way to hide when he feels too much.* "I want to know what you want. I want to understand why you think you must protect me from yourself when we have given each other so much."

He took in a long, deep breath and let it out again,

wreathing his face in mist. "Will you come with me, now?"

"What?"

"I asked you once before," he said. "Will you come with me—away from Denver, from Colorado, taking nothing, giving up everything you've known? Will you, Athena?"

Yes, her heart cried. *Yes, yes, and yes.* But there was something wrong with his question and her own response to it. She hesitated, and in that hesitation lay the cold, hard seed of doubt.

So much had altered since the first time he had asked her to abandon her life. She had remembered how to Change, and healed herself. She had begun to discover that what seemed important was only window dressing and false pride. She had learned to love, not with charitable dispassion, but with her entire soul.

She was not the person she had been a few months ago. But Morgan demanded her complete surrender without offering his trust in return. He had tried to drive her away even as he claimed her for his own. He asked her to run, not toward a real life together, but away from what he feared in himself.

"You want me to go with you," she said. "But you expect me to do so in ignorance. You want me to trust you, when you will not trust me with the things that have hurt you and made you what you are. You refuse to believe that I'm strong enough to accept whatever you tell me." She held out her hand, cupping her palm as if she could touch his face. "All I ask is that you confide in me, Morgan. Confide in the woman who loves you. If you do that now, for me, I will go with you to the ends of the earth."

Dry leaves rustled across the cavern floor. Athena's heart beat five, ten, twenty times before Morgan moved. He smiled, only with his mouth, and she knew that she had lost her gamble.

"Your love is not enough," he said, almost gently. "The answers you want are only the beginning. You would find no contentment, no peace. You would always expect what I can't give you."

"You mean that you could not love me."

"Love breaks like thin ice on a lake just when you think it is sound to cross." He lowered his head so that the dark mass of his hair concealed his face. "It's a hard lesson, but it will make you stronger in the end."

"Strong . . . as you are? Is this your example, Morgan?" She uncurled and stood to face him. "Is it strength to pretend that none of this ever happened? Should I let my past determine my future, crawl back into my chair and play at being helpless so that I will be safe until the day I die?"

"You will not be safe in Denver."

Such irrational anger stirred in Athena that it was as if the wolf had taken her mind without Changing her body.

"Oh?" she choked out. "What danger will I face, once you are gone? My heart will be cast in iron, but I'll still be able to help those who can find some use in hope. If I'm careful, I can concoct an explanation for my recent behavior that may convince society to accept me back into its midst."

His eyes burned through the veil of his hair. "You will not be safe as long as your brother is alive."

"I know . . . I know that he tried to kill you, but he is not an evil man. I will talk to him. I'll make him understand, and he'll regret what he did—"

"No." Morgan stood, moving as if every bone and muscle in his body had been torn apart. "Niall told me the truth about your mother, Athena. He hid it from you all these years. He wanted you to remain dependent and weak, so that he wouldn't have to remember the woman who stole your father's love."

"What truth?" she whispered.

Morgan hesitated, staring toward the mouth of the cave.

"What truth?" She strode toward him and stood so close that he had no choice but to meet her gaze. "Tell me!"

He lifted his hand and let it fall. "He told me that he got rid of your mother."

Her knees locked, keeping her on her feet. "I don't understand."

"He hated her. He hated what she was, and that your father loved her more than he did his own mother. He was still a boy when he—"

"No." She pressed her hands over her ears. "I don't believe it."

"He had no reason to lie to me." The gentleness of Morgan's voice pierced her shock as no shout could. "Listen to me. You must be on guard against him. He knows what you are, and he hates you for it, just as he hated your mother. You betrayed him when you came to me. He will not forgive you, Athena. If he killed once, he can kill again."

"Like you?" She backed toward the entrance. "Do you presume to understand what Niall is because you have committed murder?"

The words were out of her mouth before she could stop them. She had sworn not to judge him, not to use his past against him, and she had failed in her promise. "Morgan—"

His eyes were frosted glass. "I should have killed him."

In that moment she believed that he had done what Cecily claimed, that he could kill a man without compunction or regret. She stood on the lip of the cave, half in light and half in shadow, riven just as surely between woman and wolf, trust and betrayal, love and hate.

There was no certainty, no peace. The two men she loved most had become deadly strangers. Doubt ate at her like a cancer. Her familiar world had done more than change; it had shattered. She had only the smallest hope of putting it back together again. And she must do it alone. For Morgan's sake, for Niall's . . . and because she had no right to happiness she had not earned.

"I am going," she said. "I'm going to find my brother and make him tell me the truth." She stepped into harsh noon light, and Morgan tensed to follow. *"No.* Don't come after me. You owe me nothing." She closed her eyes to the sight of his beloved face. "You are free."

He laughed wretchedly. "Don't trust him. Athena—"

She Changed and was ready when he followed. She turned on him, snapping and snarling, until he had to retreat or defend himself. But he did not Change. He knelt in the snow, hands on his thighs, and watched her go.

Phantom tears gathered behind her wolf's eyes. *It must be this way. Niall is still my brother. You would destroy us both if you killed for my sake. And I am not strong enough, my love. Not strong enough to believe in you.*

Athena lost herself in the wolf and ran, with all her strength, until she knew nothing but the flex of muscle and the rush of wind through her fur. When she reached the ranch she traced a wide circle around the buildings and approached from the rear of the house, a shadow all but invisible to human eyes. At the door she Changed, slipped into the house, and dashed up the stairs to her room. There she hastily donned a calico skirt and shirtwaist, barely enough to cover her nakedness.

Voices echoed downstairs, but none of them was Niall's. She took the stairs two at a time and confronted a pair of startled troupers, men she recognized as Harry's star aerialists.

"Where is Mr. Munroe?" she demanded.

They exchanged glances. "Miss Athena?" one of them said. "He left with Caitlin, just after dawn."

She had no time to consider the implications of Caitlin's involvement. "Where did they go?"

"I heard it was to look for you in Denver," the other man said. "Harry and Ulysses left last night. They said you might be in trouble." He paused. "Can we help, Miss Athena?"

She shook her head and tried to clear her mind. Did Harry and Ulysses know that Niall had tried to kill Morgan? Was that why they had gone to Denver? Why had Niall taken Caitlin, when surely he must believe that Morgan was dead and he was returning to face his sister's anguish? Caitlin would hate him just as much for what he had done.

Without another word to the troupers, Athena ran back upstairs and threw open the wardrobe. On one of the shelves she found a pair of trousers and a flannel shirt. She pulled out a pair of old boots and quickly made a bundle of the clothing, cinching it with a braided leather cord. She carried the bundle outside, dropped it in the snow, stripped, and Changed.

Wolf's jaws closed around the cord. She could reach Denver much more quickly in wolf shape, but there was no telling when she might catch up with Niall. If she found him in the city, she would need the clothing.

She would need every tiny advantage she could get.

Human voices shouted, severing her thoughts. She had been seen, and no rancher would balk at shooting a wolf. She burst from a standstill into a dead run. Rifle shot cracked in her wake. Pellets of snow brushed her fur, and a second bullet exploded in the ground where she had been an instant before. Then she was beyond human reach, headed unerringly toward Denver.

It was when she had reached the foothills, just as the sun was sinking behind the Front Range, that she remembered the significance of this night, the detail she had so completely put from her mind. It was the night of the Winter Ball.

She barked a wolf's laugh around the leather between her teeth. The ball. The very pinnacle of her social life, the event of which she had been so inordinately proud. What had once seemed worth a year's painstaking effort had become just another self-indulgent folly, a consolation prize to a woman who had misplaced the true meaning of life.

Cecily would be at the ball, lording it over everyone. Nothing would stop her, not even Athena's escape and its possible consequences to her designs upon Niall. Niall would expect Athena to be there under Cecily's vigilant eye. But he would not find his sister. Not before she found him.

Tonight's Winter Ball would indeed be one to remember.

I am sorry, Mr. Munroe," the unfamiliar servant said with a diffident shake of his head, "but Miss Hockensmith has gone to the ball."

The Winter Ball. Dammit, he had entirely forgotten about that bit of foolishness. Cecily had mentioned that she'd changed the venue to the Windsor, but he'd forgotten that as well.

Nothing tonight was what it should be. There had been no groom lodged in the rooms over the stable to take his and Caitlin's weary mounts. Romero was gone. The house was noticeably devoid of servants. Niall stood in the hall of his own home, staring into the face of a man he did not know. Caitlin waited behind him, her gaze taking in the vastness of the high ceiling and the gilt and marble embellishments. She was no more lost than he.

"Who the devil are you?" he demanded, tossing the servant his gloves. "Where is Brinkley?"

"I regret to say that Mr. Brinkley has tendered his resignation," the man said with an air of false regret. "Miss Hockensmith felt it necessary to replace him and the other servants who have since departed."

Good God. Had the entire world fallen apart in the short time he had been gone? "The other servants?"

The man cleared his throat. "There have been a number of changes in the staff during the past several days, sir. You may wish to consult Miss Hockensmith for the details. Would you and the young lady care to rest in the parlor while I send for tea?"

"Miss Munroe has accompanied Miss Hockensmith to the ball?"

This time the butler was not so quick with an answer. "I . . . am not informed as to Miss Munroe's whereabouts, sir."

"What do you mean?" Niall seized the man's collar. "Where is my sister?"

"Sir . . . I . . . ah—" He choked and went very pale. "She has not been in residence since my arrival. Miss Hockensmith said that . . . that she had run mad, threatening to . . . to kill Miss Hockensmith if she attempted to restrain Miss Munroe. That is . . . all I know!"

Niall let him fall to the ground. Athena, run mad? Escaped? And Cecily had traipsed off to the ball as if all was well, knowing where Athena must have gone. The sudden resignation and hiring of servants was nothing compared to this.

"She went to warn Morgan," Caitlin said behind him. "She must have, knowing how much you hated him. Lord, if she made it to the mountains—"

"She could be anywhere. Lost . . ." *Or with* him. Niall stumbled toward the door.

"You can't go back to the mountains now," Caitlin said, grasping his arm. He tried to shake her off, but her grip was sure and fearless. "You're exhausted, and you would not know where to look. She will find Morgan if he hasn't found her first."

"If you are right, and he is alive." Niall stopped at the door, leaning his head against the paneled wood. "He may have her now."

"Then you have a chance to do right, Niall. Let them go. Let them live the life they were meant to have."

Niall ignored her, icy panic racing through his veins. "Cecily," he said, biting off the name. He snatched his coat from the stand where the new butler had hung it and threw it around his shoulders. He didn't bother to question the servant further, but strode down the hall and to the rear door facing the carriage house. Caitlin's footsteps drummed at his heels.

He harnessed one of the horses to the fastest buggy and swung into the seat. Caitlin climbed up beside him. With a grunt he lashed the chestnut out of the carriage house, down the lane and into the street.

In a matter of minutes he had reached Eighteenth and Larimer. The carriages of ballgoers made the streets almost as congested as they were during the business day, and as he neared the Windsor every available space was occupied by a conveyance. He drew the buggy as close to the Windsor as possible and tied the horse to a lamppost.

"You have no part in this," he told Caitlin. "Stay here."

She shook her head, jaw set. He jumped down from the seat and started for the Windsor at a furious pace, not looking behind to see if she followed.

Only two hours into the ball, Cecily reflected, and everything was utterly perfect.

She gracefully deflected a compliment from one of Denver's leading dowagers and waved her fan with an elegant tilt of her wrist. The Windsor ballroom was crowded from end to end with Denver's elite and visiting dignitaries, many of them people that bitch Athena would never have thought to invite. The orchestra played sparkling melodies to delight every ear, and the refreshments in the adjoining room had been created by some of the city's most skilled chefs. This was Cecily's triumph, and hers alone.

As long as Athena and her brother did not spoil it. Cecily glanced about the mirrored chamber for the hundredth time. It was sheer foolishness to think that the bitch would return after her escape four days ago. Doubtless she had either perished in the mountains or found her lover and run off with him—if she had miraculously managed to reach him before Niall.

Nevertheless, Cecily had circulated sly rumors about the reasons for Athena's sudden disappearance. When she had told a few choice gossips that Athena was able to walk—that she had doubtless been deceiving society for years—she had spiced the narrative with the hushed, embarrassed account of how the girl had run mad and attacked her like a wild beast, threatening her very life.

How ready were the bored matrons and misses of Denver to believe such a lurid tale, especially when Cecily encouraged speculation that Athena had manipulated them into making excessive contributions for pity's sake. Cecily showed them the substantial bruise on her arm where Athena had grabbed her. She expressed compassion for the young woman who had fallen prey to bad elements and her own weak nature. A little truth here, a bit of exaggeration there, and she had laid the groundwork to explain Athena's violent deterioration.

Cecily had alerted the police, of course, and told them that Miss Munroe had declared her intent to travel into the mountains alone. If they had found the girl, Cecily would be seen as having done her duty, and Niall could not fault her. Any accusations Athena might make could be explained as resulting from her lunacy; Cecily had every confidence of victory in a contest of wits. But the police had not found Athena, nor had anyone been able to contact her brother because of the bitter storm. It was a tragedy indeed.

But the ball must go on. Everyone agreed, most solemnly, that Cecily was holding up very well. She had done everything she could, but Munroe had expected too much in asking her to care for a madwoman. Poor, demented Athena had done so much to create the ball, even if she had turned her back on society as well as sanity. It would be the height of irresponsibility to cancel the affair and deprive the blameless unfortunates who would benefit from the money collected.

So Cecily had forged ahead, swallowing her unease. She well knew she had Niall to face, assuming he returned from his confrontation with Holt. Perhaps he would not. Cecily felt only a lingering regret at the prospect. If Athena was mad—and clearly she was—*he* might be unstable as well. She could no longer bring herself to believe that marriage to Niall Munroe brought advantages enough to outweigh the disadvantages—particularly when she had begun to make some very promising acquaintances among Denver's wealthy bachelors.

Cecily issued a brave smile for the benefit of her peers and declined a dance offer from one such gentleman. Best to appear a little reserved, a little sorrowful over the recent events than seem too quick to dismiss them. There would be ample time for celebration after the ball, when her new social position was firmly established and she had dealt with Niall. If he survived.

She was speaking to Mrs. Gottschalk, her back to the ballroom doors, when the murmur of many voices swelled to the buzzing of a disturbed hive of bees. The music lurched to a halt. Cecily paused in her solemn speech and turned around.

Niall Munroe stood in the doorway, mud-splattered and dressed as if he had arrived straight from the wilderness, which very likely he had. At his shoulder stood the red-haired creature Caitlin, as bedraggled as he.

Cecily shrank in on herself as if she could hide from the gaze that raked the crowd. Voices lifted in question, but no one approached Niall. He exuded violence like a rabid dog.

"Does he know?" someone whispered behind her.

"Why would he be here if he did not? Look at his face!"

"The poor man . . ."

"He must have known she was mad."

Oh, he knew; of that Cecily was certain. He had concealed Athena's lunacy behind a mask of propriety and dependence. And he also knew that she was missing. He had surely been to the house and spoken to the servants.

Cecily tried to breathe and felt her corset tighten about her chest. She should be well prepared for this moment. She knew what she ought to do. She would appear all the more heroic if she placed herself at Niall's disposal before he came in search of her.

But her feet would not carry her. Niall scanned each corner of the room, and at last his gaze fell upon her.

He moved like a man bent upon murder. Cecily braced for attack.

"You let her go," he snarled, oblivious of several hundred pairs of eyes. "Where is she?"

Cecily drew upon her dignity and clasped her hands in an attitude of deep concern. "Mr. Munroe. I understand why you are upset. I am sure this has been quite a shock. If only I had been able to reach you." She would not ask him to find a more private place to talk. She wanted the safety of witnesses.

"I trusted you to watch her!" he shouted. "You let her go . . . you always wanted her out of the way, didn't you?"

A woman exclaimed in frightened tones. "He is as mad as she!" another cried.

"Mr. Munroe," Mr. Osborn said, moving to Cecily's defense. "Please lower your voice. There are ladies present, and this is not the time or place to—"

Niall struck out and sent the man staggering back. Caitlin caught his arm and hung on as fiercely as a bulldog. A wave of motion rippled outward from the disturbance as ladies and gentlemen scurried away.

"It is not . . . it is not what you think," Cecily said. "She attacked me. She threatened me with serious harm. The servants took her part against me. I had no choice but to allow her to leave. Of course I contacted the police immediately, but . . . your sister is not well, Mr. Munroe. You must believe I would never have willingly let her go."

"She attacked you? Athena?" He laughed. "You're lying."

She flushed. "You are distraught. You know she is able to walk. Her strength is greater than it appears. She was determined to go after her lover—the murderer Morgan Holt."

A fresh swell of exclamations followed, but Niall's wild glance imposed silence once more. He loomed over Cecily. "He has not come here?"

"Here?" Cecily shuddered. "But I thought you—" She bit her lip. "I warned you about him. You said that you would deal with him yourself!"

He seized her upper arms and shook her. "If anything has happened to my sister—"

"But nothing has, Niall," a hoarse voice said from across the room. "Not in the way you mean."

Chapter 23

Cecily felt her knees begin to buckle. *A figure draped in* oversized trousers and shirt walked down the open path the crowd had made for Niall's entrance. Athena's approach was not nearly so violent, but every eye turned to her and the silence became even more profound.

Athena's face was white, her hair a rat's nest, her breathing ragged. But she stood before her brother as if she were the taller and more powerful, capable of felling him with a single blow.

"Athena!" Caitlin exclaimed.

"Athena," Niall stammered. "You are . . . Where have you been?"

His attempt to regain control of the situation failed miserably. Athena stared up at him, unblinking.

"Did you kill my mother?"

Niall's mouth fell open. She showed him no mercy. "I know you were responsible for her disappearance just after I was born. Did you kill her?"

Cecily had never seen Niall turn white as he did now. "Athena, what are you doing?"

"I am seeking the truth." She smiled, a look that sent a

chill down Cecily's spine. "It's too late to worry about my reputation now, isn't it? I am sure that Cecily has told everyone what they didn't already know." The smile vanished. "Tell me."

"Athena . . . you don't understand." He looked about as if for support and found only one gaze that would meet his. Caitlin Hughes stepped up beside him. It was a measure of how far he had fallen that he seemed to take comfort in her presence.

"I did not kill her," he said in a firmer voice. "I drove her away. I had to. She was ruining our father's life, and she would have ruined yours. I tried to save you."

"To save me," she whispered, "or yourself? Are you that afraid of me?"

Niall's face darkened in fury. "Who told you about your mother?" he demanded. He swung on Caitlin. "Was it you?"

"No." Athena glanced at Caitlin with a remote gentleness in her eyes. "Morgan told me. You thought he was dead, didn't you? You believed you'd killed him. But you didn't succeed, Niall. He deceived you. And I found him."

The expression on Niall's face transformed from consternation to contempt in a handful of seconds. "You . . . you have been with him, haven't you? Turning against your own family, your own kind . . . Lying with him like any whore, just like your mother—"

A blur of motion was all Cecily saw before Niall crashed onto his back on the ballroom floor. The blur resolved into another man, barefoot and wearing only a calf-length greatcoat. He stood over his fallen victim with teeth bared and eyes ablaze.

Morgan Holt. Morgan Holt had come. Those terrible eyes turned from Niall, rested briefly on Athena, and fixed unerringly upon Cecily.

With a mindless shriek, Cecily turned and fled.

Athena watched her go, feeling nothing, just as she suffered no regret or embarrassment under the horrified and titillated stares of those she had once called friends. All the emotions that had driven her for the past hours—rage, confusion, terror—had deserted her; it was as if she stood at the eye of a tornado, hearing it howl about her while she remained untouched.

It was a way of protecting herself from hurt, just as she had made a fortress of her lameness and the chair that restricted her freedom. From the chair she had watched the world go by, seeking to affect it while remaining unaffected, a serene goddess of mercy and charity who had forgotten what it was to be human.

She had run to Denver to demand the truth of Niall, and all the while she had been running away from the truth of her heart. The truth she was still afraid to feel. Because of her weakness Niall lay sprawled on the polished floor, waiting for a mortal blow. As Morgan waited to give it.

Morgan had followed her. She should have known he would. She should have known he'd endanger himself to protect her from her brother . . . and take his revenge.

He had looked at Athena but once since she had entered the room—met her gaze like a stranger, as emotionless as she. The man she had loved was gone, replaced by a cold-blooded killer. And only she could stop him.

She, and Caitlin. The equestrienne knelt beside Niall at the same instant Athena placed herself between Morgan and her brother.

"You cannot hurt him, Morgan," Athena said. "You know you can't."

The stranger's merciless eyes hardly touched upon hers. "He will destroy you, as he destroyed your mother."

"He did not kill my mother," she said. "He drove her away, but he says he didn't kill her. I believe him."

Though she had not lifted her voice, Morgan flinched as if she had struck him. The frightening, alien mask dropped away, replaced by naked pain. Pain that cut through her own detachment and left her raw and defenseless.

"You believe him," Morgan said. He looked down at Niall and took a step back, his muscles loosening from their posture of threat. "You still trust him."

"Yes, Athena. You must trust me." Niall got to his knees, his attention on Morgan. "I know the truth about this man. He is a convict and a murderer." He raised his voice to reach the farthest corners of the ballroom. "Morgan Holt killed his own father."

A collective gasp rose from the onlookers. Several women appeared on the verge of swooning, and no few of the men looked about for possible weapons. Athena ignored them all. Morgan's anguished eyes had become her world.

"It is true," he said, speaking only to her. "I killed my father. I served nine years in prison. And I would have murdered your brother to protect you." He held up his hands and turned them palm up, flexing his fingers into fists. "Maybe he speaks the truth. I am a killer at heart. You were right to leave me."

Like a dam bursting under the weight of a raging spring flood, her heart gave way. Everything she had been holding inside, every doubt, every unbearable image was dislodged by the deluge until she was scoured clean and bright and new.

"No," she said. "I was wrong. I said I would listen, and trust you, but I was deceiving myself." She glanced at Niall with profound sorrow. "I came after my brother because I couldn't face the one who mattered most. Niall was an enemy I could conquer. My feelings for you were not. I was afraid that Niall was right, and that I had loved a murderer. I would rather have lost you forever than find such a crippling flaw within myself."

Morgan shook his head. "The only flaw is in me."

Athena held out her hand. Morgan gazed at it, unmoving. She kept her hand in place, fingers extended, offering him the forgiveness he refused to permit himself.

"I will tell you what I believe," she said. "I believe that whatever crime you committed was done only because you had no other choice. I believe that you paid in full for your mistakes. I believe that there is great good in you, Morgan Holt, and someone must make you see it."

"You're the only one who can," Caitlin said, restraining Niall with a hand on his shoulder. She gave him an apologetic glance and lifted her voice to address the crowd. "Morgan has had two chances to kill Mr. Munroe, and he could easily have escaped. But it was Niall who left Morgan for dead in the mountains. Morgan chose to feign death rather than be forced to kill his enemy."

"As he was forced to kill his father."

Athena turned toward the cultured tenor voice, recognizing it at once. Very little had the power to shock her now, and all she felt was gratitude and heartfelt joy as Ulysses Marcus Aurelius Wakefield and Harry French walked into the ballroom.

A distant part of her mind acknowledged how out of place they seemed in this glittering company—Harry in his loud waistcoat and red jacket, Ulysses a golden-haired mannequin of a Southern gentleman. But they were her family as these wealthy, distinguished people could never be. They were showmen, professional charlatans, and yet they were the most honest of all. She loved them only a little less than she loved Morgan. And they were here to save him.

Ulysses paused in the center of the room, standing as tall as his stature permitted. He did not wear the protective robes and anonymity of the Little Professor. He was entirely exposed to the fascinated distaste of those who should have been his peers, and Athena knew how difficult it must have been for the gentle man who had been cast out of his own elite world.

"Ladies and gentlemen," he said. "I see that Mr. French and I have arrived at a most propitious moment. We are members of French's Fantastic Family Circus, who have recently been in the employ of Miss Athena Munroe." He executed a bow in her direction. "I am Ulysses Marcus Aurelius Wakefield, and the gentleman beside me is Harold B. French. We have observed the events that have recently occurred involving Miss Munroe, Mr. Munroe, and Mr. Holt. It is now necessary to clarify statements that the latter two gentlemen have made with regard to Mr. Holt's more distant past."

Morgan took a sharp step toward Ulysses. "No."

Ulysses lowered his gaze. "I regret breaking a confidence, my dear friend, but it must be done."

Turning her back on Niall, Athena went to stand beside Morgan. She took his hand in hers. The tendons below his knuckles stood out like steel cords. She held him all the more tightly.

"It is true," Ulysses said, "that Morgan Holt committed patricide, a most heinous crime among civilized peoples. Mr. Holt was tried and convicted and spent many years in prison. If it had not been for a single witness in his favor, he would have been sentenced to death. He neither defended himself nor attempted to escape, though he had many opportunities to do so during his incarceration." He met Morgan's gaze again. "I made it my business to learn all I could of the circumstances of this affair. I know the truth behind the tragedy."

The ballroom might as well have been empty in its absolute silence. Heads topped by gleaming tiaras and meticulously pomaded hair turned from Ulysses to Morgan.

He stared at the floor and closed his eyes. His protest was so soft that Athena felt rather than heard it.

"Ladies and gentlemen," Ulysses said, "Morgan Holt's father left his wife, son, and daughter in California to seek a fortune in mining when Morgan was but a lad of thirteen. He promised to return but did not. His family was compelled to fend for itself with no source of income, until Morgan determined to go after his father and bring him home.

"He was fourteen when he left his mother and sister. I will not relate all the tribulations that he was forced to overcome in his journey, or how his childhood was lost before he attained the age of fifteen years. But when he reached Colorado Territory and found his father at last, he had learned how to hate."

"Morgan," Athena murmured, resting her forehead on his shoulder. "Oh, my love."

"The claim his father had staked in the mountains was poor," Ulysses went on, "but Aaron Holt would not give it up. He refused to return to his family, no matter how his son tried to persuade him. His lust for wealth was greater than his love. And so he and his son quarreled bitterly, and Morgan departed with many harsh words and an even greater despair.

"Many months later he returned and found his father again. But Aaron Holt had changed. He had fallen prey to men who make their living from cheating and theft, and they had left him—" Ulysses paused. "I beg your pardon, ladies, but what I am about to relate is not for delicate ears. You may wish to leave the room before I continue."

No one stirred. Morgan heard the faint shuffle of slippered feet, the rush of breath from a hundred throats, the creaking of corsets as women shifted for a better view of him. He heard the steady beat of Athena's heart and felt her warmth along his side. But Ulysses's voice had become a drone, a meaningless jumble of words that had no power to describe what had happened on that terrible day in the Colorado mountains.

It had been sunny, an unusually warm late spring afternoon. But Morgan scarcely felt the sun and balmy breezes, nor noticed the riot of wildflowers growing fat and lush on the hillsides and in the meadows.

All he could see was Aaron Holt—not the hearty, stubborn man he had left in such anger, but a wasted, hollow-eyed invalid who was more of a stranger to Morgan now than he had ever been. He lay against a boulder at the heart of his claim, stinking in soiled clothes and lying in his own waste.

Morgan knew that he was dying.

"They tried to jump my claim," Aaron Holt said, his voice like a rusty hinge. "The thieving bastards. I fought 'em. Didn't . . ." He coughed, and the motion jarred his gangrenous leg.

It was a miracle that he could speak at all. Morgan could smell the poison, the swift rotting of flesh. The smell of death—lingering, painful death.

"They were scared enough not to come back," Aaron whispered. "But . . . they left me with a memento." He gestured at his seeping left leg, deep bronze and purple with infection, no longer recognizable as living tissue. The original wound had been lost in the swelling.

Aaron was skeletal from lack of food, half-delirious with fever. The first thing Morgan had done was bring him water and try to make him eat the jerky and day-old bread he'd brought, but his father had pushed it aside untouched.

"I'll find a doctor," Morgan said, half-afraid that Aaron Holt would not be alive when he returned. But his father laughed, a sound more dreadful than weeping, until tears ran down his cheeks.

"I'm dying," he said. "Can't eat, can't sleep. My leg is rotting. No doctor can save me now." He shook his head at Morgan's mute denial. "I wouldn't go to town . . . when there was some chance for me. Now all I can do is—" He stopped, and he looked at Morgan with such desperation that Morgan's eyes filled with tears. "I know I haven't . . . been much of a father to you, boy. I know you hate me. I reckon you don't owe me any favors. But now I've got to ask you one." He drew in a deep breath and let it out again with a rattling wheeze. "I hurt, boy. Can't take it no more. Don't have the strength to end it myself. You got to do it for me."

Morgan heard the words, but it took him several minutes to understand. *End it.* His father wanted him to end his misery, and there was only one way to do that.

"I've . . . got a gun, hidden under those rocks," Aaron said. "All it takes . . . is one bullet, boy."

"No." Morgan stepped back, stumbled on a stone, caught his balance again. "I won't do it."

"You got to. You got to, boy. I'll be dying another week, and I can't . . ." He coughed again and sank back against the boulder. "I'm beggin' you. Please—"

After that Aaron Holt was quiet for a time, exhausted by his efforts to talk. Morgan tried to make him drink, but his father refused every attempt to help. That evening, Morgan made a fire and covered his father with all the blankets he could find. During the long night, Aaron dreamed. He wept and shouted and screamed in agony, and Morgan could smell the rot spread, inch by inch, eating Aaron's body from within.

By dawn, Aaron could barely move. It was as if he had used up all the life left within him . . . all but the pain. Every breath he took was a struggle. He screamed when Morgan touched his leg to adjust it under the blankets.

There was no hope for Aaron Holt. Morgan knew it. He had become familiar with death in the past several years of searching. He had seen it take many forms, but none so horrible as this.

"You . . . want revenge," his father panted, opening one red-rimmed eye. "You want to see me die slow, don't you?"

Morgan hung his head, the emotion so choked up inside him that he thought he would strangle on it. "I don't hate you, Pa."

"Then help me!" Aaron moaned. "Have mercy. Mercy."

The sun rose higher, promising another warm day. It traced all the tendons and veins standing out in Aaron Holt's neck and hands. Nothing in its caress could comfort Morgan's father, now or ever.

Morgan got up. He walked to the pile of rocks where Aaron had concealed his revolver, and shoved the stones aside. The gun felt heavy and awkward in his hand. He had never carried one; he didn't need it, being what he was.

But Aaron Holt was human.

"Bless you, boy," he whispered. "God . . . bless you."

With the gun loose at his side, Morgan stood over his father and stared up the hillside where rows of evergreens marched upward to the sky. "Is there anything you want me to tell Mother and Cassidy?"

His father only closed his eyes. "The head," he croaked.

"That's the fastest way. I won't . . . feel it. No more pain. Blessed . . . peace."

Morgan hated him then, more than he had ever done. He lifted the gun and thought of all the times he had dreamed of facing Aaron Holt and making him wish he were dead.

Aaron Holt wished he was dead. That was all. He had nothing to give, no amends to make, no regrets. Only one last demand from the son he had abandoned.

"Please," he whispered. "Damn you. Damn you."

The sun wheeled madly overhead. Morgan's hand began to tremble. He made a fist. The trembling stopped.

"Now. Do it . . . *now.*"

Morgan raised the revolver and took aim with exquisite care.

"Thank . . . God," Aaron whispered.

Morgan fired once. Between one moment and the next, Aaron Holt's pain was over. The echo rang across the hills, and crows rose up from a nearby pine with raucous cries.

An old miner and his mule emerged from the underbrush. Morgan was distantly aware of the man's frightened face and the way he glanced from Morgan to the body and back again.

"You kilt him," the old man said.

"He was my father," Morgan said. There were no tears. No feeling at all.

The old miner gripped his mule's halter as if for dear life. "We was comin' to check up on 'im. Hadn't heard in a week. Now he's dead." He narrowed his eyes. "You were his son?"

Two other men came up behind the miner, both in rough garb and weathered with years in the mountains. "Hank! You all right?" one of them said. He stared at Morgan. "We heard the shot. What the hell?"

"Aaron's dead," Hank said. "His own son shot him."

The newcomers started for Morgan and stopped at the sight of the gun. Morgan let it fall from his fingers. One of the men circled him cautiously and darted in to snatch the gun.

"He's dead, all right," the second man said grimly, bending over the body. "You saw him do it, Hank?"

"Well, I . . ." The old man chewed the frayed ends of his moustache. "I heard them quarrel afore, back in March during the thaw. Didn't know the boy was Aaron's son. But . . ."

"We got to take you to town, boy," the man with the gun said, aiming it at Morgan's chest.

"I did hear Aaron tell him to do it," the old miner stammered. "He looks in a bad way. Maybe it was a mercy."

"That's for the law to decide." The first man nodded to the second. "Get some rope, Bill. Can't take no chances with a man who'd murder his own pa."

Hank opened his mouth as if to speak, but quickly closed it again. Morgan waited quietly while Bill tied his hands behind his back. He welcomed the discomfort when the men dragged him back to their claim a mile away and talked of how they would get him to town and hand him over to the law. He could have escaped them easily, but he did not.

He didn't defend himself when he went to trial. Old Hank spoke of what he had heard, how Aaron Holt seemed to beg to be killed, and the local doctor testified that Aaron had been in the grip of fatal gangrene poisoning and must have been suffering unbearable pain.

In the end, that was what had spared Morgan death. What they gave him was worse. They locked him up in a place that would have driven him mad at any other time. They caged him for nine years, and when they judged his silence as rebellion they beat him. He let them. He always healed. After a while they left him alone. Alone with his own thoughts and memories.

That was the true punishment, the one he could never escape. Only the wolf gave him peace. And then that, too, was taken away.

"Why didn't you tell me?"

Morgan climbed out of the pit of memory, reaching toward the light of the voice.

Athena's voice. She held him, and her hazel eyes glittered with tears.

"I would have understood," she whispered. "It wouldn't have changed anything between us."

Ulysses's voice rang in dramatic conclusion. "And so Morgan Holt paid for his crime. A crime of mercy, a reluctant easing of inconceivable torment. He has served his sentence. He has been punished enough, and must be punished no more."

People in the crowd began to murmur, a tide of sound suddenly released by the end of Ulysses's tale. Morgan found his mind remarkably clear. He eased his arm from Athena's grip and turned slowly to Niall, who had scrambled to his feet, Caitlin solemn and pale at his side. Niall's gaze slid away from his.

"I offer a bargain," Morgan said. "Let Athena go. She is not what you are. Give her what is hers, and I will leave and not return."

"No, Morgan," Athena said. "It's not your bargain to make." She swung on her brother, head lifted, and compelled him to meet her eyes.

"I loved you, Niall," she said. "I trusted you. I refused to believe ill of you, even when I should have seen the truth. You cared for me all these years. I will never forget that. But now I understand what made you so careful with me. It was guilt—not only about the accident, but because of my mother." She did not lower her voice, though she must have known how her words would be taken by the avid audience. "You robbed me of her and lied to me all my life. You were afraid that I would become just like her if I had my freedom." She gave a heartrending smile. "You were glad when I was hurt, weren't you? I was safe in my chair, with my domestic and charitable work. I let you convince me that it was all I could aspire to. Your mistake was trying to take even that away. And my great good fortune—" She reached for Morgan's hand. "My great joy is that someone came along to teach me about courage and daring to hope. Someone who has suffered more than you or I can imagine."

"Athena," Niall said, swallowing heavily. "You must understand—"

"But I do, Niall. And I pity you." She looked at Caitlin. "If anyone can help him, you can."

Caitlin bent her head. "Thank you."

Niall looked at Caitlin as if she had grown horns and a tail. "You," he whispered. He stared at Morgan and Athena in turn. It was no longer merely fear in his eyes, but something more complex made up of equal parts bewilderment and desperation. Morgan recognized the kind of madness that came to a man when everything he had believed, every foundation of his world, disintegrated beneath his feet.

As Cecily had done before him, he turned hard on his heel and fled the room at a run. Caitlin hesitated, anguish in her eyes, and ran after him. A hum of excited comment rose and fell about the ballroom.

Athena clenched her fists at her sides and did not follow. Morgan wanted to hold her, comfort her with all the loving words he had never been able to say. He remained still.

Ulysses and Harry came to join them. Ulysses nodded to Morgan, eloquent in his silence. Harry's eyes were moist.

"My boy," he said. He reached out as if to pat Morgan's shoulder and tucked his hand into his waistcoat instead. "My dear boy." He cleared his throat. "I know . . . I know that your father loved you, and you loved him in spite of everything. What lies between a parent and child is not easily torn asunder."

"He's right," Athena said. She was not afraid to touch him, no matter how little he responded. "You have lived with this for too many years. Let it go. Walk away from it, just as I learned to walk away from my chair and everything that held me prisoner." She placed her hand on his chest, fingers spread, as if she could reach inside his ribs and replace what was missing. "Forgive your father, Morgan. Forgive yourself."

"Listen to her." Harry blinked, and a tear leaked from the corner of his eye. "Morgan . . . I am as proud of you as if you were my own son. That is why I must insist that you do not throw away the one thing that can give you peace." He took Morgan's hand and then Athena's. Gently he placed her fingers in his. "Love one another. That is all that matters."

Morgan could not have spoken if he wished. The obstruction in his throat had grown and grown to fill all the hollow places in his body, pressing on his eyelids and the casing of ice around his heart.

He looked into Athena's eyes. They were clear, sane, bright with love. For him.

"I cannot stay here, among men," he said, so that only she could hear.

"I know."

"I won't let you give up all this for me."

"All this?" She glanced around the room, her gaze sweeping over the sea of faces as if they were so many antique paintings on a wall. "Do you think I want this now? They would not have me again even if I did. And I wouldn't have them." She cupped his hand between hers. "I decided even before I returned to Denver that my old life was over. I should have known before, but a part of me was still bound to that chair. The one you made me recognize for what it was. *You,* Morgan."

"You knew I had killed."

"And I doubted, for a while. But love—" She glanced at Harry with a warm smile. "Love is stronger than doubt."

Still he refused to let himself believe. "The people you help . . . you cannot abandon them."

"For all the mistakes he made, my brother was right in one way," she said. "He accused me of trying to do everything myself, as if I could save all of Denver single-handedly." She dropped her gaze. "I was arrogant. I wanted to make myself indispensable—to Niall, to society, to the needy, because I had nothing else then." Her eyes found his. "There are many good people in my employ who can do what I did. All they need is money. After what has happened, I think I can convince Niall to release my fortune so that I can give the charities whatever they require to go on without me. And—" She turned his hand over in hers and kissed his palm. "There are people who need help everywhere. It doesn't matter where we go or what we do. I choose a life with you, Morgan Holt. I love you."

Morgan's chest rose in a great, heaving breath. The frigid sheath behind his ribs cracked in one painful, miraculous spasm. Melting droplets rushed up his throat and into his eyes. He heard the hoarse sound of sobbing and realized the tears were his own.

"Athena," he said. He took her face between his hands. "My love." He kissed her, tasting salt on his lips and hers, daring the entire world to judge. All the anger, the self-contempt, the grief that had consumed him flowed out with that kiss, passed into Athena and came back to him cleansed and purified.

"I love you," he said. "Will you have me, Athena?"

"Yes. Oh, yes." She kissed him boldly, passionately, spitting in the collective eye of shocked society matrons. "But only if it is forever."

Morgan responded as ardently as Athena could have wished. She rejoiced in his tears, for she knew they came as a release—release from the prison in which he had bound himself since his father's death. She felt no shame for her own silent weeping. Only three people in this grand ballroom mattered to her now.

"Athena," Morgan murmured into her hair. "Will you dance with me?"

She drew back in amazement. "You know how to dance?"

"Ulysses showed me once. I have never practiced."

"And I," she said, "have almost forgotten how."

With solemn deliberation, Morgan placed one hand on

her waist and took her other in his. There was no music. Athena didn't need it. It sang out in her heart, a melody too perfect to be rendered by human hands.

Morgan took an awkward step, and then another. It was the first time Athena had ever seen him less than graceful. She loved him all the more for his imperfection, and the courage he showed in a place so alien to his nature. She followed him, gazing into his eyes, as he grew more sure and his steps took on a smooth, three-quarter rhythm.

Then they were flying about the ballroom and Athena was laughing, glorying in the dance and the man who held her. Morgan smiled. He waltzed her with wild abandon to the ballroom doors and carried her with him down the stairs. The same flabbergasted hotel staff and patrons who had seen them enter singly watched them leave together, hand in hand.

They dashed into the street, past the waiting carriages and out of the business district to the very edge of town. Morgan shed his clothing, eyes alight with challenge. Athena never hesitated. She flung her clothes aside and took Morgan's hand. He bent back his head and howled loudly enough to wake the dead. Naked man dissolved into great black wolf.

In seconds Athena was beside him. He licked her muzzle tenderly, and she could hear the words he did not speak, the words that had set them both free.

I love you.

Ulysses gazed at the open doors, vaguely surprised at the tightness in his chest. It was not his way to become sentimental, particularly when matters had resolved themselves so fortuitously.

Harry's broad hand came to rest on his shoulder. He didn't speak; no words were adequate to the occasion. Unlike Ulysses, Harry felt no compunction about his tears. He sniffled, dug about in his pocket for a handkerchief, and blew his nose.

The din in the ballroom had reached a high pitch, men and women competing with each other to exclaim most volubly upon the appalling events that had just taken place. Ulysses glanced up at Harry. Harry nodded, and a smile spread across his round, florid face.

Together they turned to face their audience. Harry raised his hands dramatically. The roar of voices faded to a murmur, and them into silence. Harry bowed and came up with a broad grin that lifted his moustache nearly to his eyebrows.

"Ladies and gentlemen," he said. "The performance is finished. Good night."

Epilogue

D enver looked very small from the top of the hill, and very far away.

Athena adjusted her knapsack and leaned against Morgan. He would have no regrets about leaving the city far behind. What surprised her most was that she had so few.

The only matters she had left undone since the ball had found their own sort of resolution. Niall had fled Denver that very night, and so had Caitlin. When Athena had returned to Fourteenth Street the following evening, she had found a message from the family banker informing her that she had been given full control of her inheritance, as well as a substantial portion of the Munroe fortune.

Niall, wherever he had gone, had made that one last act of atonement. The money was more than enough to keep Athena's charities going indefinitely, under the care of trusted employees. As she had told Morgan, her direct supervision was hardly necessary. And whatever the Denver society ladies thought of her now, they would not entirely stop their own contributions. Athena had them too well trained.

Cecily Hockensmith had certainly believed she had all

of Denver at her feet. Athena could not guess what she was thinking now. Since the ball, she had remained locked up in her house and had issued no invitations or ventured out to a single luncheon. Once it might have mattered to Athena whether or not the harpy received her just punishment and became persona non grata among the very people she wished to impress. Now her fate was unimportant. No matter how she schemed and simpered, she would never be happy.

And as for French's Fantastic Family Circus . . .

"Where do you suppose Harry will take the troupers after the winter is over?" she asked Morgan.

He reached for her hand and squeezed it gently. "I don't know. He will need to find replacements for Caitlin and Ulysses—and Tamar." His lips wrinkled on that last name. Tamar and her serpents had been gone when Harry and Ulysses returned to Long Park, and no one had bothered with inquiries as to her whereabouts.

Only Ulysses, Harry had told her, seemed troubled. A few days later he had announced his intent to return to the Wakefield mansion in Tennessee, there to face his family for the first time in many years.

"It took great courage for Ulysses to stand before Denver society as he did," Athena said. "I think that was what made him decide to go back home."

"He has always hurt because of their treatment of him," Morgan said. "It will not be easy."

"But it is worth it." She laced her fingers through his. "It's worth it to know what you are truly meant to be, without fear. And yet—" She sighed. "I worry about Caitlin. If she went after Niall, she cannot expect happiness. He will have to change a great deal before he can accept love."

"As I did?" Morgan gave her a twisted smile. "I didn't think I needed anyone. You proved me wrong." He kissed her fingers. "Do not be concerned for Caitlin. She can take care of herself. You didn't think she was an ordinary woman?"

She peered up at him. "Are you saying . . . She is not . . . not—"

"No, not like us. She was traveling this country alone before you and I were born."

Athena was well past the point of amazement at such revelations. "I see. And yet she chose Niall."

They were silent for a while, watching light and shadow roll across the prairie beyond the city's edge. Snow settled lightly on Athena's hair. A new, increasingly familiar restlessness came over her, and she knew that the time of farewells was over. She tugged at Morgan's hand.

He held back, scanning the horizon once more. "Are you sure, Athena?"

She knew what he asked. Quickly she stepped up behind him and wrapped her arms around his waist. "I'm sure, Morgan. As sure as I am standing here with the man I love."

He twisted around and looked into her eyes. "Then let's go," he said. "The whole world is waiting."

Susan Krinard graduated from the California College of Arts and Crafts with a BFA, and worked as an artist and freelance illustrator before turning to writing. An admirer of both romance and fantasy, Susan enjoys combining these elements in her books. Her first novel, *Prince of Wolves*, garnered praise and broke new ground in the genre of paranormal romance. She has won the *Romantic Times* Awards for Best Contemporary Fantasy and Best Historical Fantasy, the PRISM Award for Best Dark Paranormal Fantasy, and has been a finalist for the prestigious RITA Award.

Susan loves to hear from her readers. They can reach her at:

Susan Krinard
P.O. Box 51924
Albuquerque, NM 87181
(please send a self-addressed stamped envelope for a reply)

or via e-mail at: Sue@susankrinard.com.

Her web page, http://www.susankrinard.com, contains information on all her books and a link to receive her monthly and quarterly newsletters.